Stoking
Hope

C. K. McDonough

D. X. VAROS

Book cover design and layout by
SelfPubBookCovers.com/VercoDesign

ISBN
978-1-955065-10-8 (paperback)
978-1-955065-11-5 (ebook)

To Jennifer and Stephen.
Dreams do come true.

PROLOGUE

November 1909
Webster Hill, Pennsylvania

The nest was empty. Frederic said it would be but Martha had to see for herself. She hooked her arm around the oak's thick trunk and peered down through the few remaining leaves, finally spotting Frederic's blond head several branches below. Commotion on the ground caught her attention and she scanned the crowd of roaming classmates, narrowing her eyes at her older sister, Klara. Too bad the acorns have all dropped, Martha thought with a smile, as tossing one at her sister would be great fun. She raised her head and looked towards the mine. The tipple, twice the height of the towering oak, was easy to spot. She couldn't see the gangway but she could hear the buggy's wheels grinding on the iron rails and the mules' sharp brays as they made their way in and out of the mine.

The colliery whistle sounded, the shriek making her teeth rattle and her stomach drop. All movement stopped, her classmates frozen, every face towards the mine. Fingernails digging into the ridged bark, Martha climbed to Frederic's side.

"It's too early for a shift change," he whispered.

She searched for smoke, listened for an explosion. It was quiet, too quiet. The coal patch was never silent, the mine and the mountain always at odds. One tense minute stretched to two. Five agonizing minutes later the whistle blew again—two sharp blasts, the all-clear signal—and she let out a grateful breath.

"Martha Kraus! Frederic Albrecht! Out of the tree. Now," Miss Pennington, Webster Hill's one and only teacher, called from the doorway of the schoolhouse. Recess over, mine disaster thwarted, the teacher was doing her best to wrangle the students back inside.

"Bet I can beat you, Frederic," Martha said. She turned ten last month and Frederic would be eleven in November, but Martha was half a head taller. She jumped from the lowest tree branch, hiked up her skirt and sprinted towards the brick building, blond braids flying. She was long-legged and athletic, a sharp contrast to Frederic's stocky build, and skidded to a stop in front of Miss Pennington a step before Frederic. "I won!" She threw her arms up and followed Miss Pennington inside, giggling when Frederic tugged her left braid. Martha was never angry with Frederic. Unlike her near-constant feuding with her four younger brothers. And her sister.

The school's floor vibrated with two dozen boots tramping across the oiled boards as Martha made her way to her desk, the fourth one in the second row. Seated behind Frederic, she watched his checkered shirt strain across his back when he leaned forward to copy numbers from the blackboard. They were both in fifth grade, although every grade was in the same room. She glanced towards the first graders, catching her youngest brother, Jakob, elbowing the boy sharing a desk with him. She quelled a snicker with her hand and pulled her composition notebook from the desk's shelf. Bored with equations and multiplications, she printed *Martha Albrecht* at the top of a blank page. Wrote it again in cursive. Once more, in German. Frederic was the one who taught her German. He knew the language well since he shared his bedroom with his grandmother who refused to speak a word of English. Frederic straightened and Martha felt his hand tap her knee. Without looking down, she eased the scrap of paper from his fingertips, burying the forbidden message in her hand. When she was certain Miss Pennington wasn't watching, she unfolded the note, and smiled.

In late afternoon, students ran from the building and scattered in every direction when the bell atop the schoolhouse tolled three times. Martha walked with Frederic, ignoring her siblings, but Klara caught up to her.

"Take little Karl and Kristopher with you," Klara said. "I'll take Albert and Jakob."

"I don't need no watching." Nine-year old Karl Junior, the oldest of the Kraus boys, stalked towards a group of kids gathered at the water pump. Kristopher followed but Karl pushed his younger brother away.

"Kristopher," Frederic called to the eight-year-old. "Come on. Walk with me and Martha."

Martha gave Frederic's arm a soft punch and rolled her eyes when he looked her way, but he just shrugged and took her books, tucking them beneath his arm. No matter how much she complained, Frederic, an only child, didn't understand Martha's aversion to her brothers and sister.

They cruised two blocks up steep Lincoln Street to the double house the Kraus and Albrecht families shared, Kristopher disappearing inside the Kraus half. Martha stood on the porch and wrinkled her nose. "Smells like sauerkraut again."

"Why don't you like sauerkraut?" Frederic asked.

Martha shrugged. "I like it," she said. "But not every day."

"Would you rather eat potatoes every day? Like the McMurphy's? Or the Doyles?" Frederic lifted his chin, tented a hand over his eyes and looked towards the apex of the street, the steepest section of the patch where the houses were nearly stacked on top of each other. The Irish section.

"I like potatoes," she said.

"You like Peter Doyle, too!" Frederic nudged Martha.

She pushed Frederic's arm away. "Do not."

"He likes you. Always pulling on your braids. You want me to make him stop?"

"You? You're no fighter."

Frederic balled his hands and boxed the air in front of Martha's face. "I can fight."

She laughed, batting his fists. "Peter Doyle would knock your ears off. Said his father boxed in Ireland. Nearly killed a man."

"Rubbish," Frederic said. "You stay away from those Doyle hooligans."

She settled on the porch railing and leaned back to admire the blue sky, a rarity. Eyes closed, sun warming her chilled cheeks, she grinned when her fingers found Frederic's note in her pocket. *Ich lasse dich hübsches Mädchen gewinnen.* "I let you win pretty girl," the note said.

The screen door's squeak evicted Martha from her brief respite. She opened her eyes to find her mother standing in the doorway with a silver bucket in each hand.

"Your turn to get water, Martha," her mother said.

Klara, moving up the porch steps with the two youngest Kraus's in tow, let out a snigger.

Martha stuck her tongue out but resisted the urge to smack the smile off her sister's gloating face. Striking a sibling meant her mother would take action. Probably paddle her with the wood spoon. The paddling didn't hurt much but it was humiliating to raise her skirt, especially in front of Klara. Maybe her mother would send her to bed without supper, she thought, brightening. With an exaggerated sigh, she stood and took the buckets from her mother, refusing to look her in the eye. She pounded down the steps.

"Wait up," Frederic called.

Martha stopped. She never passed up the chance to spend time with Frederic.

PART ONE:
NECESSARY EVIL
1918 – 1919

CHAPTER ONE

September 1918
Webster Hill, Pennsylvania

Martha sat up, picking straw from her hair. "Stop it," she said and tucked stray strands back into her thick braid.

"Lay back down, Martha," Peter Doyle said, tugging on the long plait.

"I have to go home." She jumped from the back of the wagon and walked away, her homespun skirt flapping about her ankles. One month shy of her nineteenth birthday, Martha was tall, just three inches south of six feet, her lengthy strides putting quick distance between herself and Peter.

He caught up to her, wrapping his arms around her waist. "I love you lass. Marry me, Martha Kraus. How many times must I ask?" he whispered into her neck.

"Father won't allow it," she said.

"We won't tell him. We'll take the trolley to the city. Get married at the courthouse. My cousin Timothy did it."

"He only married Paula to keep from going to the war," she said, disentangling herself from his embrace.

He toed a pebble in the dirt. "This dang war. I have to register next week."

"What? Why? You're not yet twenty-one."

"New law. Ages eighteen through forty-five have to register."

"No!" Martha said, a hand on her chest. "Karl Junior is eighteen. And Father is forty-three. They'll have to go to war like my Uncle Emil." Frederic came to mind, too, but she pushed him from her thoughts.

Peter held Martha's hands. "No. They'll be exempt. They're both married."

"So that's why you want to marry me? To avoid the war?" Martha pulled her hands from Peter's grasp.

"No. I am already exempt," he said, shaking his head. "I bring in the money. My ma, and all my brothers and sisters depend on me since Pa died." He paused and looked at his boots, jamming his hands into his pockets. "That's why I work for the Johnson Brothers. I don't make enough in the mine. And the prices they charge at the company store..." He lifted his chin, let out a long, low whistle. "I see what other stores charge. Things are cheaper at the shops in the city. But those stores won't take our script. Or the ones that do, don't pay face value. A nickel of our script is only worth three cents. It ain't right."

"What do you do for the Johnson's?" Martha asked.

He hesitated, glancing at the mule when it stamped its heavy hooves. "I just load crates into the wagon. Meet some boys in Claysville."

"What's in the crates?"

"Beer," Peter said. "The Johnson's get it at the brewery. Store it at their barn. You can't get beer in West Virginia no more so the boys in Claysville buy ours. Take it over the state line to Wheeling." He pulled bills from his pocket. "I been saving for us. There's a vacant house on Buchanan Street."

Martha eyed the wad of money, lifted her gaze to study Peter. He was a handsome man. One of the few men she knew taller than herself. Broad-shouldered with thick hair the color of cinnamon. A kind man, despite his outlaw reputation. And, really, what other options did she have? The old butcher at the company store? The dim-witted farmer's son? It was time she was married. Hopefully, that would bring her happiness. Lighten her dulled temperament. She raised to her toes and kissed Peter's full lips. "I will marry you."

His green eyes widened and his face split into a smile. "Hot damn!" he yelled and pulled her into his arms, lifting her off her feet and adding two spins, and a long kiss. "Do you work tomorrow?"

She shook her head. A clerk at the company store, Martha worked two, sometimes three, days a week.

"Tomorrow, it is," Peter said. "I have to take a load to Claysville at dawn. Meet me at the trolley stop. Noon."

Martha nodded and turned away. She walked out of the woods and on to the narrow trail leading to the village, leaves crunching under her feet. Gazing at the treetops, she smiled. Fall was her favorite season. When she was young, it meant going back to school, and she liked school. Less time for chores, more time with Frederic. Her smile faltered and she pushed Frederic from her thoughts again, reminding herself she was marrying Peter tomorrow.

***

After a killing frost, Martha's wedding day dawned cool and crisp. She and her mother, Marie, got an early start, canning two dozen quarts of tomatoes and beets. Her legs ached from the countless trips up and down the stairs to stack the jars on the shelves in the basement.

"Mom, I'm going to Klara's," she said half an hour before noon. "I finished the booties for the baby." She held up a bundle of muslin wrapped with twine.

Her mother, scrubbing her prized sink, nodded, her gaze never leaving the porcelain.

Martha pulled her sweater from the hook on the wall and paused, taking a long look around the kitchen. Would this be her last time here? Her father would be

11

furious about Peter becoming her husband. She glanced at her mother. How would she react? There was no question her brothers would be horrified. They called the Doyle boys rogues. Ruffians. Martha thought Peter charming. All the Doyle boys were. They laughed. They sang. Her father wouldn't even sing in church. She shrugged into her cardigan and slipped out the door.

The trolley stop was a ten-minute walk from Martha's house. She knew the route well, having walked it with Frederic for four years to attend high school in the nearest city. It was her mother who insisted she go to high school despite most of the kids in the patch ending their schooling after the eighth grade. Education for her children and running water had been her mother's mantra for as long as she could remember. Grateful the stop's small shelter was empty, Martha sat on the lone bench, her arms wrapped around her knees. She studied her boots, frowning at the leather patch her father had sewn onto the toe of her left one last week. She and Klara hated wearing patched shoes. It was one of the few things she and her sister agreed on, both complaining to their mother.

"Don't bother him with such petty grouses," her mother had said when Martha threatened to take her complaints to her father. "Look at your *vater's* boots, Martha. They have more patches than yours and Klara's shoes combined. He works hard. Show some appreciation. Many men cannot be counted on. We are lucky."

From listening to the other clerks at the company store gripe about their husbands, Martha knew that was true. She was the youngest worker there, and the only unmarried woman.

A low rumble and clanging bell announced the arrival of the trolley. Martha stepped from the shelter and looked towards the patch. No Peter.

"Good morning, miss," the trolley driver said as he pushed the twin doors open. Extracting his watch from his pocket, he corrected himself. "Sorry, good afternoon, it is." He came down the steps, extending his hand.

"I'm waiting on someone," Martha said.

The driver gave his head a shake. "Can't get off schedule, miss. I'll return at two." He climbed back into the trolley, the doors folding closed behind him.

The trolley looped and headed back the way it came, Martha watching the orange tram until it disappeared around a bend. She looked towards the patch again. Nobody in sight. She returned to the shelter and dropped to the bench, fuming. When the approaching trolley's rumble told her two hours had passed and still no Peter, Martha gave up. Her father was right. Peter Doyle was a scoundrel. Full of empty promises. She ran from the shelter and didn't stop running until she was back in Webster Hill. Not wanting to go home, she went to the company store.

"Hello, Martha!" Old Earl called from behind the meat counter. "Got some of that cheddar cheese you like. Want a taste?"

Martha shook her head and continued on to the dry-goods counter where Edith was stacking cans on the shelf behind and Margaret was boxing up an order.

"Martha, have you heard?" Margaret leaned forward, her elbows on the countertop. "Peter Doyle's dead. Shot in Claysville this morning. His brother Patrick caught a load of buckshot in his backside but the doc said he'll recover. Wonder what those boys were up to."

CHAPTER TWO

December 1918
Webster Hill, Pennsylvania

Her shift over, but in no hurry to go home, Martha dawdled for an hour in the back room at the company store. Eventually, her boss told her to move along. She slogged up Lincoln Street, her head bent against the wind and sleet. Halfway home, she stopped to catch her breath. A month ago she moved up and down the hill easily but her growing baby was stealing her air. *Her baby.* She put a hand on her belly and quickly pulled it away, looking left and right, fearing someone would guess her secret. She trudged on, determined to tell her mother today.

"*Hallo,*" Martha said as she walked into the kitchen and dropped into a chair.

"Boots off, Martha." Her mother stood at her usual place in front of the sink.

Martha burst into tears.

Klara, sitting at the table with her two-month-old daughter, Eleanor, balanced in the crook of her arm, narrowed her eyes. "What's wrong?"

Marie put a hand on Martha's shoulder. "Martha, what is it?"

"I-am-going-to-have-a-baby." Her voice hitching after each word, Martha kept her face down, staring at the floorboards.

Her mother pulled her hand away and stepped back, slumping against the sink's apron. "*Oh mein Gott!*"

"Who?" Klara asked.

"Peter Doyle," Martha whispered.

"*Oh mein Gott!*" Marie repeated, her hand over her heart. "Your father..."

Two-year-old Paul toddled from the front room at his grandmother's cries and, wide-eyed, looked at Klara. "Mommy?"

"We're going home." Klara pushed Paul's arms into a coat and shrugged into her own. She wrapped a blanket around her infant daughter and grabbed Paul's hand, dragging the bawling tot out the back door.

Martha locked eyes with her mother, yearning for a kind word, just one, but Marie turned away and ran up the stairs.

The pot on the stove gurgled and Martha pushed to her feet to dip the wood spoon in the cabbage. She stirred lazily, eyes closed. Sweat trickled down her back but despite the heated kitchen, she shivered. Lightheaded, she stumbled to a chair and laid her arm on the table, resting her forehead on her wrist. Her stomach roiled. She ran out the door towards the outhouse, holding her hand over her mouth. She didn't make it inside. Her palm against the rough boards, she emptied her stomach on the frozen ground as voices drifted up the alley, moving closer. Panicked, she kicked snow over the steaming vomit and wiped her mouth with the back of her hand just as her father and another miner rounded the coal shed.

"*Gute Nacht, Karl,*" the other miner said, and shuffled down the alley, his lunch bucket bouncing against his thigh.

Her father grunted at her and limped towards the house.

16

She followed, praying her mother would be in the kitchen so she wouldn't have to face her father alone but the room was empty, the only sound the bubbling sauerkraut. "Father, I am going to have a baby," she blurted, surprised at her steady voice. Back straight, shoulders squared, she took a step forward. "I know this is wrong but I..."

His hand was so quick she didn't see it coming. The shocking crack rang in her ear, the blow knocking her off balance. Pain seared her face as she clung to the edge of the sink.

"You lay with a man who was not your husband," her father said, his voice a growl, his hand in mid-air, thick fingers splayed.

Martha had expected yelling. Or silence. Her father had gone days without speaking to her after a mishap or improper remark, her brothers lashed with his belt when they misbehaved, but never had her father raised a hand to her or Klara. Stunned, she touched her fingertips to her stinging face.

"You have disgraced me," he said, turning his head, looking at his hand as if seeing it for the first time. His arm fell to his side and he fixed his gaze on the window. "I do not want to see you again. Leave this house. You are dead to me." Shoulders slumped, he walked to the front room.

Martha stumbled outside and ran the two blocks to Klara's house, clambering up the back porch steps and pounding on the door. "Klara, I'm freezing," she yelled, rubbing her arms, stomping her feet. "Let me in."

Her sister opened the door, glaring. Slowly, she let her hand fall from the doorknob and stepped aside. "Keep your voice down. Henry and Paul are asleep. And don't wake the baby."

"I need to stay here tonight," Martha said.

Arms crossed over her chest, Klara glanced at the cradle in the corner. She sighed and disappeared into the living room, returning with a blanket. "You will have to

17

sleep on the floor in the front bedroom, next to Paul's crib," she said. "Henry won't like having you here. If word gets out, it could hurt his chances at becoming shift leader. The boss hears you're mixed up with them hooligans he might take it out on Henry. Or Father."

"You're worried about Father? He hit me, Klara." Martha turned her head to expose her cheek, pushing her heavy braid from her shoulder.

With a light touch, Klara ran her fingers across Martha's inflamed skin. "I'm sorry," she whispered. "But, oh Martha, why Peter Doyle?"

Martha sat. She sighed, her attention on the tabletop. "He made me laugh. After Frederic died I didn't think I would ever laugh again." She looked up, her gaze meeting Klara's. "There aren't many men left in Webster Hill. This awful war. Frederic's dead. Mother's brother and cousins dead. And we haven't heard from Uncle Emil in months." Martha looked at her niece, asleep in her cradle. "I want a family. Peter had plans, Klara. He worked hard. Saved money for us."

"Did he give you any of that money?"

Martha shook her head, wrapped the blanket around her shoulders. "I went to see Mrs. Doyle. Told her Peter was going to marry me. I told her I was having his baby. She said she couldn't help me. Whatever money Peter had was stolen when he was killed. Said she can't feed the mouths she already has."

Klara frowned. "I don't think you should tell anyone else, Martha. You don't want word to get around the patch you're that kind of girl." She caught her lower lip in her teeth. "I've heard of girls going away to have their baby. They say they're going to care for a sick friend, or ailing relatives. Then they come home like nothing happened."

"What about their babies?"

"They are given to some other family. Adopted."

"No! I would never give my baby away." Martha stood so quickly she knocked over the chair, sending it to the floor with a thud. Eleanor's eyes popped open.

"Shush!" Klara moved to the cradle, nudged it into a gentle sway. "Think about it, Martha. How will you provide for a baby? They are more work than you think. Go upstairs now. Don't come down tomorrow until after Henry leaves."

***

Martha woke when daylight seeped through the space between the window and the blinds, her cheek throbbing. Paul jumped up and down in his crib, squeaking "up, up," his breath a white wisp in the cold room. She gathered her nephew into her arms and pulled the blanket from the floor, wrapping it around herself and the child. Her ear against the door, she listened for her brother-in-law's voice. Klara's double house, identical to the one she grew up in, didn't offer much privacy. Voices, even when using hushed tones, could be heard through the thin walls and Martha was caught more than once eavesdropping on her parents.

She kissed Paul's head and lowered him to the floor. "Let's get you changed." Her nephew twisted and kicked as Martha pulled the soaker off and unpinned the wet flannel. "Hold still now, Paulie, I don't want to stick you," she mumbled, two large safety pins clamped between her teeth. Drawing the corners of a fresh cloth together, she slipped the pins in without incident and closed the clasps. The soaker back in place, she stood with the restless toddler in her arms.

"You look funny," he said, his tiny fingers brushing her cheek.

She winced. Using the tin of pins as a makeshift mirror, she looked at her distorted reflection. Her left eye was swollen, circled by a thick swatch of black and purple.

19

"Let's go downstairs," Martha said. She paused on the bottom step, peering in the kitchen.

"Mommy!" Paul cried, fighting his way to the floor. He ran to Klara, his small hands clutching the fabric of her skirt.

Klara lifted the toddler, kissed his forehead, and put him in the highchair.

"I changed him," Martha said, still standing by the stairs.

"Come sit. Henry's gone." Klara spooned a dollop of oatmeal in Paul's mouth.

He spit it out.

"Paul!" Klara scolded. She draped a bib across the toddler's small chest and pushed another spoonful in his mouth.

He spit it out again.

With a sigh, Klara slid the bowl out of Paul's reach and turned her attention to Eleanor, the infant kicking and whimpering in her cradle, hands balled into walnut-size fists. "She needs fed. I'll take her to the front room.

Martha pushed her chair towards her nephew. "Let's eat, Paulie." After three spoonfuls of oatmeal on his bib, she finally got him to swallow one. She repeated until the bowl was empty, much of the porridge on the bib.

"Not so easy, is it?" Klara stood at the doorway, Eleanor on her shoulder. She moved to a chair.

Martha didn't respond. She had foolishly hoped for compassion from her sister. She stood, releasing her nephew from his chair. With a glance at her sister's cup, she lifted the coffee pot from the stove and filled Klara's cup, pouring the remainder in a chipped cup for herself. She sat just as a knock on the back door sounded and her mother walked in.

"Grandma!" Paul scrambled to his feet.

Martha hung her head, her unbraided hair falling over her face.

Marie gave Paul's blond crown a quick rub and stepped to Martha's side, cupping her chin. "*Das tut mir Leid*. Your *vater* regrets his actions. But not his words."

Martha jerked her head from her mother's grasp, anger rising. Did her mother agree with her father? She glared at her mother, readying nasty words, hurtful words, but she swallowed them when she noticed tears welling in her mother's eyes. Those eyes, so much like her own, were dull, the blue nearly faded to gray. Martha looked away, her chest tightening. The room tilted, the air thickening. This was real. Her father would not back down, her mother would do as her father said. She closed her eyes, opening them again at the knock on the front door.

"I will get it," Marie said. "I invited Mrs. Kaczmarek over." Make more coffee, Klara."

The portly mid-wife swept into the kitchen and pushed back the hood of her cape. "Hello, Klara. And how is the babe?" Mrs. Kaczmarek pulled Eleanor out of Klara's arms and inspected the infant's face. "Beautiful. Told you she was going to be a pretty one." She handed the now-crying baby back to Klara and sat, the fabric of her worn cape puddling at her feet.

Marie returned to the kitchen, the mid-wife's bulky medicine bag in her arms. She put the black satchel on the table and Martha coughed as a pungent odor filled the air.

"Creolin. A disinfectant," Mrs. Kaczmarek said, tapping the bag. "Kills germs but stinks to high heaven." She moved her hand to Martha's arm. "Why don't you move my satchel to the front room, dear?"

Martha sidled from the kitchen, face turned to keep her bruised cheek from Mrs. Kaczmarek's sharp eyes. She lowered the satchel to the floor by the front door, resting her hand on the doorknob. Whatever the mid-wife had to say, Martha didn't want to hear it. And she didn't want to look at her mother's heartbroken eyes again. Or Klara's pinched brow. Another wave of nausea stirred her stomach and she pitched forward, one hand on her belly, the other gripping the knob. She contemplated a run. But where would she go? She had no money. Nowhere to hide. No one willing to help.

"Martha?"

Her mother's voice brought her upright. Jaw clenched, Martha returned to the kitchen on shaking legs, dropping into her chair.

"It is not the end of the world, dear," Mrs. Kaczmarek said. "You are hardly the first girl to get in the family way without a husband. There is a home in Wheeling for unwed mothers."

The knot in Martha's stomach loosened. The mid-wife just uttered the first soothing words she had heard in the past two days. "I'm not giving my baby away," Martha said. She lifted her face, giving Mrs. Kaczmarek a full view of her black eye.

"They will not make you give away your baby," the mid-wife said. "You can stay there for a year. With your baby."

"Then what, Martha?" Her mother asked. "Come back here with a baby? Disgrace your father?"

"You would rather I give my baby—your grandchild—to strangers?" Martha sat back, arms crossed over her chest. "I won't do it." She was a little surprised by her own strong words. But she meant them. Her dropped a protective hand to her belly, her gaze shifting between the mid-wife and her mother.

Marie shook her head, focused on a spot beyond Martha's right shoulder. "Such disobedience," she said. "Never would I have rebelled against my *mutter* in Germany."

Martha steeled herself for another exaltation on Germany. Her mother spoke of her homeland as if it was paradise. The people were kinder. The hills greener. The streams clearer. "Nothing is clean in the patch," her mother said, often. Martha had to admit that much was true, black dust, fine as sifted flour, filled every crevice

22

on the floorboards. The soot was everywhere. It might clear for an hour after a heavy shower but the rain turned the streets into a river of red sludge.

"What will you do, Martha?" Marie said. "No man will marry you with a baby."

Martha held on to her defiance. "I'll get a job. I've learned so much working at the company store. They like me. I'll work there."

"No. You cannot return. This choice—keeping your baby—will make your life hard," Marie said.

"Your mother is right, Martha, your life with a baby will be a struggle," Mrs. Kaczmarek said. She paused, frowning at Martha's eye. "But, you do not have to choose today. You can decide later, after you have settled into the rescue home. Dr. Medford is not in today so I can use his telephone to make arrangements for your arrival on the train."

"Train?" Martha asked, her boldness slipping.

"You will take the trolley to Little Washington. Then the train to Wheeling," Mrs. Kaczmarek said.

Martha's chest squeezed, her courage drained. She looked at her mother. "By myself?"

"I certainly cannot afford two tickets, Martha," Marie said. "And I would have to buy a ticket to return. As it is, there will be no Christmas presents for your brothers this year." She let out a long breath.

With a groan, Mrs. Kaczmarek pushed to her feet. "Thank you for the coffee, Klara." She turned her attention to Martha. "Good luck to you, dear. I will leave some salve for that eye."

Martha watched the mid-wife sashay from the room, wishing there was a salve for a broken heart.

CHAPTER THREE

December 1918
Wheeling, West Virginia

The train stopped but Martha didn't move from her seat. She stared at the window, gazing at her reflection, her black eye a reminder of her shunning, her very own scarlet letter. The hour-long journey was harrowing, her thoughts running amuck. One minute she was remorseful, sorry she hurt her mother, the next she was angry, believing her mother, and her sister, wickedly unkind. Once, she touched her swollen cheek and her father's words rushed back to her in an agonizing torrent. She wished him the same pain, hoping for a cave-in or explosion, then feeling overwhelming guilt for her nefarious thoughts. Peter crossed her mind, too, but Martha couldn't decide what she felt about him.

"Miss, this is your stop," the conductor said. He had validated Martha's ticket in Washington, Pennsylvania, directing a porter to stow her trunk in the train's belly, and led her to a seat by a window for the journey. "Is someone meeting you?"

Martha nodded, still frozen to her seat.

The conductor sighed and disappeared down the aisle. He returned with a tall, thin woman, a white cap on her head, six inches of white skirt hanging beneath her dark coat of rough wool.

"Martha, I am Miss Elizabeth Rungee, matron of the Florence Crittenton Home. Come with me, please," she said, raising her palm, fingers joggling.

Martha stared at the hand, holding her breath.

"Come, please," Miss Rungee repeated, her voice soft but stern.

Martha forced herself to her feet, dropping her chin and angling her head to hide her bruised face. She followed Miss Rungee to the platform where a scowling man, his arms crossed over his chest, waited. The conductor pointed to Martha's trunk sitting next to the train, the only baggage still on the platform. The man hoisted the trunk to his shoulder and headed inside, moving through the station with long strides, forcing Martha and Miss Rungee to a brisk pace. As they crossed the lavish, two-story lobby, Martha was so awed that she forgot to keep her head down, her gaze traveling from the sparkling skylights overhead, to the floor where grey veins ran across the gleaming marble. They exited under a clock, green pine wreathing the massive face, and followed the man to a truck with "Wilson Storage and Van Co" painted on the side. He heaved the trunk into the back and stalked to the driver's seat, not offering his hand to Miss Rungee or Martha as they climbed into the cab. When he swung behind the steering wheel the man glanced at Martha's belly, then locked his eyes on hers. She sucked in her breath at his unmasked contempt, her hands dropping to her stomach. She felt naked, exposed, her shame searing like a poker in a bed of hot coals. No words were spoken during the twenty-minute drive.

The truck jerked to a stop in front of a large clapboard house painted the color of a fresh egg yolk. The window frames and shutters were white, the lacy trim at the peak of the second-story roof also white. It reminded Martha of the gingerbread houses Frederic's mother used to make at Christmas. It even smelled like gingerbread when she followed Miss Rungee inside.

The matron led Martha and the truck's driver up a narrow flight of stairs, the man cursing under his breath as he struggled to get the trunk around two sharp bends.

"Martha, this is your bed," Miss Rungee said as she pointed at one of three single, white iron beds. "Mr. Wilson, put the trunk at the end of the bed, please."

Martha jumped as the trunk thudded to the floor.

Miss Rungee sighed. "That is all, Mr. Wilson. Thank you." She paused, waiting for the man to exit the room. "This is your space in the closet, Martha. The bottom drawer of the bureau is yours." She put a hand on the folded privacy screen to the side of the bureau. "Do you know how to use this?"

Martha shook her head.

"It provides modesty. When you're dressing. See?" She pulled the three sections open and stepped behind the five-foot screen, peering over the top.

The screen would have come in handy at home in her bedroom, Martha thought. Keep her nosy brothers at bay. She was vexed by the tightness in her chest, finding it difficult to believe she was actually missing her brothers. At least she got to say goodbye to Jakob, her youngest brother, now a brawny lad of sixteen. Allowed back into the house this morning while her father was in the mine, Martha and her mother packed up her belongings and Jakob had unexpectantly come home. He had frowned at her black eye, but said nothing, and carried the trunk to the trolley stop, giving her an awkward hug before leaving her and her mother in the shelter.

Miss Rungee collapsed the screen with three quick clicks. "Dinner is at five. Do not be late," she said, giving Martha's arm a pat as she walked from the room.

On her knees in front of the trunk, Martha ran her hand along one of the three-inch wide wood slats bowed atop the lid. For as long as she could remember, the trunk filled a corner of her parents' bedroom, her and her siblings daring each other to open it. They never did. No longer able to hold back her tears, she let them fall, a small pool gathering in a hollow gouged in the tin between the slats.

"That's a big trunk you got there. Don't think it's all gonna fit in your closet."

Martha wheeled around to a very pregnant woman standing behind her, pointing at the trunk. Martha pushed to her feet.

"Don't mean to be spying on ya, but we gonna be sharing this room. My name's Dorothy Shoaf but everyone calls me Dottie."

Martha towered over her roommate, frowning at the short fuzz on Dottie's scalp.

With a loud chuckle, Dottie rubbed her head "Had to have it shaved off back in July. Lice. But it's all cleared up now. Don't you worry none." She dropped her hand to her belly. "The baby's kicking up a storm today. Wanna feel?" Not waiting for a reply, she grabbed Martha's hand and held it to her belly. "Feel it?"

Martha shook her head and tried to pull her hand away.

Dottie held tight. "Mrs. Hinkle—that's the nurse—swears it's a boy since it's always kicking. I was hoping for a girl. Afraid he's going to come out looking like his daddy, and I don't want that. His daddy's uggg-ly. Swivel-eyed. And mean. And a liar. Said he was gonna marry me but he ran off with my cousin. Took a boat downriver." She moved Martha's hand a few inches to the left. "Good riddance, I say."

"Oh! It kicked. I felt it," Martha said. She couldn't help but smile, wondering if the fluttering she sometimes felt in her own belly could be kicking.

Dottie released Martha's hand and eyed Martha's stomach. "You don't look like you having a baby. So skinny." She lifted the end of Martha's braid and rolled it between two fingers, the nails bitten to the quick. "I used

28

to have hair long as yours. 'Course it weren't yellow, like yours." She dropped the plait and squinted up at Martha's face. "You a pretty one, ain't you? Except for that shiner. But that'll be gone soon. Mine take about two weeks to disappear but I got thin skin. That's what Momma said, 'fore she died." She turned her head and pointed. "That's Priscilla's bed. She's down in the nursery with her baby boy. Want some help putting your things away?"

Martha looked at the trunk and shrugged. "If you want." She knelt. "How long have you been here?"

"Got here in October." Dottie put a hand on Martha's shoulder as she lowered herself to the floor. "Mrs. Hinkle says the baby will be here next month. Mildred. Millie. That's what I wanna name it if it's a girl. My granny's name. Don't got no boy names in mind. What about you?"

Another shrug. Baby names had not crossed Martha's mind. She pushed the trunk's lid up to reveal a wood tray, five inches deep, filled with underwear and woolen hose, a book, a photograph and a doll made from a sock.

Dottie reached for the doll. "Yours?" She stroked the braids of yellow yarn on the doll's head, then picked at the eyes, bright blue buttons.

Martha nodded.

The doll discarded, Dottie picked up the photograph. It was taken in eighth grade, Martha's last year at the Webster Hill school.

"That you?" Dottie pointed.

Martha nodded again. She was the tallest kid in the back row, Frederic beside her, his shoulder touching her arm, his head turned towards her. Both wore broad smiles.

"That boy next to you likes you, don't he? He's looking at ya."

"Frederic." The name sounded hollow, her voice not her own. What would he think of her now? She let herself remember the last time she saw him, one year ago, one knee on the schoolhouse floor, his cap held over his heart with both hands. "I'm leaving tomorrow, but the war won't last long. Will you wait for me? Marry me when I return?" he had asked, beaming, so proud of his uniform with "PVT ALBRECHT" stenciled on the flap of the right chest pocket. Martha had said yes without hesitation.

"He the baby's daddy?" Dottie asked. "Why ain't you two hitched?"

"He died in the war." *The Battle of Cantigny*, Martha was going to add, but the words caught in her throat. She pulled the photo from Dottie's hand.

"Sorry." Dottie reached in the tray again. "That's a fat book. You like to read? Hey, this ain't English."

"It's German," Martha said. It was her father's English-German translation book, banished long ago to the bottom of the trunk. Although German was no longer taught in school, Martha continued to learn the language from Frederic so she could listen in on her parents' forbidden conversations.

"I don't read so good," Dottie said. "I only went to sixth grade." She put the book aside and pulled two satin ribbons from the trunk, one blue, one green. She dangled them from her fingertips. "You wear them in your hair?"

"Yes." Martha watched Dottie run the blue ribbon through her fingers. Frederic gave it to her on her sixteenth birthday. Said it matched her eyes. The green ribbon was once her mother's. She pulled it from Dottie's hand, her thoughts returning to her mother as they sat side by side on her bedroom floor this morning, the open trunk at their backs. Martha had found yellowed papers from the RMS *Lucania* in her father's book and asked about them.

"From 1894. Our passage on the ship to America," her mother had said, rubbing the brittle paper between her thumb and index finger. "I was number 1532. Your *vater* number 1531. Group C. Steerage." Her mother had snapped to her feet, tearing the papers in two, then tore them again, tossing the remains on the dresser.

Martha hadn't been surprised by her mother's actions. The journey from Germany was never talked about but her mother had said, more than once, it was not her idea to come to this country. After destroying the papers, her mother pulled the quilt from Martha's bed and stuffed it in the trunk. Stitched when Martha was an infant, the quilt had a dozen blocks with Dutch girls in oversized wood shoes, each wearing a different color bonnet.

Her meticulously-made bed, just like Dottie's and her other, unknown roommate's, was covered with a white spread. Martha decided her humble quilt would stay in the trunk.

"So, what's your name?" Dottie asked.

"Martha." She tugged the blue ribbon from Dottie's hand and tossed both ribbons in the trunk. They landed on the photograph, the blue satin circling Frederic's face. She stood. "Martha Albrecht."

Lifting the tray from the trunk, she carried it to the bureau and dumped the contents into the bottom drawer. She slammed the drawer closed and walked to the closet, flinging the door open and yanking the one empty hanger from the rod. She clutched the hanger to her chest, tears flowing again.

"It's not so bad here," Dottie whispered. She worked to her feet and backed out the door, closing it softly behind her.

Martha lay on her bed, her booted feet suspended over the side, and cried silently. *Move forward,* she told herself, repeating her mother's parting words.

"Hold your head up." Her mother had lifted Martha's chin with icy fingers as the trolley rumbled towards the Webster Hill shelter. "I came to this country filled with hope, filled with dreams," her mother said, her voice hitching. "I let life steal them from me. Whatever hope I have left, I am giving to you. You will have to find your own dreams." She had gripped Martha's shoulders, forcing Martha to look her in the eye. "Never let go of that hope. Remember where you came from, but do not dwell on the past as I did. Move forward. Always forward."

Martha wiped away her tears with the back of her hand. She was finished crying.

CHAPTER FOUR

December 1918
Wheeling, West Virginia

Martha buried her face in the pillow and pushed away the hand on her shoulder, thinking it was one of her brothers waking her. Slowly, the memories came back. The train, the hateful man at the station. She jolted awake, cheek throbbing, and stared at Miss Rungee.

"Dinner is ready, Martha. We're waiting on you," the matron said.

"I'm not hungry." Martha wrapped her arms around her shivering body. "I'll just stay in my room."

"No. No, you won't." Miss Rungee took a step back. "Every woman here eats breakfast, lunch and dinner in the dining room. The residents and the workers all eat together. Like a family." She raised her eyebrows, swept her hand towards the door.

Martha dropped her feet to the floor and stood, a steadying hand on the bed. She looked at Miss Rungee. "I really don't feel well. I'm not sure I can eat."

"Well, then, you will just sit quietly at the table. You've already met Dottie, she will be seated beside you, and you can meet your other roommate, the other residents, and the workers." Miss Rungee moved towards the door, stopped and turned back when she realized Martha hadn't moved. "Don't get off on the wrong foot, Martha. The other women are hungry and they can't eat until you've been seated."

Resigned, Martha followed the matron down the stairs. As they rounded a corner, she heard a buzzing, voices, lots of them, rising and falling. They walked into a large room and the buzzing quieted, dozens of faces turning towards her. Her face warmed as Miss Rungee led her to a round table draped with white linen.

"Howdy, Martha," Dottie said, patting the chair next to her. "This here's Priscilla."

Martha tried to smile but her trembling lips wouldn't cooperate. She nodded and dropped into the chair, Miss Rungee taking the seat next to her.

"That is Miss Yoho, one of the home's workers," Miss Rungee said, nodding across the table at a young woman about Martha's age. "Mrs. Graham, our assistant matron, is beside her."

Both workers were dressed in blue checked dresses, pinafore aprons and caps, the caps and aprons as white as the tablecloth. They smiled at Martha, Miss Yoho, murmuring "hello" just before she bowed her head.

Miss Rungee led them through grace, Martha sneaking glances around the table from beneath her lashes. There were four other women, ten total, seated around her. A pasty woman beside Priscilla, thinner than Martha, her black hair cropped short, caught Martha looking and stared back with eyes as dark as her hair.

"Amen," Dottie said. She elbowed Martha.

Martha frowned, then realized the entire table had repeated "amen" when Miss Rungee ended the prayer. "Amen," she whispered, taking the basket of bread from Dottie's hand.

"Yum, spaghetti! My favorite," Dottie said, scooping long noodles from a platter. She handed a long, wood-handled, two-pronged fork to Martha. "Don't forget the meatballs. They're darn good."

"Dottie, language," Miss Rungee said. She nodded at the serving fork in Martha's hand. "Go ahead, help yourself."

"I really am not hungry," Martha stammered as her stomach growled. She hadn't eaten since breakfast but, although it smelled fine, the mound on the platter didn't look good to her. She never had spaghetti. Tomatoes on skinny noodles? Round meat? She grew up on sauerkraut and sausages, the rare spaetzle on holidays being the closest thing she got to a spaghetti noodle.

Miss Rungee studied Martha for a moment, held up the basket of bread. "At least have a slice of bread." She looked across the table. "Charlotte, please pass the butter to Martha."

The thin woman with the short hair picked up a round, lidded dish and handed it to Priscilla, who held it out towards Dottie. Hunched over her plate, intent on her spaghetti, Dottie didn't notice until Priscilla elbowed her.

"Hey!" Dottie said, mouth full.

Miss Rungee sighed. "Manners, Dottie."

Dottie swallowed, took a swig of milk. "Yes, ma'am. Sorry." She took the dish from Priscilla and set it in front of Martha.

Martha stared at gold-rimmed edges and the small, gold loop atop the dish's domed lid. She raised her chin, her gaze sweeping the table, looking for the crock of butter. Charlotte met her eyes again, unblinking.

Miss Rungee lifted the dish's lid, grasping the delicate loop between her thumb and index finger to expose a creamy block of butter. "All our dishes and silver were donated," she explained to Martha. "The patterns are mismatched but the appropriate china and tableware help our residents learn proper dining etiquette."

Martha watched as Miss Rungee sliced off a pat of butter with a short knife and added it to Martha's plate.

"Now use your own knife to butter your bread," Miss Rungee said. She took a pat for herself, raised her chin, and smiled. "This is my favorite room in the Home. Bright and airy."

It was bright, but not from the windows at this time of day. Martha squinted at the glowing globe suspended from the ceiling on gold chains. It lit the entire room, and this was a large room, as big as her kitchen, living room and bedroom at home combined. Four round tables, all draped in white, a mixture of workers, all dressed alike, and residents filled each table of ten.

"We added this room three years ago," Miss Rungee said. "And the four bedrooms and another bathroom above it."

To Martha it was a mansion, the largest house she had ever been in. "How many bedrooms are here?" she asked.

"Eleven. Three to a room, just like yours. All furnished the same."

Martha did a quick calculation in her head. Thirty-three women. Thirty-three strangers to avoid. But Miss Rungee had a different idea. After dinner, the matron led her around the room, introducing her to every worker, every resident. Martha remembered just a few of the names and was relieved when she was allowed to return to her room with the stern warning of "lights out at eight."

Dottie was pulling a grey nightshirt over her head when Martha walked in their room. "Oh, sorry." She turned her face, trying not to stare at Dottie's belly and bulging navel, the skin stretched and mottled.

"What you sorry about? Ain't you that looks like a cow," Dottie said, laughing. She turned and faced Martha, bloated breasts swaying. "Better get used to it, you'll be busting out all over soon enough."

"Dottie, have some humility." Priscilla's head popped up behind the privacy screen and she stepped out in an ankle-length pink gown of thick flannel, white

36

ruffles at the neck and sleeves. She looked at Martha. "You want me to leave the screen up?"

Martha nodded. She dug her night clothes, an oversized shirt of muslin, from her drawer and went behind the screen. Her dress off, she lifted the waist of her bloomers, inspecting her still-flat stomach. Camisole, bloomers and wool stockings still on, she pulled her sleep shirt over her head and hurried to her bed.

"You need to put the screen away," Priscilla said from her bed.

"And hang up your dress," Dottie added. "The workers can stop in anytime for inspection."

"Did you clean your teeth?" Priscilla asked.

Martha bristled. She didn't need reminding about everything. Priscilla was starting to sound like her sister.

"Oops, I forgot again," Dottie said, sitting up. She lay back down. "Ah, never mind. I'll do it in the morning."

"You are supposed to clean them twice a day. Once in the morning, once before bed," Priscilla said. "Don't you listen to anything they say in hygiene?"

Dottie giggled. "Miss Yoho don't like teaching that class. She gets all red talking about body parts. Specially the men parts."

"Class?" Martha sat on her bed and worked her braid loose.

"Didn't Miss Rungee tell ya? We have classes every day," Dottie said.

"Penmanship on Monday. Geography Tuesday morning. History on Wednesday. Reading and spelling on Thursday," Priscilla said.

"And hygiene on Friday," Dottie added with another giggle. "You'll get to go to that one tomorrow."

Martha nearly dropped her hairbrush. "We have to go to school?"

Priscilla shook her head. "Oh, no. The classes are in the dining room. After breakfast."

"Yeah, after us kitchen helpers clean up," Dottie said.

"Thought you liked working in the kitchen," Priscilla said. "What's your assigned duties, Martha?"

"Assigned duties?"

"Chores. Just another way of saying chores," Dottie said. "I work in the kitchen. Cutting up vegetables, washing pots. Priscilla works in the laundry."

"I don't know," Martha said, slowly realizing her time at the Crittenton Home was not going to be easy. There were rules, lots of them, and she had never been good with rules. She lay her head on her pillow and pulled the blanket to her chin, her thoughts going to her family. It seemed ages ago that she said goodbye to her mother. Was it really just this morning she stood at the Webster Hill trolley stop watching her brother walk away? She wondered if Jakob made it home for dinner tonight. He had been staying out late the last few weeks, her mother getting no answers when she asked him where he had been. She heard he was skipping school, too. That would really make her mother angry. What did her family eat for dinner, she wondered, deciding on sauerkraut. Her stomach rumbled and she rolled on to her side, surprised to find she actually missed sauerkraut, and drifted asleep with the smell of cabbage vivid in her dreams.

***

A loud rap on the door woke Martha at dawn. She had to wait ten minutes for her turn in the bathroom but the wait was still better than having to run outside on a cold morning to use the outhouse. Breakfast was oatmeal. Not her favorite but she ate two bowls. She watched as the tables were stripped, paper and pencils replacing the forks and spoons. Dottie giggled her way through hygiene class, earning steely looks from Miss Yoho, and Martha stifled her own sniggers, agreeing that much of the class was silly. Who didn't know you had to wash your hair and clean your privates? She tried to limit her looks around the room, but she couldn't help herself. The women were fascinating. All different shapes and sizes, some very pregnant, others thin as a willow tree. Most were around her age but a few were older, or maybe they just looked older. Two women wore bright blouses with knee-length skirts, the rest in dark dresses that fell to their ankles.

Lunch was a thick soup of potatoes and green beans and after a quick trip to the bathroom, Miss Rungee led Martha outside into a wide yard at the back of the house. There were no other houses in sight.

"Privacy is one of the reasons we moved here," Miss Rungee said. She pointed to a grove of squat trees and chuckled. "Our neighbors are apple and cherry trees. But that's a good thing. Most communities don't like having us around." She paused, pursed her lips, her gaze on the treetops. "We had to leave the building on Sixteenth Street even though five months' rent had already been paid." She stopped in front of a windowless, one-story building painted the same yellow as the Home. "Our laundry shed," she said. "We need help in the laundry so you will spend your afternoons here. Priscilla has agreed to train you."

Martha was relieved. She feared her assigned duties would be in the kitchen, and she had never been much help to her mother at mealtime. Laundry was not difficult, just rub the soiled cloth across a washboard and hang it on the line. Or so she thought.

Priscilla laughed at her hubris. "Laundry is a little more complicated here." She pointed at a silver tub large enough to bathe in. "Linens go there, towels in that tub. Aprons and caps in that one." She scrunched her snub nose, jutted her sharp chin at a round tub in the corner. "Diapers only in that one. Always use hot water. Heat it on the stove." She wagged her hand at the large, coal-burning stove in the center of the room. "We have two plungers." She held up a funnel-shaped hunk of copper attached to a three-foot wood handle and dunked it in a tub of tablecloths soaking in lye.

Martha learned to agitate the soiled cloth with a plunger until it was clean, and how to send the fabric through the wringer without catching her fingers in the clacking rollers. She learned to mix starch and how to iron without scorching. It was all new to her. In the patch she had no need for ironed clothes. No need for starch, either, since muslin was already stiff.

Late in the afternoon, the thin woman at the dinner table last night, Charlotte, helped Martha feed a tablecloth into an electric wringer. "Thank you," Martha said.

Charlotte turned and fished another cloth from the soaking tub. "Watch your fingers," she said, her voice soft.

Martha nodded. "Looks like you know what you're doing. How long have you been here?"

"Six months."

"You have a boy or a girl?" Martha asked, assuming Charlotte had a baby in the Home's nursery.

Charlotte dropped her hands and moved to the other side of the wringer. She pulled a tablecloth from the basket and stalked across the room, tossing the cloth over a rope stretched from wall to wall.

"Her baby died. Stillborn," Priscilla whispered in Martha's ear.

Martha's mouth fell open, her stomach flipped. She glanced at Charlotte, returned her attention to Priscilla. "Why is she still here?"

Priscilla shrugged. "Nowhere else to go, I guess." She grabbed the other side of the cloth. "Not so fast, Martha. You'll jam the wringer."

For the next hour, Martha worked through several apologies in her head, none of them sounding right. The moment she learned Charlotte's baby died was the moment Martha realized how much she wanted her baby, how much she loved her baby already. A fierce love that was a little frightening. She knew she would do anything to protect her child. Charlotte stayed on the other side of the shed, head down, disappearing behind the cloths hanging on the line whenever someone came close. Women came and went from the laundry—Priscilla explaining that they had to feed and care for babies—and Martha was kept quite busy, never getting the chance to speak to Charlotte.

***

Martha spent the night tossing and turning, her stomach rebelling against a strange dinner Miss Rungee called Shepherd's Pie. She had searched the dining room for Charlotte but the woman wasn't there. Nor was she there for breakfast or after breakfast when a group of ladies from the YWCA visited, the residents were herded to the parlor where the contemptuous Mr. Wilson angled an upright piano in the corner. One of the visitors, a Mrs. Richards, played the piano and the other ladies sang, encouraging the residents to sing along but only Priscilla joined in. Martha was astounded. Who knew her prudish roommate with the pockmarked face could sing like an angel?

"Where did you learn to sing like that?" Martha asked when they returned to their room just before lunch.

"I sang in the choir at school," Priscilla said.

"You sang at school?" Martha was intrigued. "What kind of school did you go to?"

"An academy. For girls."

"Rich girls," Dottie said.

Priscilla ignored Dottie. "I can play the piano, too. My school had a music room so we could learn many instruments." She sat on her bed, running her hands down her skirt. "My little sister plays the harp. And the guitar." She looked off to the side, pressing her lips together. "I didn't get to hear my sister play," she said, her voice hitching. "Father brought me here the night of her recital. Said I was an embarrassment. Said he didn't want to see me again."

Martha turned away. It didn't matter if you were once rich or poor, respectable or scorned, the women here could never go home.

CHAPTER FIVE

June 1919
Wheeling, West Virginia

Martha sat next to Dottie in the nursery on the Crittenton Home's first floor, hands crossed over her belly. At nine months pregnant, she was due any day and spent extra time in the nursery, watching, learning, constantly on edge.

Dottie encouraged a burp from her five-month-old son, Mickey. "Ah, that was a good one!"

Martha smiled at the baby, stroking his small foot. She turned her attention two cradles down where Miss Rungee, a mewling newborn in her arms, stood next to Lena, the Home's newest resident. Lena showed up on the doorstep three mornings ago, feverish and heavily pregnant, her baby boy arriving just hours later.

"He is hungry," Miss Rungee said, lowering the baby to Lena and signaling to Miss Yoho. "We will use a feeding bottle again, but you must learn to nurse."

"How are you feeling today, Lena?" Miss Yoho asked, bottle in hand.

"Tired. Scared." Lena's brow furrowed. "What will I do with a baby at the house? He cries so much. Madame Ada will be angry. *O mójboże*," she said in broken English.

"No, Lena, you mustn't go back to Madame Ada's. Do you have family here?" Miss Rungee asked.

Lena shook her head. "My aunt has a cousin in Baltimore. I was to stay with her." She took the bottle from Miss Yoho and pushed the rubber nipple in her son's mouth. The infant turned away, his cries increasing.

Her hand cupping the baby's crown, Miss Rungee raised the small head an inch. "Do you have an address for your relative?"

"No." Lena shook her head again. "My aunt works at a bakery. I was to work there. I gave the address to a man at the docks, but he did not take me to the bakery."

"What man, Lena?" Miss Yoho asked.

Lena shrugged and put the nipple back in her baby's mouth. After a moment, he latched on, his cheeks dimpling with the effort. "Oh! He is eating." Lena looked up and smiled, until she caught sight of Martha watching her. Her face went slack and she glared at Martha, the circles beneath her glistening eyes dark against the sallow skin.

"What man?" Miss Yoho repeated.

"A man in a cab." Lena pulled her angry gaze from Martha, focused on Miss Yoho. "He had a white horse," she added, and lifted a shoulder. "Took me and two other girls from the ship to the train. We came to Wheeling. Madam Ada's house. She fed us. Gave us clothes. Put us in a bedroom in the attic." She paused, ran her fingertip down her baby's cheek. "There were already five other girls there. The men came that night," Lena said, voice cracking, tears dripping on her baby's blanket. "I never even kissed a boy in Poland."

"Oh my word," Martha blurted, her hand on her chest. "I thought the women wanted to be at those places."

Miss Rungee turned. She studied Martha for a moment, then walked to her side. "It is unmannerly to eavesdrop, Martha." She sighed. "Your belief is not

44

uncommon. Brothels are often called a 'necessary evil.' They say..." she paused, her cheeks reddening as she threw a glance at Lena. "It is often said that sexual indulgence is vital to men's health. That the brothels kept decent women safe. I, and every other matron at the Florence Crittenton homes, say they are wrong." She put a hand under Martha's elbow and helped her to her feet. "Today will be your last day in the laundry since you are close to delivery." She looked at Dottie. "Put Mickey down for his nap and return to your duties in the kitchen. We have much to prepare before Doctor Barrett's visit tomorrow."

Martha left the nursery, loitering outside the door with her back against the wall, hands under her belly, and waited for Dottie.

"They're all a titter in the kitchen," Dottie said. "Don't know who this doctor is, but he must be important."

"She," Martha said, moving down the hall towards the dining room.

Dottie stopped. "What?"

"Doctor Barrett is a woman."

Dottie eyed Martha. "How do you know?"

"I heard Miss Rungee talking about her."

Dottie chuckled. "You got big ears. What else you hear?"

Martha shrugged. "Doctor Barrett is important. Lives in Washington D.C., just like the President. She's in charge of these Homes. All seventy of them. Some as far away as California."

"Hmm. All I know is I had to cut the carrots twice. Mrs. Gaines said they was too big but that's the way I always cut 'em." Dottie pushed open the door at the end of hall.

"There you are!" The cook, Mrs. Gaines, stood in the dining room with a basket of potatoes on her ample hip. She puffed her cheeks and blew a strand of grey hair from her face, chucking her chin towards the kitchen door. "Hurry up, now."

With her back to Mrs. Gaines, Dottie rolled her eyes at Frances. "See you later," she said, and followed the cook.

Martha looked out the window, scowling at the laundry shed. It would be hot as an oven in there today. She pulled out a chair and lowered her bulk to the seat, using a fingernail to scratch at a stain on the tablecloth. She grimaced. There were several stains scattered across the white cloth. It would take work to get this one clean.

"Martha!" Miss Yoho strode into the room. "Take these to the laundry. Now." She put a basket of soiled diapers in Martha's lap.

Martha got to her feet, surprisingly quick, considering her size. "Yes, ma'am." The basket wasn't heavy, but it smelled. She sucked in a breath, holding it until she was outside. The sun was shining and she turned her face towards it, savoring a moment of fresh air. Lowering the basket to the ground, she dug her cap from the pocket of her apron, yanking the despised hat over her coiled braid.

"The cap and apron in our home is a badge of authority," Miss Rungee had said when Martha balked at wearing a cap. "I wear one. Every worker wears a cap. When the women leave here, many will become domestics. Some may become nurses. They will be asked to wear a cap and apron and should not feel it to be a badge of inferiority. Soldiers, sailors and policeman are all proud of their uniforms. Why should not the serviceable cap and apron be looked upon with pride instead of being considered a mark of servitude?"

Martha didn't agree. Life in the laundry would be much easier if she didn't have to starch and iron dozens of caps every day. The door to the laundry was propped open but the building was still steamy. She tossed a handful of cornstarch in a bucket and moved to the sink, giving the faucet a solid twist. Water splashed into the pail.

"Don't pick that up. It's too heavy," Priscilla mumbled, a clothes pin clamped between her lips. She dropped the wood pin in her apron pocket and lifted the full bucket from the sink, carrying it to the large ironing board.

"Thank you," Martha said.

An hour later, her stack of ironed aprons a foot high, Martha had to sit, a pain in her belly sending her to her knees. She had been warned the pains would become more common as her delivery neared.

"How will I know when it's time?" Martha asked Dottie.

"Oh, you'll know," Dottie said.

She also asked about the actual birth but Dottie wouldn't give details. Neither would Priscilla. They shrugged at each other with a look Martha didn't like. "You'll be fine," Priscilla said. "Miss Rungee will tell you what to do."

***

The next morning, after an abridged breakfast, the tables in the dining room were stripped, fresh cloths draped, and the parquet floor buffed to a high sheen. Dr. Kate Waller Barrett arrived just before noon. Martha stood against the wall along with the other residents and workers and watched the guest-of-honor shake hands with the Board of Directors and newspaper reporters. Dr. Barrett was short—a full head shorter than Martha—and older than she had expected. The doctor's face was lined, her white hair pulled into a tight bun, but Dr. Barrett's light grey eyes were clear when she stopped in front of Martha.

Extending her arms, Dr. Barrett pulled Martha's hands into her own—just as she had done with each resident. "What's your name, dear?"

"Martha."

Dr. Barrett gave a nod towards Martha's bulging belly. "May I?" she asked.

Martha nodded.

"You will be a mother very soon," Dr. Barrett said, her veined hand on Martha's belly. She raised her gaze to Martha's face and smiled. "I hope you'll do me the favor of having your baby while I'm here. I never tire of bringing a new life into the world." She turned away, moving to the small table serving as a makeshift podium.

Martha worked her way to a table, squeezing her bulk into the chair between Priscilla and Dottie. She watched Dr. Barrett pull papers from her pockets, spreading her notes on the table before her, studying them as she smoothed the creases.

The room quieted when Dr. Barrett looked up from her papers. "It's been twenty-five years since a group of women put aside their fears and ventured into the dark depths of your city jail," she said, her voice strong and steady. "Their goal? Helping the female inmates turn their lives around. These heroic women tried to raise the funds necessary to open a rescue home, but despite their best efforts, they collected little. Then Charles Crittenton visited your fair city and pledged his support." She swept her hand in a wide arc. "Now, you have this exceptional home."

For such a small woman, the doctor could talk awfully loud, Martha thought. She looked around the crowded room as people applauded, finally finding Miss Rungee. The matron sat very straight, her focus on Dr. Barrett.

Dr. Barrett held one of her papers aloft, waiting for the room to quiet again. "Three hundred twenty young women. One hundred seventy babies. That's who this home has served. Those are the statistics on this report." The page fluttered in her fingertips and she paused as a few board members clapped. She let the paper fall to the table. "Statistics are for the politicians. What interests me is the life that goes on within these walls." She rapped her knuckles on the table. "This Home teaches by example. Every worker. Every day. They influence and shape our women. Our residents leave here equipped to meet the world. Equipped to earn an honest living, regardless of their pasts.

"What a burden would be removed from the taxpayers if every unmarried mother was given the chance to earn that honest living, not only for herself, but also for her child. What if the ban of illegitimacy was removed? What if every struggling boy and girl born to an unwed mother was given the chance to shine? It is of far greater importance to the world what a man's grandchild is going to be, than who that child's grandparents were." Dr. Barrett paused, murmurs and coughs reverberating. She paused, encouraged quiet.

"Now, back to the politicians," she said, raising her hands, palms up. "Those men in Washington who have the power to change not only laws, but an unjust, un-American way of thinking. There has been change. The Mann Act. Protections for immigrants." She shuffled through the papers, pulling one into her hand. "Our honorable President Wilson sent this letter. He said our work should command the interest and support of every good citizen."

Dr. Barrett searched the crowd, her eyes locking with the board treasurer, the lone man on the board. The only person in the room able to vote.

"There is more to do," she said. "We need forward-thinking men in government. Men unafraid to fight for women and children. Unafraid to fight for what's right."

The clapping was sparse, at first, then all joined in. Dr. Barrett folded her papers, returned the stack to her pocket. "Thank you," she said, allowing Miss Rungee to guide her to the table with the Board of Directors.

***

Exempt from her duties, Martha went back to her room after lunch. All her books had been returned to the library downtown so there nothing to read in the room except her father's German books and a small pamphlet about the Crittenton homes. With a grunt, she unhooked her boots and lay on the bed, reading about Charles Crittenton's young daughter, Florence, who died from scarlet fever when she was four-years-old. Martha chocked back a sob. Now that she was about to become a mother, tears seemed to come unannounced. One minute she was laughing, the next she was crying. She watched Dottie and Priscilla and all the other mothers in the nursery and wondered how she would measure up. It kept her awake at night, her sister's warning of "being a mother is harder than you think" running through her thoughts.

She forced her focus back to Charles Crittenton. He was a wealthy man. She closed her eyes. Even a rich man could lose his child. The thought brought on another sob but she continued to read through bleary eyes. After his little girl died, Mr. Crittenton opened the Florence Night Mission in New York City to help prostitutes. He gave money to Dr. Barrett for a rescue home she opened in Atlanta, and when Dr. Barrett moved with her preacher husband and six kids to Washington D. C., she became General Superintendent of the Mission.

Martha put the pamphlet to the side. The only superintendent she knew was the mine super. A nasty man, her father said. She pushed her father from her thoughts and moved her hand across her belly, cupping a small foot. Or maybe it was a little hand curled into a fist. Whatever it was, it moved, sending a searing pain straight through to Martha's spine. She closed her eyes and lay back on the bed, waiting for the pain to ease.

"Hello?"

Martha opened her eyes to find Dr. Barrett standing at the doorway. She pushed to her feet. "I'm due to give birth," she stammered. "I have been dismissed from my duties."

Dr. Barrett nodded and walked to the table by the bed. She picked up one of the books. "German?"

"My father's," Martha said.

Dr. Barrett sat and patted the bed. "Sit with me. Do you like to read, Martha?"

"Yes, ma'am. Miss Rungee brings me books from the city library. Says I can go myself once the baby is born."

"Wonderful. All our young women are encouraged to read, but most have to be taught to love books. Very few come to us with a natural fondness for reading. I was glad to find many books and magazines in your sitting room." Dr. Barrett chuckled as she tapped the book's cover. "But they are in English."

Martha smiled. "Yes, ma'am."

"Do you have a favorite book, Martha?"

"I liked *The Secret Garden*, even though it's for kids," Martha said. "I'm going to read it to my baby, ma'am."

"Why don't you call me Mrs. Barrett?"

"Miss Rungee calls you 'Doctor.' Are you a real doctor, ma'am?" Martha asked.

"Yes, but I don't treat patients. Not like most of the doctors you know."

"I only knew one doctor, ma'am...ah, Mrs. Barrett. He had an office at the patch but I never had to see him. My sister went once." She raised her chin, fingers tapping her neck. "She had a bad throat. And my brother went to the doctor when he cut his hand. Jakob, my brother, was always getting into trouble..." Martha bowed her head, concentrating on her hands squeezed together in her lap. Thoughts of her family still made her weepy.

"I'm sure you miss your family, as I miss mine," Dr. Barrett said, resting a hand on Martha's.

"I miss my mother. And Jakob." Martha raised her head and shrugged. "I even miss my sister."

"And your father?"

Martha put her palm on her cheek, let her chin fall to her chest. "My father made me leave the house."

"Ahh." Dr. Barrett nodded. "Fathers often find it difficult to accept their daughter's choices. My own father could never quite reconcile himself to my path in life. I was the eldest of eight daughters. Many things were expected of me. And many more things were forbidden."

"My father forbade me to see Peter," Martha said. "I am ashamed. I know what I did was wrong, but Peter and I were to be married."

"We all make mistakes." Dr. Barrett said, patting Martha's hand.

"Yes ma'am." Martha gritted her teeth, sweat beading on her forehead. Another massive cramp was coming.

Dr. Barrett frowned. "Are you in pain?"

Martha nodded, her belly on fire.

"Let's get you downstairs." Dr. Barrett gripped Martha's elbow and helped her to her feet and into the hall, waving her hand at a passing worker. "Alert Miss Rungee that Martha is in labor."

As they neared the small room at the end of the nursery, the delivery room, Martha stopped. She had heard the cries of agony coming from inside. Dr. Barrett urged her on and helped her into a cotton gown as Miss Rungee hurried in, Dottie on her heels.

Dottie dropped to her knees and grabbed Martha's hand. "I won't let go. You can squeeze as hard as you want."

Martha nodded, another contraction taking hold. She grimaced and twisted but didn't utter a sound. She had been taught to keep her pain to herself, that it was unseemly to cry out. "It is our way, Martha," her mother had said. "I did not shed a tear when I left my home."

"I have sent word to the doctor," Miss Rungee said to Dr. Barrett, moving to end of the bed and raising the sheet draped over Martha's knees. "But, you never know when he will arrive." She put her hands on Martha's tightening belly, fingertips probing, palpating.

Martha gripped Dottie's hand. "I'm scared."

Dottie gave a little cry. "You got strong hands, Martha." She laughed. "Bet you could whip Mr. Rake."

Martha managed a giggle. Mr. Rake was the stunted man with the tongue-twisting Italian name who tended the lawn. Only Dottie could make her laugh in the middle of labor but Martha's mirth didn't last long. The next contraction was sharper and a small moan escaped her lips as she squeezed her eyes closed. After a few intense minutes the contraction eased and Martha opened her eyes, looking up at Miss Rungee. The matron had gold eyes, Martha noticed, wondering why she never took note of the unique color before. They were kind eyes, Martha decided, and managed a weak smile.

Miss Rungee returned the smile. "You are doing fine, Martha. Just fine." She ran a cool, wet rag across Martha's forehead.

Unprepared for the next contraction, Martha didn't have time to steel herself. Her vow of silence forgotten, she cried out a torrent of nasty German words she had overheard her father use.

Dottie giggled. Miss Rungee and Dr. Barrett said nothing, but two red circles bloomed on Miss Rungee's cheeks.

Martha wanted to apologize for her outburst but she was in agony again. She lost track of time, voices fading in and out, the pain becoming constant.

A voice cut through the fog. Martha thought it was Dr. Barrett's.

"Not much longer, now. Push, Martha. Push."

The voices faded again, the pain threatening to overwhelm, and then it was gone.

"Oh, Martha, she's beautiful!"

Martha knew that voice. Dottie. She turned. Her friend was smiling at a small head covered with red-gold hair.

"Do you have a name picked out?" Dr. Barrett asked as she pulled the corners of a flannel blanket over the baby's chest, wiping the tiny face with a damp cloth.

"Frances," Martha said. She licked her parched lips, swallowed hard. "Like the writer. And her middle name is Hope."

PART TWO: STAINED GLASS 1925 – 1933

CHAPTER SIX

February 1925
Wheeling, West Virginia

"Martha, this tablecloth is wrinkled." Ruth Pickett, the wife of Martha's employer, pointed to a two-inch crease at the corner of the white linen cloth spread across the mahogany table. "Mr. Pickett's guests tonight are important and I want dinner to be perfect. Iron it again. I'm going to lunch out the pike at Mrs. Harper's. I expect the table to be set for inspection when I return. Did the florist bring the flowers yet?"

"No ma'am," Martha said. She kept her head down, hands clasped at her waist, doing her best to look compliant. Obedience did not come easy to her.

"Where's Mrs. Roth?" Ruth asked.

"At the market, ma'am."

"Then you must call the florist, Martha." Ruth walked into the hall, her steps heavy as she moved down the polished oak floorboards towards the front door. She ran a finger along the carved spindles along the open stairwell. "This needs dusted, Martha."

"Yes, ma'am." Martha took the coat draped over Ruth's arm and helped her into the soft wool. "Here's your muff, Mrs. Pickett."

"Is Vickers there?" Ruth asked, forcing her plumb hands into the rolled leopard fur.

Martha pulled the thick door open, passed through the marble vestibule, and peered out the entrance door. The green Franklin sedan idled at the curb. "Yes, ma'am." She opened the door and nodded at the driver.

Dennis Vickers, chauffer and handyman, ran up the sidewalk, hurdling the three marble steps to the porch. He came to a stop in front of Martha, his smile wide as he pulled his cap off.

"Morning, Martha. Ready to go Mrs. Pickett?"

"My hat, Martha." Ruth bowed her head, though there was no need as Martha stood a foot taller. She faced the oval mirror on the wall and moved her head from side to side, inspecting the six-inch hat of the same fur as her muff. "Tell the florist I want peacock feathers. And lilies, not roses," she said to Martha's reflection.

"Yes, ma'am." Martha closed the door behind Ruth and walked back to the dining room, blowing on the spindles as she passed by. She gathered the tablecloth into her arms and moved into the kitchen, relieved to see the housekeeper, Mrs. Roth. "Mrs. Pickett asked about the flowers. Wanted me to call the florist," Martha said. "Peacock feathers and lilies."

Mrs. Roth waved her hand in front of her face. "She can't change the order now. The florist will be here at two o'clock. Mrs. Pickett gets herself worked up every time the mister has guests for dinner."

"She gets worked up about most everything these days. Lacing her corset sent her into tears this morning," Martha said.

Besides the laundry, Martha attended to the lady-of-the-house's needs and whims. Ruth, thankfully, spent a great deal of time out of the house socializing, but when she was around she was formidable, chastising household staff and making difficult demands. Last week she had a hankering for black walnut fudge and sent

Mrs. Roth on a frantic search for a nut that was out of season and nearly impossible to find.

"I would cry, too, if I was married to George Pickett." Mrs. Seighman, the cook, turned from the pot on the stove, oversized spoon in hand. "Miserable cheat."

Tablecloth hugged to her chest, Martha ran down the stairs to the basement. She spread the linen across the ironing board and dipped her hands in a small tub. With a flick of her fingers, she sprinkled the starch across the fabric. Two irons rested in the gas fireplace and she attached a wood handle to one. Ironing was her favorite part of laundry. Quiet. Calming. She thought of Priscilla as she glided the hot metal across the cloth. "Always moving, Martha," Priscilla had said in her songful voice as she hunched over the Crittenton Home's large ironing board. Where was Priscilla now, she wondered. Does she still sing to her son? When Priscilla left the Home, Martha took charge of the laundry, and ran it well. Miss Rungee noted Martha's laundry prowess and when it was Martha's time to leave, the matron helped secure the job as laundress at the Pickett house five years ago.

Martha still kept in touch with Miss Rungee. Just yesterday, she received a sad letter from the matron, informing her that Dr. Kate Waller Barrett had passed away.

"I'm heart-broken. We were all devoted to her," Miss Rungee wrote. "Her son, Robert, will be taking over as president of the Mission. I don't know how he can possibly fill her shoes but we all agreed to soldier on, as Dr. Barrett would want us to do. We are planning a celebration of her life on Sunday, March fifteenth from one o'clock until three o'clock. All the women who passed through the doors of the Wheeling Home, and their children, are invited to the celebration."

It would be nice to attend but Martha knew better than to ask Mrs. Pickett for the time off, the household was already short-handed on Sundays since it was Mrs.

Roth's day off. The rest of the staff worked every day. Martha was permitted to arrive three hours later than normal on Sunday, at ten o'clock, so she could attend church, and she had Monday afternoons off. Usually Mrs. Seighman left after lunch on Saturday, unless there was special dinner planned, like tonight. It would be midnight before the household staff finished their duties this evening.

"Hello, Martha."

She wheeled around to face her boss, George Pickett. Last month, George started coming in the house through the basement door, claiming the walk from the garage was shorter to the basement than to the back door on the first level of the house. It wasn't.

George laughed. "No need to arm yourself, Martha." He took the iron from her hands, licking his lips as he ogled her body. "I'm quite harmless. You must be used to admiration from men. Have you a boyfriend, Martha?"

"No, sir." She stared at the scuff on the right toe of George's polished shoe. Her boss wasn't a tall man, his height and hers same, but he had a presence, a commanding voice, intense eyes. Feral was the word that came to mind, along with a few unspeakables.

With a finger under her chin, George raised Martha's head. "I hear you are a widow, Martha, so I know you have experienced the pleasures of a man."

She turned her head, but George gripped her chin, forcing her face back to his. He kissed her. A quick touch to her clamped lips. He held her hands, his thumbs rubbing her calloused knuckles. "I hope you liked the gloves I gave you. So many gifts I would give you. I could make your life easier, Martha. Think about it." He smiled and released her hands. Whistling, he went up the stairs.

She blew out a breath and wiped her mouth with her sleeve. His breath smelled of tobacco and decay, his lips dry and scaly. She stomped to the fireplace and, palm against the warm stone, took in a deep breath, let it out slowly. Eyes closed, she took another deep breath,

60

pictured Frances Hope. Her anger ebbed. Just the thought of her daughter made Martha smile. Made the work bearable. She retrieved the other iron from the coals and moved it across the tablecloth until it was flawless, draping the warm fabric over her arms for the trip upstairs. After setting the china, crystal and silverware for ten, she pulled the dining room pocket doors closed and went into the kitchen.

"I don't want chicken. I want lamb," Russell, the Pickett's ten-year-old son, said to Mrs. Seighman.

"The lamb is for tonight, Master Russell. Your father is having the chicken for lunch." Mrs. Seighman raised her eyebrows at the nanny who was standing in the doorway with nine-year-old Randolph, the Pickett's other son.

Maureen Hodgins, the third nanny in as many years, remained quiet. She had been with the Pickett's one month, hired when the previous nanny was discovered in George's bed. Maureen, grey haired and heavy set, was hand-picked by Ruth Pickett. Mrs. Roth and Mrs. Seighman had to make room in the cramped third floor quarters for Nanny Maureen when Ruth insisted the boys no longer needed their nanny sleeping in the bedroom on the second floor in the room across the hall from George's bedroom.

"Your father is expecting you. He is in the second floor dining room," Mrs. Roth said to Russell. She looked at the nanny. "Mr. Pickett does not like to be kept waiting."

"Come, boys," Maureen said. She clapped and motioned the Pickett sons out of the kitchen.

"Laura, help Martha take lunch upstairs. But let Martha serve," Mrs. Roth said.

Laura, Mrs. Seighman's daughter, spent her days toiling at a glass factory and helped her mother in the Pickett kitchen on special occasions. She was not permitted to wait on guests as Ruth labeled her "unrefined" and deemed her serving skills an embarrassment. Another girl, Mary McIntyre, would help Martha and Mrs. Roth serve guests tonight in the main dining room.

With Laura on her heels, Martha climbed the narrow back stairs. They walked down the hall to the spacious room just outside Ruth's bedroom that served as an upstairs dining area.

"I said I don't want chicken." Russell pushed his plate away as soon as Martha put it in front of him.

Martha glanced up, watching Laura hurry from the room. Coward, she thought. But she would escape from Russell, too, if she could. She lowered a plate in front of Randolph. He looked up and gave Martha a quick smile. She returned it, just as quick.

"Didn't you hear me? I said I don't want this," Russell repeated.

George lowered his newspaper. "What's wrong, son?"

"I want lamb."

George looked at Martha.

"The lamb is for tonight's guests, sir," Martha said, her gaze leveled at her boss.

George looked at Randolph, then back at Russell. "Your brother likes the chicken."

"He likes anything." Russell snickered. "That's why he's fat."

"I am not fat!" Randolph said, his mouth full of food.

"Are too."

"That's enough. Give him lamb, Martha." George went back to his newspaper.

Smirking, Russell's eyes had a triumphant glow as he looked at Martha. She picked up his plate and turned away, smiling, wondering what Russell would do if she stuck her tongue out at him like she used to do to her sister. It puzzled her, Russell being such a nasty child. There were kids in the patch that teased and bullied, but they were dirt poor, no shoes, their clothes ill-fitting and

62

filthy. They had reason to be mean. But Russell, he had everything. No excuse for his outbursts, if you asked her.

Nanny Maureen followed Martha down the stairs. "He's quite a handful, isn't he?"

"Yes." Martha didn't slow her steps.

"Randolph's very sweet."

"Yes."

"Where should I eat lunch?"

"The other nannies ate with the boys."

"Even when the boys dined with their father?"

Martha laughed. "Especially when they ate with their father." She pushed the door to the kitchen open. "Russell got his way, as usual, Mrs. Seighman. I need lamb," Martha said, handing the plate of chicken to the cook. The kitchen was crowded, Laura peeling potatoes, Mary snapping green beans, and Mrs. Seighman's sister kneading dough.

"Hi, Martha," Mary said. She looked at the nanny, standing at the bottom of the stairs.

"That's the new nanny. Maureen," Martha said. "She wants to know where to eat."

The room erupted in laughter.

Mrs. Roth clapped. "Enough. You can eat here. Mrs. Seighman will fix you a bowl."

"Hello!" Vickers walked in, stomping his feet at the doorway. "Can a man get a hot meal around here? Smells wonderful, Mrs. Seighman." He pulled his cap from his head and stood by the stove, closing his eyes as he took in a noisy breath.

"Ain't I got enough to do without feeding the help?" Mrs. Seighman shooed Vickers away but ladled cabbage into two bowls, handing one to the chauffeur, the other to Maureen.

"What time is Mrs. Pickett returning?" Martha asked, glancing at the clock on the wall.

"I'm to pick her up at three o'clock." Vickers tossed his cap on the table and dropped into a chair. He raised his spoon just as one of the servant bells on the wall sounded.

Mrs. Roth frowned. "The dining room?"

Martha darted from the kitchen.

Russell sat at the head of the table in the dining room, a fork grasped in his hand. "Where's my lamb? I want to eat it here."

"Russell! That table is set for tonight's guests," Martha hissed.

"So what?"

Martha stared at the boy, hooking her thumbs under the strap of her apron, tamping her anger. "Your mother would not be happy that you are in here." She dropped her arms to her sides, hands pressed against her thighs.

"My mother's not home." Russell picked up a crystal glass, and with his smirky smile, licked it.

Martha pinched her thighs, twisting the skin, the pain distracting her from her growing rage. "Shall I tell your father what you just did?"

Russell shrugged. He put the glass down and wiped his greasy hands on the corner of the tablecloth. When Martha took a step forward, he jumped from the chair and bolted from the room.

Martha blew out a breath as she stared at the chandelier, the crystals quivering from Russell's hasty exit. "Do it for Frances," she whispered. With a sigh, she moved the china, glass and silverware to the sideboard and pulled the tablecloth into her arms to wash and iron again.

CHAPTER SEVEN

February 1925
Wheeling, West Virginia

Five minutes after midnight, Martha stacked the last of the bone china plates into the Pickett's mahogany hutch and hung up her apron in the kitchen. She and Mary went out the back door and headed north on Main Street. They walked arm-in-arm, both fighting to stay upright on the icy bricks.

"Oh drat, it's starting to snow," Martha said, looking up at the flakes illuminated in the dim light of a lamp post. Her fingertips were numb and she regretted, for a moment, throwing the gloves George Pickett gave her into her coal stove. After trudging eight blocks, the women crossed the street, careful to avoid the slick trolley tracks, and started up Pike Street. When Martha moved to her apartment near the top of Wheeling's steepest hill, she was reminded of her childhood walks up and down the red streets of Webster Hill.

"At least the cold keeps the men inside," Mary said, peering down a dark alley.

In warmer months, the walk on Pike Street meant eluding the men loitering outside the speakeasies and brothels tucked behind legitimate businesses.

"Good night," Mary said. She lowered her head against the wind and moved down Market Street. Her apartment was two blocks north.

Martha continued up Pike Street for another block to a three-story, brick building. In the unadorned entranceway, she unwrapped the scarf from her head, her eyes slowly adjusting to the darkness. During the day, the stairs were brightened by the skylight but once darkness fell the stairs could be treacherous. At the first door on the second floor, she knocked softly and pushed the door open.

"Mommy!"

"Shush." Martha put a finger to her lips and dropped to one knee, gathering six-year-old Frances into her arms. Her daughter's warm body melted away the day's woes.

Dottie stood by the lone bed, watching, rubbing her arms against the cold. "She woke an hour ago and wouldn't go back to sleep," she said.

"I'm sorry she kept you up." Martha stood, keeping her daughter in her arms. She pulled the door closed behind her. "How's Mickey?"

"Sleeping. Not much coughing today. 'Course I kept him inside. Out of the cold."

The two women looked at Dottie's sleeping son, curled into a ball under two quilts on the narrow bed in front of the coal stove. He was a fragile boy, his health always a concern.

Martha put Frances on her stocking feet and pulled a loaf of bread and three oranges from her pockets. "Wish I could have brought more but I swear Mrs. Pickett counts the leftovers." She cut the loaf in two and put a half and one orange back in her pocket. She smiled down at her daughter and pushed a silky tendril from the small face. "Let's go upstairs, Sunshine."

"Will you read to me, Mommy?"

"Tomorrow."

"That child loves her books," Dottie said. "Wish my Mickey could read as good as her."

Whenever Mickey stayed with her while Dottie worked, Martha read to him and tried to help him with his letters. The boy's struggle with concentration reminded Martha of her brother Jakob. She wrote two letters to Jakob, and one to Klara, since moving to Wheeling and got one letter from Jakob in reply. She hadn't heard from her mother since she left Webster Hill.

"Good night, Dottie," Martha said. "Thank you." She bent, pulling Frances to her hip and took her daughter's battered boots from Dottie's hands. She climbed another flight of stairs to the last apartment on the top floor. Identical to Dottie's, her apartment had one room with a coal stove for cooking and heating, a sink with a cold water tap, a wood icebox lined with tin, and one single bed. She salvaged a small table from the Pickett's trash and found two mismatched chairs at the thrift store. With rags collected from the Pickett's, Martha had braided a rug and made curtains from discarded tablecloths but the thin fabric did little to keep the cold air out and a thick layer of ice coated the inside of the window during the winter months. She pushed the switch on the wall and her lone light sputtered to life.

"I'm cold, Mommy."

"I know." Martha lowered Frances to the bed. "Get under the covers. I'll get the stove going."

Gently tucking her Dutch girl quilt under Frances's chin, Martha kissed her daughter's chilled forehead. She yanked the stove's door open, the rusty hinges creaking, and dug through the ashes with an iron rod. One glowing nugget, not much larger than a marble, sparked, and she added three baseball-sized chunks of coal, stoking the glossy lumps into a glowing fire. She emptied her pockets, unbuttoned her boots and crawled in bed beside her daughter.

"Good night, Mommy."

"Sleep tight, Sunshine." Martha buried her face in her daughter's hair. It was fair, like hers, but when the sun glinted on Frances's waves there was a hint of red. That red, and the smattering of freckles across Frances's nose, reminded Martha her daughter's father was Peter Doyle.

***

Early the next morning, as light filtered through the transom above the apartment door, Martha woke with a firm shake from her daughter.

"Mommy. It's time to read."

Martha rubbed her eyes. "Another book?"

"Miss Gongola let me bring it home," Frances said.

Halfway through the first grade, in a classroom with second and third grades, the teacher, Miss Gongola, said Frances read better than her third graders. At the Crittenton Home, Martha started reading to Frances when her daughter was just a month old. She would read from her German books, or from one of the day room magazines, until Miss Rungee took her on the trolley to the library. Martha was awed by the large collection of books.

"Shelves and shelves. All the way to the ceiling. And you can take the books home with you as long as you promise to bring them back," Martha had told Dottie, dumping an armful of books on the dresser they shared at the Home.

Dottie was unimpressed. She struggled to read and write but encouraged her son to learn his letters. Every weekday morning, Dottie walked Mickey and Frances to the school at the bottom of Pike Street then continued downtown to her job rolling stogies. It was Dottie who found the apartment building she and Martha lived in. It wasn't the newest building and it wasn't in the best part of town, but it was clean. Mrs. Hofmann, the widow on the first floor, lived rent-free in exchange for sweeping and scrubbing the hallways and stairs. She even kept the sidewalk out front clean. The widow had a phone, used mostly to cajole the maintenance man, but she let the other tenants use it sparingly. Mrs. Hofmann's children and grandchildren visited every Sunday, but during the week the widow watched Mickey and Frances when both Dottie and Martha were working. She also watched another tenant's four-year-old daughter, Pamela, on the nights Pamela's mother painted on her face and strutted down one of the blighted allies.

Martha sat up and pushed the pillow behind her back, Frances nestling into the bend of her arm. She opened the slim book. "The elderly lady-bee who helped the baby-bee Maya when she awoke to life and slipped from her cell was called Cassandra and commanded great respect in the hive," she read aloud, pausing to make a soft buzzing sound.

Frances giggled. "Will the bees come back this summer, Mommy?" She looked up with eyes the same blue as Martha's. The same as Martha's mother.

Frances was obsessed with the bees' nest hanging outside their window last summer. Martha wanted to knock it down but her tender daughter protested, worried that the bees would be without a home like old Mr. Craig who panhandled at the corner of Market and Pike Streets.

"Yes, the bees come back every summer but hopefully they'll build their home elsewhere," Martha said, closing the book. "That's enough reading for now, Sunshine. Let's have breakfast. Then off to church."

Frances groaned. "Do we have to go to church today, Mommy? It's so cold."

After seventeen hours at the Pickett house yesterday, Martha was tired so skipping the long walk to the church was appealing. It wouldn't be the first time she missed a visit to Saint James during the winter. "If there is enough snow to cover my ankles, we'll stay home."

Jumping from the bed, Frances raced to the window and scraped at the ice with a fingernail, clearing a jagged spot to peer out. "Yippee! Look at all that snow on the roof."

Martha sat up, swinging her feet to the floor. She emptied her scuttle bucket into the stove's belly and, while the coal scraps smoked and smoldered, cut the orange into wedges and the bread into thick slices. They had no eggs, and no syrup, but the bread fried in ham grease was still a treat for her daughter. Martha watched Frances eat and sucked on an orange wedge, shaking her head at the thought of all the grapefruits and oranges tossed in the trash at the Pickett house because Ruth Pickett tired of the "Hollywood Eighteen Day Diet." Ruth was trying to conform to the new, slimmer ideals of beauty promoted in the fashion magazines but lasted just two days on the restrictive diet of grapefruit, oranges and Melba Toast.

"Drink your milk, Sunshine." Martha stood and poured the last of the milk from the bottle into Frances's glass, stowing the empty quart on the windowsill with two other empties. Once she got her weekly wages tomorrow, Martha was heading to Dawson's Market, plus a stop at the thrift store for new shoes for Frances, and maybe gloves for herself.

***

Monday dawned cold with another inch of snow. Martha kissed Frances goodbye at Dottie's door and skidded down Pike Street, her years of practice on the slippery streets of Webster Hill keeping her upright. She thought of her nephew and niece, making their way to school this morning. How tall was Paulie, she wondered. Did Eleanor look like Klara or Henry? Frances often asked about her relatives, especially after listening to classmates chatter about dotting grandmothers and fun cousins. Martha explained that her family lived far away.

70

"Could we visit them?" Frances asked.

"Maybe someday," Martha always said, feeling bad about the fib, but she couldn't tell Frances that they weren't welcome in Webster Hill. She swallowed hard, feeling the familiar sadness along with a tightening in her chest, whenever her family intruded on her thoughts.

At the Pickett house, Martha spent her entire morning doing laundry but at noon several loads still remained. Her arms throbbed and her back ached as she knelt to drain the iron tub. She twisted the spigot and stood, arching her back, and watched the tub fill as the gas pipe beneath slowly warmed the water. Dumping the Pickett boys' pants in the tub, she worked the plunger up and down, back and forth, so intent on her task that she didn't hear her boss come in.

"How would you like one of those new, electric washing machines?" George Pickett said.

Martha dropped the plunger in surprise, the copper head clattering to the stones.

George retrieved the plunger and extended the wood handle towards Martha. When she reached for it, he grasped her hand, tender and chafed from the morning's efforts, and traced his thumb across her red knuckles.

"We don't want your skin to get chapped and calloused, do we? No man wants to be touched by rough hands," he said.

Martha pulled the plunger, and her hand, from his grasp.

He laughed. "Come to the kitchen. It's payday."

Today, like every Monday, George came home from his job as bank president to pay the household staff. Each person stepped forward as he called their name and waved an envelope, keeping it out of reach until he was properly thanked. Martha refused to look at her boss, mumbling "thank you" as she stuffed the envelope into the pocket of her apron. She followed George to the second floor, a silver tray topped with a bowl of beef

71

stew, bread and coffee, in her hands. As she poured coffee in George's cup, Mrs. Pickett emerged from her bedroom.

"I'll be eating with Mr. Pickett today, Martha." Ruth lowered into the chair across from George and snapped her fingers, pointed at the coffee pot. She looked at her husband's bowl. "I'll have the same, pronto."

"Yes, ma'am," Martha said. She tucked the tray under her arm and jogged down the stairs. "Mrs. Pickett has decided to join her husband for lunch," she said to Mrs. Seighman.

She want the stew, or is she on another crazy diet?"

Martha laughed. "Stew, please." She returned to the upstairs dining room and hovered in the corner as the Pickett's ate, George's face buried in the newspaper. Serving food was not a favorite task, but she was thankful she had learned the skills at the Crittenton Home. Serve and remove plates from the left, serve and remove beverages from the right. Who knew there were rules? In the patch, people were just happy to have food and water.

"Lucinda Stewart told me at Saturday's dinner they are moving out the pike. Buying the Pavlick's house," Ruth said. With her fork, she picked three cubes of potato from her bowl, dropping each one on the tablecloth. "Did you hear me, George?"

"Yes, I heard you, Ruth." He lowered his newspaper. "The Stewarts are moving to Woodsdale."

"Why can't we move to the country?"

"Too far from the bank." He returned to his newspaper.

"Psst," Ruth waved a hand in front of her face. "You don't walk anymore. Not since you got the Dodge. The air here is horrid now with that train going by at all hours of the day. We can't even enjoy the summer house."

When Martha first came to work for the Pickett's, the family often sat out in the backyard in a small,

72

covered pavilion Ruth called "the summer house." In recent years, the railroad increased its travel on the tracks running along a narrow strip of land between the Ohio River and the western edge of the Pickett property, filling the air with soot as the engine chugged past the house.

"I like this home," George said.

"It's dark. Dreary."

"Buy another lamp."

Ruth had a dozen Tiffany lamps, trying to compensate for the home's many stained glass windows. "It's cold. Drafty," she said, forking another potato cube from her bowl. It skidded across the table, leaving a brown trail on the white cloth.

Without looking up, George pointed at the fireplace. "Martha, turn up the gas."

The house was warmed by gas fireplaces with asbestos fronts in all the major rooms, except the top floor. One coal-burning fireplace provided heat for the entire third floor. Martha knelt and nudged the small handle to the right, a rush of warm air heating her cheeks.

"I'm retiring to my room, Martha," Ruth said, glaring at the newspaper in front of George's face. "Bring me tea."

"Yes, ma'am." Martha watched Ruth disappear into her bedroom. She glanced at Mr. Pickett but his face remained hidden behind his newspaper. This couple was a mystery to her. Always bickering. Her parents never spoke to each other like this. She remembered a few disagreements when she was growing up, mostly over running water or the charges at the company store, but her mother and father didn't squabble constantly like the Pickett's. She shrugged, scooping Ruth's discarded potatoes back into the bowl and went downstairs.

***

That afternoon, Martha left the Pickett house forty minutes later than her scheduled time but she wouldn't see any extra on payday. She hurried up Main Street, making a quick stop at the market, and greeted Frances and Mickey at the school.

"Running a little late today, Sunshine." Martha adjusted her daughter's knitted hat, tugging it over her ears. "Here, you carry this box. And Mickey, you carry this bundle." Martha was careful not to tax Mickey as they ventured up the hill. He was smaller than Frances, smaller than all the other first graders, and suffered from bouts of coughing and wheezing. When he turned three, Dottie scrapped together the money for a doctor when the arrival of spring brought weeks of struggled breathing for the toddler. The doctor called it hypersensitiveness and offered no solution.

"Let's say hello to Mrs. Hofmann," Martha said when they stepped inside their apartment building. Usually the sidewalk in front of the building would be cleared of snow and ice by this time of the day but last night's snowfall still covered the bricks.

"*Hallo!*" Mrs. Hofmann opened the door and ushered Martha and the kids inside her warm apartment.

"*Guten Tag,*" Martha said. She encouraged Mrs. Hofmann's use of German as it brought back comforting memories of her childhood, and she was passing on the language to Frances. Little Pamela sat on the floor in front of Mrs. Hofmann's stove, a rag doll in her hands.

"Her mother was ill today so I'm keeping an eye on her. I haven't made it outside to clear the sidewalk," Mrs. Hofmann explained.

Martha smiled at Pamela. The tenants didn't appreciate the girl's mother, Evelyn, living in their midst but most were civil to Pamela. Evelyn was tossed from her madam's house the day Pamela was born and, with nowhere else to go, knocked on Mrs. Hofmann's door. The widow took pity and moved Evelyn and her infant daughter into one of the apartments in the building. Martha tolerated Evelyn better than most. Proper food service and laundry was not all Martha learned at the Crittenton Home. She knew not every prostitute was nasty and remorseless like "Dreadful Darla," the bedeviled whore who frequented the boarding houses in Webster Hill. Some of them just needed a helping hand.

Martha passed a peppermint to Pamela and patted the girl's head. "Let's go," she said to Frances and Mickey.

A short time later, Dottie collected Mickey and Martha dragged a large, silver tub to the front of the stove.

"Oh, no, Mommy, it's too cold for a bath," Frances whined.

"I'll get the water really warm tonight, Sunshine."

A cast iron bathtub dominated the small bathroom at the end of the hall but there was no hot water so Martha took baths in the apartment, filling her silver tub with water heated on the stove just as she did in Webster Hill. Frances took the first bath, Martha adding another potful of hot water for her quick soak. Afterwards, she combed the knots out of her daughter's hair as it dried in the heat from the stove. They sat down to a supper of lima beans and ham hocks when there was a knock at the door. Martha pulled it open, expecting to see Dottie.

"Hello, Martha," Patrick Doyle said. He smiled and tipped his fedora as he stepped into the apartment, followed by a young woman wrapped in a sleek, black fur. Patrick looked past Martha's stunned face to Frances. "You must be my niece. I'm your Uncle Patrick. And this beautiful lady is your Aunt Susie."

CHAPTER EIGHT

February 1925
Wheeling, West Virginia

Susie Doyle strolled past Martha, the heels of her satin shoes clicking on the bare floorboards and stopped in front of Frances. "Oh, isn't she precious! Daddy will love her," she said, fingering a strand of Frances's hair. "It actually glows. I could curl it. Or maybe cut it into a bob like mine." She patted the dark tresses curling beneath her bell-shaped hat of red felt.

Frances shrank from Susie's touch.

"No need to be afraid, young lady, we're family. Isn't that right, Martha?" Patrick said, pushing his fedora into Martha's hands. He sat in the chair across from Frances and pulled Susie onto his lap. "Your Aunt Susie has been looking forward to meeting you. What's your name, girlie?"

"Frances."

"Frances. That's a beautiful name. What about your middle name?" Susie asked.

"Hope," Frances said.

"Frances Hope Doyle. I love it." Susie clapped, the sound muffled by her gloves.

"My name is Frances Hope Albrecht."

Patrick raised a russet eyebrow at Martha.

Martha stared at Patrick but couldn't hold his gaze. She looked away, wondering if he could hear her heart hammering.

"Why don't you get to know your niece while Martha and I talk in the other room," Patrick said, pushing Susie to her feet and helping her remove her long coat, revealing a red velvet dress, a black belt wrapped about her narrow hips. He gave his wife a playful slap on her bottom.

"There is no other room," Martha said, finally finding her voice. "What are you doing here?"

"Let's talk in the hall." Patrick draped the fur over the chair. He noticed Frances eyeing the coat. "You want to touch it? Maybe try it on? Aunt Susie will show it to you." He winked at Frances and walked towards the door, pausing once when his right hip hitched, his black wingtip scrapping the floor.

His limp coaxed no sympathy from Martha. "Patrick, why are you here?" she asked the minute the door closed behind her.

"Just catching up with family," he said. "You know, we been living in the same town for years. I have a house around the corner from the market in the center of town. Ma lives with me now. She told me about you. Said you came looking for money for Peter's baby." He paused to tap the flickering lamp on the wall. "I convinced your sister to tell me where you'd gone, but it took me some time, and money, to track you down. 'Course I was looking for Martha Kraus, with a kid named Doyle." He turned to Martha, his thick eyebrows knitted together. "Albrecht. Hmm. Wasn't that the fella from the patch got killed in the war?" He pointed at the apartment door. "That kid can't be Albrecht's. It don't add up. Who's the daddy, Martha?"

"Keep your voice down," she said, glancing down the hallway for nosy neighbors.

"Maybe you don't know who the daddy is?"

Her mouth fell open, cheeks flaming. "Of course I do. It was Peter. He promised to marry me!"

Patrick smiled. "Thought so. She looks like my sister, Molly. 'Cept for those eyes. Your girl needs to know who her daddy was."

"Right. I'll be sure to tell my daughter her father was a bootlegger that got killed over a wagon load of beer," Martha snapped.

Patrick's smile faded, his mouth pushed into a tight line. His hand slid to his damaged hip, his head shaking. "I knew something was hinky on that run. We were ambushed." He paused, his smile returning. "They'll never ambush anyone else."

Martha looked at Patrick. His eyes were hard. Lifeless. She shivered, looked down at the hat still gripped in her hand. "I was trying to protect Frances. She shouldn't be fodder for gossip and innuendo."

"Yes, being a bastard could make her life hard."

"Don't call her that!" Martha raised her chin, narrowed her eyes.

"Would you prefer 'catch colt?' Or just 'illegitimate'?"

"I would prefer you leave."

Patrick chuckled, lifting his heels and tossing his head back. He tapped the flickering lamp again and ran his hand along the peeling wallpaper. "I was hoping for a nephew but my wife is obviously taken with the girl. I like keeping my wife happy. I especially like keeping her daddy happy. Perhaps you've heard of him—Jeb Goodman? City council?" He paused, looked at her expectantly. "No? My father-in-law is an important man. And he is very protective of his daughter. You see, Susie's mother died so it's been just her and her daddy for a long time. He would do anything for her." Patrick leaned his back against the wall. "I run a restaurant. A nice restaurant. Your boss, George Pickett, likes our food. Eats there 'bout once a week."

"How do you know I work for Mr. Pickett?"

"I know many things, Martha. I have friends at city hall. Hell, the Chief of Police eats at my restaurant twice a week. No charge, of course. Just the other day I sat down with the judge of the new Juvenile Court. We enjoyed a bottle of my finest to celebrate his new position. Poor Judge Robinson has the terrible job of locking up delinquent and wayward children." Patrick paused, examined his nails. "Some families just can't afford to care properly for their children. Some even allow their daughters to be led down an immoral path." He dropped his hands and pushed from the wall, his eyes leveled at Martha. "What do you think the judge would say about Frances?"

Rage bubbling up inside, Martha threw her shoulders back and took a step closer, her face inches from Patrick's. "I take good care of my daughter."

"How?" He took a step to the side, widening the space between them. "I know how much George Pickett pays you. I know how much rent you pay to live in this dump. It's freezing in here." He took another step to the side and yanked on the lapels of his overcoat, pulling it closed over his striped vest. "I also know a prostitute lives here. The judge wouldn't like that a little girl lives next door to a tramp. He could take Frances away. And the whore's kid, too."

Martha's rage slipped to panic. Unbounded, terrifying panic. A strangled cry slipped out.

"Maybe I can help you, Martha," Patrick said, taking a step towards her. "We both want what's best for little Frances. I could talk to my judge friend. Tell him Frances will live with us."

"I don't want to live with you," she whispered.

Patrick laughed. "Not you. Just Frances. We will adopt her." His smile faded. "You see, Susie got some bad news from the doctor. She can't have kids. Her daddy was really looking forward to being a grandfather."

Martha shook her head. "No." Her throat was dry, her voice hoarse. She forced a swallow. "There are plenty of children you can adopt."

"I don't want another man's bastard. Frances's got my blood." He raised his arms, palms up, and looked at the ceiling. "A gift from heaven. That's what I thought when Ma told me you had Peter's baby." His gaze shifted to the apartment door. "My Susie's been so sad. She wants to be a mama. She would give Frances everything. The best clothes. The best schools. A warm house. Proper food."

"No," Martha said again. It hurt to speak, her voice trembled and her legs rubbery. She put a hand on the wall to steady herself, taking in air, her head bowed.

"I will make Frances legitimate," Patrick said. "She would have a family. Her grandmother living in the same house. Do your mother and father visit their granddaughter?"

Martha stayed quiet, chin down.

"Didn't think so. It's a great offer, Martha."

She raised her head, looked Patrick in the eye. "No-o-o." Her voice was low, a growl, camouflaging her rising dread.

Patrick took Martha by the shoulders. "Don't be stupid. Let me adopt Frances or I'll have Judge Robinson pay you a visit."

"No. Never." Martha jabbed Peter's hat into his chest and walked into her apartment.

"Look, Mommy, Aunt Susie let me wear her hat. But it's too big," Frances said, her blue eyes peeking beneath the red rim.

Martha pulled the hat from her daughter's head and extended it towards Susie. "Leave. Now. And don't come back."

Patrick strode into the room, snatching the fur coat from the chair and wrapping it around his wide-eyed wife. "It's fine, honey," he said into Susie's ear, his attention on Martha. "Don't forget what I said."

"Bye, bye, for now." Susie waved to Frances as Patrick ushered her out the door.

Frances stood and frowned at Martha, hands on her hips. "Why did you make my aunt leave?"

Martha staggered to the bed and collapsed. She couldn't get enough air. Couldn't breathe. Couldn't talk. She shook her head. They can't Frances away, can they? Should she run? Where could she go with no money? Patrick tracked her down once, he could do it again.

"Mommy?"

She focused on her daughter. Breathe, she commanded herself. "Come here, Frances. I need to tell you about your father." She patted the bed. Took a deep breath. "Your father's name was Peter. He was Uncle Patrick's brother."

Confusion clouded Frances's eyes. She had grown up believing her father was Frederic Albrecht, a brave man who died in the war before she was born.

"A soldier?" she asked.

Martha shook her head. "No. He was..." She paused. "A miner. Just like my father."

"Oh," Frances said, biting her lower lip. "Is that better than a captain on a boat?"

"What?" Martha frowned.

"Mickey's mom said his pa went down the river. Mickey said he must have been a riverboat captain.

Martha managed a smile. She took Frances's hands in hers. "Doesn't matter who your father was, you are perfect. Just the way you are. But nobody needs to know. Your father is our secret," she said, squeezing Frances's hands, her eyes fixed on her daughter's. "Promise me you'll keep our secret."

CHAPTER NINE

February 1925
Wheeling, West Virginia

A week after Patrick's visit, Dottie burst into the Pickett dining room, Mrs. Roth on her heels. "Where is Martha? Martha, oh Martha," Dottie cried. "They took Frances." She paused, pressing her palm against the sideboard as she caught her breath.

Martha, working later than usual to serve dinner to the Pickett's and another couple, let out a strangled cry, nearly dropping a bowl of soup on Ruth's lap.

George sprang to his feet. "Here. Here. What is the meaning of this?"

Dottie ignored George and the other three people staring at her with open mouths. "A policeman came. Said he was taking Frances and Pamela to 'that home for girls.' Mrs. Hofmann couldn't stop him."

Mrs. Roth shepherded Dottie and Martha towards the kitchen. "Excuse me, Mr. Pickett. I'll return shortly."

In the kitchen, Dottie, Mrs. Roth and Mrs. Seighman tried to calm Martha. She pushed their hands away.

"Do you know of this place? This home for girls?" Martha asked, her voice breaking.

Mrs. Seighman nodded. "Yes. It's run by nuns. On Edgington Lane."

Martha bolted out the back door. Dottie followed.

"Martha! Wait. You'll freeze." She shrugged out of her coat. "Here, take this."

Martha sprinted east, pushing her arms into the thin coat that was several sizes too small and smelled of tobacco and grease. She ran until she no longer could, the feeling gone from her feet and hands. Her thoughts on her daughter, she paused, gulping air, and leaned against a stone wall. Frances must be terrified. Dragged from her home. Stranded among strangers. Her daughter had never spent a night apart from Martha. She doubled over, a hand to her mouth to keep from screaming. Footsteps neared and she forced herself forward.

It was well past sunset when she got to the behemoth monastery, three stories of brick surrounded by a four-foot stone wall topped with foot-long iron stakes. She walked along the wall, looking for an opening, finally finding the gates, a padlock larger than her hand securing the rusty chain. She pushed. The gates didn't budge. She rattled the chain, and wailed, her piercing screams bringing faces to the windows on all three floors. A tall nun in a long, black habit finally came to the gate.

"Is my daughter here? Her name is Frances. Frances Albrecht. She did nothing wrong. Please, I must see her," Martha said. She peered between the bars, her hands wrapped around the freezing metal.

The nun stared at Martha, her face haloed by a white wimple, "I am Mother deSales, the prioress of Our Lady of the Valley monastery and school." She made no effort to open the gates.

"Please," Martha whispered.

"Are you able to compose yourself? Keep your voice down and not disrupt our girls?"

Martha nodded. She watched the nun pull a large key from the folds of her habit, the padlock opening with a click, the chain clattering as she pulled it free. The gates swung open on complaining hinges and Martha followed the nun into the building.

"Sit here. Do not move," Mother deSales said, pointing at a bench just inside the door.

Martha sat on the hard wood, shivering uncontrollably. She looked down the long corridor of red tile that sloped into the monastery's dark depths. Where was Frances? This was a massive building. She would never be able to find her daughter before the police came and dragged her away.

The nun returned with a glass of milk.

Her hands numb, Martha struggled to hold the glass, lowering it to the bench. "Did you see my daughter?"

"Yes. I saw Frances this afternoon. She came in with a younger girl. Are they sisters?"

Martha shook her head. "Pamela is Evelyn's daughter. A neighbor." She looked down the hallway again. "Is this a jail?"

"No. These girls have nowhere else to go. We feed them. Clothe them. Provide schooling."

"An orphanage? Frances is not an orphan."

"It is not an orphanage," the nun shook her head, her wimple twitching. "Although we do have girls who have lost both parents. Some of the girls are sent by their own parents when they are unable to care for them."

Martha bristled. "I did not send my daughter here. This is a mistake."

Mother deSales sighed, the lines around her mouth deepening. "I saw the authorization papers. Judge Robinson can intervene in a family for reason of neglect, crime, drunkenness or other vice of parents."

"Frances is not neglected!" Martha said.

"You must keep your voice down," Mother deSales said. She placed a hand on Martha's arm. "What is your name, child?"

"Martha." She picked up the glass, her fingertips gray against the white milk. She managed a sip without spilling. "This is because of Patrick," she whispered.

"Is Patrick your husband? The father of the child?"

"No. Her father is dead. Patrick is her uncle. He is not a good man." Martha told Mother deSales of Patrick's visit to her apartment the week before. Told her of his threats. Told her of his plan to adopt Frances. "It's not fair."

"I'm afraid life is not fair, Martha," Mother deSales said. "Frances will have to stay here. It is the judge's order. But, it does not have to be forever. I promise you, your daughter is safe here. She will not be adopted. Not when she has a mother who loves her." She paused. "Frances needs time to adjust to her new surroundings. Come back in two weeks. During the day, please." She patted Martha's hand and pushed to her feet. "Drink your milk. Our laundry delivery driver will take you home tonight in the truck."

***

Martha stared straight ahead as the truck chugged up Wheeling Hill. The driver had been polite, kind actually, but Martha was too muddled to respond to his remarks. "Stop here," she said when the truck turned on to Pike Street. She jumped out without a word and climbed the dark stairs to her apartment. She clutched Frances's sweater to her chest and dropped to her knees, sobbing. When her tears ran dry, she got up and paced the small space until Dottie knocked on her door as the sun was beginning to rise.

"Did you see Frances?" Dottie asked.

Martha shook her head and resumed her pacing.

86

Dottie lingered by the door. "I didn't know Frances had an uncle in town."

Martha halted and looked down at the balled sweater in her hands, picking at a strand of frayed yarn. "I didn't know until last week. He's a bad man."

Dottie hesitated. "Will you still get Mickey from school today?"

Martha was about to agree, but she suddenly shook her head. "No. I'm going to the courthouse," she said, straightening her back and turning towards Dottie. "Going to see that judge."

She handed Dottie the coat she had worn last night, her eyes locking on her friend's. "I will get her back," she said.

Although she had just a knitted shawl draped across her shoulders, Martha didn't notice the cold as she trudged south. Her thoughts were on Frances. What was her daughter doing this morning? Was she warm? Were the nuns kind? Would she get enough to eat? As she neared the Pickett house, she eyed the windows of Ruth's bedroom, wondering if she still had a job. She dropped her head and ducked around the side.

Mrs. Roth opened the back door and motioned her into the kitchen. Mrs. Seighman stood at the sink, head bowed. Vickers downed his coffee and made a hasty exit after a quick nod.

"Mrs. Pickett wants to see you," Mrs. Roth said, helping Martha into her apron. "She's waiting in the upstairs dining room."

Unable to look at Mrs. Roth, Martha nodded and moved up the back stairs, her steps slow, her attention on the door at the top. It was slightly ajar. She paused, listening to George.

"I'll talk to Thorne today. I can count on his discretion," he said.

Howard Thorne and his wife were the couple at the dinner table last night when Dottie stormed in.

"I abhor being the topic of gossip," Ruth said.

George chuckled. "Won't be the first time."

"George!"

"Good help is difficult to find, Ruth. She stays. I'll see you at dinner."

Martha heard George's heavy footsteps on the front stairs and waited for the sound of the door. Once it slammed, Martha stepped into the upstairs hall.

"Good morning, Mrs. Pickett," Martha said. She stood at the doorway, her gaze fixed on Ruth.

"Last night was unacceptable, Martha."

"Yes, ma'am." Martha's face flushed, but she didn't turn away.

Ruth stared back, lips pursed. "See that it never happens again." She looked at her plate, waving her hand over it. "Take this away and send up a fresh pot of tea. And one of those pecan rolls."

Martha escaped from the room and spent the rest of the day in the basement, happy to put space between herself and Ruth Pickett. When her workday was complete, she ran out the back door and climbed on the trolley for the short ride downtown. At the corner of sixteenth and Market Street, she eased down the trolley steps and stood on trembling legs, looking up at the courthouse's clock tower. The building covered a city block with dozens of people crowding both entries. She worked her way up the steps of the Market Street entrance.

"Judge Robinson?" she asked the uniformed man standing by the door.

"Juvenile Court. Third floor."

After wandering the marble hallways, Martha finally found the door with "Juvenile Court" stenciled on the glass. She locked her knees to quiet the shaking and knocked.

"Yes?" The door was opened by a glowering young man, no older than her own twenty five years. He frowned at Martha, his hand on the brass doorknob.

"Judge Robinson?" Martha asked.

"Who are you?"

"Martha Albrecht. My daughter, Frances, was taken away. I want her back." Her voice hitched. She dug deep, found a scrap of courage. Eyes level with the clerk's, she said. "I am a good mother."

The young man laughed. "That's what they all say. The court will decide. Don't come back here." He closed the door.

Although she heard the click of a lock, Martha tried to turn the knob. She put her hand on the glass and leaned close. "Please. I did nothing wrong."

"Go away or I'll call the police," the clerk yelled from the other side of the door.

Martha took a step back, her heel catching a spittoon's funnel and sending the cast-iron globe across the hall. It crashed into the far wall, greasy contents spewing on to the white marble. Heads turned, hands flying to their noses at the foul scent. Martha darted down the hall and into the stairway. She paused, hand on the railing, head spinning, legs quivering. With slow, unsteady steps, she inched down the three flights and out the building. She pushed through the crowd to the wall circling the dry fountain and sat on the cold concrete. *No.* She would not cry. Not here. Not with an audience of strangers. She staggered forward, one wobbly step at a time. Outside the American Legion on Twelfth Street, she stopped and stared as a soldier on crutches, one empty pant leg pinned up, hobbled past. She was just like this crippled veteran without Frances, a part of her missing.

CHAPTER TEN

March 1925
Wheeling, West Virginia

Martha avoided Dottie and Mrs. Hofmann, and she couldn't look at Mickey without crying. At the Pickett house, she caught her fingers in the wringer and burned her wrist on the iron. She broke two glasses and a china plate, Mrs. Roth covering for her when Ruth questioned the shattered glass.

With nothing to lose, Martha went to George for help. "You are an important man, Mr. Pickett. Surely you know Judge Robinson?"

George paused, his gaze wandering down Martha's body as usual. "As much as I'd like for you to be indebted to me, I cannot get involved in the court's business."

A day later, a new washing machine was installed in the basement.

"How do you like it, Martha. Just for you," George said, brushing his fingers along her cheek. "See, I do care for you."

She turned her head.

At daybreak on the second Sunday after Frances was taken, Martha waited outside the gates of the monastery. Hands in her pockets, bouncing from foot to foot for warmth, she could barely contain her excitement. She wanted to cry out, scream Frances's name as loud as she could.

"We were not expecting you quite so early," Mother deSales said and led Martha to a small room in the front of the monastery. "This is our parlor, where families can spend time with the girls in our charge." She lowered to a threadbare couch, tucking the folds of her habit under legs, and motioned for Martha to sit next to her. Two straight-back wood chairs sat on either side of the fireplace where coal embers smoldered. A marble Madonna, the baby Jesus in her lap, gazed benignly from the mantle. A wood clock ticked beside the Madonna.

"Sister Mollie is getting Frances dressed. She will be here momentarily," Mother deSales said.

Martha nodded, squeezing her hands together in her lap and staring at the small stained glass window tucked near the ceiling. It was a simple design—unlike the intricate patterns of the windows in the Pickett house—with uneven squares of blues and greens arranged around a cross of the palest yellow.

Mother deSales caught Martha looking at the window. "From our convent in Toronto," she explained. "Five of us arrived here twenty-five years ago with that piece of glass and the clothes on our back." She cleared her throat. "You appear much better than our previous meeting, Martha. I know seeing your daughter will be emotional, but I must request that you refrain from hysterics. It will only make it more difficult for Frances, as she must remain here."

"For how long?" Martha asked, her attention still on the glowing cross.

"That is unknown at this time. But be prepared. The court often moves slowly."

Martha looked at her hands, forcing them apart. She swallowed. "Is my daughter well?"

"Yes. Frances is fine. Eating. Doing very well in her classes."

Martha couldn't hold back a smile. "Her teacher said Frances is the best student she ever had."

The mother superior returned the smile. "Frances is a good girl. She has been quite helpful with Pamela, also." She paused. "Do you know Pamela's mother?"

"Evelyn. I don't know her last name. She's disappeared. Left the day after Pamela was brought here. Has she visited?"

The prioress shook her head and was about to say more when the door opened and Frances ran in, diving into Martha's lap.

Martha wrapped her arms around her daughter's quaking body, pulling her close. She kissed the red-gold hair, locking eyes with Mother deSales' over the top of Frances's head.

"Remember our talk." Mother deSales stood. "I will return in one hour."

"I'm sorry, Mommy," Frances sobbed into Martha's chest.

Martha leaned back and lifted Frances's chin with her finger. "Why would you be sorry, Sunshine? You did nothing wrong."

"I told Mickey about Uncle Patrick," Frances said. "That's why I'm here. I didn't keep our secret."

"Oh, Frances. That's not why you're here." Martha cupped her hand over Frances's hair, and buried her face in the curls, breathing in, wanting—needing—to take her daughter's familiar scent deep into her lungs. She frowned. The smell wasn't right. Unfamiliar soap, incense, disinfectant. Her daughter smelled of the monastery. She raised Frances's head and searched her face, making sure it hadn't changed, soaking in every detail, wiping a tear from the smooth cheek.

"You did nothing wrong," Martha repeated. "You won't be here forever, Sunshine. Listen to the Sisters, and study hard." She paused when her voice hitched. "I will find a way to bring you home." She had to. She couldn't live without her daughter.

***

The following Sunday, after another visit with Frances, Martha remained seated on the couch in the monastery's parlor as Patrick and his mother were led in. It was the first time she had seen Mrs. Doyle since the day she cried on her shoulder after Peter died. She barely recognized the woman. The frizzled hair the color of coal ashes was smoothed into soft waves, the homespun skirts replaced by a fur coat and a Copenhagen blue dress of fine wool. Mrs. Doyle sat in one of the wood chairs, concentrating on the Mother Superior, never once glancing at Martha. Patrick remained standing, his hand hooked on the fireplace mantle, his other hand tapping his fedora against his thigh.

"A child belongs with her mother," Mother deSales said to Patrick. She sat next to Martha on the couch. "I am giving Frances's mother every chance to reunite with her daughter." She looked at Mrs. Doyle. "It's obvious Frances has not suffered abuse. The girl loves her mother, and there is no doubt her mother loves her daughter."

"I think Judge Robinson will see it differently," Patrick said.

Mother deSales smiled. "How is the Judge? I look forward to seeing him again. He has enjoyed many a tea with me as we discuss ways to solve the world's ills."

Patrick's mother tried another tactic to sway Mother deSales, saying she would raise Frances Catholic, just as she raised her own children, and as she herself was raised in Ireland. "Martha's family is not Catholic," Mrs. Doyle said. "Maybe if she had a proper upbringing, if she had proper morals, she wouldn't have corrupted my Peter."

"*Das stimmtnicht!*" Martha snapped. "Peter promised to marry me."

94

Mother deSales silenced Martha with a pointed index finger and stern look.

Martha sat back, chin down. She had not told the prioress that she and Frances's father were not married. Nor had she told Mother deSales that Frances's birth certificate listed another man as her father.

"We are well-equipped to instruct Frances in our traditions, Mrs. Doyle," Mother deSales said.

Her face red, Mrs. Doyle pulled her coat closed and threw an angry look at Patrick.

"We'll see about this," he said, palming his hat on his head and pulling his mother to her feet.

Several unkind words passed through Martha's thoughts as she watched Patrick and his mother stalk from the room. She felt Mother deSales gaze but she stared obstinately at the door, her lips pressed together, the ticks of the clocks the only sound in the stuffy room.

"I'm sorry," Martha finally said. She turned, looking at Mother deSales. "I should have told you the truth."

The prioress sat quiet for a long moment, her fingers stroking the silver heart dangling from the chain around her neck. "Some things are best left unsaid."

CHAPTER ELEVEN

January 1927
Wheeling, West Virginia

"Flopsy, Mopsy, and Cotton-tail, who were good little bunnies, went down the lane to gather blackberries," Martha said, reading aloud from Frances's favorite book. It was the second day of the new year but nothing had changed for Martha. She was struggling to keep her voice upbeat, not allow her despair to overwhelm both her and her daughter.

"I like blackberries," Frances said. She sat on the couch in the monastery's parlor, her head on Martha's shoulder. "There are oodles of blackberries on the hill behind the school. Do you think bunnies live there, Mommy?"

Martha nodded. "Yes, I think so."

"Maybe I'll see one when we visit Lady Victory." Frances sat up and looked at Martha, her blue eyes intent. "I get to be in the procession this year after my First Holy Communion."

"Is Victory one of the nuns?"

Frances laughed. "No, Mommy. It's a statue. On the top of the hill."

"Oh." Martha managed a smile but her heart ached. Her daughter had a life she wasn't part of. During

Frances's nearly two-year stay at the monastery, she had grown three inches, her cheeks had plumped into rosy globes, and she excelled in all her classes at the grammar school run by the nuns.

The clock chimed the top of the hour and Martha turned toward the mantle, her attention on the marble Madonna. She swallowed the lump in her throat. It didn't get any easier, the end of each visit was a like a knife in her side. She closed the book and stood.

"Don't go yet, Mommy. Please." Frances inched to the edge of the couch and grasped Martha's hand.

Martha pushed a curl from her daughter's forehead. "I'll be back next week, Sunshine. Do you have any special books you want me to bring you from the library?"

"Do they have any with fossils?" Frances looked up, her hand still clinging to Martha's.

"Fossils?" Martha asked.

Frances nodded. "Sister Agnes showed us a rock with a leaf on it," she said. "It was a million years old."

Martha smiled, feigning interest in her daughter's words. She let Frances pull her back to the couch and draped her arm across her daughter's shoulders, her cheek against Frances' crown. They sat silent until Mother deSales whisked into the parlor, her wool habit sweeping the floor.

"Time for supper, Frances," the Mother Superior said. "Sister Mollie will walk you back to your dormitory." She nodded at a young nun standing in the doorway, her hands steepled at her chest.

Martha helped Frances to her feet, closing her eyes when Frances wrapped her arms around her legs. The prioress made a small sound in her throat, and Martha took a step back, separating from her daughter. Not trusting her voice, she nodded a silent farewell, remembering Mother deSales' mandate of no crying.

"Goodbye, Mommy." Frances walked to Sister Mollie's side, turned to give a quick wave, and followed the young nun out of the heated room.

Watching the closed door, Martha shook off a shiver. She bent and gathered the stack of books on the table into her arms. Every Monday, after she completed her morning work at the Pickett's, she went to the library downtown. Usually she walked the twenty blocks, but when it was bitter cold, like today, she splurged on trolley fare. Counting every penny, Martha clung to the hope she would one day bring her daughter home.

The prioress tucked a jar of hot chicken soup into Martha's pocket. "For your supper. And it will warm you on the way home. God Bless."

"Thank you." Martha paused, swallowing twice. "Have you heard from the judge?" She asked the same question every week. Every week she got the same answer.

"Sorry, no word yet." Mother deSales sighed. "These things take time."

"Time. Yes, as you've said. How much time?" Martha tapped her foot, her boot drumming against the worn carpet. She knew her tone was sharp but she couldn't help her seesaw emotions. Her mood swung from debilitating sorrow to blinding rage, sometimes in a matter of minutes.

"You have to be patient. The courts..."

"I have been patient!" Martha snapped. "That judge won't even talk to me." She went to the courthouse a dozen times but on each visit the arrogant clerk in the juvenile court office wouldn't let her in. He stood at the door, arms crossed over his chest, leaning back slightly, as if she was diseased. On her last visit, three weeks ago, she pounded on the locked door until a policeman seized her arm and escorted her from the courthouse.

"Making a nuisance of yourself will not help," Mother deSales said.

Martha turned, eyebrows raised. "What will help?"

The prioress sighed again. "I do not know."

Martha's shoulders sagged, her anger sapping what little strength she had. She savored the warmth in the parlor a moment longer, then, with a glance at the door where her daughter disappeared—and a pointed non-look at the prioress—stepped outside.

The sun dipped behind the hills as she walked down the lane, her right arm filled with books, her left hand in her pocket gripping the warm jar. She paused at the south end of the monastery, gazing at the lights in the third story windows. Smoke poured from the tall chimney at the rear of the building. Comforted that her daughter was warm and well-fed, Martha picked her way across the frosty bricks to the junction of National Road, ducking under the awning of a drug store. She pulled coins from her pocket and sighed. A penny short for the trolley fare. It would take nearly an hour to walk home but it didn't matter since there was no reason to hurry to her cold, lonely apartment.

She put her head down and moved west along National Road, the coins in her pocket rattling against the jar. Her steps slow and cautious, she took in her surroundings, trying to keep her thoughts from Frances. She passed through the Woodsdale area, the houses large and well-lit. She imagined the people behind the walls, the owners eating in the dining room, the help busy in the kitchen. Maybe there was a child in that room upstairs where a light glowed, working on a spelling lesson. The small window next to it, also glowing, could be the bathroom where a little brother or sister splashed in the tub. A church bell rang seven times as Martha passed into Fulton, a community of factory workers and tradesmen. On the banks of the wide creek bisecting the neighborhood, a foundry was still active, the sky overhead bright, cacophonous grinds and clangs making her teeth rattle. She quickened her pace, legs burning, her breath frosty gasps as she labored up a lengthy slope.

100

At her apartment building, she crept in the front door, hoping to go unnoticed by Mrs. Hofmann but the widow's door opened and she called out to Martha.

"How is Frances? Pamela?" Mrs. Hofmann asked. She held a tattered robe closed at her chest, chunky-knit socks on her feet. "I worry so for those little girls. My heart aches."

"Frances is fine," Martha said. She knew Mrs. Hofmann felt remorse, the widow saying, more than once, that she blamed herself for letting the police take the girls away, but, cold and tired, Martha wasn't in the mood to ease Mrs. Hofmann's guilt tonight. It wasn't Mrs. Hofmann's fault, she knew that, but a part of Martha did blame the old widow. If she hadn't invited Evelyn here, if she hadn't allowed a prostitute and her offspring to live in this building, maybe Patrick's evil plan wouldn't have worked.

"Did you see Pamela?" Mrs. Hofmann took a step into the hall when Martha started up the stairs.

"No," Martha said, not slowing her steps. She heard Evelyn was working on Water Street in the south part of town, never once visiting her daughter at the monastery. Poor Pamela. At least Martha was able to feel tenderness towards a motherless child but her empathy didn't extend far. These days, she avoided people, and most people avoided her. Dottie had finally stopped asking about Frances since Martha alternately burst into tears or spit out "fine." Mickey was often the target of Martha's sharp tongue—he made her miss Frances all the more—and Mrs. Roth, Mrs. Seighman and Vickers had all been victims of Martha's misplaced anger. Mrs. Pickett lessened her demands, or when she did have a request, she passed it on via Mrs. Roth. The only one at the Pickett house who didn't avoid her was George. She rejected her boss's advances out of habit, rather than outrage, too despondent to care.

Tiptoeing past Dottie's apartment, Martha made her way to the third floor and opened the door to her apartment. She didn't bother to lock it anymore. Without Frances, there was nothing she valued in the small space. She crossed the dark room and lay on the bed, the jar of soup still in her pocket. A prayer came to mind but she pushed it away. She hadn't been to church for six months. When Frances was first taken, she went to Saint James every week and prayed harder than ever. Was this punishment for her sins, she asked God, and vowed to be better. She left an extra penny in the collection basket, went to her knees every night before bed, but Frances remained at the monastery and Patrick continued his quest to adopt her. Mother deSales said she would fight until her dying day to keep Frances from her uncle but what if something happened to the prioress? She wasn't a young woman. Would the other nuns fight so hard to keep Frances or would they be happy to have one less mouth to feed?

Sleep didn't come and images of Frances worked their way into her head. Newborn Frances, cocooned in a blanket, Martha counting every finger and toe, kissing the puckered forehead, tiny nose and silky hair. Frances taking her first clumsy steps the week after they moved to the apartment, giggling as she careened across the bare floor, the tattered sock doll in her hand. The first day of school, Frances waving from her desk, blue eyes shining. She rolled to her side and clasped her knees to her chest. These reminisces hurt. Every moment away from Frances was a memory missed.

***

The next morning was cold and clear, with an inch of snow. Martha left her apartment early, making sure she would not run into Mickey on his way to school. As usual on Monday morning, Martha did laundry in the basement, not emerging into the kitchen until noon. "Mr. Pickett come home yet?" she asked Mrs. Seighman.

102

The cook dried her hands on her apron, shaking her head. "He won't be coming home for lunch today. Big meeting at the bank. Said we'll get paid tomorrow."

Martha heaved a sigh. It would be another cold night in her apartment since coal was on her very short shopping list. She yanked her coat from the hooks by the door and was shrugging into it when Mrs. Roth walked into the room, a tray of food in her hands.

"Mrs. Pickett refused to eat." Mrs. Roth lowered the tray to the table, steam rising from the bowl. "Martha, she didn't touch it—why don't you eat it?"

Martha eyed the plump dumplings, the smell of chicken spilling into the warm kitchen. Her mouth watered. "She on another diet?" Martha asked, admiring the food.

"Said she's not feeling well. I do believe she is running a fever."

Martha sighed. She shook her coat off and returned it to the hook. "She'll want a bath."

"I can do it," Mrs. Roth said.

Martha forced a smile. "Thank you, Mrs. Roth, but the missus's bath is one of my duties."

"Eat first, Martha." Mrs. Seighman stepped from her place in front of the sink and pulled a chair out. "You are far too skinny." She moved the bowl to the table, adding a spoon and a cup of coffee next to it.

"Go ahead, Martha, eat," Mrs. Roth said. She looked up when the back door opened and Vickers stomped into the kitchen.

"The Franklin don't like this weather," he said. "Colder than a..." he stopped when he caught sight of Martha. He walked to the stove and filled a mug with coffee.

"Let's eat," Mrs. Roth said. "It's been quite some time since we have all had lunch together. She rubbed her palms together and looked at the cook. "You have soup for us, Mrs. Seighman?"

"Of course," the cook said, ladling creamy broth into three bowls.

"Potato, huh?" Vickers sat in the chair next to the one Mrs. Seighman had pulled out for Martha. "My grandma made a mean potato soup," he said. "Onions and something green." He slurped a spoonful into his mouth. "Hmm, better than granny's."

Still standing, Martha watched Vickers until Mrs. Roth nudged her elbow and Martha slipped into the chair next to him. She kept her head down as she ate, the dumplings melting on her tongue, the consonant chatter of her co-workers lifting her mood. She willed herself to slow down, savor the meal, and be cordial. "Something wrong with the car?" she asked.

Vickers swallowed, wiped his mouth with the back of his hand. "Getting old and cranky, just like Mrs. Seighman." He winked across the table at the cook.

"Cranky? I'll show you cranky," Mrs. Seighman said and pushed to her feet. She gave the handyman a firm rap on his head as she refilled his coffee cup. "You ain't no spring chicken anymore."

"Don't I know it." Vickers took a noisy slurp. "I'm not sure which aches more, my back or my knees."

"Back. Definitely my back," Mrs. Roth said.

Martha smiled. Between the warm food and light conversation, she had a brief respite from her worries. "I better get upstairs." She stood, tying an apron around her thin waist. "Thank you," she said to Mrs. Roth, giving her a sincere smile, and went upstairs, her thoughts drifting back to Frances. She paused outside Ruth's bedroom door, steeling herself for unreasonable demands and whining complaints. One knock and she pushed the door open.

The room was dim, the drapes pulled closed, and it was hot, the gas stove in the fireplace glowing red. And it smelled. Martha moved towards the bed, the stench growing stronger. She turned on the lamp on the bedside table and sucked in her breath. Ruth's face was crimson and slick with sweat, her hair damp and matted. Martha recoiled. The smell was coming from the bed, Ruth must have soiled herself. With her forearm covering her mouth and nose, Martha moved to the fireplace to lower the heat. She turned the water on in the tub next door, lighting the stove in the bathroom's fireplace.

Ruth mumbled "no" a few times and swatted uselessly as Martha undressed her. Hooking Ruth's arm over her shoulder, Martha heaved her boss to her feet and staggered to the bathroom. Once in the half-full tub, Ruth opened her eyes, patted Martha's cheek, and said "thank you." When Mrs. Roth came in a few moments later, Ruth had closed her eyes and the crimson had moved down to her chest and torso.

"She doesn't look well," Mrs. Roth said from the doorway.

"She thanked me," Martha said, pressing a damp cloth to Ruth's forehead. "She never thanks me." Martha turned to Mrs. Roth. "She's burning up. I think she needs a doctor."

Mrs. Roth nodded. "I'll make the call." She returned ten minutes later. "We are to take her to the hospital. Vickers is bringing the car around."

When George arrived at the hospital an hour and a half later, he was greeted by two doctors. They led him away. After another hour, and no sight of George or the doctors, Victors announced that he was leaving.

"I'll drop you at your apartment, Martha," he said.

Martha crept up the stairs to her apartment and sat at her small table, staring at the jar of soup Mother deSales had sent home last night. She couldn't heat it since there was no coal for the stove. No ice for the ice box, either, but the apartment was cold enough to keep perishables fresh, if she had any. The books from the library were next to the soup jar but, after a glance at the gray sky outside her window, she decided to wait until tomorrow to return them. She crawled beneath her quilt, hoping for a dreamless sleep.

CHAPTER TWELVE

January 1927
Wheeling, West Virginia

Back at the Pickett house early the next morning, Martha asked Mrs. Roth for word of Ruth's condition.

The housekeeper shrugged. "I don't know. Neither the mister nor missus have returned from the hospital."

Just before noon, George strolled into the kitchen as if nothing was amiss. "Mrs. Pickett has passed away," he announced as he paid the staff. He looked at Martha. "Pick out a dress for the undertaker. I'm going back to the bank."

Stunned, Martha walked slowly up the stairs. Ruth Pickett seldom had a kind word for her, or anybody else in her orbit, but Martha never wished her dead and was sickened by George's callousness. In Ruth's bedroom, Martha found eleven-year-old Randolph sitting on his mother's bare bed and her heart sank lower. The foul odor still lingered and Martha fought the urge to escape the room, sitting beside Randolph and draping her arm around his thin shoulders. He leaned into her and sobbed. After several minutes he sat up and wiped his eyes with back of his hand.

"Don't tell my father I cried," Randolph said.

"I won't."

"Don't tell Russell, either. He'll make fun of me."

Martha nodded. "Can you help me pick out a dress for your mother? Do you have a favorite?"

"The green one she wore on Christmas."

"That's a fine choice, Randolph. Now, let's get you something to eat."

***

A week after Ruth's funeral, George propositioned Martha. "I am a man. I have needs," he said, cornering her in the basement.

She stared at him but said nothing.

He didn't try to kiss her or grab her hand as he usually did. They stood eye to eye for a long moment, the corner of his lips twitching, his head slightly tilted. He raised an eyebrow.

Martha didn't flinch.

He blinked and turned away.

Martha watched her boss go up the stairs, his leather soles slapping against the wood planks. A plan was forming. George's needs could be useful. Maybe there was a way to bring Frances home, after all. She dismissed the notion, closed her eyes. The thought of George's hands on her body made her stomach retch, but she forced his leer from her mind, replacing it with Frances's innocent face. Reuniting with her daughter was all that mattered. Two days later, when George again cornered her in the basement, she surprised him by taking a step closer, her left palm on his chest.

"I have two conditions," she said, holding up her right index and middle finger. "One," she folded her middle finger, "you will marry me. Two," she folded her index finger, "you will have my daughter released from the monastery. She will live here, and you will grant her the same education as your sons."

It took George three days to accept Martha's terms. They married at the courthouse and went to a downtown hotel for the night, Martha focusing on Frances to get through her vows and honeymoon. The next morning, George went to the bank as usual, and Martha rode with Vickers to the monastery. She waited in the parlor, a room she knew so well, but today it looked different. Felt different. The cross in the small window seemed brighter, the Madonna on the mantle wore a tranquil smile. Frances burst through the door, Mother deSales and Sister Mollie following.

"Is it true, Mommy? I'm going home?"

Martha knelt. "Yes!" She pulled Frances into her arms.

Frances stepped back, put a hand on Martha's lapel.

"New coat, Mommy?" She looked at Martha's feet. "And new boots, too?"

"Yes. Gifts," Martha said, her cheeks warming as she stole a glance at Mother deSales. Once he accepted Martha's terms, George had insisted on several new dresses with shoes to match, plus a new wool coat and boots. A seamstress had come to the house to take Martha's measurements and George picked the fabrics.

"Good luck to you, my dear," Mother deSales said, laying a hand on Martha's shoulder. She bent, cupped Frances's chin. "We will miss you, child. Sister Mollie has your possessions."

Frances looked up, her smile slipping. "Can I come back to visit?" She turned to Martha. "What about Pamela?"

"We will take good care of Pamela," Mother deSales said. "And you can come to Mass every Sunday and visit with Pamela in the parlor, just as your mother did."

Martha stood, Frances's hand firmly in hers. "Goodbye." Her focus stayed on Mother deSales. What else should she say? Did the prioress know how she freed Frances? How wrong was it to give yourself to a man you didn't love for the sake of your child? "Thank you,"

Martha finally said and let her gaze drop to her daughter. She smiled. She couldn't help it. "Let's go, Sunshine."

Frances stopped when she saw the car, Vickers standing beside it. "Mommy?"

"It's fine, Frances. Mr. Vickers works for Mr. Pickett." She put a hand on Frances's back and lowered her lips to Frances's ear. "He's very nice," Martha said. "And he will drive us wherever we want."

Frances climbed into the back seat, Martha sliding in beside her. "I can't wait to see Mickey," Frances said.

Martha bit her bottom lip. She had tried to come up with the right words to tell Frances they no longer lived on Pike Street, the only place Frances had ever called home. She didn't tell Dottie, yet, either. Things had happened so fast. George sent Vickers to the apartment, instructing the handyman to pack up any worthy property and Vickers returned with two crates of clothes and a few other items. Their belongings now sat in what was Ruth Pickett's bedroom.

"Do you have to go back to work?" Frances asked when the car stopped at the Pickett house.

Martha turned to her daughters, putting both hands on the thin shoulders. "Remember, how I told you the Pickett house is very large with lots of rooms? Well, now we get live in that house, Sunshine."

"Why would we live here? I want to see Mickey." Frances's voice quivered.

"We will see Mickey, and his mother, in a few days." Martha squeezed Frances's shoulders. "Let's go in and say hello to Mommy's friends. And wait until you see your new bedroom." Martha gave Vickers a nod and he hopped out to open the door.

"Let me help you, Miss Frances," Vickers said, extending his hand. "I think you will like living here."

Frances frowned at Vickers's hand, turned back to Martha.

"Go on, Sunshine, hold his hand. He won't bite."

When they walked into the kitchen, Mrs. Seighman wiped her hands on her apron and smiled. "She's a beauty, Mrs. Pickett."

Frances looked at her mother, her confusion obvious.

"This is Mrs. Seighman," Martha said quickly, turning her attention to Mrs. Roth. "And this is Mrs. Roth.

Mrs. Roth gave Frances a quick smile and looked at Martha. "Are we to call her Miss Albrecht? Miss Pickett?"

Martha studied Mrs. Roth for a moment. "Frances. Call her Frances." She put a hand on her daughter's back and nudged her towards the back stairs. "Let's go see your bedroom."

Frances's head swung left and right, her mouth hanging open, as they walked down the hall. She stood speechless at the doorway to Ruth's bedroom.

"There's your books," Martha pointed towards one of the crates. She turned at the sound of heavy footsteps.

"What are you doing in my mother's room?" Russell stood tense and rigid in his gray school uniform.

"This is Frances. My daughter." Martha wasn't sure how the Pickett boys reacted when George told them he was marrying her. When she asked, George had deflected, changed the subject, simply saying his sons had no say in the matter.

Russell eyed Frances from head to toe, just as his father had done many times to Martha. "Look at that dress," he said with a laugh.

Martha felt Frances stiffen. She looked down at her daughter, still dressed in her handmade jumper and white blouse, a yellow bow tied at her neck. The younger girls at the monastery all wore yellow bows, the older girls green or blue bows so the nuns could easily discern ages. What little sympathy Martha had for Russell vanished. "Go to your room," she said and turned away, Frances's hand still in hers.

111

"No. You aren't my mother." Russell grabbed Martha's other hand. "I don't want you in my mother's room."

Anger erupting, Martha wheeled around, pulling her hand from Russell's grip. She nudged Frances behind her legs and bent forward, her face inches from Russell's. "You are never to touch me again. You are never to touch my daughter. You are not welcome in this room." She straightened, catching sight of Nanny Maureen, wide-eyed in the hallway with Randolph at her side. Martha ran her hands down her skirt, forced a smile. "Maureen, I'm sure Russell has some homework you can help him with. Randolph, come here and meet Frances."

CHAPTER THIRTEEN

April 1927
Wheeling, West Virginia

Frances sat at the table in the Pickett house kitchen, a green crayon in her right hand, her left hand twisting one of her braids. Her mother tried to redo the uneven plaits this morning but Frances was in a hurry to get her day started. She was so excited. After three months at the Pickett house, Mickey was finally able to visit since George was out of town. She looked across the polished wood at her mother, sitting between Mickey's mother and Mr. Vickers. Her mom was smiling, but it was an odd smile, not all the way there. Frances called it her half smile. Not that she would tell her mother that. The sisters at the monastery said if you can't say anything nice, don't say anything at all. She didn't remember her mother having a half-smile before she went to the monastery but that wasn't the only thing about her mother that had changed. Of course, her mother's clothes were different, and she was taller since her shoes now had little heels that made tapping sounds when she walked across the wood floors, but she also talked differently. Softer, like she was whispering all the time. Her mother caught her looking and Frances shifted her focus back to the coloring book. She filled in another leaf, stealing glances at Mickey sitting on her left. His head was down and wisps of brown hair hung in his face but she could still see the pink tip of his tongue caught between his lips as he worked a brown crayon across the page.

"There. I colored the dog," Mickey said, raising his head and smiling at Frances.

She returned the smile. It felt so good to be with Mickey. Like she could finally be herself. Besides her mother, Mickey was who she missed the most while at the monastery. When she learned she was leaving the monastery, she thought she would be going back to the school at the bottom of Pike Street but instead she was enrolled at an all-girls academy on the outskirts of town. It was bad enough not living in the same building as Mickey but not going to school with him was dreadful. Not at all what she expected. She begged her mother to change her mind but her mother wouldn't budge.

"You are going to college, Frances," her mother had said. "The academy will prepare you. It will teach you other things, too. Social things. How to dress. What to say. I don't want you to be like me."

That had confused Frances. Why wouldn't she want to be like her mother? She adored her mother, although her mother's watchfulness was getting a little frustrating. When she was at the Pickett house her mother seldom let her out of her sight. At the monastery, Frances was expected to take care of herself, had learned to change her own bed, take a bath and wash her hair. She didn't need her mother's help, especially not in the bathroom. It was still hard for Frances to believe that entire bathroom was hers. One toilet, one tub, just for her. The thirty girls in her wing at the monastery shared one sinkhole with five toilets and three tubs. When she arrived at the monastery, she didn't use the toilet for an entire day, embarrassed to sit on one with other girls watching.

114

Mickey touched her hand. "Want me to color the cat?"

Frances studied the page. "Let's make a rainbow above the tree," she said, drawing a wide arc with the violet crayon.

Mickey picked up the red crayon.

"No, that goes on top of the rainbow," Frances said. "Red, orange, yellow, green, blue, indigo and violet."

"Indigo?" Mickey wrinkled his forehead.

"It's a dark blue." Frances searched through the crayons until she found the one she wanted and handed it to Mickey. She gathered the rest of the rainbow colors, passing each crayon to Mickey with a smile.

"There. All done." Mickey turned the book around and pushed it across the table. "Look, Mom, we made a rainbow!"

"That's nice." Dottie nodded and drained her glass. "Nothing better than lemonade on a hot day," she said.

"'Cept an ice-cold beer." Vickers, on the other side of Martha, leaned forward and winked at Dottie.

"Hush, you," Mrs. Seighman said and turned from the sink. "If you are going to sit here, make yourself useful. Peel some carrots." She snapped the green stems off a dozen carrots and dropped them on the table.

"Oh, no!" Mickey yelled, grappling with his half-full glass as it upended, lemonade splashing to the wood.

Quick to her feet, Martha snatched a towel from the counter and blotted the table.

"I'm sorry," Mickey said.

"It's fine." Martha said. She looked up as Mrs. Roth came in the room with a bundle of towels and sheets. "Sunshine," Martha said, her gaze still on the housekeeper, moved her hand to Frances's shoulder. "It's a lovely day. You and Mickey go on outside for a bit."

Frances watched Mrs. Roth toss the soiled linen into a basket. She was still leery of the housekeeper, staying out of her way, although the woman had never

115

been nasty to her. Mr. Vickers was her favorite worker at the Pickett house and Mrs. Seighman was second favorite. The cook sometimes let her help in the kitchen and she didn't mind when Frances washed her own dishes. Mrs. Roth, on the other hand, didn't appreciate when Frances stripped the sheets off her bed on laundry day and told Frances that cleaning her own bathtub wasn't necessary. At the monastery, every girl knew how to scour the tubs and sinks.

Mrs. Roth surveyed the table. "Mr. Vickers, I am sure there are things need done in the garage."

"Yes, ma'am." He got to his feet and walked out the back door.

Martha picked up the empty pitcher and wiped the table. "Do you have more lemons, Mrs. Seighman? I'll make more lemonade."

"I'll get that," Mrs. Roth said, taking the pitcher from Martha's hand. "Perhaps you and Miss Dottie would be more comfortable in the parlor, or the library? I will be happy to refill your glasses, Mrs. Pickett."

There it was. The half-smile, and a flash in her mother's eyes. It happened every time someone called her Mrs. Pickett.

"Come on, Mickey." Frances returned the crayons to the box and went out the back door.

Russell and Randolph were sitting in the pavilion and Randolph stood, waved his arm. He ran down the steps. "Hello!" He thrust his right hand towards Mickey. "I'm Randolph Pickett."

Mickey frowned at Randolph's hand, looked at Frances.

She giggled and elbowed Mickey in the ribs. "Go ahead. Shake his hand." She moved her lips to Mickey's ear. "He's the nice one."

Mickey smiled and grasped Randolph's hand. "I'm Mickey."

"Mickey who?"

"Oh. Mickey Shoaf."

116

"Nice to meet you Mr. Shoaf."

Mickey giggled. "Nobody's ever me called me that."

"You can call him Mickey, Randolph," Frances said. "Want to play with us?" She glanced at the pavilion, hoping Russell wouldn't hear. She was relieved to see he hadn't moved, his head bent over a book. "Let's look for barges on the river."

They ran to the fence at the west end of the yard and wrapped their hands around the black iron. The railroad tracks ran along the other side of the fence atop a twelve-foot stone wall and twenty feet separated the bottom of the wall from the shore of the brown river.

"Aww, we just missed one," Randolph pointed north at several flats heaped with coal, the black nuggets glinting in the sun. He looked south, a hand tented over his eyes. "No other barges. No boats at all." He focused on the Ohio shoreline.

Frances followed Randolph's gaze and watched smoke pour from a tall smokestack. There were six more stretched along the river in both directions. She gripped the fence and leaned forward, craning her neck to the left. "I can see cars on the bridge."

"I want to see a train," Mickey said.

"There won't be a train for another hour, idiot." Russell stood behind Mickey, his pocket watch in his hand. He returned the timepiece to his pocket and eyed Mickey from head to toe. "You're short. How old are you, kid?"

"He's eight, just like me," Frances said.

"He can't be," Russell said. "He's shorter than you,"

"Mommy says I'm tall for my age. Like her." Frances let her shoulders droop and tried to look shorter. She hated being tall. The girls at her new school made fun of her height and it didn't help that she was two years older than most of the girls in her class. Even though she had gone to first grade at the public school, and had two more years of schooling at the monastery, the academy had made her start in the first grade. During one class

117

about animals in Africa, the teacher held up a picture of a giraffe and one of the other students, Joan Whitman, yelled out, "look, it's Frances." The name stuck and now most of her classmates called her "Giraffe."

"Girls aren't supposed to be tall," Russell said.

"Why not?" Randolph asked.

"They're just not. The man is always supposed to be taller." Russell looked at Frances. "Your mother's as tall as my father. Good thing she's pretty."

Frances didn't know what to say so she walked away, Mickey and Randolph following.

"Want to play Duck, Duck, Goose?" Mickey asked.

"I don't know what that is," Randolph said.

"It's a dumb game for little kids," Russell said, giving Randolph a shove.

"Is not," Mickey said.

"Shut up, runt." Russell pushed Mickey.

Mickey stumbled, pinwheeling his arms for balance, but he fell forward, his face hitting one of the pavilion's columns. He screamed as blood poured from his nose and dripped on to his shoes.

"Mommy!" Frances yelled.

Mrs. Seighman ran out the door. "Good Lord," she mumbled and ran down the steps, jamming a rag into Mickey's face. "Put your head back, child." She led him, Frances following, into the kitchen. "Mrs. Shoaf! Mrs. Pickett!"

At the sight of the blood-soaked rag, Dottie stopped, let out a shriek.

Martha pushed past Dottie and hustled Mickey across the hall and into the bathroom, tilting his head back. She pulled a towel from the wall hook and pressed it against Mickey's nose. "What happened?"

"Russell!" Frances hissed. "He pushed Mickey."

"Did not. The stupid kid fell." Russell stood in the hallway, smirking, Randolph behind him. "Right?" He turned and backhanded Randolph's arm.

Randolph looked at his shoes.

"Right?" Russell repeated, and whacked Randolph again.

Randolph, chin on his chest, nodded.

"You are twelve years old, Russell. Too old to act like this. Go to your room," Martha said, lifting the towel from Mickey's face. She smiled. "It's fine, Mickey. The bleeding has stopped."

"My hand." Mickey raised his palm to reveal three scratches oozing blood.

"Whiner," Russell said.

"Go to your room, now," Martha repeated. She wet the towel and dabbed Mickey's palm.

"He pushed him," Frances repeated. "Why is Russell so mean?"

"I don't know," her mother said. "There, good as new, Mickey."

Mickey turned, burying his face in his mother's skirt.

Dottie patted Mickey's back "Time to go."

Frances wiped away a tear. Her day with Mickey was ruined. She looked at her mother. Was she going to punish Russell? Or do nothing, like every other time he misbehaved. Her mother didn't look at her, but turned to Dottie, giving her one of her half-smiles.

"Take some biscuits with you," Martha said.

"I don't want your charity," Dottie snapped and led Mickey out the back door, neither saying goodbye, neither looking back.

Mrs. Roth appeared in the doorway and cleared her throat. "Mrs. Pickett, Mr. Pickett is on the phone.

Martha let out a long breath. "I'll take it in the library," she said and hurried from the room, eyes straight ahead.

Frances went to her room and flopped face first on her bed, hot tears soaking the pillow. She hated it here. She pounded the mattress with her fist. When Sister Mollie told her she was going home, Frances had been so happy. Then they came to this house and Frances's joy

119

faded. Her mother tried to cheer her, gushing about the new bedroom. Told her how lucky she was to have such a beautiful room. She rolled on to her back, looked towards the windows. It was a beautiful room. A rounded bay with floor-to-ceiling windows. Burgundy drapes in soft velvet. Every morning, Frances pulled back those drapes so the rising sun could brighten the space, but, despite three lamps, the room was dark, especially in the afternoons when the sun passed to the back of the house. Like now. She raised to an elbow and flipped on the light on the bedside table.

"I'm sorry," Randolph said. He stood in the doorway.

Frances sat up and ran her fingers across her damp cheeks.

"I wanted to tell the truth," Randolph stammered. "But I have to go to school with Russell. And he's bigger than me."

Frances nodded. "I know." She knew very well what it was like to be tormented at school. There was no doubt Russell would punish Randolph if he didn't do what Russell said.

"Can I eat dinner with you tonight?" Randolph asked.

"We can all eat in the kitchen since your father is out of town."

Randolph shook his head. "He's back from Pittsburgh. Your mother has to meet him at the club downtown for dinner and I don't want to eat with Russell."

Frances felt her lips quiver, tears burning at the back of her eyes. Her mother had promised today was Frances's day, said that they could do anything they wanted since Mr. Pickett was out of town and Frances had picked a visit from Mickey. Look how that turned out. She raised her head and glared at her mother standing behind Randolph, wearing one of her fancy dresses, white gloves and hat in her hand.

"I have to go out, Sunshine," her mother said, the half-smile in place. "Mrs. Roth will bring your dinner up." She put a hand on Randolph's shoulder. "You'll keep Frances company, won't you?"

He nodded.

Frances glowered, said nothing, and turned her head.

"Goodnight, Sunshine."

Frances refused to look at her mother. When the sound of her mother's heels on the front stairs faded, she swung her feet off the bed and walked to the table in the room just outside her bedroom. This is where she ate most of her meals, except the rare breakfast when Mrs. Seighman let her eat in the kitchen.

"My mother used to eat here," Randolph said, running his palm over the wood.

"Do you miss her?"

He shrugged. "Sometimes. She wasn't like your mother. Didn't talk to me much. 'Children are to be seen, not heard' was her favorite saying."

It was obvious to Frances that Mr. Pickett felt the same way. At least when it came to her. Her mother made it clear that George Pickett was never going to be a father-figure, telling Frances it would be best to steer clear of him. "Speak only when he addresses you," her mother said. He still hadn't spoken to her, and that was fine with Frances. She wished Russell would so the same.

***

Frances woke with a start, heart pounding, breaths shallow as she dreaded another day at school. Then she smiled. It was Sunday, her favorite day of the week. After breakfast, she and her mother and Randolph climbed into the Franklin and Vickers drove to the monastery.

"Bye, Mommy. Bye Randolph," Frances said, hopping out of the car when Vickers held the door open.

"Pick you up in two hours, Miss Frances," Vickers called. He slid back behind the wheel to drive Martha and Randolph to a downtown church.

Frances skipped up the stone steps leading to the monastery's three-winged chapel, pausing at the heavy door to pull her veil from her pocket and drape it over her hair. Inside, she inhaled deeply, breathing in the lingering scent of incense from the last Mass. She dipped a finger in the font, crossed herself, and walked to the front pew of the public wing. Lowering to the kneeler, she leaned forward and craned her neck, hoping for a glimpse of Sister Agnes or Sister Christine, but they remained hidden behind the cloister grille in the nuns' wing. The third wing of the chapel was reserved for the Catholic girls of the monastery and Frances resisted the urge to wave to the few girls she recognized. She concentrated on the priest's words, singing and praying as she had been taught, the smooth rosary beads—a gift from her teacher Sister Agnes—slipping soundlessly through her fingers. While her eyes were closed during the final hymn, she picked out Sister Gertrude's gravelly contralto and Mother deSales surprising soprano, the nuns' melodic voices soaring to the rafters, three stories above.

After mass, she stowed her beads and veil in her pocket and walked to the parlor where Pamela was waiting, her friend talking before Frances even sat down.

"We went to the farm yesterday. I got to pet a cat. It lives in the barn with the cows," Pamela said, her voice squeaking with excitement. "Sister Agnes showed us a turtle at the pond. Remember those special flowers that grow in the water. They are sooo pretty. And Wendy moved to the third wing. You remember Wendy?" She took a breath, then chattered on, not giving Frances time to respond. "I got a new jumper." Pamela patted her chest. "I outgrew the other one. Sister Mollie says I'm growing like a weed." She jumped to her feet and put a hand over her head. "See how tall I am?"

Frances nodded and smiled, letting Pamela fill their short time together. She had hoped to visit with Sister Agnes, or Sister Christine, but neither were granted permission for visitors. It was confusing, missing the nuns and Pamela. When she lived at the monastery, she thought of her mother constantly, a dull ache in the pit of her stomach never lessening. All she wanted to do was go home. She did as her mother asked—listened to the Sisters, ate everything on her plate, studied hard—and her wish came true. Sort of. She was glad to be with her mother, but Frances was more comfortable at the monastery than at the Pickett house. A feeling she could never share with her mother.

Thirty minutes later, Mother deSales came into the parlor. "Time's up," she said.

"Oh no." Pamela ran to Frances and held tight, just like Frances used to do every time her visit with her mother ended.

Mother deSales cleared her throat and Pamela dropped her arms to her sides and disappeared out the door.

"This is for you," Frances said, thrusting a small book towards the prioress. Her mother always sent a gift for the sisters. Sometimes it was a bolt of cloth, other times it was a few coins, or a can of sardines.

Mother deSales nodded her thanks. "Give my best to your mother," she said and walked Frances to the door.

Head hanging, Frances descended the steps of the monastery, watching the delivery truck pass through the iron gates and stop outside the laundry building. The laundry would be quiet today but during the week it bustled. Businesses and a few, well-heeled families paid to have their clothes and sheets washed, and before and after their classes, the older girls helped. Frances had stood at the laundry door many times, fascinated by the assembly line of girls and the odd-looking machinery. They ironed and mended the freshly-washed shirts, one girl at the dampener, another at the finisher, another running the shaper. Frances actually looked forward to working in the laundry with the other girls. She sighed, the rackety Franklin interrupting her recollections as it pulled to the curb.

Vickers jumped out. "Why so glum, Miss Frances? It's a knockout day."

She shrugged.

"You want to sit up front?"

"Sure." She ran to the passenger door and hopped in, pulling the door closed before Mr. Vickers could offer help.

"Mr. Pickett is getting us a new car. A Hudson," he said.

As they bounced over the uneven bricks, Frances ran her hand along the dashboard. "I like this one." It was far different than the first vehicle she was in, the police car that took her and Pamela to the monastery. One minute they were warm and safe in Mrs. Hofmann's apartment, the next they were bundled into the back seat of a car, both panicked and uncomprehending. They had clung to each other during the ride, keeping their hands entwined as they were ushered into the massive building that looked like a prison. "I want to go home," Frances had said over and over, but Pamela didn't utter a sound, and after three days of muteness the sisters wondered if she would ever speak. At the beginning of their second week at the monastery, Mother deSales carried a brown puppy into the dormitory and placed the wiggling dog on Pamela's lap, prompting Pamela into a gap-toothed grin, and to say her first word, "doggie."

"Want to take a ride through the park?" Vickers asked.

"Are we permitted?"

"Why not? Your ma and Mr. Pickett went to lunch out the pike and the boys went to the movie house."

Frances shrugged and they cruised east, slowing when Vickers thrust his arm out the window, signaling a turn. He added the Franklin to the long line of cars inching down a road paralleling the golf course. She laid her chin on her hands as she gazed out the open window, watching men in plaid knickers stride across the manicured grass, small boys hauling oversized bags trailing behind. They drove by the two-story white pavilion, past a small lake and a playground filled with children.

"You want to get out and play a bit, Miss Frances?"

She looked closely at a group of kids near the swings, recognizing her most vicious classmate, Joan Whitman. "No thanks, Mr. Vickers." The last thing she wanted to do was spend more time than she had to with the cruel girls from the academy. "Let's just go..." she paused, nearly saying home. But home to her was not the Pickett house. Frances wasn't sure where home was anymore.

CHAPTER FOURTEEN

February 1933
Wheeling, West Virginia

Frances lifted the cloth covering the two dough balls resting on the counter in the Pickett kitchen and poked one ball with her finger. She smiled. She was happy to be in the kitchen, and it was Saturday, so no school, and George Pickett was not around. Laura, Mrs. Seighman's daughter, stood beside her, rolling pin in hand. At thirteen, Frances was already as tall as twenty-three-year old Laura. Though Laura was ten years older, Frances liked spending time with her. Much better than spending time with the girls in her class. By second grade, Frances stopped trying to make friends at her academy and planned her movements throughout her days to avoid the worst of her classmates. She concentrated on her studies, excelling in every subject and showing exceptional aptitude for science. That distinction earned her additional rolled eyes and belittling comments from the group of popular classmates led by Joan Whitman. It also led to her new nickname, "Freaky Frances." The only saving grace was the lie Frances had been living all her life —her brave father sacrificed his life in the Great War. The students were taught about the war and told to appreciate the soldiers who fought it.

"Your turn," Laura said, handing the rolling pin to Frances.

***

Flour drifted to the floor and dough splattered the tiled backsplash as Frances worked the wood roller back and forth. She liked helping in the kitchen. At the monastery, every girl took a turn in the big kitchen, filling milk pitchers or spooning oatmeal or soup into bowls, and in the fall, the girls helped the nuns can tomatoes and beans and peaches from the farm. The rolling pin veered off course, plowing a trail of flour across the countertop. She giggled and turned to her mother and Vickers at the table. They both shrugged. Mrs. Seighman would not be happy with such a mess in her kitchen but the cook wasn't there to scold, Laura filling in for her ailing mother on a Saturday morning.

"Think your biscuits will be as good as your ma's?" Vickers asked Laura.

"Better!" Laura laughed. "But don't tell her I said that." She flipped a small glass jar upside down and pushed it into the flattened dough to make a round cut. "Bet our factory made this," she said, squinting at the embossed trademark on the bottom of the jar.

"I get to visit your factory next week," Frances said, lifting to her toes, working the rolling pin forward. "Our whole class is coming to see how glass is really made. We created little marbles in chemistry." Frances was looking forward to the field trip to the factory. From the first day of fourth grade when she stepped into the small laboratory carved out of a corner in the academy's basement, Frances was fascinated. A few chemicals were brilliantly colored, many smelled foul, some had no color and no odor. Meter, kilogram, kelvin, ampere, candela...everything was carefully measured, and when mixed, or heated, a reaction occurred. Unlike people, chemical reactions were the same every time. The exactness of chemistry was appealing. No secrets. No surprises. She dropped her heels and peeled excess dough from the counter, leaving behind rows of round discs. "My marble was supposed to be green but I added too much chromium oxide. It turned black."

Vickers let out a low whistle. "Listen to them big words. That fancy school sure making your daughter smart, Mrs. Pickett."

Frances glanced at her mother, who smiled back over the rim of her cup, but Frances caught the familiar flash in her mother's eye, that quick flare at the sound of "Mrs. Pickett."

***

Sunday passed as it had for the past six years: Mass and a visit with Pamela. Pamela chattered away, just like always, asking about Pike Street, Mrs. Hofmann and Mickey.

"I haven't seen them for a while," Frances said. 'A while' was six weeks. The longest Frances had gone without seeing Mickey since she left the monastery. At first, her mother walked with her every Saturday afternoon to Pike Street. They often took a gift—a pie, a loaf of bread or some fruit—and sat for hours in Mickey's apartment, the mothers talking, she and Mickey spinning tops or shooting marbles. When she turned ten, Frances was allowed to walk up Main Street by herself and she would stop at Mrs. Hofmann's apartment and then run upstairs to Mickey's. Her mother still went with her from time to time but George's demands increased and Martha's excursions to Pike Street had dwindled to just a handful last year.

"Any news on my mother?" Pamela asked.

Frances contemplated the yellow cross in the parlor's small window. "No one has seen her," she said, just as she did every other time Pamela asked.

Pamela simply nodded. No tears. No disparaging words. A quiet acceptance. She smiled at Frances across the couch. "I like your dress."

Frances looked at her lap, ran her palm across the worn chambray. She had a closet full of dresses in fine-spun wool and linen, many of them trimmed with ruffles and lace, but Frances always wore a simple cotton dress to the monastery. Or when she visited Mickey. It was as if she lived in two worlds, the Pickett house and the academy in one world, the monastery and Pike Street in the other.

The visit left Frances drained. They often did. Her mother said she didn't have to see Pamela but Frances shook her head. She refused to abandon her friend.

Her mood buoyed with her upcoming field trip, Frances woke on Monday with a smile. She took extra care with her appearance, heeding the headmistress's threat that any student not reflecting the academy's high standards would be excluded from the field trip. She pulled the school's standard black jumper over her head, smoothing out the creases. Stretched black wool stockings up her legs and weaved her hair into a braid, scrutinizing the long plait in a silver hand mirror leftover from Ruth Pickett. Many furnishing in the room were from the days of the first Mrs. Pickett. She still felt uneasy in the room. Her first night here she had expected her mother to stay with her, not understanding why they had separate bedrooms.

"We have to live by Mr. Pickett's rules now," her mother said. "Life is full of compromises."

"Compromises?" Frances had asked, bewildered.

"Give and take. You have to give up some things to have other things." Her mother tucked the Dutch girl quilt tight against Frances's chin. "I know you don't understand but someday, you will." She smiled and kissed Frances's forehead. "Now go to sleep, Sunshine, there is nothing to fear. I'm just down the hall."

Despite her mother's encouraging words, Frances had trouble adjusting and after two sleepless nights in her new bedroom, she had padded down the hall to her mother's bedroom. Once the nanny's room, it was simply furnished with a single bed and a dresser, the plaster walls bare. The room was empty. Frightened to search the big house by herself, Frances sat on the narrow bed, and waited. She grew tired and laid her head on the pillow that smelled of her mother, lulled to sleep by the comforting mix of witch hazel and ivory soap. George Pickett's voice woke her. She sat up, listening. His words were slurred, unintelligible, and dissolved into grunts and moans. Frances jumped from the bed and ran, taking cover under the table in the room outside her bedroom. From between the table legs, she watched her mother leave George's room and cross the hall. Frances crawled from her hiding spot and crept down the hall, quietly pushing open the door to her mother's room. Her mother was in bed, her face buried in the pillow, but Frances could hear muffled sobs. She tiptoed back to her bed and pulled the quilt over her head, never venturing out of her bedroom at night again.

In front of the full-length mirror, Frances turned from side to side. She stepped closer, rubbed at a freckle on her cheek, took two steps back, tugged on her stockings and buffed the toe of her left boot. This was far longer than she usually spent in front of the mirror. In the monastery, the only mirrors were small squares hanging above each sink and the girls were taught not to dwell on their reflections. During one of Aunt Susie's and Uncle Patrick's rare visits, Aunt Susie had pulled a small mirror from her handbag and, with a pout, colored her lips bright red. Frances was so enchanted by the mirror and its silver case that her aunt said she could keep it but Mother deSales, watching from the parlor's corner, intercepted the mirror and told Susie that vanity was not encouraged under her roof. That was Aunt Susie's last visit.

Frances took one more look in the large oval and went downstairs. Her first stop was the kitchen, but Mrs. Roth shooed her to the dining room, a plate of scrambled eggs in her hand. Since her mother was the only one in the room, Frances relaxed.

"Ready for your field trip, Sunshine?"

Frances nodded and slipped into the chair across from her mother.

"How is school?" Her mother asked.

Frances swallowed a bite of eggs. "Same as always."

"I spoke to Sister Mayme. She said you're an exceptional student."

"Hmm." Frances pushed another mouthful of eggs in her mouth. Sister Mayme taught chemistry at her academy, and the nun had taken a special interest in Frances. The teacher allowed her to spend extra time in the laboratory, let her complete experiments meant for the older students. Frances stood, empty plate in her hand. "I have to go." She kissed her mother on the cheek and returned to the kitchen, running out the door with a wave to Mrs. Roth.

Randolph stood beside the car, holding the back door open. "Come on, I want to show you something."

She climbed into the back seat, Randolph sliding in beside her.

He grinned and unrolled a large square of paper. "What do you think?"

Frances scanned the large sheet. It was two maps of the world with each country hand-colored a different hue. One map identified present-day countries and their territories, the other map showed countries and their colonies a hundred years ago. Randolph had worked on it for months.

"It's wonderful," she said.

He pointed at Europe. "Things really changed after your father's war."

Frances's smile wavered, guilt from her deceit clouding the moment.

132

"It's for geography," Randolph said.

"You will get an 'A,' I'm sure," Frances said. "Of course, you always get 'A's."

"Look who's talking." Randolph nudged her with his elbow. "I hear your mother bragging about your grades all the time. Already talking college."

Frances waved a hand in front of her face. "I'm only in the seventh grade." She sighed. Not once did her mother ask her if she wanted to go to college. She did...but it would have been nice to be asked.

"I can't believe you will be going to Penn this fall. I will miss you."

"Aww, shucks, I will miss you, too." Randolph patted her hand. "At least my brother isn't around anymore.

Russell was in Ohio, struggling through his first year at the state university. Unlike Randolph, Russell was not a straight A student and Frances had overheard George's rantings about Russell's poor reports from the college. It wasn't just Russell's low grades that earned him reprimands.

"Have a good trip, Frances," Randolph said when they pulled up to his school. He stepped from the car, and waved his right hand, his map rolled and tucked safely under his left arm. He was enveloped by a crowd of young men, all well-groomed and smiling, the sun glinting off the brass buttons on their uniform jackets.

Frances watched her stepbrother, admired his easy way with the other students. Most everybody liked Randolph. Especially girls. At seventeen, he already towered over his father and was at least three inches taller than his older brother. He had changed much since the day Frances met him, growing from a shy, plump boy into a lean athlete with the brains of a scholar. One thing that hadn't changed was Randolph's kindness towards her.

At Frances's school, Vickers pulled next to the bus for the field trip. She remembered to let him open the car door for her, thanked him, and climbed into the bus. The seat next to her remained empty on the short ride to the glass factory.

Sister Mayme barked instructions and pointed as the girls filed into the factory's lobby. "Fifth graders, line up here. Sixth graders, here. Seventh graders, over there."

"Such a tyrant," Joan Whitman whispered to the girl next to her. "Bet her tail is the longest."

"Tail? What tail?" The girl asked.

"The nuns are really monsters," Joan said. "They have tails. That's why they wear all them clothes. To hide their tails."

"That's not true!" Frances said, much louder than intended, causing Sister Mayme to turn.

Joan pointed at Frances and, with her trademark giggle, shrugged. Frances moved to the back of the group as the seventh graders followed Sister Mayme and a short man down a long hallway. They moved into a cavernous room, two large furnaces glowing, molten glass bubbling in their bowels.

"Do not move. Do not touch anything," the man leading the tour warned. He tugged at his tie, pulling a handkerchief from his pocket to wipe his forehead. "Seen enough, Sister?" he asked.

Sister Mayme nodded and herded the students out the door. They followed their tour guide down another hall to a smaller room. "This is the packing room," he said.

Fifty women stood elbow to elbow at two conveyers, pulling glass jars from the moving belt and stacking them in wood crates. The room was nearly as hot as the furnace room, the heat and stink of sweating bodies hastening the students through the stifling space. As they neared the door on the opposite wall, Frances spotted Laura Seighman at the second conveyor. She waved and smiled, but Laura dropped her head. Frances frowned,

134

her smile still in place, and waited for Laura to look up again.

"Move on, Frances," Sister Mayme commanded.

With one more glance at Laura's downturned head, Frances followed her classmates from the room.

"The laboratory is more comfortable," their guide said. "Follow me."

They moved upstairs to a large, narrow room, fans whirling overhead, a dozen men in dark ties and white shirts standing at waist-high counters. A small group gathered at the chalkboard, one man scribbling across the black surface.

"Hello, ladies." A thin, balding man with thick glasses broke from the gathering and walked towards the students. Nodding, he stopped in front of Sister Mayme and pulled his glasses off for a quick polish.

"This is Mr. Latter, girls," Sister Mayme said. "Mr. Latter is in charge of the laboratory. This is where new glass colors are created."

"Not just new colors, Sister. New patterns, new shapes, new moulds, new finishes. Look at this." Mr. Latter picked up a plate from the nearest counter and held it towards the ceiling light. "We call this Platonite. It might look like ordinary milk glass, but it's nearly translucent. See?" He moved his other hand behind the plate and waggled his fingers. "You can almost see through it. We have several more years of testing and refinements to do before it can be made in one of our factories."

"Years?" Frances asked. "Why does it take so long?"

Mr. Latter looked at Frances, his eyes bulging behind the thick lenses. "Making glass is not easy, miss. Cool it too fast, and it cracks. Add too much uranium or copper, and the color is wrong."

Frances bobbed her head. "Like mine." She pulled a small marble from her pocket. "I made this in chemistry class."

Mr. Latter leaned forward to study the black dot in Frances's palm. He laughed. "You should stick to typing classes, little lady."

CHAPTER FIFTEEN

March 1933
Wheeling, West Virginia

Martha pushed scrambled eggs around her plate. She had no appetite. Russell's impending visit had her stomach in knots. A college freshman, he was coming home for his spring break and Martha was not looking forward to her stepson's return. "What time does your brother arrive?" she asked Randolph. It was a warm day for mid-March, and she sat with Frances and Randolph in the solarium, the windows open wide. The room was at the back of the Pickett house on the second floor, its wall of windows offering a view of the river and the buildings on the Ohio shoreline. Today, the smog hung low in the valley, obscuring the sights.

"He was leaving early, so I expect he'll be here before noon," Randolph said. "I was hoping he would stay in Columbus during his break." He shook his head, with a smile, at Mrs. Roth when she moved the coffee pot over his cup. "No thank you." He stood, laying a hand on Martha's shoulder and giving it a gentle squeeze. "Ladies, try to have a pleasant day, although I know it won't be easy with my brother around."

"More coffee, Mrs. Pickett?" Mrs. Roth asked.

"Just half, please," Martha said, frowning. She would never enjoy the "Mrs. Pickett" moniker.

The housekeeper collected Randolph's empty dishes and left the room.

"I stopped by Mickey's yesterday," Frances said. "He's dropped out of school. Going to work at the glass factory."

"He's too young."

"Fudging his age."

"Does Dottie know?" Though she rarely saw Mickey these days, he was still in Martha's thoughts. Just like her mother, she believed education was important and was sorry Mickey wouldn't finish high school.

Frances nodded. "They need the money."

The Depression was taking a toll on most everyone, including the staff at the Pickett house. Mr. Vickers was released the first of the month and Mrs. Seighman reduced to three days. The entire staff at the Maxwell house next door was let go. She worried about Mrs. Seighman and Mrs. Roth, but Martha was most concerned that George would renege on his promise and pull the plug on Frances's schooling.

"I have some reading to do." Frances stood, taking her cup and saucer into her hand.

"Leave the dishes, Sunshine. I'll take them downstairs after I finish." She watched Frances move down the hall, wondering, again, if she made the right choices for her daughter. She had dismissed Frances's objections to her new school, ignored her daughter's wistful memories of the Pike Street apartment. Yes, they had been happy at that apartment but a little less joy was worth a college education, wasn't it? Her daughter had a full belly. Opportunities. And they were together, living in a grand house. She scanned the room, taking in the hardwood floor and paneled walls, gleaming and scented by the morning's polish. She ran her finger along the rim of the china cup on the marble-topped table. Yes, it was a fine place to live, but the elegant house was also home to a ghost and a demon—Ruth Pickett haunted her nights and Russell terrorized her days. Martha shook her head to loosen the distressing images, exiling them deep inside where they would lie in wait, attacking during her next weak moment. She gathered the dishes and went downstairs, finding Mrs. Roth at the kitchen table with a cup in front of her. The housekeeper pushed her chair back.

"Don't get up," Martha said. She poured herself another cup of coffee and filled Mrs. Roth's cup. The aging housekeeper nodded and gave Martha a quick smile.

"I miss Vickers," Martha said, sliding into a chair.

"He did know how to tell a joke," Mrs. Roth said.

"Do you keep in touch?"

"Yes, ma'am."

Martha took a sip, waiting for Mrs. Roth to say more, but instead, an uncomfortable silence filled the room. Her gaze swept over the counters and cabinets, the ice box and potato bin, the large stove. When she worked for the Pickett's, this had been her favorite room. Warm, seldom empty. Comforting. The staff congregated to share laughs and secrets, sometimes a tear or two. It was the heart of the house, nourishing the body of all who lived and worked there, but it also nourished the soul of the staff. Since she married George, the staff treated her differently. When she walked into the kitchen their conversations ended. They exchanged glances. She was no longer welcome in their world, but not accepted in George's world, either. At the parties she attended with her husband, his friends and their wives were cordial, nodding and smiling to her face, whispering as she walked away...*Ruth must be turning over in her grave. But so gracious of George to help a war widow. Taking in the poor soldier's daughter.*

A pounding on the front door brought Martha from her musings. "I'll get it," she said and hurried down the hall. She opened the door to a red-faced Dottie.

"I want my money, Martha. I had ten dollars in Mr. Pickett's bank but when I went there this morning, it was closed." Dottie stepped into the vestibule. "Your husband's a shyster," she said, pointing her finger at Martha's face. "Look at this house. Look at your clothes. He's using our money to keep you happy."

"Miss Shoaf, the bank will reopen soon. It will be better than ever," Randolph said as he jogged down the front stairs. "Did you hear President Roosevelt on the radio?"

Dottie moved into the hallway, standing in front of Randolph, arms crossed, head titled. "I ain't got no radio."

"The president said it's safer to keep your money in a reopened bank than it is to keep it under the mattress," Randolph said. He smiled.

"Phooey. Your pa told you to say that. I don't believe a word. Shame on you, Martha."

"Dottie, if I had money I'd give it to you," Martha said. "Come in. Have some coffee."

"I don't want coffee. I want my money."

Randolph dug in his pockets and extended his hand towards Dottie. "Here's a dollar. And some change."

After the briefest hesitation, Dottie plucked the cash from Randolph's palm and stuffed it in her own pocket. She squared her shoulders and faced Martha. "Don't give me that look. You ain't no better than me. Your kid's a bastard, just like mine." She walked out the door.

Martha turned and caught sight of Frances, frozen at the top of the front staircase. She looked away and stepped out the door, wanting to call out to Dottie but she couldn't find her voice. Instead, she let her friend march up the street, years of treasured memories going with her. When she stepped back inside, Frances had disappeared but Russell was standing next to Randolph, a wide grin on his face.

"Well, well. Our little stepsister's a field rabbit, brother." Russell slapped Randolph's back. "What does that make you, dear stepmother? Obviously not the sad war widow we thought you were." He laughed and turned away, his cackles echoing as he sauntered down the hallway. Randolph remained.

Her hand gripping the carved knob atop the newel, Martha avoided Randolph's eyes. She looked up the staircase. "I was trying to protect Frances. Didn't want her being judged." She spoke quietly, as if her hushed voice could soften the blow.

Randolph put his hand on Martha's. "I won't repeat it. And it doesn't change the way I feel about Frances. Or you."

Still unable to look him in the eye, Martha whispered, "thank you." She wondered if her kind stepson would be so accepting if he knew Frances's real father was a bootlegger and her uncle a gangster living on the other side of town. But she had no time to dwell on Randolph's reaction, it was George's she was most concerned about. Certain Russell would tell his father, Martha needed an answer. Another lie to cover the original lie. She moved through her day in a determined fog, her mind turning over options. Twenty minutes before George's expected arrival, she went to her room and removed her girdle, inserted her sponge, and waited.

George bellowed her name the minute he burst through the back door.

Martha ran her hands down her skirt and wordlessly counted her husband's weighty steps on the back stairs.

He stood at the door to her room, breathing heavy, eyes narrowed. Slamming the door closed behind him, he stepped forward, and bent, his face inches from hers. "Not married to the girl's father? That true?"

Martha took a breath, rehearsing her story in her head, one more time. "Of course it's not true." She put a hand on his shoulder.

He pushed it away.

141

"Calm down, George. You know what the doctor said." Her voice was low, soothing, the special tone crafted in his bedroom. She stood, touched his shoulder again. He didn't resist. Her hands under his lapels, she massaged his chest and eased his jacket off. "Relax, dear," she whispered, her lips brushing his ear. She turned him around, coaxing him to sit on the bed. She remained standing, her knees touching his.

George lifted his chin, eyebrows raised. "Russell heard your friend, Martha. Why would she say that?"

"Dottie was muddled. Angry," Martha said. Her heart squeezed, making her best friend—her only friend—into a raving loon was painful, but Frances came first. "This Depression has upset everyone." She laid her hands on her chest, over her heart. "I am so lucky. My daughter is lucky." She moved her hands to George's shoulders and leaned close. "We are thankful. To you."

"You should be grateful," he said, still glowering, but his voice had lost its rancor.

For a moment, Martha thought of Patrick Doyle. He had the power to destroy the life she built for Frances. She pushed the thought away. Pushed all thoughts away, closed down, just as she had done since her first night with George. Her hands moved of their own accord, well-trained from the years of her husband's demands, unbuttoning his vest, unhooking the suspenders, working their way beneath the tight waistband of his trousers. She straddled him and closed her eyes, unwilling to watch his face contort with pleasure. Patrick drifted into her thoughts again and she wished him dead. Her breath caught at the morbid thought. George, taking the sound as encouragement, maneuvered Martha to her back, hips thrusting. Martha's thoughts remained on Patrick, speculating if she could kill the man, if given the chance. Yes, she decided and felt the smallest bit of guilt. At least she felt something. She added this guilt to the long list she already had, slightly alarmed at the length, and wondering how much you can live with.

PART THREE:
EDUCATED SECRETS
1940 – 1942

CHAPTER SIXTEEN

April 1940
Philadelphia, Pennsylvania

Frances pointed out the grimy window as the train pulled into the Philadelphia station. "There he is!" She pounded on the glass and waved both hands at Randolph.

On spring break from her first year of college, the last time Frances saw her stepbrother was eight months ago when he drove in from Philadelphia to help her move into her dormitory. After graduating from Penn, Randolph continued his education at Wharton and took a job at *The Philadelphia Bulletin*.

"He's more handsome than I remember," Christy, her college roommate, said.

"Never you mind, Christy. He's a married man now." Frances shook her head. She and Christy had become good friends, in spite of Frances's standoffish efforts. Once she had been accepted by Margaret Morrison Carnegie College in Pittsburgh, Frances had tried to back out. It wasn't the classes that frightened her, it was the curious students. They would ask about her family. Want details on her father. She was weary of the I-am-the-daughter-of-a-war-veteran fabrication.

And, it had been a long time since she shared a room. She didn't expect to be friends with her roommate. Didn't want to be friends. Friends hurt. Like Mickey. She thought they would be friends forever—maybe more than friends—but once their mothers' friendship ended, Mickey's resentment bubbled up. He refused to let Frances pay for a movie, or buy dinner. She stopped by his apartment the day before she left for college but he ended the visit after five minutes, reminding her he had to work for a living.

Sitting in the seat by the aisle, Martha stood and pulled her gloves on. "Make sure you have all your belongings, girls."

Frances and Christy ran towards the door, bouncing from foot to foot as they waited for the conductor to release them. Scrambling onto the platform, Frances nearly knocked Randolph over when she launched herself into his arms.

"Good to see you, too," Randolph said, laughing and patting Frances's back. He smiled at Christy. "Hello, Christy." He released Frances and moved down the platform towards Martha. "I am so glad you came." He extended his hand and pulled her into an embrace.

Frances couldn't stop smiling. It took months of convincing to get her mother on the train. In early December, Randolph invited his entire family to spend Christmas with him, enticing them with tales of a beautifully decorated city and the opportunity to meet his girl, Lily. Russell refused immediately, saying he had his holiday celebrations already lined up, and George declined soon after. Frances begged her mother to go— she had no desire to spend Christmas with Russell—but George forbade his wife to leave him alone during prime dinner party season. Not wanting to spend Christmas apart from her mother, Frances endured her break at the Pickett house, vowing to visit Randolph during her spring vacation.

"Oh, my," Christy said, stopping to admire the modern train station. Built seven years ago with a roof large enough for small aircraft to land on, the elaborate waiting area had travertine walls and a coffered ceiling of red and gold. Born and raised in the small mill town of Donora on the Monongahela River, and the first of her Irish-Catholic family of seven to attend college, Christy had not travelled further than the twenty miles from her home to Pittsburgh.

As they drove through center city, Randolph pointed out the newspaper building where he worked and next to it, the ornate city hall where he and Lily married in January. He pointed out a few other landmarks and pulled to the curb in front of a four-story, red brick row house. "This is it," he said. The houses stretched the length of tree-lined Spruce Street, young leaves of vivid green shrouding the sidewalk.

"Hello!" A dark-haired woman waved from the arched doorway. She was dressed in a crisp, white blouse and sailor-style, navy pants, gold buttons tracing up each hip. She skipped down the two stone steps and moved to Randolph's side, standing eye to eye with him.

"This is Lily." Randolph slipped his left arm around his wife's shoulders and pulled her close. With his right hand, he pointed. "This is Martha, Christy and Frances."

"So glad to meet you," Lily said, her voice husky. She had large, brown eyes fringed with dark lashes, the same color as her glossy hair. "Would you like some cawfee? Worter?"

Frances frowned and Randolph laughed.

"That's 'coffee' and 'water,'" he said. "You'll get used to my wife's accent. Go on, ladies. I'll get the bags."

They followed Lily into a large room with dark oak wainscoting, two narrow windows facing the street. The fireplace was bordered with dark green tiles, a long sofa stretched across the opposite wall. Two bookcases, the shelves overflowing, filled a corner.

"Our living room," Lily said. She walked through, past the staircase and into a smaller room. "The dining room." She paused, using her sleeve to wipe a smear from the glass pane on the china closet door. "And, this is the kitchen." She maneuvered around a range and refrigerator to open the back door. "Our yard. It's small but room enough to grow tomatoes. At home—in Jersey—we grew tomatoes bigger than my fist." She raised a balled hand for emphasis.

"That's a big tomato," Christy blurted.

Frances's face flamed at Christy's bluntness. Lily was a sturdy woman, tall and buxom, with generous hands but Frances was most taken by the flawless skin and lustrous hair.

Lily laughed and looked at her fist. "One shake of this and my little brothers ran." She dropped her hand. "Come on, I'll show you to your rooms. Martha, you'll be on the third floor. Frances, you and Christy get the top floor."

They moved upstairs, Martha taking a seat in the wicker rocking chair in her room, and Frances and Christy following Lily to the fourth floor. It was an open space with a vaulted ceiling. Two narrow beds sat side by side, a small table between them.

"Hello?" Randolph called from the bottom of the stairs. "Can I bring up your bags, ladies?"

"Yes. I'll help." Lily ran down the stairs and reappeared with a suitcase in each hand. "Hope you like spaghetti. It's my specialty." She turned and started back down the stairs.

"It's the only thing she knows how to cook," Randolph whispered.

"I heard that!"

He winked at Frances and disappeared down the stairs.

France smiled. She was happy for Randolph. He hadn't changed – still full of kindness. The opposite of his brother. She shivered at the thought of Russell.

"You all right, Franny?" Christy asked.

"Yes. Just thinking of my other stepbrother."

"Oh. The rotten one."

Frances laughed. From the minute she moved into the dormitory, the diminutive Christy had surprised her. Made her laugh. Called her Franny in her big voice that belied her small stature. The first afternoon they met, Frances planned to tell Christy her name was Frances, not Franny, but she never got the chance as Christy pulled Frances along with her to a movie, and afterwards, danced out of the theater singing, "follow the yellow brick road," at the top of her lungs. Heads turned, but Christy was oblivious to the attention. In their first week together, Christy had convinced Frances to join a sorority, shorten her skirts, and change her hair. For as long as she could remember, Frances wore her hair braided. Two braids when she was young, one braid once she got older. Christy persuaded her to wear her hair 'half up, half down,' pinning a few waves on top of her head, the remainder of her thick tresses curling around her shoulders.

"Here, let me fix your hair." Christy nudged Frances to a chair by the lone window.

"Look." Frances pointed. "You can see the statue on the top of city hall."

"Hmm," Christy said, bobby pins between her lips.

"I can't wait to see the sights. So much history," Frances said.

"Uh-uh," Christy mumbled.

Frances smiled. Her roommate wasn't interested in history. Or literature, science or any of the other subjects at college. She was interested in dances, parties and men. "The sororities mingle with the fraternities," Christy had said when Frances balked at joining a sorority. After being snubbed by her fellow students at her high school, Frances wasn't sure she wanted to give another group of girls the chance to wound her. She grudgingly admitted she enjoyed the handful of sorority events they attended,

149

but she hadn't enjoyed the fraternity dances, nor the few dates that came afterwards.

"Simon Michelson asked about you in biology," Christy said, pushing a pin in Frances's hair.

Frances rolled her eyes. "He's a bit of a snob. Talked incessantly of his family's summer home."

"What about John Furness? He seemed nice. We could double date."

Frances wrinkled her nose. Her few dates had been awkward. Uncomfortable. In truth, it really wasn't the men's fault. On every date, Frances found her mind wandering, her thoughts turning to Mickey, wishing it was him sitting across from her. "No more dates right now," she said. "I'm behind in my reading."

"You always have your head in a book," Christy said. "How are you going to meet your husband if you never go anywhere except the library?"

Frances snorted. "I just want a good grade in economics. I'll worry about a husband later." Margaret Morrison Carnegie College was a women's college, one of the reason's Sister Mayme recommended it and Frances's mother had eagerly agreed. But there were plenty of men around since her campus and the Carnegie Institute of Technology were closely aligned and her co-ed science and chemistry classes were held at Carnegie Tech. Becoming a chemist was her goal, but tired of the skeptical laughter her ambition elicited, Frances kept her lofty wish to herself. Randolph and her mother were the only ones who encouraged her dream. Even Sister Mayme suggested a more traditional profession, steering her towards teaching.

After pinning one more wave to Frances's crown, Christy dropped her hands. "There. Much better." She raised her head, sniffing the air. "Something sure smells good. Let's go."

They went to the kitchen but Lily shooed them to the living room, where Martha sat in one of the chairs by the fireplace, Randolph in the other.

150

"Were you kicked out the kitchen, too?" Martha asked with a chuckle.

Lily came in behind Frances and Christy and sat on the sofa. She patted the cushion next to her. "Have a seat, gals. It's almost ready. You can't rush spaghetti sauce," she said, smiling at Randolph.

"That's why I married her," Randolph said. "One meal at her house and I was hooked. Little did I know the only thing she could make was spaghetti." He laughed and blew a kiss across the room. "My wife had her first story printed yesterday. Show them your byline."

"It's just an article about a women's club," Lily said, but she sprang from the sofa and pulled a newspaper from the stack on the bookcase. She folded the broadsheet and handed it to Martha. "It's in the life section, below the fold. But it's a start." She lifted a shoulder. "I want to be like Margaret Bourke-White. Go overseas and write about the war. She's from Jersey, you know." She paused to pat her chest and smile. "Like me."

"My wife is rather ambitious." Randolph winked at Lily and she beamed.

"I'm proud of you, Randolph," Martha said. "Your home is lovely. And your wife...," she raised the newspaper in her hand and smiled at Lily, "is a delight." She turned back to Randolph. "You have a great life ahead of you."

"I wouldn't be half the man I am without you," Randolph said, his voice soft. "I fear I would have turned out like my brother had I not had you and Frances around." He looked at the cup and saucer in his lap. "I know your life with my father hasn't been easy. And Russell, well," he shrugged, raising his eyes to Martha's. "What can I say about my brother? He still at the house making life miserable for everyone around him?"

"He is the same," Martha said. Russell was once again living at the Pickett house after being fired, for the second time, from a bank in Columbus. "He's currently interviewing for a wife."

"What?" Randolph nearly dropped his cup.

"To avoid inscription," Martha explained. "Your brother reported to the draft board late last year but was rejected for his poor eyesight. Terrified he will be called back, he's looking for another exemption. Wants a wife that will produce offspring immediately to further increase his exemption options."

"Not very honorable." Randolph shook his head, lifted a shoulder. "But nobody ever accused my brother of being honorable. I'm going to make more coffee."

"I'll help." Lily jumped to her feet.

Frances watched her stepbrother and his wife walk from the room, Lily laying her head on Randolph's shoulder, he slipping his arm around her waist.

"I want to fall in love." Christy sighed and slapped her hand over her heart. "They can't stand being apart."

"You fall in love every other week, Christy." Frances turned towards her mother. "You should see her in chemistry class. It's full of men." The class was a beginning chemistry course, and she learned nothing new—Sister Mayme's class had been more stimulating—but Christy had certainly made the class interesting.

"The fellas are why I signed up for it!" Christy said. "Thank goodness I have you because I would never make it through those silly experiments. Who knew that little stove could make such a big flame?"

"Burner, Christy. It's called a Bunsen burner," Frances said, shaking her head.

"Burner. Stove. Who cares?" Christy winked at Martha. "I got the attention of my handsome lab partner."

Frances shook her head as her mother laughed.

Randolph returned with a tray in his hands, Lily following. "Here we go. Better enjoy the sugar while we can. I hear it will be in short supply soon." He lowered the tray to the table in front of the sofa.

152

"Another war." Martha spat out her words. "They called the last war 'the war to end all wars' but here we are again on the brink of another."

The room fell silent, Randolph throwing glances at his wife. He cleared his throat, twice. "I've enlisted. I hope to be a pilot."

Frances let out a stunned gasp as Martha's cup clattered to the floor.

CHAPTER SEVENTEEN

June 1940
Wheeling, West Virginia

Back at the Pickett house for her summer break, Frances sat on the bed in her room, buttoning her blouse, running her sweating palms across the rough fabric of her brown skirt. She tied her oxfords and picked up her handbag, taking one look in the mirror. Drab. There was no other word for it. Although this is what she wore nearly every day to her college classes, the outfit suddenly seemed overly plain. What would Mickey think? Was she trying too hard to fit into his lifestyle? A life she struggled to understand. Or maybe he would think she didn't care enough to wear something more attractive. Christy was always commenting on her fashion choices, pulling dresses from Frances's closet in their dorm room and demanding to know why Frances kept wearing the same white blouse and brown skirt. "I wish I was your size," Christy said. "I would raid your closet every day."

Frances tossed her bag on the bed and returned to her closet. It was filled with dresses, most of them refashioned from her mother's wardrobe. When she was a child, mother didn't stitch more than a torn seam or replace a missing button. Their clothes were practical, made of sturdy fabrics at low prices but since marrying George, her mother had taken an interest in fashion, learning from the seamstress who visited the house regularly to create new dresses for Martha. Her mother's closet overflowed and she decided her dresses, many only worn once, could be re-created into something for Frances. At first, her mother made simple jumpers or skirts but as Martha's sewing skills improved, she took to making dresses with flowing skirts and matching jackets. The seams were not always straight and the sleeves were often not the same length, but the fine fabrics made up for the sewing faults. Frances only wore the dresses around the house anyway, except for the rare occasion she had been forced to a social outing at the academy. She pulled a dress of red and pink flowers from her closet and walked to the mirror. After two more dresses she finally decided on a green dress with a silk bodice, the sleeves and skirt of linen herringbone. She considered a hat, decided against it, and kept on her brown oxfords since they would be walking to the Rex Theater on the south end of town.

Three weeks ago, on her first day home for the summer, Frances visited Mickey's apartment and they set a date for lunch and a matinee. He still lived with his mother on Pike Street although they had moved to a one bedroom unit on the first floor. When Dottie answered the door, her grey hair cut as short as Mickey's, she eyed Frances through a cloud of cigarette smoke and coughed out a clipped "hello." She went into the bedroom, never reappearing during Frances's hour-long stay. Frances had written to Mickey at least once a month while she was at college and he had written back twice, his handwriting the same childish scrawl she remembered from grade school. Her letters were filled with Christy's antics, no details on her classes or how much she liked college. She did tell him about her disastrous, final date with Simon Michelson, and asked him if there was a special girl in his life. When he finally replied, firmly stating he was an unattached man, Frances had been elated.

She walked down the front stairs and out the door, her smile widening the minute she saw Mickey strolling down Main Street. Her heart sank. He was in blue dungarees and a dark shirt, the sleeves rolled to his elbows, a tweed flat cap perched on his head. She wanted to run inside to change clothes but it was too late.

He waved his cap, broke into a jog, stopping on the sidewalk in front of the house.

"Hello," Frances said and moved down the porch steps. She tried to hold her smile but it faltered under Mickey's scrutiny.

"We ain't going to the steakhouse, Frances. My friends gonna think I'm crazy taking you for a hotdog at Louis's." He slapped his cap back on his head, tugging the short brim to his brows.

"I've always wanted to go to Louis's. Randolph talked about it. Said it was the best..." Her words trailed off at the sight of Russell's red Chrysler pulling to the curb. She grabbed Mickey's arm. "Let's go."

"Frances? Wait a minute."

Frances tuned. She was speechless. Joan Whitman, her former classmate, and nemesis, had her left hand on Russell's arm.

Joan stepped towards Frances, her flowery perfume smothering. "Thought that was you." She turned her attention to Mickey, eyeing him from head to toe. "Who's your friend, Frances?"

"That's Mickey," Russell said with a snort. "Didn't grow much, did you kid?"

Frances felt Mickey's arm tighten under her palm, saw the muscles clench in his jaw. "Come on, Mickey," she urged.

"Mickey who?" Joan asked.

"Shoaf," Mickey said, nudging his cap off his forehead and glaring at Russell.

"Is this who you're bringing to the wedding, Frances?" Joan asked.

"Wedding?"

"Oh, didn't your mother tell you?" Joan smiled, linked both arms around Russell's. "Russell and I are getting married next week."

Frances stood rooted, a chill running down her back as Joan glided up the steps, turning back at the top to display the sly smile Frances knew all too well from her days at the academy. Married to Russell, Frances was horrified. Would she be living at the Pickett house?

"Friend of yours?" Mickey asked, slipping his arm from Frances's grasp.

She shook her head.

"Too embarrassed to introduce me?"

"What?" Frances turned to Mickey. "What?" she repeated.

"You didn't tell that woman my name," Mickey said, eyes narrowed, thumbs hooked under his suspenders.

Frances stared at Mickey, watched the muscle in his jaw twitch. "I was surprised," she stammered, turning back towards the front door of the house. "Joan hates me. I didn't know what to say."

"Right," Mickey said. "Let's go. Don't want to be late for Grapes of Wrap."

"Wrath. Grapes of Wrath," Frances said, immediately regretting her words. The movie had been her choice, the book being one of her favorites. Mickey had never heard of it but agreed to go.

"Right," he repeated in a flat voice.

He set off down the street and she had to hurry to catch up. They walked in silence, Frances's high hopes for the afternoon slipping away. Inside the restaurant, a small, one-story building painted bright red, Mickey pointed to a bare table in the corner, telling her he would order at the counter. Her eyes watered from the heavy scent of onions as she watched him from the table, other young men dressed similarly rapping him on the head, chuckling, stealing glances at her. He sauntered to the table, two glasses of Coca-Cola in his hands.

"Jane will bring our dogs," Mickey said, sliding into the chair next to her.

"Do you work with them?" Frances asked, titling her head towards the men at the counter.

He nodded, gulped his drink. "Hank's shipping to Fort Bragg in the morning. The boys are sending him off with a bang. Heading to the Green Lantern."

Frances nodded like she knew about the Green Lantern, a notorious bar she had never set foot in. She looked around the room and smiled. "This is nice. I like it."

"I like the prices."

Frances scanned the menu and prices on the blackboard above the counter. Seven cents for a hotdog with all the "fixins." She wondered what the "fixins" were as she watched the group of men slap coins on the counter. "I'm glad it's not you going to Fort Bragg," she said, turning back to Mickey.

"I wish it was me." He pulled his cap off and ran his hand through his cropped hair. "I tried, you know. I want to do my part but, my lungs." His hand rubbed his chest and he coughed to emphasize his point. "Well, you know. Won't ever be nothing but a shipping clerk. Can't work the ovens. Sure as hell can't be a glassblower."

She felt her face redden at the harsh words.

"Sorry," he said, studying his fingertips as they drummed the table. "Hard to accept that this is as good as my life gets." He raised his head, his eyes misty. "I wish..."

"Hey, Mickey, last chance to say goodbye to ole Hank," one of the men yelled across the room as the group moved towards the door. They all laughed, whacking one young man on the back.

Mickey ran a sleeve across his eyes and waved the men out of the restaurant. He nodded at the waitress as she put two plates and two napkins on the table, no

159

silverware. "Thank you," he mumbled and picked up his hot dog. He ate silently, his head bowed.

Frances watched Mickey, mimicked his motions, and turned her head to the side and took a bite. Covered with a meaty sauce, onions and a ribbon of yellow mustard, the hotdog was delicious. "This is really good," she said.

He looked up, an eyebrow raised. He shook his head but said nothing, went back to his meal.

Frances took another bite and retuned the bun to the plate. "Mickey, would you rather go with your friends? We can go to a movie another time."

He swallowed the last of his hotdog and emptied his glass. "You wouldn't mind?"

She shook her head, tears burning at the back of her eyes but she refused to give into them.

He jumped to his feet, palming the cap on his crown. "I'll walk you home."

Frances stood. "No, that's out of your way. I'll be fine. Do a little shopping." She managed a smile.

They parted on the sidewalk outside the restaurant door, Mickey promising to see her soon. She didn't let her tears fall until he was out of sight, silently weeping until she was a block from the Pickett house. Drying her eyes with her handkerchief, she went in the front door and directly upstairs, closing her bedroom door behind her. She kicked her shoes off and flopped on the bed, digging in the nightstand drawer for pen and paper. She would write to Christy. Write away the day's fiasco with Mickey. She wanted to write about the run-in with Joan and expunge her former classmate from her thoughts but Christy didn't know about Joan or any other of her academy classmates. Frances merely hinted that her memories from her high school days were not as pleasant as Christy's. She also never told Christy about her real father. She never told anyone except Mickey and although her mother said that wasn't the reason she went to the monastery, there was a small, dark part of

Frances that still believed it was her fault. Her door opened and Frances looked up, expecting her mother, but instead it was Joan, barging in unannounced, uninvited.

"This room looks like it's from the dark ages," Joan said to a short woman hovering behind her. "But I can make it work."

"What are you doing?" Frances put her pen and paper to the side.

"Getting measurements," Joan said. As her companion dropped to a knee, releasing a tape measure from a round case, Joan preened in front of the mirror, pushing her fingers into her hair, throwing her shoulders back. With a smile at her reflection, she wandered into Frances's bathroom.

"This is my room, Joan." Frances stood and moved to the bathroom door. "Russell's room is down the hall."

Joan dodged around Frances and flung open the closet door. "Oh my. This simply won't do." She looked at the woman with the measuring tape. "I'll need at least two wardrobes, Miss Johnson." Joan walked to the nightstand, eyeing Frances's stack of textbooks. "Economics. Good God." She shook her head and walked to one of the windows, running her hand down the velvet drape. A trolley bell clanged and Joan peered out the window, wrinkling her nose. "Not much of a view. And the noise. I don't know that I want this room, after all." She snapped her fingers. "Follow me, Miss Johnson."

Frances sank to her bed and watched Joan prance from the room, Miss Johnson running behind. Less than a month into her summer break and she was already counting the days until she could go back to her college dormitory.

***

After a lavish wedding, which Frances did not attend, Joan and Russell embarked on a six-week honeymoon.

161

The day after the wedding, Martha moved her clothes into Frances's bedroom since Joan had decided to take over Randolph's old room, next to Russell's, and across the hall from Martha's room. Russell's current bedroom was to become Joan's dressing room, and Martha was relinquishing her room to Russell.

"I'm sorry about this, Frances," her mother said, dropping several dresses on the bed.

Down the hall, workers hammered, sawed, and swore, trying to meet Joan's impossible deadlines. The new bride expected the renovations to be completed when she returned in early August. George stayed from the house from early morning until early evening, taking most of his meals downtown at the men's club.

"I don't mind. I'll make room," Frances said, pulling her school uniform from the closet. "This can go."

"Was the academy that bad?" her mother asked. She sat on the bed and sighed. "I wanted the best education for you, Sunshine. Wanted you to have opportunities I didn't."

"It was a good school," Frances said. "I just didn't fit in." She walked to the window and watched a woman cross the busy street, a child hanging on to her skirt. She never told her mother the extent of her classmate's tormenting. Joan had been the leader, once calling Frances's mother a gold digger. Said it to Frances's face, in front of her classmates. "Did you marry George for his money?" she asked, her hands wringing the uniform, her gaze on the street.

Her mother moved beside her and pushed the drape aside. "This street has changed since the day I first came to the Pickett house. Back then, I was just happy to have a job. Happy to have an apartment in the same building as my best friend. Happy to have a healthy, beautiful daughter." She turned, laying both hands on Frances's shoulders. "The money meant nothing to me. Marrying George meant reuniting with you."

"Hmm," Frances managed. She had little insight into her mother's relationship with George. She wondered if there was love between them. Her mother explained the mechanics of what a man and woman did in bed and the brief conversation had been awkward for both of them. Being the reason her mother was with George didn't feel good. Didn't feel right.

"I would have done anything to bring you home," her mother said. "It hasn't turned out so badly. George kept his promises." She smiled, giving Frances's shoulders a squeeze. "And raising Randolph has been a joy."

"Have you heard from him lately?"

"Yes. Getting ready to leave Oklahoma. Going to Texas," Martha said.

Accepted into flight school, Randolph wrote letters to Martha faithfully. When Frances learned his training would take nearly two years, she was relieved, clinging to the hope that the United States would not join the war, or the war would be over by the time Randolph got his wings.

"The training sounds exhaustive," Frances said. She paused, catching her lower lip between her teeth. "Do you think I could call Lily before I leave?" Frances kept in touch with Lily through letters and the occasional phone call. Her stepbrother's wife was putting on a brave face, but Frances saw cracks in Lily's cheery persona and knew she missed Randolph desperately.

"Perhaps a letter would be better." Martha sighed. "George questions every bill, every phone call. Russell makes a handsome salary at the bank, but he never offers to help with household expenses. Joan's renovations are costly, and George grumbles nightly about money. But he never could say no to Russell."

"It's fine. I'll write," Frances said. "I just feel my letters aren't near as interesting as Lily's."

"I do enjoy her letters, she's a lovely writer." Martha smiled. "But I like your letters, too. Just wish I would get

163

them more often." She winked. "I need to empty the drawers of my dresser. Don't want the new Mrs. Pickett snooping through my things."

Frances followed her mother into the room outside her bedroom and paused, tracing her index finger over a deep gash in the large table where she spent hours conquering homework and eating her meals. "Do you think 'bad' is passed down?" she asked. It would be easy to blame her imperfections, her mistakes, on her heritage. Her propensity for saying the wrong thing at the wrong time would be her father's fault, not hers. Maybe Mickey would forgive her then. She hadn't seen him since day of the hotdogs, although she stopped by his apartment twice, his mother saying he wasn't home, not inviting her in. "Whenever I have bad thoughts, like wishing something terrible happening to Russell, I wonder if that's my nature," she said, a finger tracing a long gash. "I'm afraid I'll turn out like my father and uncle. That badness runs in my blood."

Martha stepped to Frances's side and put a finger under her chin, forcing Frances's eyes to hers. "Your father was not a bad man," she said, her voice low. "He made mistakes. But the things he did, he did them to help his family. He would have loved you fiercely."

"Then why did you not claim him as my father?"

Her mother shrugged. "I didn't plan it." She shook her head and sighed. "Guess I didn't want to be a Kraus anymore. Not after what my father said. And once I used Frederic's name I couldn't go back. The lie just kept growing, and after a time, even I believed it."

"Until Patrick came around," Frances said. "A horrible man."

"You are not anything like him," Martha said. "Besides," she smiled, sliding her arm through Frances's, "everyone who's met Russell has probably had unkind thoughts about him at least once. Or twice."

Arm in arm, they walked down the hall, making an abrupt stop at the doorway of Martha's bedroom. It was

164

still sparsely furnished with a bed and dresser, a sewing machine below the lone window. A man, his overalls splattered with paint, was on a ladder scraping at the wall.

"What are you doing?" Martha asked.

"Taking down the wallpaper, ma'am. I was told to strip this room today."

"She's not yet moved her things out," Frances said.

"It's fine." Martha looked at the man on the ladder. "Can you come back in an hour?"

The worker didn't budge. "My boss said I'm to finish this room today. Or else."

"Help us move the furniture down the hall, and the room's all yours." Martha patted her dresser, head at an angle, a smile on her face.

The worker sighed but he backed down the ladder.

Frances studied her mother as they cleared bottles and tins from the dresser's marble top. Changes were coming to the Pickett house, probably none boding well for her mother, but if she was worried about it, it didn't show in her face. Still beautiful, her mother's skin was line-free, her blue eyes clear. George had not worn her down. Russell had not worn her down. Would Joan? Frances thought not. Her mother worn her optimism like a coat of armor, the glass always half-full, the past behind her. Frances, on the other hand, wasted far too much time in the past. Rewriting it. *What if her father had lived, he and her mother married?* They would be a legitimate family, living in Webster Hill. But then she would never have met Mickey. *What if her mother didn't marry George?* They could still be living on Pike Street. But Randolph wouldn't be in her life. No college. No Christy. Round and round it went in her head. Thinking about it didn't change a thing, and it could make her crazy, if she let it.

CHAPTER EIGHTEEN

December 1940
Wheeling, West Virginia

Martha hit the brakes as she cruised out of Pittsburgh's Liberty Tunnel, her right arm extended to keep Frances secure in the passenger seat. It was Christmas break for Frances's second year of college and Martha was so glad to see her daughter. So glad to have someone to talk to. "The first thing Joan did was hire a new cook," Martha said, her foot moving to the accelerator. "I came downstairs one morning to find a strange woman in a black dress with a white apron in the kitchen. She has gray hair pulled straight back into a tight bun." She tried to demonstrate the cook's hairstyle but the car swerved as both hands left the wheel.

"Mom!" Frances yelled.

Martha righted the car and continued her tirade, deepening her voice to mimic Joan's raspy sound. "Mrs. Manning cooked for my momma for years. Why don't you show her around the kitchen, Martha? I'll have my breakfast in my bedroom. And remember, I'm eating for two, Mrs. Manning."

"Lest we forget about the baby." Martha returned to her normal voice. "It's not Mrs. Manning's fault but I wasn't very kind to her. Told her I don't like surprises. Mrs. Manning says, 'in my experience, ma'am, Miss Joan is full of surprises'." Martha snorted. "An understatement. Thank goodness Mrs. Roth retired. Joan would have pushed her over the edge."

"Mom, maybe you should slow down a little," Frances said.

"Sorry." Martha glanced at her daughter's hands gripping the Hudson's dashboard and eased up on the gas pedal. Grousing about Joan felt good. So good that she couldn't seem to stop. "Joan hired her own maid. Linda. She rings her bell and calls out for Linn-daaa. Linn-daaa. Then she hired an upstairs maid. A downstairs maid. Mrs. Manning and Linda moved into the third floor, always at Joan's beck and call."

Frances let out a sigh.

"Sorry," Martha repeated, giving Frances another sideways glance. "How is Christy? I'm sorry I didn't get to see her."

"She left school before the break started. Her father's not well," Frances said.

"How is school?"

"Fine. I'm expecting good grades in all my classes."

"Are you doing anything fun?"

Quiet for a moment, Frances wrinkled her forehead in thought. "We went to a football game," she finally said.

"That's good." Martha was concerned about Frances's grades but she also wanted her daughter to enjoy her time at college, hopefully making up for her dismal high school days. "Who won?"

Frances laughed. "I don't know. I was paying more attention to the band in their plaid kilts than the game."

Martha waited but her daughter remained quiet. Frances obviously wasn't in a talkative mood. Martha had more to say about Joan, so much more, but she bit her tongue and an amiable silence settled in, Martha savoring the nearness of her daughter.

At the Pickett house, Martha crept up the back stairs, Frances on her heels. They both wanted to avoid Joan and her gathering of friends in the parlor. They were halfway up when Joan summoned them.

"Frances, please join us," Joan called from the bottom of the steps, her fingers drumming on the railing. "I've told everyone you were coming today and they can't wait to see you."

"I'm a little tired after the drive back," Frances said, running her hands down her worn skirt.

Her back still turned towards Joan, Martha rolled her eyes. She saw plenty of Joan's old schoolmates. They visited nearly every week, chattering through the afternoons, wearing flashy fashions and gaudy jewelry, each hoping to outshine the other. Parties were planned for the week between Christmas and New Year's Day, with a big bash scheduled for New Year's Eve. Martha would need to warn Frances to have an excuse ready.

"You can rest later, Frances. Look at me, expecting a baby, and I haven't missed one celebration. And I promised the girls you'd stop in," Joan said, sticking out her bottom lip and patting her rounded belly.

"All right. Just for a minute." Frances walked past Martha, the chunky heels on her scuffed oxfords thudding on the worn boards.

"You, too, Martha. Come say hello," Joan said.

Martha followed Frances, not wanting her daughter to deal with the room full of old antagonists on her own. As they walked down the hallway, she looked at Frances, waiting for her reaction to the framed seascapes that had replaced the painted portraits of Pickett ancestors. Wait until she sees the parlor, Martha thought. Joan had outdone herself in that room. Gone was the Turkish rug of rich reds and dark greens, and in its place was a pink carpet. Bright pink. The sofa was green, the chairs blue, the windows in the round bay framed by flowered curtains instead of velvet drapes. A fifteen foot Christmas tree, decorated in gold and blue, replaced the

169

baby grand piano. As Martha expected, Frances's mouth fell open when she walked into the room, but she closed it with a cough, probably from the noxious blend of heavy perfumes.

"Beautiful, isn't it?" Joan said. "Sarah helped me decorate. You remember Sarah Decker, don't you?"

"It's Norton now. I married Jonathon Norton." A dainty woman in a red dress waved her left hand, her hefty diamond flashing. "Any marriage plans for you, Frances?"

"No." Frances continued to study the room.

"You look the same, Frances. Even looks like you're wearing your uniform." Evelyn, a tall, thin woman gave Frances a look from head to toe.

"Oh, you know Frances. Fashion was never her thing," Joan said, lowering into a chair. She lit her long cigarette, the sterling holder adding another six inches.

"What is your thing, Frances?" Sarah asked, raising one perfectly arched eyebrow.

"I-I-I don't know," Frances stammered. "I like chemistry."

"Chemistry? Yuck. I hated that laboratory at school." Joan paused to exhale. "Sister Mayme was a tyrant. Who cares what's in water? Or at what temperature it boils. That's why we have cooks!" Joan said, setting off a round of giggles.

Martha put a hand on Frances's back. "Ladies, always lovely to see you, but we have some unpacking to do."

"Sit down, Martha. I have news to share," Joan said, her eyes narrowing as smoke seeped between her lips. "War widow. Ha! Everyone thought you were raising poor little Frances on your own because her father died in the war, but Russell set me straight." She smiled. "My husband and I were enjoying a little pillow talk."

Martha remained standing, moving her hand to Frances's shoulder. She squeezed. "Joan, I hardly think this is the time to discuss family matters."

Joan leaned forward. "Oh, I think it's the perfect time. All the ladies here were misled." She waved her hand, the cigarette leaving a thin trail of smoke. "You see, girls, Martha was never married. Well, not until she tricked Russell's father into marrying her. Quite a secret, huh?" Joan sat back, reveling in her friends' startled expressions that quickly melted into wry smiles.

"Rumors, Joan. Old rumors I settled with George years ago," Martha said. She turned to her daughter. Let's go, Frances."

"Wait, I'm not finished," Joan said.

Martha bumped into Frances as her daughter remained in place, rooted to the floor. Frances turned, eyes blazing, Martha unsure if they were fueled by fear or anger.

Joan let loose another loud exhale, her hand raised, flakes of grey ash fluttering to the carpet. "I wondered what other secrets you have been keeping so I tracked down an old friend. Mickey Shoaf. Surely you remember him, Frances?"

Martha watched her daughter's eyes go dull.

"Poor Mickey's health is bad. He can't breathe," Joan said, patting her chest. "He needs medicine. Expensive medicine. I helped him out. He was so grateful that he shared a bit of information with me. Turns out Frances's father—her real father—was a bootlegger. The brother of a gangster working for Big Bill."

A collective gasp filled the room as Frances fled. Joan inhaled deeply, noisily, the cigarette snaking to a long ash. She grinned at Martha. "Russell is passing on this information to his father today."

Martha couldn't move for a moment, the room falling out of focus, a whistling in her ears. Fearing she might faint, she closed her eyes and fought for control. What could she do? What should she do? All those years, bowing to George, enduring Russell, biding time for Frances's future. Her eyes snapped open and the room was back in focus, Joan's triumphant face all too clear. She backed slowly from the parlor and went up the front stairs, her steps accelerating as she ascended, but it didn't matter how fast she went, she wouldn't be able to outrun her lies. In the room outside Frances's bedroom, she sank into a chair, searching for words that would comfort her daughter. She had none. Still sitting at the table an hour later, she heard George's heavy footfalls.

"Martha!"

She walked down the hall, staring at George. Russell stood behind him, grinning.

"How could you?" George said, glaring at her as she walked into his bedroom. "Get in here, too, Russell." He slammed the door closed.

Martha sat in a chair by the lone window. She never liked this room. It was cold and colorless, the wallpaper and carpet faded shades of brown and grey. The bed, with its towering mahogany headboard dominated the space, and it certainly didn't hold happy memories. Once George was finished with his lovemaking, which didn't take long, he turned away, discouraging coddling or conversation. When they first married, she waited until he fell asleep before going to her own room but now she left the minute he rolled off.

"That Doyle man always came to my table, smiling like a cat with a canary," George said. "Now I know why." He tugged at his tie, trying to undo the knot but his shaking hands failed. Pulling the looped silk over his head, he knocked his hat to the floor, leaving his few remaining hairs standing on end. With a grunt, he retrieved the hat.

Russell stood by the door, bobbing his head. "I know who Doyle is. A real crumb."

"Quiet!" George turned to his son, the folds of his neck rippling. Too much rich food, along with too many drinks, showed in George's bulging gut and fleshy face. "Your wife had to make her announcement in a room full of blabbering women? Half the town will know by

172

tomorrow." He paused, considering the hat in his hands. Sucking in a long breath, he raised his head, looked at Martha. "You lied to me. I would throw you out tonight but a divorce would only add to the scandal. I won't shell out another cent on Doyle's kid."

"George, no!" Martha sprang to her feet. "You promised to pay for Frances's college."

His hat dropped to the floor and George strode to Martha, stopping inches from her face. "The girl's tuition is already paid for this year. I would get my money back if I could do it without raising questions. Once she leaves, she will not return to this house."

"But George..."

He raised his hand and Martha took a step back. His eyes blazed, reminding her of her father's enraged face moments before he slapped her.

"Get out of my sight," George said. He lowered his hand and turned away.

Martha refused to look at Russell as she hurried from the room, but she heard his laugh. She also heard George say "son, you better learn how to control your wife."

Her heart breaking, she stood outside the door to Frances's bedroom, her forehead and palm resting against the wood. All her efforts to protect her daughter, to give Frances a good life, an education, thwarted in an instant. The weight of kowtowing to George all these years, the countless taunts from Russell she absorbed, it was too much. She sank to her knees, her fist in her mouth to keep from screaming. How could she tell Frances that those unhappy years at the academy, her hard work at college the past year and a half, were all for naught? Her daughter was so smart. Always curious, even the workers at the Crittenton Home commented about it. She was different. Crawled, talked and walked before the other babies. Her first grade teacher said Frances was especially bright and the nuns at the monastery confirmed it. Sister Mayme said Frances was remarkable, could be a scientist, if women were allowed. She suspected Frances was like Martha's father. "Your vater is very intelligent," her mother often reminded Martha and her siblings as their father spoke about the gases in the mine, throwing out complicated words while they ate supper. Martha shook her head, pulled herself to her feet. Her father didn't deserve her thoughts. He gave up on her. She would not give up her daughter. The years at the monastery instilled anxiety and doubt, and the academy with its gaggle of tormenting classmates eroded Frances's confidence, but Martha knew, with the right education and encouragement, her daughter could do great things. She would find a way.

CHAPTER NINETEEN

January 1941
Pittsburgh, Pennsylvania

Frances was glad to be back at her dormitory. After her mother broke the news that George would not pay for college after this semester, she spent the remainder of her break in her bedroom watching her mother pace the room, angry and unrepentant, but confident of a solution, her trademark optimism on full display. Frances was oddly calm. While sequestered in her bedroom, she realized there were few things in the room with meaning—a few books, a stuffed bear from Randolph, and a cigar box of letters. Her fingers fumbling through the letters, she pulled out those from Mickey, ripping them into shreds without reading them. His betrayal cut deep, a scar that would never heal. She wrote to both Lily and Randolph the day after Joan's grand revelation. It was hard to find the words to explain the lies, especially to Randolph, but once the letters were mailed, she felt better. Lighter. Carrying a secret for so many years was a heavy burden.

Randolph called when he received Frances's letter. "I don't feel any differently about you," he had said.

"Neither does Lily. You will move in with her this summer. Stay as long as you want."

Lily had a friend in the Wanamaker's advertising department who could find a job for Frances at the large department store. The conversation was cut short when Russell walked into the library, snapping his fingers and demanding the phone.

Her mother told her to not give up, she would find a way to pay for college. Frances wasn't convinced, her pessimism mushrooming, her mother's bright outlook nettling. The life she dreamed of—working in the research laboratory at the glass factory, taking lunch breaks with Mickey—was gone.

From the window of her dormitory room, Frances scanned the crowd of returning students as they disappeared under the building's plaid awning. She couldn't wait to see Christy. Her roommate would cheer her up. She always did. Frances practiced her speech again. "My stepfather is having money problems. He can't pay for college next year." It wasn't a complete fabrication. George always complained about money. She couldn't bear to tell Christy the truth and watch her eyes cloud the way Pamela's had. Although it had been five days since her visit with Pamela at the monastery, the harrowing memory still made her stomach turn. Her face placid, hands folded in her lap, Pamela had kept her head lowered as Frances told her about her real father. Told her about her uncle. Told her about George's banishment. Frances poured out everything as she sat with her friend on the sofa in the monastery's parlor. Old enough to leave the monastery, Pamela chose to stay and become a Magdalene, destined to live out her days with nuns. Pamela had stood, staring at the small statue of the Virgin Mary, rosary beads in her left hand. "May God forgive you and your mother. I will always pray for you." She fled the room, leaving Frances stunned and shattered.

A knock at the dormitory room door startled Frances from her memories. Her smile grew as she ran across the room and flung the door open, expecting Christy's cherubic face.

Beatrice, the dorm monitor, stood in the hall. "May I come in, Frances?"

"Yes, ma'am." Her smile fading, Frances cleared her desk chair and offered it to Beatrice. She sat on her bed.

"Christine will not be returning. Her father passed away," Beatrice said, pushing to her feet. "You will be assigned a new roommate."

Frances waited until Beatrice closed the door to cry. Ten minutes later, she bolted from the dormitory. The day was bitterly cold, dry leaves, twigs and trash swirling around her feet. It was early afternoon but with Pittsburgh's perpetual cloud of smog, it looked close to sunset. She lowered her head, keeping a lookout for icy patches and doing her best to avoid collisions with passersby. The vibrant area around the college was always crowded and this afternoon was no exception with students and faculty hurrying by, their arms filled with books. They shared the sidewalks with families, the little ones bloated by layers, dashing towards the museum and library.

On the bottom step of St. Paul's Cathedral, Frances paused and swiped her knitted glove across her eyes. She looked up the broad steps to the arched doors and stained glass window, to the twin steeples piercing the clouds. Christy had been the one to find this church. Faith was one thing the two girls always had in common. She slowly climbed the steps and once inside, pulled off her gloves, keeping the wool scarf wrapped over her hair. The nave was still half full, despite Mass ending hours ago, coughs and sniffles echoing, the lingering scent of incense giving way to damp wool. She slid into the first empty pew and bowed her head, waiting for peace and calmness. Nothing. Today, the church wasn't consoling. She didn't belong here. Her secret was out, she was exposed. Unworthy. A sob escaped. She retreated to the narthex and huddled in the corner, taking deep breaths as she fumbled with her coat buttons.

"Miss? Are you all right?" A tall, young man, stood at her side. He held a black wool cap in his hands, nervously turning it through his fingers. "I couldn't help but notice you're a tad upset. Thought maybe you could use a friend. I know I can."

Frances had to raise her chin to look at the man's face, a rarity at her height. He was a head taller than her five foot eight inches, with a pair of blue eyes. Or were they green? His eyes seemed to change colors as she stared at them. What didn't change was the sparkle. She noted the soft lines at the corners of his mouth, carved by his wide, lopsided, smile, and a dimple split his chin. Frances didn't speak but didn't walk away.

"I'm new to town. A student at Carnegie Tech," the man said, extending his hand. "Joe Ferguson. The third."

Frances stared at his hand and finally extended her own, a tingle creeping to her elbow when his warm hand enfolded hers.

"Could I buy you a cup of coffee?"

She shook her head. "I need to get back to my dormitory."

"So, you're a student? This your first year, too?"

She shook her head again. "No. I'm a sophomore."

"Well, then you know your way around. Is there a restaurant nearby?"

"Go down to Forbes. There's one on the corner of South Craig Street." She looked down, fumbling with her gloves.

"Are you going that way? Can I walk with you?"

She continued to fight with her gloves, thinking she should tell this stranger to go away. Finally pushing her fingers into the left glove, she thought of his heated hand on hers, the prickle of his touch. "Fine," she said.

"Swell!" He slapped his hat on his palm and planted it on his head. He offered his arm. "It's a little slick out there."

Frances hesitated, feeling she should move along, but something held her back. She looked at his hopeful face and despite her somber mood, a smile threatened.

"What's your name?" he asked as she grasped his elbow.

"Frances."

Joe took long strides and they covered the four blocks to the restaurant quickly. They talked and sipped through three cups of coffee, Frances learning that Joe was raised on a dairy farm in New Kensington, a town twenty miles up the Allegheny River. His mother died the day he was born.

"Dad and my Uncle Bill run the farm," Joe said. He looked down at his coffee. "Grandpa died last year."

He went on to explain his farm was started by his grandfather when he moved west from Baltimore. Raised in the Irish countryside, city life didn't suit Joe Senior so he bought a Conestoga wagon, loaded up his wife and joined a wagon train going west on the National Trail. When the trail hit the Youghiogheny River, he headed north and kept going until a wagon wheel broke, stranding him and his wife in New Kensington. While searching for a new wheel, Joe Senior spotted twenty acres with a neglected house for sale. Joe the second was born later that year, followed by daughter Emily the next year, and another son, William, ten months later. As the children grew, so did the farm. It was now sixty acres.

"I worked at the aluminum plant for a year and a half. Hated it. But we needed the money once the Depression hit. Thought we were going to lose the farm," Joe said, his eyes growing dark. "But things are looking up. Have you seen the milk posters?"

Frances shook her head.

"Advertisements. So folks drink more milk. Part of President Roosevelt's New Deal," Joe said. He paused and smiled at the waitress standing by the table, coffee pot in hand. "I'm fine. No more coffee for me." He looked at Frances.

She shook her head.

The waitress didn't move. "We get people in here all day long in the winter who just want to drink coffee to stay out of the cold," she said. "Order some food or move along. I'm trying to make a living."

Joe's smile faded. "Right. Sorry ma'am. You like apple pie, Frances?"

She nodded.

"We'll each have a slice of apple pie. With whipped cream, of course," Joe said, his smile restored. He turned his now-blue eyes back to Frances. "I've been doing all the talking. Tell me about you. What made you so sad in church?"

She told him about Christy, how entertaining her roommate was and how much she would miss her, but not a word about her own troubles. Frances wouldn't say anything that might change the way Joe Ferguson the third was looking at her.

CHAPTER TWENTY

March 1941
Pittsburgh, Pennsylvania

Frances smiled as Joe dashed into the chemistry laboratory and dropped onto the stool beside hers, his face flushed. She leaned closer, listening to his labored breaths, taking in his familiar scent of dried grasses, ripe soil, and something distinctly masculine. Musky. She liked how he smelled. She liked the way he scratched his eyebrow when an experiment baffled him. How he moved her away from the curb when they walked, putting himself between her and traffic. A dozen little things that made her heart swell and her pulse quicken.

Dr. Robinson paused at the blackboard at the front of the lab, pulling back his sleeve and frowning at his watch. He was head of the chemistry department and a stickler about punctuality. A stickler about everything. He pushed his black rimmed glasses up his nose and peeled off his rumpled tweed blazer, shrugging into a white, knee-length jacket with his name embroidered on the pocket. The students stood, each pulling on a generic lab coat.

"Let's begin," Dr. Robinson said. "Mr. Ferguson, what is the first step in determining the empirical formula of copper chloride?"

Joe adjusted the knot of his tie and cleared his throat. "Measure twenty five milliliters of copper chloride solution in a graduated cylinder."

Frances beamed with pride. Joe was smart. He had a thirst for knowledge, just like her. And she didn't have to hide her inquisitiveness from him like she did with other classmates. He encouraged her curiosity. Suggested books to read, asked her what she thought of them afterwards. Being with Joe was easy, comfortable. The last time she had felt this at ease was with Mickey. She scowled, dismissing Mickey from her thoughts and pulled on her lab coat, giving the sleeves two quick rolls. The coat was made for a man and, even though she was tall, hung to mid-calf. "I'll get the cylinder and a beaker," she said to Joe.

He put a hand on her arm. "We need an evaporating dish, too."

She nodded and moved towards the shelves in the back of the room, her arm tingling from his touch. On the first day of this course two months ago, Joe walked in and her heart skipped. It had been nearly a week since they met at the church and, despite Joe's urging when they parted ways after their pie and coffee, she was unsure she wanted to see him again. Still intent on her grades—though her college future was doomed—Frances didn't want the distraction of a boyfriend. But Joe walking into the class changed her mind. The stool beside her was already filled with another student that day but Joe somehow convinced his classmate to change places with him, becoming Frances's lab partner for the semester. She smiled at the memory and absently pulled a glass cylinder from the shelf, juggling it before clasping it to her chest. Joe, just as she suspected, could be very distracting.

"How was the tea yesterday?" he asked once she had returned to her stool.

"I didn't go," Frances said. Once a month, Dr. Robinson and his wife hosted afternoon teas for the chemistry students, quizzing and probing for the brightest prospects. Joe had convinced her to go to the tea in February, and with him by her side, she had enjoyed it. Felt like she belonged. Joe turned heads—his height, his grin, his dimple—people were drawn to him and she was happy to be in his orbit. She was proud walking into the theater on his arm or sitting across from him at the college cafeteria. He told her she was beautiful and, even if she didn't fully believe him, he made her feel as though it was true. They had planned to go to this month's tea but Joe cancelled, telling her it was calving season and he needed to go home for the weekend. Still hesitant around strangers, she didn't go without him. "Maybe we can go to the next one." She leaned closer, catching his appealing scent again.

"I missed you," he whispered in her ear as they measured and mixed.

She smiled shyly, feeling heat rise to her cheeks, and glanced at him out of the corner of her eye. Now spending most of their free time together, Frances was surprised at her strong feelings. Reading, studying, eating...anything taking the slightest bit of concentration had become more difficult since her thoughts were on him, no matter how hard she tried to steer them in another direction. "Everything all right at the farm?" she asked and lit the flame on the burner. "How many calves?"

"Eleven." Carefully measuring hydrochloric acid into a beaker, he dropped in a zinc strip and flipped the two-minute hourglass, turning his gaze on her. "My grandmother wants to meet you," he said, his breath warm, faintly scented with coffee. "Come with me to the farm this weekend. You can see the calves. Meet my father and my Uncle Bill." He chuckled softly, his grin widening. "And probably several other Ferguson's. There's always a bunch of relatives at grandma's, especially around supper time."

Frances stiffened. His family would ask about her father and she would have to tell another lie.

He nudged her with his elbow and put his mouth to her ear. "Don't worry, they'll love you."

She turned and gave him a quick smile. He was so mindful of her. Watched her expressions. Mined her thoughts. When she was quiet and withdrawn, he guessed she was thinking of Christy. And sometimes she was. But her most distressing thought was that this could be the end of her college days. End of her time with Joe. In two short months she would be on her way to Philadelphia and not returning. If she told Joe he would ask why, and if he knew the truth, she wondered, would he still want her? Randolph said it didn't matter to him, but even he admitted that many men would be off put by her illegitimacy. And what would Joe think of her mother? She couldn't stand the thought of Joe not liking her mother.

They finished their experiment without any mishaps and walked out to a sunny, brisk day. The grass on campus was stiff and brown but a few bright green tufts promised spring was on the way. Joe took her books and added them to his, tucking the stack under his arm.

As they strolled, she read the hand-painted messages on the fence stretching across the campus — Kappa Sig was having a social, Alpha Tau a dance. She stopped, a frown furrowing her brow. "Are you joining a fraternity?"

He glanced at the fence and shook his head. "No, I don't have the time. Nor the money."

"Good," Frances said, then bloomed red. "I don't mean it's good that you don't have money. I meant about not joining a fraternity."

He laughed. "I know what you meant. Are you cold? You want to go to your dorm?"

She shook her head and took a step, giving his arm a squeeze.

They crossed the bridge guarded by bronze panthers and walked into a park bordered with towering sycamores. She scanned the treetops, searching for signs of spring but the limbs were bare, the glass spires of the city's conservatory clearly visible through the branches.

Joe stopped and stomped his feet, staring at the glass building. "It's cold. Let's go inside and warm up." He emptied his pocket and gave the coins to the woman working at the conservatory's gate.

Her mouth fell open, ready to decline since Joe being indulgent with his scant funds brought her a twinge of guilt, but the warmth of the building was so welcoming that she closed her mouth, her concerns unspoken. The air was heavy and damp, full of ripe scents. They walked through a dozen rooms overflowing with exotic plants and flowers, pausing to read the small identification tags and trying to pronounce the long names aloud.

"Good thing I'm trying to be a chemist, not a botanist," Joe said, squinting at the name printed beneath a tall plant with leaves as large as elephant ears, hairy vines as thick as her finger snaking up the trunk. He pushed open the door to the Orchid Room.

"Mmm," Frances mumbled, overwhelmed by the intoxicating scent flowing from a hundred blooms in a dozen colors, the delicate flowers quivering atop rubbery stems. She bent, her nose inches from violet petals. Two women approached, the only other people in the room, and Frances murmured a greeting, straightening to let them pass. She worked her way further into the tight space, closing her eyes and taking a deep breath, dewy air inflating her lungs. Joe moved to her side and she opened her eyes. The women had disappeared, she and Joe were alone. She raised her chin, and he leaned down,

185

his eyes a brilliant shade of green, mimicking the lush plants. She melted into his arms and his lips pressed against hers. Their first kiss. Her first kiss ever. It was the best sort of shock—just as her high-school-self imagined it—pulse racing, knees wobbling, lips tingling. Except it wasn't Mickey.

CHAPTER TWENTY-ONE

May 1941
Philadelphia, Pennsylvania

Free! Martha wanted to stand up and shout. Free from George. Free from Russell. Free from Joan. For a week, anyway. She leaned her head back and closed her eyes, the rocking of the train lulling her towards sleep. Pittsburgh, then on to Philadelphia. She smiled. In less than an hour, her daughter would be in her arms.

When Frances left the Pickett house in January to take the train back to college, Martha stood outside until her hands grew numb. She watched her daughter disappear down Main Street, not knowing when she would see her again. She tried to change George's mind about Frances's tuition, serving his favorite meals, spending more nights in his bedroom, but he held firm on his decision, referring to Frances as "Doyle's bastard." Those words, every time he uttered them, stung worse than a hive of bees.

Russell, thankfully, ignored her. Joan, on the other hand, took every opportunity to taunt. A week after Frances left, Joan announced that Frances's old bedroom would become the baby's nursery and the space outside the bedroom that once served as an upstairs dining room, would be the nanny's room.

"And where will I go?" Martha asked.

Joan exhaled, blowing out two perfect rings of smoke. "There's a spare bed on the third floor. Or perhaps the basement?"

George refused to intervene. Martha moved her things to the third floor, sharing the space with the cook and maid.

Not permitted to use the phone to call Frances, Martha mustered up the nerve to visit Mrs. Hofmann on Pike Street, the only person she knew with a phone. A stranger answered the door, telling Martha the widow passed away last year. In the hallway of her old apartment building, she looked up the stairs, wondering if Dottie was home, if Mickey still lived there. She turned away. If she were to see Mickey, there was no telling what she might say. Or do.

She wrote to Frances, using coins from her daughter's piggy bank to buy stamps and included one with the letter, anxiously awaiting a reply. It came a week later.

"Your daughter has learned quite the vocabulary," Joan said, dropping an opened envelope on the kitchen table.

Martha grabbed it. "This is addressed to me. You have no business opening it." She pushed to her feet, fists resting on the table. "Do not open my mail."

Joan laughed. "Or what?"

Mrs. Manning stood at the stove, frozen.

"Well?" Joan said, taking a step forward.

Martha stared, seething. *Well, what*? What could she do? Tell George? He wouldn't care. The urge to strike out festered. She forced her hands open. *No.* She was not her father. She walked from the room and wrote another letter to Frances. Told her to send future letters to Mrs. Roth's apartment. She tracked down Laura, Mrs. Seighman's daughter, and asked about a job at the glass factory.

"They don't hire married women," Laura said.

Even if she left George and got hired at the factory, Martha knew she could never make enough to pay for Frances's college. The bright future she had forged for her daughter was slipping away and she was running out of options.

***

The train lurched to a stop and Martha pushed out of her seat. She ran down the narrow aisle, apologizing over her shoulder to a young woman she nearly bowled over in her haste to get to Frances. Oblivious to the other passengers filling the platform, Martha stood in an embrace with Frances for a very long time. Eventually they sat on the trunk, talking and laughing until the time came to board the train to Philadelphia.

"I can't wait to see Randolph," Frances said after they settled into their seats.

A recent graduate from flight school, Randolph was spending two weeks in Philadelphia before his combat training began. He had been in Oklahoma, Texas and Missouri, and gone through primary, basic and advance training, plus ground school and pre-flight. He invited his father and Russell to Philadelphia during his short leave, but both declined.

"I knew they wouldn't come," Randolph said to Martha when he called two weeks ago. "Honestly, I don't care if I see either of them but I made my father feel bad. Told him I was hurt that my family couldn't find time for a soldier. Told him it was unpatriotic. Then I said, 'send Martha.' And I didn't allow him any excuses."

George bought Martha's roundtrip ticket and handed it to her without a word. Randolph paid Frances's fare.

"I'm so proud of Randolph," Martha said. It baffled her how two sons from the same parents, raised in the same house, turned out so different. Naively thinking fatherhood would bring about a positive change in

Russell, she was, once again, disappointed. His daughter, Judith Pauline, was born the last day of March, and Russell spent little time with his colicky child.

"Is Judith doing better?" Frances asked.

Martha shrugged. "Poor thing still cries. Russell took a room at the club for the entire month of April. He still spends several nights a week out of the house but Joan doesn't seem to mind."

Frances sighed. "How is Joan?"

"She hasn't changed. When her friends visit, the nanny parades little Judith through the parlor in a fancy dress, and all the women coo. Ten minutes later, the nanny and Judith are back in the nursery. The other days, Joan goes to her friends' homes. Or her mother's. The more time she spends out of the house the better." Martha patted Frances's hand. "And that's the last time we will speak of Joan, or Russell, on this trip." She leaned forward to look out the window. "Much has changed since our last train ride across Pennsylvania."

Frances nodded, ran a finger along the glass. "I wish Christy was here. She kept us laughing."

"How is she doing?" Martha had found Christy's lively personality a good balance for her daughter's thoughtful nature and her heart ached that Frances was without her friend, especially during this difficult time.

"Making the best of it," Frances said. "Her letters are always cheerful but when I saw her she looked tired."

"You saw her?"

"Yes, took the trolley to Donora to return what she left behind in the dorm. Christy works in the office at the mill. The same mill where her father, two brothers and a sister work. They're a close family," Frances said. She chuckled and turned towards Martha. "They better be close, all living in a house of six rooms. It's made of concrete. Rows and rows of these houses. The company owns them."

"Sounds like Webster Hill, except our company houses were wood," Martha said, her words garnering a quizzical look from Frances. How many times had her daughter asked to visit Webster Hill? How many excuses had Martha given throughout the years?

Frances turned back to the window. "Christy is dating one of the workers. Seems serious, but we didn't get to meet the fella."

"We?" Martha asked.

"Yes, Joe went with me."

Martha fought the urge to ask about Frances's relationship with Joe. Her daughter had mentioned him more than once in her letters but gave no indication of the seriousness of their relationship. "How do you like your new roommate?"

"She's nice, I guess." Frances shrugged. "Studying interior decoration so we don't have any classes together. I don't expect to be friends with her. She has her own group of friends, anyway." Frances quieted and turned back towards the window. She pointed. "That barn looks like the one at Joe's farm. See the black rooster on top? It's the same."

She couldn't hold her tongue any longer. "You care for Joe?" Martha asked.

Frances looked down at her hands folded in her lap and nodded. "Yes," she whispered. "But I fear I will never see him again. He'll be back at college this fall," she paused, her voice breaking, "but I won't."

"I'm sorry," Martha said. There was nothing else she could say. Frances's head fell back on the seat, eyes closed, and Martha watched her daughter drift to sleep, resisting the urge to run her fingertips across the delicate cheeks. When they lived on Pike Street, she spent hours watching Frances sleep. She didn't worry about the future then. She lived happily, day by day. Patrick stole that happiness. She let her own head fall back and closed her eyes. Her anger towards Patrick had dulled over the years, but she had never found a way to forgive him. Just like she would never forgive Joan. Or Mickey. Or herself.

She built a future on secrets and lies, and her innocent daughter was paying the price.

***

"We're here." Martha tapped Frances's shoulder as the Philadelphia station came into view. "There's Randolph."

"Oh my. Look at his uniform," Frances said.

Randolph stood on the platform, wings shining on his lapels, an arm draped across Lily's shoulders. He pulled his cap off and waved.

Martha struggled to keep up with Frances as her daughter bolted down the aisle, burst out the door, and threw herself into Randolph's arms. She pulled away to hug Lily.

"You look so handsome in your uniform, Randolph," Martha said, touching one of the gold wings with a gloved finger. She turned to Lily and smiled. "How are you, dear? You look lovely, as always." She leaned forward, kissing Lily's cheek.

"I am fine, now that Randolph's home. I've been a wreck. An absolute wreck since he left," Lily said.

"That's not true." Randolph put a hand on Lily's shoulder. "My wife is a full-fledged reporter now. Doesn't need me anymore."

Her head nestled against Randolph's chin, Lily patted her husband's chest. "I will always need you."

Martha turned away, a lump rising in her throat. She walked towards the train, watching the porter lower her battered suitcase and scarred trunk, now Frances's, to the platform. Both had seen better days. She ran her hand along the trunk, memories of her mother and Dottie coming to mind. Thankfully, Randolph coming aside saved her from her melancholy thoughts.

He looked at the trunk, looked at Frances, and shook his head. "What on earth did you bring?"

"Everything I own!" Frances chuckled and rushed to Randolph's side. "Here, I'll help you." She grasped one of the trunk's handles.

He moved her hand away. "Don't be silly. After all the training I've had, I'm stronger than ever." He started to lift the trunk, but quickly put it back down, grabbing his back with a groan.

"Oh, no!" all three women said, encircling him.

His head tossed back, he let out a whoop. "Just kidding. I like having my favorite gals fussing over me." He hoisted the trunk to his shoulder with ease and grabbed the suitcase with his other hand. "Follow me, ladies. Hope this monster fits in my car."

Randolph's street was ablaze with white blossoms, a slight breeze scattering the petals like snowflakes. Martha plucked one from her cheek, caressing it between her thumb and index finger. She and Frances settled into the guest bedroom, deciding to share the room so they could spend as much time as possible together. Within the hour, Lily called them to dinner.

"I promise I can cook more than spaghetti," Lily said, spearing a meatball with her fork. "I made lasagna, manicotti and cannelloni with my mother. I plan to practice my cooking skills on you this summer, Frances."

"I'm easy to please," Frances said. "Maybe you can teach me a few things?" She looked at Randolph and smiled. "On your next trip home, I'll be the one making your dinner."

He returned the smile and lowered his fork to the table. After a glance at Lily, he looked at Martha, then settled on Frances. "That sounds nice but you won't be here. You will be back at college, cooking in the chemistry laboratory, where you belong. I am paying your tuition."

Frances's mouth fell open and Martha gasped. Recovering quickly, Frances shook her head. "I can't take your money."

"It's not my money. It came from my father's father. A man I never knew. An inheritance when I turned twenty-five."

Her face crimson, Frances looked at Lily.

Lily nodded. "We want you to have it." She grasped Randolph's hand. "We have everything we need."

Overwhelmed, Martha's tears ran down her face like they hadn't in decades. Years of practice had made her stoic, suppressing her tears now second-nature, but this was so unexpected. So generous. Unselfish. So unlike the people she lived with. She put a hand to her chest, her heart thumping against her palm.

"How can I ever repay you?" Frances whispered, patting her napkin against her wet cheeks.

Randolph smiled and waved a hand across his face. "Easy come, easy go. Do your chemistry thing. Invent something. Change the world."

That evening, as Martha settled into the bed beside her daughter, she reflected on the change in Frances's demeanor. Her daughter chattered throughout their dinner, talking of classes, chemistry experiments and the Ferguson family farm, smiling shyly when Lily probed about the mysterious Joe.

"Is this Joe being a gentleman?" Randolph had asked.

"Of course," Frances said. "We've gone to a movie or two, some gatherings at our professor's. I am always back in my dorm by curfew."

"But no chaperone," he said. "I am not sure I approve."

Frances had laughed. A loud, genuine gaffe and Lily joined in.

"A chaperone?" Lily asked between chuckles. "Really, Randolph, what century are you in? I don't remember you lining up a chaperone for our dates."

Martha had found the conversation heartening— Randolph acting just as a big brother should. "Randolph is so fond of you," she said, smoothing the quilt over her legs. "You warm enough, Sunshine?"

"Yes, I'm fine," Frances said. She raised to an elbow and turned off the light on the bedside table. "Do you really think it is all right to accept his money?"

Martha turned on her side, trying to see her daughter's face, find her hand, but the room was dark. "Randolph wouldn't have offered if he had doubts."

Frances was silent for moment. When she spoke again her voice was very soft, a whisper. "Mom. You could leave George now."

Martha rolled on to her back. "Where would I go? I can't live with you in the dormitory, Sunshine."

"You could live here. With Lily."

Martha sighed. The thought had crossed her mind. But that would put Randolph in the middle of a mess. He would have to choose sides and although Randolph seldom agreed with his father and brother, they were his family. She would not do that to him. "It's not so bad," Martha lied. Her days and nights at the Pickett house were ghastly. George didn't take her to his bed very often but when he did, he was forceful. Punishing. She would creep to the third floor afterwards and crawl into her bed beneath a small window in the west corner. There were no walls to separate her from Mrs. Manning and Linda, but she had two large wardrobes moved to the top floor and positioned her bed behind them, creating a small bit of privacy. The cook and the maid didn't speak during the day—she hoped they were discreet outside of the house—and she steered clear of Joan, spending time in the library or outside in the pavilion, taking long walks when the air was clear. She endured life, considered the lack of amenities comeuppance for her decades of deception.

***

Martha's week in Philadelphia went fast. Too fast. Randolph was the perfect host, showing off his adopted city's best known landmarks.

"It's cracked," Martha said, pointing at the Liberty Bell on her last day in town.

Randolph laughed and led Martha, Frances and Lily out of Independence Hall. They walked three blocks, adding themselves to the crowded lobby of a popular restaurant.

"Oh, dear," Martha said when she caught sight of a large tank full of lobsters.

Lily sighed, but she couldn't hold back a giggle. "I feel sorry for the poor creatures but lobster is quite tasty."

"As is their turtle soup," Randolph said. "Four," he told the tuxedoed maître d'.

"Good afternoon, Officer." The man ran his finger down his clip board. "It'll be just a moment. Busy day today. Lots of new recruits here for their complimentary lunch."

"A toast," Randolph said after they were seated. He raised his glass of beer. "To my stepmother."

Martha blushed and cried again. The next day, on the train platform, she vowed to keep her tears at bay, hoping she was cried-out and wouldn't embarrass her family with a public display of weeping. She did. It was as if she had been storing her unshed tears, depositing them in her own personal bank throughout the years and spending them all this week. She hugged Lily, then Frances, then Randolph, and returned to Frances, refusing to let go until the conductor announced the final boarding call.

Once more, Martha was on a train alone, wondering when she would see her loved ones again.

CHAPTER TWENTY-TWO

September 1942
Pittsburgh, Pennsylvania

Back for her senior year after another summer in Philadelphia, Frances watched the ROTC drills from her dormitory window. At first glance, the uniformed students all looked similar but it didn't take her long to pick out Joe. She knew him well, having spent every spare minute with him last year. There had been movie dates at the Schenley, the theater a few blocks from the campus, and Joe taught her to bowl on the theater's second floor when the weather turned too cold for walks in the park. They studied together, read the same books, and had long discussions over cups of coffee. They never missed Dr. Robinson's teas, Frances watching Joe banter with the professor and the other students as she drank neon punch from beakers. She wished she had the nerve to join in the chemistry conversation, like Dr. Robinson's bold wife did, but when she thought about it, her cheeks heated, her heart pounded and her mouth went dry. Joe had boosted her confidence but she was still reserved, especially timid among large groups.

Frances sighed as Joe stopped, turned and marched on, head at a slight tilt, steps purposeful. She didn't want him to join ROTC but it was better than enlisting. Hopefully the war would be over by the time he was obligated to become an officer. "Why won't he use that damn exemption?" she muttered. Since farming was an essential industry, Joe could be exempt from serving in the war but he refused. She wrapped her arms around herself to quell a shiver. The same shiver she felt the first time she saw Joe in his uniform. He had been proud, turning from side to side, grinning. So handsome. But she never told him because her initial admiration dissolved into uneasiness. The same feeling she had when Patrick Doyle walked into the apartment on Pike Street. Before her uncle entered her life, she had felt safe. Comfortable. Then she learned she had been lied to her entire life. She wondered what else she had missed. Were there more secrets? More unsavory details to be revealed? Always waiting for the other shoe to drop kept her on edge. Hesitant. But Joe had calmed her. She felt safe with him. So safe that she considered telling him the truth about her father but a niggling voice at the back of her head told her to keep quiet.

She turned, listening, thinking she heard a knock at the door. Nothing. She turned back to the window. Another knock, so soft it was barely audible. She sighed and walked across the room, pushing the door open with more force than necessary.

"Oh!" A young woman jumped back, stumbling, a notebook falling from her arms.

Frances looked down, watching the woman scramble across the hallway floor. The woman raised her head and Frances frowned, trying to place the face staring up at her.

"Sorry," the woman said, jumping to her feet. "Hope I'm not bothering you, but you did say stop by anytime. I have a question."

Frances continued to stare. The woman was slight, a head shorter than Frances, with amber eyes, the same shade as her dress. It was a fashionable dress, fitting her small frame perfectly with a cinched waist and full skirt of a dozen narrow pleats. Frances expected to find trendy pumps on the woman's feet, but instead, she wore scuffed oxfords, black as the frames of her glasses perched upon her up-turned nose.

"Stephanie. Stephanie Kwolek," the woman said.

"Right." Frances forced a smile. "Joe's friend."

"Yes."

Both hailing from New Kensington, Joe and Stephanie went to the same high school, although several years apart, and attended the same church. Last week, when Frances walked into the college's chemistry building, Joe was talking to Stephanie, and he introduced her.

"Stephanie is a freshman," Joe had said. "Maybe you could help her get settled?"

Distracted and late for class, Frances scarcely registered the woman. "Sure, stop by anytime," she had mumbled and moved on quickly, intent on a front row seat in the lecture hall.

Stephanie pushed her glasses further up her nose and hugged the notebook to her chest. "Is this a bad time?"

Frances found her manners and shook her head, taking a step back. "Actually, I'm glad for the company. Come in." She moved to her desk, stacked with textbooks and notebooks, but tidy, and pulled out the chair. She followed Stephanie's gaze and sighed. Her roommate's desk, and the floor next to it, was strewn with sketch books, colored pencils and squares of fabric. "My roommate's majoring in interior decoration," Frances said, feeling the need to explain the clutter.

Stephanie picked up a scrap of fabric, something purple, and rubbed it between her thumb and index finger. "I once thought I would be a dress designer," she said, carefully replacing the scrap. She caressed another square, this one plaid, replaced it with a sigh, and took the seat at Frances desk. "My equation can't be right," she said and opened her notebook, balancing it on her knees. She looked up, frowning. "Can I look at your notes?"

"Which experiment?" Frances asked.

"Alchemy. Changing the copper token." Stephanie tapped her pencil on the page. "What's the zinc solution?"

Frances rummaged through her stack of notebooks, extracting one and carrying it to the bed. She sat, flipping through pages. "It's dissolved in sodium hydroxide to form sodium zincate. Here's the ionic equation." She handed the open book to Stephanie.

"Oh. I forgot the sodium." Stephanie slapped her forehead. "How could I miss something so elementary? She lowered her hand and scribbled on the page. "It's not like me to overlook a detail."

Frances smiled, her eyes on the red handprint emerging on Stephanie's brow. "You are just a freshman. Takes time to get used to college."

"Mr. Eskens said it would be different," Stephanie said. "He was my high school teacher. Taught chemistry. Helped me get into college."

Her smile still in place, Frances nodded.

Stephanie returned the nod. "Thank you," she finally said.

"You're welcome."

"All right, then, I suppose I will see you in class." Stephanie closed her notebook. She threw another look at the fabric squares and pushed to her feet.

Frances was looking forward to spending time alone with Joe but she felt bad for this young woman, remembering her years of being an outsider. She stood. "What are you doing for supper? I'm meeting Joe at the Beanery. Would you like to come?"

"Yes!" Stephanie said, raising to her toes, the pleats of her dress swaying. "I mean, only if I'm not intruding."

Frances shook her head. "Joe will be glad to see you."

"Joe is nice," Stephanie said, lowering her heels and hugging the notebook to her chest. "His whole family is. They were kind to me and my mom and brother after my father died. Gave us extra milk. For free." Her face reddened and she looked at her feet.

Frances fell quiet, frowning at the bowed women's head. "Sorry about your father," she said.

Stephanie kept her attention on the floor. "It was a long time ago. I was ten. But I still miss him. We used to take long walks in the woods and he would point out the different trees and plants. He knew all the names." She paused and looked at Frances. "What is your father like?"

"He died before I was born." Frances moved to the window, putting an end to the father conversation. "They are still practicing."

"Practicing?"

"Yes. Joe is in ROTC."

"Oh." Stephanie came to stand beside her.

Frances turned, waiting for Stephanie to say more but she just continued to stare out the window. The silence grew long, uncomfortably long. Frances sighed and walked to her desk, rearranging the notebooks. She looked at Stephanie again, let out another sigh, realizing it was up to her to keep the conversation going. "So, you're interested in chemistry?"

"Yes." Stephanie stayed at the window, her back towards Frances.

"I want to be a chemist, too," Frances said.

Stephanie wheeled around, her eyes wide. "You? A chemist?"

Frances raised an eyebrow. "You don't sound convinced."

"Ah, well, it's just. You don't look..." Stephanie pushed her glasses up, meeting Frances eyes. "None of the other girls in my school were interested in chemistry."

Frances laughed. "Mine either."

"I am going to be a chemist, but not forever," Stephanie said. She returned to the desk chair, letting out a loud breath as she sat. "I want to be a doctor. But I don't have the money. Yet. I'm going to work for three years as a chemist—four years at the most—then go to medical school."

Frances studied Stephanie, unable to define her. She dressed well, her interest in fashion reminding her of Frances's academy classmates but Stephanie wasn't haughty and money was a concern, unlike those snobbish classmates. Stephanie was also the first woman Frances had met at college with an ambition other than securing a husband. She stood and returned to the window. "They're finished. Let's go," she said and pointed at her desk. "You can leave your book here and pick it up after we eat."

At her usual brisk pace, Frances strode across campus, not noticing Stephanie's labored breathing until they neared the college fence. She stopped, letting Stephanie catch her breath, and pointed. "They used to print fraternity party dates and events on it." The fence was now painted with "Remember December 7th" and "Victory Begins at Home" and other war slogans. Everywhere you looked there was a reminder of the war and how every citizen could help. It was impossible to avoid all the ads, posters and pamphlets promoting war bonds, victory gardens and salvage programs. Ration books, air raids, death toll—words seldom uttered before the United States declared war—were now part of everyday life.

They moved on again, Frances shortening her strides.

Still in his uniform, Joe stood at the college café's door. He smiled, taking one of Frances's hands in his. He looked at Stephanie. "Glad you two met up. You getting use to college?"

Stephanie bobbed her head and stammered, "yes."

202

Few of the tables in the restaurant were occupied but the wait for service was long since many of the women who normally worked as waitresses moved on to jobs in the mills and factories, filling the void left behind by the men going to war. It was the same story most everywhere: short-handed businesses. Frances spent her summer working long hours at Wanamaker's and Lily worked from sunup to sundown, but Lily welcomed her busy schedule.

"Less time to worry about Randolph," Lily had said, tearing up. Captain Randolph Pickett was nearing his thirtieth mission, piloting a B-17 from his station in England for the past year.

The waitress put a basket of rolls and a pot of tea on the table, hurrying away before Frances could ask for sugar.

"They probably don't have any," Joe said, breaking a roll in two. "No butter either."

"Do you really think they will start rationing gasoline?" Frances asked, wrinkling her nose as she took a sip of her bitter tea.

Joe nodded. "Many states already have. Voluntary conservation isn't working."

"We have a fuel shortage?" Stephanie asked.

"No. That's not the problem. It's rubber," Joe said. "The Japs control all the plantations so we can't import rubber. Less driving helps conserve tires so the rubber we do have can go to the Army and Navy." He paused, letting out his breath. "That's what we should be doing in chemistry. Looking for ways to make rubber instead of cooking copper to see what colors we get. Sometimes, it feels like I'm doing the same experiments I did in high school."

"Was Mr. Eskens teaching chemistry back then?" Stephanie asked.

Joe laughed. "Yes, way back then. Mr. Eskens' been teaching for years. You probably used the same Bunsen burners I had."

Stephanie's cheeks reddened. "He was my favorite teacher." She bowed her head down, hands wrapped around her cup.

"Joe's going to be a chemical engineer," Frances said, placing her hand on his. "Maybe he'll invent something that helps our troops."

"I'd like to be helping the troops right now," he said and slid his hand from Frances's grasp. He pushed back from the table, his chair scrapping loud enough to turn heads. "I have studying to do. See you later." Joe dodged two students, uttering an apology, as he stalked out the door.

"He wants to enlist," Frances said with a shrug. "We argue about it every day." She turned away, wondering why she would share something so personal with this woman. She was, after all, still a stranger and Frances's experience with classmates had left her skittish about sharing. Christy had been the exception, but even Christy didn't know the whole truth. She smiled, thinking of Christy. Her Christmas break was spent in Donora, sleeping on the floor of Christy's bedroom, talking and laughing into the wee hours of the night until Christy's sisters scolded them quiet. It was a merry holiday, the modest house filled to capacity, but all the festivities couldn't keep Frances from missing her mother so Christy borrowed the family's old Ford and drove to Wheeling the day after Christmas. Frances and her mother met for a few hours at Mrs. Roth's apartment but George somehow found out about the meeting and Martha was now forbidden to leave the house without a chaperone. Frances yearned for the day her mother would be free of George, Russell and Joan. Though her mother said very little about her life at the Pickett house, Frances knew it was taking a toll. She could see it in her mother's eyes. A nervousness that wasn't there before. Her mother had always walked with purpose, head held high, back straight, but now her gait was slowed and her shoulders sloped. Getting her mother out of the Pickett house was extra incentive— a driving force—for Frances to graduate and find a job. She would take her mother away. Return her freedom.

Frances stood. "Let's go."

When they returned to the dormitory, Beatrice was waiting in the lobby. She looked at Frances. "Your mother called. She wants you to call her. You can use the phone in the office."

Frances froze. It had to be an emergency for her mother to call. Her feet like blocks of ice, she forced herself forward, her shaking hand making it was difficult to spin the dial. When her mother's voice came on, it was thin, cracking. Frances collapsed, the receiver gripped in her white-knuckled hand.

Stephanie rushed forward and dropped to the floor, her hand on Frances's shoulder. "What is it?"

"My stepbrother," Frances whispered. "His plane was shot down."

CHAPTER TWENTY-THREE

September 1942
Pittsburgh, Pennsylvania

The nights were the hardest. During the day, Frances had classes and Joe to keep her mind occupied, but at night, the terrifying dreams came. She woke screaming, her frightened roommate running from the room. Yesterday, a week after news of Randolph's death, Frances fell asleep in her history class and today, in the chemistry lab, she was having a difficult time staying focused. She reached for her notebook, knocking a beaker of sodium sulphate to the tiles.

"I'm sorry, Stephanie," Frances said, looking down at her shoe where glass shards and white powder collected in the creases. Stephanie was now her laboratory partner since Joe dropped out of chemistry courses this semester, deciding to concentrate on mathematics and geometry.

Stephanie put a hand on Frances's arm. "Don't move. I'll get the broom."

Frances continued to stare at her shoe, fighting tears, fighting to stay upright. It felt as though the room was tilted and she gripped the cold slate of the counter with one hand, reaching behind with the other to find the stool. She sat, closed her eyes.

"You all right, Frances?"

Stephanie's voice was muffled, the rush in Frances's ears dulling the sound. She nodded but kept her eyes closed, feeling the stiff stalks of the broom through the worn leather of her shoe. She took a long breath, let it out slowly. When she had these overwhelming feelings, Joe told her to concentrate on something else—a sound, a smell, anything—to distract her, keep her in the present. The laboratory was seething with smells. In her mind, she named the ones she recognized, keeping her eyes closed. *Sulfur*. That one was easy. She breathed in again. Oranges? She frowned. Definitely a fruity scent but no food was allowed in the lab. "Oh, right," she said aloud and nodded. *Acetone*.

"Frances?"

Frances opened her eyes. "Yes, I'm fine. Sorry." She looked down at Stephanie's concerned face and managed a tight smile.

Stephanie rose, dustpan in her hand. "I'm ready to call it a day, anyway. I have a composition due tomorrow."

They parted ways outside the science building, and Frances wandered along the fence. It was a lovely day, the sun warm but a hint of fall in the air, a scattering of leaves on the ground. She raised her face to a cloudless, blue sky, not something found very often in Pittsburgh's soot-filled environs. How could Randolph not be alive on such a day, she wondered. She turned, tented a hand over her eyes, and scanned the sky, seeking the cathedral's steeples. *Why, God, why?* No answer. She walked to hers and Joe's favorite bench and sat, concentrating on the passing students, keeping her thoughts from Randolph and the fact that she would never see him again.

"Hello, Beautiful," Joe said as he lowered to the bench beside her. He kissed her on the cheek, took her hand in his. "Lovely day, isn't it?"

Frances nodded. "Why aren't you in your uniform? I thought you had practice this afternoon."

208

Joe raised his chin, focused on a spot just over her shoulder. He squeezed her hand, brow furrowed, eyes narrowed.

Frances went cold.

"I have enlisted," he said, turning dark eyes to her.

She tried to pull her hand from his grasp but he hung on.

"I can't sit around here playing solider in ROTC. I want to help win this war, Frances. Put an end to all this death and misery," he said.

"Please, don't..." she hiccupped, swallowed twice. "I can't lose you, too. Please."

He angled his body closer, held both her hands. "You won't lose me. But will you wait for me? Marry me?"

"Oh Joe, yes. I'd marry you tomorrow."

"You would? Then let's do it. Get married. Now." He kissed her full on the lips and jumped to his feet, pulling Frances up with him. "I'll call Grandma and she'll call the priest. We'll get married this weekend and you can move in with Grandma. There's plenty of room and she will be glad to have you living with her." He started walking, her hand in his.

Frances halted. "I want to finish college." She swallowed, her voice soft. "Randolph paid for it. I won't let him down."

Joe turned, studied Frances for a moment. He nodded and they started walking again, remaining quiet until they reached her building. "See you later, Mrs. Ferguson," he whispered in her ear and brushed his lips across her cheek.

She hurried into her dormitory's office, begging to use the phone. Beatrice finally agreed, giving her five minutes of talk time. Linda, Joan's maid, answered at the Pickett house and asked who was calling.

Joan came on the line. "Frances, your mother is unavailable," she said, exhaling loudly into the phone.

Shocked to hear Joan's voice, Frances was speechless.

"Frances?" Joan said. "Is there something you would like me to pass on to your mother?"

"No," Frances said.

"Well, then, don't call here again." Joan hung up.

Frances wrote a letter to her mother, keeping her comments free of malice, since her words would most likely be read by Joan. Since their clandestine Christmastime meeting, her mother was no longer allowed to visit Mrs. Roth so Frances had to mail the letter to the Pickett house. She told her mother how happy she was to be marrying Joe, how much she missed Randolph and how she was not giving up on college. What she didn't say was how jittery she was about the wedding night. She knew the mechanics, but she had so many questions. Would it hurt? Do you talk during it? Should I touch Joe? Can you make a baby the first time? She put her pen to the side and lay her palm on the paper. When her mother read these words, Frances would be a married woman.

**

Joe greeted Frances at the New Kensington train station on Saturday morning and drove directly to the church where the Ferguson family, all eighteen of them, filled the first three rows. She wore a light blue dress of linen, the best dress she had, and carried a wilting chrysanthemum as she walked down the long aisle on Joe's father's arm. The priest who baptized Joe led them through their vows and they had punch and cake in the basement. There were many new faces and Frances did her best to remember names but she was preoccupied, the ache for her mother crushing, her apprehension over the upcoming night distracting.

After dinner at a small restaurant in town, Joe drove to his grandmother's house and led her upstairs.

She stood at the doorway of the bedroom, trembling, her stomach knotted, her face on fire.

"Don't be scared, Frances," Joe said, holding her hands. "I'm probably as nervous as you are. This is my first time, too."

Frances dropped her head and fumbled with the buttons on her dress.

"You want me to help?" he asked, pushing his shirt off his shoulders.

She shook her head and managed to unhook the buttons. In her slip, she sat on the bed and worked to unclip her nylon stocking from her garter belt.

Joe put a hand on hers. "Let me do that, Mrs. Ferguson."

He slowly slid the stocking down her leg, his fingers igniting a warm trail. She worried about getting a run in her stocking—nylon stockings were hard to get and she only had two other pair, hoarding and protecting them as if they were made of cash—but when Joe's hand inched up her thigh, her thoughts of stockings vanished. All thoughts vanished, her body taking command.

Afterwards, Frances lay very still, anchored to the bed as she fought to make her fragmented mind whole. She shifted closer to his heated body, resting her head on his shoulder, her fingers exploring the whorls of dark hair on his muscled chest.

"I'm sorry your mother and stepfather couldn't come today," he said, tugging a quilt over their bodies.

"Hmm." She kept her words about her stepfather to a minimum, never disparaging him, but never complimenting him, either. "Your father was kind to walk me down the aisle," she said. "He didn't say much."

"Don't take it personally. Dad is a quiet man." Joe slid his hand down her arm, letting it rest on her hip. "He prefers working to talking. Likes getting his hands dirty. Fixing fences, planting corn. He takes care of the horses, too. Does his own shoeing. 'Course we only have two horses now, since we got the tractor."

"Do you ride the horses?"

"No. They're work horses," Joe said. "My Uncle Bill's in charge of the barn and the cows. They are milked twice a day. You ever milk a cow, Frances?"

"Me?" Frances giggled. "No, but I watched."

"Oh? Where?"

Frances bit her lip. She wanted to tell Joe about the monastery. About the farm she visited with the nuns and how Sister Agnes was proclaimed the fastest "milk maid." She didn't want to keep secrets from her husband but there was still a part of her that believed he would love her less if he knew the truth. "The county fair," she lied.

"Well, you'll have to give it a try. Can't live on a dairy farm and not milk a cow." His hand dropped to her buttock, patting it twice.

They slept very little that night, nor the next night at a hotel in downtown Pittsburgh, both evenings filled with talking and lovemaking. Frances was astonished at how her body responded to his touch, how the sound of his voice fueled her longing, her doubts and inhibitions disappearing. The morning after their second night together, they walked across the street and Frances said goodbye to her husband at the train station. She returned to school as though nothing changed so she could continue to live at the dormitory. Her marriage would be a secret—she was, after all, well-rehearsed in keeping secrets—as she was determined to keep her promise of a college degree to her mother and Randolph. She would move to the farm after she graduated, with the hope the war would be over quickly and Joe, and all the troops, would be home soon, celebrating victory.

CHAPTER TWENTY-FOUR

December 1942
Pittsburgh, Pennsylvania

The ring was a plain gold band. No diamond. No engraving. Nothing special, but to Frances, it was perfect. Sitting on the bed in her dormitory room, she extended her left hand and admired the ring, remembering her wedding two months ago. She glanced at the clock on the bedside table and pulled the ring from her finger, returning it to its black velvet pouch and tucking the pouch in her pocket. She pushed to her feet and smiled. Time to meet Joe. She couldn't wait. He just completed his basic training at Fort Lee and had one week of leave before his infantry unit boarded a ship bound for England. After a hurried run down the dormitory stairs, she ran out the door and into Joe's waiting arms. They embraced for a long moment, enjoyed an even longer kiss and set off in the spitting snow.

He wrapped his arm around her shoulders and they headed across campus. "God, it's good to see you." He dodged a half-frozen puddle and pulled her closer, away from the curb, as a trolley sluiced down Forbes Avenue. "Boot camp was tough. Never been so tired," he said. "I thought the farm was hard work, but..." he let out a long whistle and shook his head. "Jumping jacks and push-ups at dawn. Marching for hours. Loading and unloading my gun until I could do it with my eyes closed."

Frances was quiet as Joe's words tumbled out, his voice a comforting lullaby. She didn't notice the cold but Joe steered them towards the conservatory, a warm place with peaceful memories.

Once they settled on a bench in a corner of the Palm Court, Joe pulled his cap from his head. "What do you think of the hair?" He chuckled, his dimple deep. "Or lack of it. First thing they did was shave our heads while we stood in our skivvies."

Frances rubbed his head, the stiff bristles tickling her palm. "I like it."

He kissed her. "You are a sight for sore eyes."

She burst into tears.

"Frances, what is it?"

She bowed her head, unable to look him in the eye. She was pregnant. Would he blame her for her ignorance? Be angry? Or even worse, regret he married her? "I'm going to have a baby," she whispered. "I'm sorry."

Joe cupped her chin with his hand, forced her eyes to his. "Sorry? Don't be sorry. I'm the luckiest fella around." He pounded his thigh. "Grandma will be thrilled and my father will be over the moon. You'll come home with me tonight to stay. We'll tell the family together."

She shook her head. "I want to finish this term. There's only a couple weeks left."

He stared at her, nodded. "All right."

"You sure you're happy about the baby?" Frances asked, laying her hand on his. "You're getting ready to sail across the ocean, facing a war, and I'm making it more difficult."

"No. Not more difficult." Joe shook his head. "This baby's another reason to fight hard and come home." He moved his hand to her stomach, she covered it with her own.

"I won't be allowed to attend school next term," she said. "What will your grandmother say?"

Joe waved his hand across his face. "She will be glad to have you." He kissed her again. "You'll be a wonderful mother."

"I'm scared." Frances said, squeezing his hand.

Joe touched his forehead to hers. "Me too."

***

They walked to the train station and Joe wiped her tears away, reminding her she would see him in just a few days. He planned to spend time with his family, then return to a Pittsburgh hotel for three days and nights with Frances before rejoining his unit. Back at her dormitory, Frances asked to use the phone in the office. This time, when Joan's maid answered, she said she was Lily Pickett, calling to talk with Martha Pickett. Feeling a bit breathless, she picked at the frayed cord and willed herself not to cry but the minute she heard her mother's voice, the tears flowed, her buried fears and worries exploding like one of her chemistry experiments gone awry.

"Frances, what is it? Are you ill? Is it Joe?" Her mother asked, her voice panicked and shrill.

This was not how Frances planned this conversation. "Mom, I'm having a baby." She blurted much too loud, her eyes sliding to the office door, hoping no one was within earshot. There was no reason to be ashamed—she was a married woman—but nobody knew, and anything with a hint of scandal spread like fire through the dormitory.

The phone was quiet.

Frances frowned. "Mom? Are you still there?"

"Yes, I'm here. I'm just...surprised. I thought you would wait to have a baby until after college. When Joe was home."

Frances's angst turned to indignation. Maybe if her mother had been more forthcoming about sex, and how not to have a baby, they wouldn't be having this conversation. "Aren't you happy?"

"Of course I'm happy, Sunshine. I just need some time to get used to the idea of being a grandmother." Her mother paused. "Are you feeling well?"

"I'm fine." Frances snapped, holding on to her umbrage.

"I miss you terribly."

Frances sighed, her anger melting at the quiver in her mother's voice. "I miss you, too. How are you?"

"Fine."

Frances knew that wasn't true, but she went along with the ruse. "What are you doing with your time?"

"Knitting. Baking cookies," her mother said with a snort. "Joan gave me a list of parties she is having for Christmas, and which ones I am expected to attend."

"After what happened to Randolph, they're having parties?"

"Joan said 'life goes on.' Poor Mrs. Manning. She's had a heck of a time getting the food she needs. Bartering with her other cook friends for extra rations."

"What does Russell say?" Frances asked.

"He goes along with whatever his wife wants," Martha said. "Especially now that another baby is on the way."

"What about George?"

"Doesn't say a word. He stayed at the club for two weeks after the news of Randolph. When he returned to the house, he took to his bed. Stayed there for a week."

"I miss Randolph," Frances said, her voice hitching. "Something happens and I think, 'I can't wait to tell Randolph about that.' Then I realize I won't be seeing him again."

"Yes, it's hard," Martha said, the quiver back in her voice. "Every room in this house has a memory of Randolph." She paused. "Have you spoken to Lily?"

"Yes. Still at her parents' house," Frances said. "She wants to go to England. A part of her refuses to believe Randolph is dead. Says she is going to look for him. And write about the war." Frances sighed, running the coiled cord through her fingers. "Randolph's plane going down motivated her. Angered her," she said. "Like Joe."

There was a knock at the door and Beatrice stuck her head in, saying she needed the phone. She stood at the doorway, arms crossed.

"I have to go," Frances said. "I'll call you as soon as I can." She took a swallow, giving Beatrice a sideways glance. "Goodbye," she whispered.

***

In the chemistry laboratory the next day, Frances found it hard to focus. Her mind wandered, thinking first of Joe, then with her hand dropping to her stomach, she thought of her baby. Would it have Joe's dark hair, or her fair hue? Blue eyes like hers, or Joe's mysterious color?

"Frances!" Stephanie said. "Turn the burner down. Your beaker's starting to smoke."

Frances tightened the valve and the flame changed from blue to orange to yellow and the bubbling slowed. She shrugged at Stephanie, feeling her face flush.

They finished the experiment in silence but as they walked from the lab, Stephanie touched her arm. "Are you all right, Frances?"

"Yes. Fine. I'm just distracted. Thinking of my stepbrother. Missing Joe."

"Going to the Beanery for lunch?" Stephanie asked.

In a hurry this morning, Frances had skipped breakfast, and supper the night before was a quick bowl of soup. "Yes. I suppose I should eat."

There were plenty of open tables as many of the students had already left for Christmas break. They took a table along the windowed wall, large snowflakes floating by.

"I like it when it snows." Stephanie smiled, a finger on one of the glass panes. "Makes everything look clean."

Frances dragged her attention to the window, trying to find joy in the falling snow. There was none. She let her eyes rove the room. Many happy hours had been spent in this restaurant with Joe. And before him, with Christy. Tears threatened and she forced her thoughts back to the present. "I hope we don't get much snow," she snapped, surprising herself and Stephanie with the sharpness of her tone. She gave Stephanie a tight smile and took the edge off her voice "It's just hard to drag my trunk through it."

"Right." Stephanie nodded, concentrating on her soup. She dipped a spoon into the bowl, frowning at the rising steam as she stirred the thin broth. After three spoonfuls, she pushed the bowl away and looked up at Frances. "What day are you returning?"

Frances tried, but she could not hold back her tears. She hung her head, embarrassed. "I won't be coming back."

PART FOUR:
THE HOMEFRONT
1943 – 1946

CHAPTER TWENTY-FIVE

June 1943
New Kensington, Pennsylvania

Frances turned her face into the breeze, welcoming the blast of air on her heated cheeks. She closed her eyes, breathing in the now-familiar scent of the farm—drying hay and fertile soil, a touch of manure. Quite different from city smells. With a contented sigh, she opened her eyes and returned her attention to the three-inch tomato plant in her hand, gently dropping the seedling into a shallow hole. The wind caught the wide brim of her straw hat and skipped it across the freshly-turned earth, and she put one hand on the ground, the other under her belly, and started the struggle to her feet. At eight months pregnant, every movement took effort.

"Don't get up, I'll fetch your hat," Stephanie said, bounding across the dirt.

Rocking back on her heels, Frances ran her hand across her damp brow and pushed her heavy braid off her shoulder. Since moving to the farm, she abandoned her contemporary, but time-consuming hair style, returning to a quick and easy plait. She smiled her thanks as she accepted the hat from Stephanie and secured the strap under her chin. She watched her friend dig into the can of bean seeds and carefully measure the space between each seed she dropped into the soil. Just like in the chemistry lab, Stephanie was exact in her gardening. It was their time together in that laboratory that sealed their friendship. Frances had never seen anyone so dedicated.

"Stephanie, I really appreciate your help but I don't want to keep you from your own plans," Frances said.

"I finished our garden yesterday." Stephanie concentrated on the spade she ran through the loose soil. "It doesn't take long since we just have a small backyard. Not anything like out here." She looked up and swept her hand towards the green fields dotted with grazing cows. She stood and watched Frances's efforts. "You should put the plants a little deeper. And mound the soil up to the bottom leaves. Here, let me show you." She hopped over a planted row and hiked up her skirt to kneel.

"This is the first time I've planted a garden," Frances said, adjusting the strap of her overalls. They were actually Joe's overalls, the only pair of pants she could fit into.

Stephanie chuckled. "You should have seen my first garden. It was the summer after my father died. The biggest carrot was two inches and the onions looked like marbles. Things don't always grow the way you want them to. You'll need to watch the leaves for disease and pull bad bugs off. But leave the good bugs."

"Bugs?"

"Most of them don't bite," Stephanie said. "You could feed them to the chickens."

"Hmm. The chickens." Frances turned to the nearby coop, brown chickens pecking the bare ground. She narrowed her eyes at the strutting rooster as the nervous hens scattered to make a path for the big bird. One of the jobs she had taken on since moving to the Ferguson farm was collecting eggs every morning and she'd had more than one run-in with the rooster. Joe's grandmother, Sarah, showed her how to collect the eggs from underneath the birds, giving the broody hens a wide berth. She felt bad, taking the eggs, and apologized to the hens, but far worse was when Sarah brought a chicken

222

from the coop for butchering. The first time she saw Joe's sweet grandmother twist the bird's neck, fling it down on a tree stump and chop its head off, Frances threw up. She blamed it on morning sickness, but her gut twisted every time she walked near the bloodied stump.

Stephanie jumped to her feet and clapped. "Git. Go on. Git!" Two black birds hopped from the cans of seeds. She stomped a foot and the crows finally took flight, landing on the roof of the house and cawing their displeasure. "A scarecrow should keep the birds out of the garden. But be on the lookout for rabbits."

"Scarecrow?" Frances frowned, her hand over her eyes as she looked up at Stephanie.

"I'm sure Mrs. Ferguson has a few around. Might need some new clothes. I can help. Gives me a reason to sew again." Stephanie smiled, clasping her hands together. "I know. I'll make something for your baby."

"Thank you." Frances grinned, Stephanie's enthusiasm contagious. It was rare to see Stephanie smile. Rare that she showed any emotion, good or bad, except during an experiment in chemistry. Frances hadn't expected to be friends with her. She didn't make her laugh like Christy, and Stephanie's interests were far different, but Frances could be herself with Stephanie. They talked of science, chemistry, literature, architecture, and their mothers. Their pragmatic, resourceful, no-nonsense mothers.

"Do you miss college?" Stephanie settled back on the ground, her bare legs stretched out beside the seed cans.

"Sometimes." Frances shrugged. "I miss reading. No time." She was glad the farm kept her busy. Kept her from thinking of Joe. The days went by quickly, but the nights were long and lonely. When she couldn't sleep, she sat by the window, twisting her ring, her eyes on the stars. She wrote Joe a letter every week, sometimes twice a week, using the special, one-sided forms for V-mail. She kept things light, aware that her letters would be opened and read by censors, telling Joe about the farm, or the weather, or how many times the baby kicked that day. When a letter came from Joe she would run to her bedroom and hold the envelope to her chest, closing her eyes, envisioning her husband putting his words on the page. She pictured him with a frown, his knuckles white as he gripped the pencil too tightly, just as he used to do when he sat next to her in the college chemistry lab. In her dream, he would turn to her and smile, showing off his dimple, his eyes as blue as the sky. His eyes would be green, like the pastures, in her next dream. His letters were always upbeat. Telling her about whatever village he happened to be in. He described the old buildings and a few of the villagers, but he never mentioned the fighting. But Frances knew. She read the newspapers. And every night, she, and Joe's father, grandmother, Uncle Bill and his wife Louise, gathered around the tall radio in the living room. It wasn't just for Joe that the Fergusons listened to the radio for news of the war. Joe's cousin, Todd, eighteen years old, left for the Pacific in March leaving his mother, Aunt Louise, devastated. Todd could have worked on the farm like his two older brothers, Bill Junior and Marvin, but he refused to use the essential industry exemption, saying there were enough Fergusons to keep the farm afloat.

Frances turned as a dusty black Ford pulled next to the house, Joe's Aunt Emily, and her two kids, Robert and Sheila jumping out.

"Hi, Aunt Frances," Sheila called as she skipped from the car. At twelve years old, Sheila was colt-like, her long arms and legs stick-thin. She dropped to the ground between Frances and Stephanie, quickly digging a hole and dropping a tomato plant in.

"This is my friend, Miss Kwolek," Frances said.

Stephanie nodded. "I've seen you in church. You can call me Stephanie."

Fourteen-year-old Robert ran in the house, the screen door slamming behind him.

"Found more of the kids' clothes from when they were babies," Emily said. She had all the distinctive Ferguson traits—tall, cocoa-colored hair, dimpled chin.

The screen door slammed again and Robert sauntered towards them. "Grandma said to get you girls moving. She wants this garden planted before fall comes around," he said, a hand tented over his eyes, a lopsided grin on his face.

"Maybe you should help plant the garden instead of milking today," Emily said.

"Aww," Robert whined. "I want to help with the milking. Look, Uncle Bill's bringing them in now."

A line of tawny cows, bells clanking, lumbered towards the barn for their afternoon milking. Robert chased after the herd and Emily shook her head, but said nothing, and plunged her hand into the tin with "cucumber" scratched on the side.

When the screen door slammed again an hour later, it was Joe's grandmother who came across the yard. At sixty-five, Sarah Ferguson was still tall, nearly Frances's height, but Joe said she used to be taller.

"Or maybe she just seemed taller when I was a kid," Joe had said with a laugh.

Sarah walked towards the garden with Rags, her elderly dog of wiry fur in a multitude of colors, trotting behind. A few stray strands of grey hair, escapees from the tight bun at the nape of her neck, blew across her tanned face as she peered into the cans of seeds. "Still some bean seeds left."

"Yes ma'am. One row left to plant," Stephanie said.

"You want to stay for supper, Miss Kwolek? We have plenty," Sarah said.

"Thank you, ma'am, but I need to get home." Stephanie rose and slapped her hands together, casting off the powdery soil.

"Let's wash up," Emily said and walked around the side of the house.

In the front yard, Sheila worked the pump's handle while the other women held their hands under the cool water and rubbed the gritty bar of Lava soap across their palms. There was a pump inside at the kitchen sink but Sarah instructed the family to wash up outside, keeping dirt, and people, out of her kitchen. Sarah was gracious to Frances, telling her to make herself at home, and Frances, for the most part, was settled in, but she still felt like an intruder in Sarah's kitchen.

"Robert. Say grace," Sarah said after they all settled at the long table in the dining room.

The minute "Amen" was uttered the room buzzed. Voices rose and fell, silverware clattered against plates heaped with food, and sweating pitchers of milk were passed. The frenzied suppertime at the farm reminded Frances of meals at the monastery, except there was talking at the Ferguson table. Lots of talking. She tried to follow all the conversations, but didn't join in, and spoke only when asked a question. It was Bill Junior's wife, Marion, who helped her through those first uncomfortable months and made Frances feel a part of the family. Marion was also a new addition to the Ferguson family, having married Bill Junior last summer. At twenty-four, Bill Junior, with prompting from his father and grandmother, decided to put his bachelor days behind him and wooed the petite, dark haired, doe-eyed Marion, just eighteen and working the counter at Jackson's Drug Store. Raised with five siblings, Marion held her own with the boisterous Ferguson clan.

Frances caught Marion's eye across the table, and Marion smiled, but it was a quick and tight smile that said she was still hurting. A second miscarriage two months ago left Marion heartbroken.

"Seven gallons today from Queenie," Bill said.

"Fike's wants more cream. John Fike said they can't make enough ice cream. Think we should start making our own?" Bill Junior asked.

"No," Bill Senior and Joe Senior said at the same time.

"I don't want a biscuit, Mom," Sheila said, shaking her head at the basket in her mother's hands.

"She's afraid of getting fat like her friend, Susie," Robert said, adding another slab of butter to his mashed potatoes.

"Go easy on that butter, Robert. Most people can't even get it these days," Aunt Emily said.

"No sugar in this week's rations," Sarah added.

"No gasoline, either," Bill grumbled.

"The horses are ready. I'll get the plow oiled tomorrow," Joe Senior said.

The talking never stopped, and there was plenty of laughter, too. Any disagreement would be quickly quelled by Sarah if the dissenting voices got too loud. Frances liked the meals, even though she didn't say much. During the few dinners she had with her husband at this table, she loved the way Joe jumped in the conversations, voicing his thoughts, his father and uncle teasing him, calling him a 'college boy with big ideas.'

The room fell silent when the phone rang. Robert jumped from his chair and ran to the living room.

"That darn phone. I don't know why you insisted I get one," Sarah said to Joe's father.

"Aunt Frances, it's for you," Robert said. "It's your mother."

The talking started again as Frances walked from the room. Her mother seldom called so she was apprehensive as she picked up the phone.

"Mom?"

"I'm fine, Sunshine," her mother said. "It's George. He died, and Russell banished me from the house."

CHAPTER TWENTY-SIX

June 1943
Wheeling, West Virginia

Martha sat straight-backed in the Pickett parlor watching Joan accept condolences from Mr. and Mrs. Harold Stevenson, longtime bank customers.

"Your father-in-law was a fine man," Harold said as he held Joan's hand.

"Yes, a fine man," Harold's wife echoed, her black hat bobbing in agreement.

Martha thought the woman's name was Carol but she had not been introduced. The couple turned from Joan and glanced at Martha, then moved into the hallway in search of food and drinks. After one more look at the clock, Martha decided twenty minutes was plenty. She slipped out the door and climbed to her bed on the third floor.

When George collapsed at the bank five days ago and was rushed to the hospital, Russell didn't call Martha until hours later. By the time she ran the ten blocks north to the hospital, George was gone, his body already at the undertaker. Joan took control of the funeral arrangements, and today, after George was buried, she insisted on this large gathering at the house.

It was hot on the top floor, as usual. Martha removed her hat and belt, rolled her stockings to her ankles and crawled beneath the sheet. Lying on her back, she stared at the window above her bed, occasional breezes ruffling the dresses in the doorless wardrobe, the rattle of the wood hangers lulling her to sleep.

"Martha, wake up," Joan said, jabbing a finger into Martha's arm.

Blinking perspiration from her eyes, Martha sat up. She ran the back of her hand across her brow and glared at Joan.

"You are needed downstairs. The lawyers are here. In the dining room." Joan turned and disappeared behind the wardrobe.

Her belt and stockings back in place, Martha made her way to the first floor. In the small lavatory, she splashed cool water on her face and leaned forward, searching the mirror. Searching for signs of sadness. Signs of grief. She knew what it looked like. When word came that Frederic died at the Battle of Cantigny, Martha had shut down. Denied it for weeks. Then there was anger followed by an overwhelming sadness. Frederic's mother had collapsed at the news. Never recovered. She died a few months later. "Spanish flu," the callous coal company doctor announced in the Albrecht's front room, a swatch of cloth held over his mouth. But everyone knew she died of a broken heart. The vacant look in Frederic's mother's eyes would haunt Martha forever. She took a step back from the mirror, straightened. George was dead but she felt nothing. Her shoulders squared, chin lifted, she walked into the dining room where Russell sat with two other men. The table, covered with trays of chicken salad sandwiches and cookies two hours ago, was now cluttered with documents and briefcases. The older of the two men looked up and nodded when Martha slid the doors open. Russell and the other man didn't acknowledge her. She sat in the chair furthest from her stepson.

"So, it's up to me?" Russell asked, leaning back in his chair and lacing his fingers across his vest, the lower buttons straining against his belly.

"Yes, since your brother is deceased," the younger man said.

Russell turned to Martha. "You are not named in my father's will. You can have the Hudson and your clothes, but I want you out. Tomorrow."

"Russell, I'm sure your father meant to provide for your stepmother," the older man said, glancing at Martha.

Russell dug into his pocket, tossing the contents on the table. "Here are some gas rations and twenty bucks." He turned his back and huddled with the younger man.

The older man averted his eyes, turning his attention to the documents in front of him. Martha stared at the back of Russell's head, watching a bead of sweat slip beneath his collar. His hair was thinning, she noted with satisfaction, he would be bald like his father. She scooped the cash and ration stamps into her hand and went to the library to call Frances. With an invitation to stay at the Ferguson Farm, she set about packing. After filling one small suitcase with undergarments, Martha opened her wardrobe and pulled dresses from the hangers, tossing them on the bed. She kneeled, digging in the bottom depths of the trousseau for her white Bible hidden under the shoes. It came with her from the Crittenton Home, each woman receiving one after memorizing the first thirteen chapters. She eased the photograph of her and Frederic in eighth grade from its place between Psalm Twenty Three and Twenty Four. Her four brothers were also in the photograph— the three tow-headed siblings standing in the third row, dark-haired Jakob sitting in the first row holding the edge of the chalkboard with "1912" and "Webster Hill" scrawled across the black slate. She moved the photograph closer, examined all the faces. Peter Doyle and his brother Patrick weren't in the photo—they had both quit school by then—but three of the young girls were Peter's sisters. She couldn't remember their names. Frances had asked about her aunt and uncles, and Martha did the best she could to describe her brothers and sister, but she never showed her daughter this photograph. The memory of Frederic was hers alone.

Her finger traced Frederic's face. She smiled, remembering the slope of his shoulders as he hunched over his desk at the small Webster Hill schoolhouse. Since she had been scribbling Frederic's name in her notebooks from the time she learned to write, it was comfortable to use "Albrecht" when she arrived at the Crittenton Home. She hadn't planned it, but when Dottie mistook Frederic for her baby's father, Martha thought, *why not?* She loved Frederic. They were to be married. He took her heart with him to his grave in France. She had cared for Peter, but her feelings were never what she felt for Frederic. Peter made her laugh, and he was a kind lover, his calloused hands always gentle. George was not a kind lover. His hands were soft—far softer than hers—but his touch was never gentle, always rough and demanding.

"I will send Mrs. Manning to assist you," Joan said. She stood at the top of the stairs, a cigarette clamped in one of her long holders.

Martha slid the photograph back between the pages and tucked the bible in the suitcase. She lowered the suitcase's lid, snapping the latches closed. "I don't need help." She opened the second, slightly larger suitcase and added a dress. She folded a blouse, then a skirt, refusing to meet Joan's gaze.

"I need to see what you are taking," Joan said. She moved to the bed and sorted through the dresses.

Now that she was leaving, now that she was free, Martha couldn't bring up enough anger to be bothered by Joan's actions. "I'm going to say goodbye to Judith," she said and hurried down the steps, the small suitcase in her hand. She stood in the nursery, looking around the room for the last time. She expected her parting to be bittersweet but if there were happy memories in this room, they remained hidden. As she kissed the toddler's sleeping head, she decided not to wait until tomorrow, choosing to leave as soon as she packed. After a night at Mrs. Roth's apartment, she would drive to the Ferguson farm the following day.

**

Early morning, Martha bade Mrs. Roth "goodbye" and climbed into her twelve-year old car. Armed with a map from Mrs. Roth's neighbor, she tussled with the gears and eased into the traffic on Market Street. As she cruised up Wheeling Hill, overtaking a trolley car trailing sparks, she realized this would be her last drive through the city. There was no reason to return. Unlike the nursery room at the Pickett house, this road did trigger memories. She remembered the feel of the bricks beneath her feet, before they went numb from the cold, as she ran to the monastery the night Frances was taken. She remembered every step she took beside this road on her lonely hikes for the year her daughter wasn't hers, her own mother's parting gift of hope the only thing keeping her upright. Patrick entered her thoughts, as did the smug young man guarding the juvenile judge's office. She would like to tell that judge what she thought of his justice system. Mother deSales' words of wisdom "some things are better left unsaid" came to her and she smiled, the kind nun one of the few bright spots in that miserable year. Her knuckles went white as she gripped the steering wheel, her anxiousness not easing until the city limits were behind. Traffic thinned and the scene outside the car transitioned from buildings to farmland, the grazing cows ignoring the passing cars. A train rumbled beside the road. The same train that first brought her to Wheeling, alone and frightened, more than twenty years ago. The landscape that chilly day in

December was barren and only a handful of cars passed by on the neighboring road, but today, the hills and trees were green, and despite gas rationing, a steady stream of cars traveled the highway.

After twenty miles, Martha signaled, and pulled into Grimes's Service Station, nosing the car next to one of two gas pumps. She had stopped at this station on her drives to and from Frances's college.

"Morning, ma'am," Mr. Grimes said and tipped his cap. He stood by Martha's open window in his usual attire—white shirt, dark pants, his cap sporting an orange globe. "Going to see your daughter?"

She smiled, touched that the man remembered her. "Yes."

"Glad to see the old Hudson is still running. Fill it up?"

"How much can I get with these?" Martha handed over the stamps from Russell.

He frowned. "These yours?"

"My stepson gave them to me."

"You got a ration book of your own?"

She dug in her pocketbook and passed her small book to Mr. Grimes.

His frown deepened as he flipped through the pages. "No stamps here for gas, ma'am."

"But I have to drive to New Kensington." Martha pulled out the twenty-dollar bill.

Eyeing the money, Mr. Grimes shook his head. "Ma'am, I'd like to help you out, you being a good customer over the years, but I could get in trouble." He looked down, nudging the toe of his boot against the front tire. "Even if I filled your tank you ain't going to make it to New Kensington on that tire, and I got no rubber to fix it."

The tire hissed and flattened as Martha stood by the bumper, watching. She raised her head, studying the road. It ran straight for a short length, then disappeared around a bend. "My husband just died." She turned and faced Mr. Grimes, her palm on the warm hood of the car. "This is everything I own. I have no home to return to."

Mr. Grimes pushed his hands into his pockets. "Come on inside, ma'am. Have a cold drink." He strode to the red cola machine by the door and slipped a coin in the slot, watching the jagged wheels squeal to life and release a captive bottle. With the metal opener hanging on a chain, he flipped the cap off and handed the chilled bottle to Martha. Inside, he pointed to a row of wood chairs along the front wall and disappeared up the stairs.

Martha sat, dabbing her face with her handkerchief, her thoughts rambling. They must have a phone here, but who could she call? No one at the Pickett house would help. She shook her head—returning to Wheeling was out of the question anyway. She could call Frances but her daughter was in no condition to drive.

Mr. Grimes returned, a plump, dark-haired woman trailing behind.

"I'm Betty Grimes." The woman said and sat beside Martha. "Bob tells me you've just lost your husband. I am very sorry."

Her chin lowered, Martha mumbled, "Thank you."

Betty put a hand on Martha's. "What's your name, honey?"

"Martha. Martha Albrecht." How easy it was for her to say "Albrecht," to truly put George Pickett behind. She raised her head, finding strength in the name.

"Where are you from, Mrs. Albrecht?"

"I've been in Wheeling for a time. Originally from Webster Hill," Martha said.

"Webster Hill?" Betty smiled and gave Martha's hand a pat. "That's not far from here. Had an aunt and uncle lived in that patch for a spell. You still got family there?"

Martha hesitated. Would her mother and father still be in Webster Hill? Yes, she decided, unable to imagine her parents moving anywhere. "I believe so," she said.

235

Betty called to her husband, lingering nearby, partially hidden behind a stack of oil cans. "Bob, has Shorty delivered today?"

"Ain't seen him yet."

"Shorty drives the cola truck," Betty said. "I've known him since grade school. He can take you to Webster Hill."

***

An hour later, the Hudson stowed behind Mr. Grimes's station, Martha was riding in a dusty truck with "Coca-Cola" in four-foot letters painted on the side.

"One mile to Claysville," Shorty said, nodding towards the mile marker cone. "Webster Hill is nine miles beyond."

Martha squinted out the smeared glass. *Claysville*. She wondered if they would pass the place where Peter died. The truck rocked and rattled, and Martha clung to the edge of the wood bench, her head pounding and her stomach lurching. The minute Betty Grimes said she could get her to Webster Hill, Martha tried to back out. But she had few options and relented. Seeing her mother would be nice, and she would like to see Jakob. She would even like to see Klara. But her father? As they passed over the stone s-bridge and the coal tipple came into view, Martha's throat tightened. She forced down a swallow filled with coal dust and regret.

"You can drop me here. At the company store," she said and climbed from the truck, her pocketbook in one hand, the small suitcase in the other. "Thank you."

Shorty called a final goodbye and pulled away, leaving her in a cloud of red. It was quiet. Too quiet. She frowned at the tipple, wondered why coal wasn't tumbling down the chute. She started walking, her feet remembering the way, the caustic smell familiar, strangely comforting. The school was larger, a brick addition on each side, swings and seesaws replacing the oak tree she once climbed with Frederic. Lincoln Street was narrower than she remembered, still covered with the infamous "red dog," the waste slag found on all coal patch roads. The houses were close together and seemed smaller, some whitewashed, others a weathered gray. Breathing heavy when she reached her childhood house, she paused and lowered her suitcase to the ground, eyeing the crumbling porch. The windows were open, no screens, and the house boards were bare and splintered. She knew immediately her parents no longer lived here, they would never let the house fall into neglect. The other side, the right side, of the house was also in disrepair, the railing where she and Frederic had spent countless hours was gone, one porch step missing, another broken in half. Once Frederic and his mother passed away, Frederic's father was forced to a one-bedroom house and the Olinski family moved in. A woman, her head wrapped in faded gingham, came out the right side door and stood on the porch. Martha studied her face, thinking it might be one of the Olinskis, but the woman was a stranger.

"I'm Martha Pickett. I used to live here." She pointed at the left side. "Kraus. I was Martha Kraus."

The woman closed one eye and tilted her head. "So, you the daughter left the patch. Thought you would be here for the funeral," she said.

"Funeral?"

"When your momma died."

CHAPTER TWENTY-SEVEN

June 1943
Webster Hill, Pennsylvania

After learning her sister still lived in the same house, Martha walked around the side of her childhood home, pausing by the back door, sadly regarding the weed-filled yard. The space had once been a garden, dense with tomatoes, cucumbers, cabbage, beans and beets. She could hear her siblings' arguments about whose turn it was to carry water from the pump to keep the crops growing in the hot summer sun, her voice usually the loudest. Her mother could silence them with a pointed finger. She tented a hand over her eyes and squinted at the coal shed, her stomach flipping as she remembered the day she told her father she was expecting. Knee-high thistles and quack grass scratched her legs, snagging her stockings, as she picked her way across the yard. At the back corner, just before the alley, she toed the pile of bricks that was once the Olinski's outdoor oven. The most delicious bread came from that oven, a mouth-watering smell filling the air whenever the bread was baking. The only smell today was coming from the outhouse, obviously still in use and in need of a good cleaning. Surprised by how much she was looking forward to seeing her sister, she picked up her pace, and came to abrupt halt. Klara was the one who told Patrick where Martha lived. If Klara had kept her mouth shut maybe Frances wouldn't have gone to the monastery. She pushed the anger aside, reminding herself it wasn't her sister's fault—the blame lay with Patrick.

Glazed with black oil, Pierce Street, where her sister lived, had been updated, no red slag, both sides bordered with concrete sidewalks. Klara's house had been whitewashed recently, her front door painted a glossy green to match the wood-slatted swing swaying on her side of the porch. Martha lowered her suitcase to the cement and patted her braid, twisted and rolled into a tight bun. She sucked in a breath, grasped the luggage handle again, and walked up the steps. Klara answered after two knocks.

"Martha," her sister said after a very long moment of staring, mouth hanging open.

Martha's mouth went dry. Although partially hidden behind black-framed eyeglasses, she recognized her sister's blue eyes, saw the judgment, the disappointment, and she was transported back to her teenaged self, running to Klara's house in the cold, hoping for kindness and understanding, receiving neither. Martha knew this was a bad idea.

"Martha," Klara repeated and stepped back from the door, eyeing the suitcase in Martha hands. "Come in," she finally said, her voice hoarse.

"Hallo, Klara." Martha managed a tentative smile. She looked down at the threshold, and with no other choice, stepped into the room. It was not as Martha remembered, the plaster walls papered in ivory and grey stripes, the worn floorboards covered with grey carpet. The mantle was still there but the fireplace below was closed with bricks. Martha walked to a long table pushed against the opposite wall and picked up a photograph of a toddler, one of the five framed pictures. "Paulie," Martha said.

Klara came to her side. "No one's called him that in years." She picked up another photograph. "These are his children, Steven and Rachel. They live in Canonsburg."

Martha studied Klara as she took the frame from her hand. Her sister had aged, her blond hair was streaked with gray, and she was heavier, her chiseled cheekbones flattened, the flowered fabric of her house dress snug across wide hips. She turned her attention to the photograph. "Your grandchildren." She smiled at the two fair-haired children, a beagle sitting between them.

"Yes," Klara said and picked up another frame. "And here's the third one. Maggie. Eleanor's first. A year old last month. She lives in Little Washington."

Martha sighed, remembering her niece as an infant herself the last time she saw her. She returned the frame to the table and tapped the phonograph with her index finger. She chuckled. "You finally got your record player." For much of their childhood, one of Edison's early phonographs sat on a shelf in the company store, gathering dust, since no one in the patch could afford the twenty-dollar price tag. When their mother took them to the store, Klara would run to the phonograph, saying someday her husband would buy it for her so they could dance the night away. "Mother always said you were a planner, just like her," Martha said.

Klara laughed. "Yes, and she called Karl Junior her fearless one, until Jakob took over that honor. Albert was the easy going one and Kristopher the quiet one."

"And me?" Martha asked.

"The smart one. A sharp mind and a sharp tongue, to match," Klara said. "Mother's words," she added.

Martha nodded. "I remember." She paused. "When did she die?"

"Four years ago. A stroke." Klara pointed to the tweed couch. "Have a seat. I'll make coffee."

Martha sat, her suitcase at her feet, and listened to her sister's movements in the kitchen, glass clinking, water running. She stood and walked to the doorway. "Looks much different." Her gaze swept over the gas

241

range and humming refrigerator, the white metal cabinets and beige linoleum. The smell of sauerkraut hung in the air.

Klara nodded. "We own our half now. Henry's done most of the work himself. Put a coal furnace in the basement, added a bathroom." She pointed to a closed door at the back of the room.

"Why did you tell Patrick Doyle where I was?" Martha blurted, her voice louder than she intended.

"Shush." Klara turned, a frown on her face. "Don't wake Father."

Martha was stunned. "Father?"

"Yes. He's upstairs, in the back bedroom."

Martha put a hand on her chest, the other on the door jamb, her legs rubbery. She stared at the stairs, expecting her father to appear, unsure what she might say.

Klara patted Martha's shoulder, their first touch. She leaned in close. "Don't worry, he won't come down. Can't come down." She straightened, let her hand fall to her side. "Black lung."

With a glance at the ceiling, Martha returned to the couch on quaking legs. *Her father, twenty feet away.* She watched Klara put a cup and saucer on the table in front of her but she didn't reach for it, not trusting her trembling hand to lift the cup without a spill. "Did he ever speak of me?" Martha whispered. "Ask about me or his grandchild?"

Klara sipped, lowered her cup to the saucer, and gave her head one shake. "Jakob mentioned you once at the supper table. He said 'Martha was the best pitcher in the family' during one of our who's the best arguments. Father pounded the table with his fist so hard the dishes rattled. Told us not to speak your name. Reminded us we had no sister."

Martha looked at the ceiling again, her hand going to her cheek, hearing, feeling, the sharp crack of her father's slap, and, once again, she was back to the day she was banished from the house. Banished from her family, no one taking a stand for her. She focused on her sister, anger simmering. She wanted to ask why Klara never wrote, why she turned her back on her, but Martha already knew the answer. Everything was black and white with her sister, always had been, always will be. In Klara's mind, Martha was the only one who did anything wrong. But was her sister so heartless that she wanted Martha punished? Is that why she spoke to Patrick? The thought made her breath catch. "What did Patrick Doyle say to you?" Martha asked.

Klara stiffened, taken aback by Martha's sharp tone. "He said he wanted to help you." Her eyes were wide behind the thick lenses. "I told him you were in Wheeling, and I remember he laughed. He was happy. Said he lived there, too, and was excited to meet his nephew or niece."

He was happy. Martha narrowed her eyes, shook her head. Patrick Doyle was about to ruin her life and he was happy. She picked up her cup and managed a sip. The coffee was strong, just like their mother's. More memories she didn't welcome.

"So, was it a nephew or niece?" Klara asked.

"What?" Martha frowned over the rim of her cup.

"Did you have a boy or girl?"

"About time you asked," Martha snapped. "A girl. I had—have—a girl. A beautiful daughter named Frances Hope." She pulled the suitcase on to her lap and flipped the latches, digging through her clothes to pull out a small, framed photograph. Frances, taken at her high school graduation. She passed it to Klara.

Klara took a brief look, handed it back. "She looks like you. Where is she now?"

Martha put the photo back into the suitcase, cushioned among her stockings and softest undergarments. She had just a handful of photographs of Frances, all taken at the academy, and only one of Randolph, his college graduation photo. They were

243

precious, more valued than anything George had given her throughout the years. Since space was tight in her suitcases, she left behind many of her dresses and jewelry, keeping only the diamond ring and ruby earrings, hoping they might be exchanged someday for cash. Slowly, softly, she told Klara the story of Frances, an abbreviated version, ending with her own aborted journey to New Kensington.

"Your car is broken?" Klara asked, glancing at Martha's suitcase.

"No, Klara, it just has a flat tire."

"Maybe Jakob can help," Klara said, biting her lip. "I think you can stay with him until your car is fixed. He has a spare room since Jakob Junior is overseas in the army."

Martha tried to picture her youngest brother as a grown man with a son fighting a war. "What about his wife? Will she mind?"

"She died years ago. Giving birth to Jakob Junior."

"He's never remarried?"

Klara shook her head, snorted. "No, but he's had plenty of offers. Lots of widows in a coal patch." She stood. "He is probably walking the line in front of the mine service garage. He's a supervisor at the garage, when they're working."

Martha frowned. "When they're working?"

"The strike?" Klara looked at Martha with narrowed eyes. "You don't know there's strike going on? Henry and his men walked off April twenty fourth. It's a nationwide strike, now."

"No, I didn't know." Martha admitted. She tried to remember the last time she read a newspaper or listened to the radio. George read his newspaper at the bank or the club and since the radio was in the parlor, where Joan spent her time, Martha avoided that room.

"Henry thinks it's going to be a long one," Klara said, crossing the room and yanking a scarf from the coat rack by the front door. "Lewis won't back down."

244

"Lewis?" Martha asked.

Klara gave Martha another dubious look. "John Lewis. President of the UMWA. United Mine Workers of..."

"I know what the UMWA is, Klara," Martha said.

Klara wound the scarf around her head and pushed the front door open, talking as she walked across the porch. "Lewis said the coal owners are using the war as an excuse to freeze wages. Says we have to stand up to Washington. President Roosevelt threatened to call out the troops to force the miners back to work."

"Hmm," Martha mumbled. Her feet hurt, her back ached, and she was hungry but she followed her sister out the door, suitcase in hand. She had never experienced a strike, although they were bantered about when she was young. She had heard the stories, disturbing stories, of miners beaten and killed during strikes, and of families forced from company houses, their furniture and clothing dumped into the streets by the coal police. She wondered if Jakob owned his house or if he could be evicted. "What about the other boys?" Martha asked as they went down the steps and started up the sidewalk. "Is Karl Junior still in the mine?"

"Yes, but he's in Kentucky. Been there five years now," Klara said. "Kristopher is dead. Mine collapse. Happened a few months before Mother died. I think that's what caused her stroke. You know Kristopher was always her favorite."

Their mother did baby Kristopher. Skinny and shy, he was often the target of the school bullies, seldom fighting back, letting Karl Junior or even young Jakob defend him. Martha's chest tightened. She too, had a soft spot for her quiet brother. "Did you keep any of his drawings?" she asked. Kristopher's sketches of trees and flowers were good, his portraits exceptional, but there was no place in Webster Hill for an artist.

"Mother did, but Father threw them away when he was clearing out the house to move in with us."

"What about Albert?"

Klara shrugged. "Last I heard he was in Detroit. Making cars. Left town in 1925 after an argument with Father. Hasn't been back since."

They turned on to Garfield Street, the road covered in red dog, and walked past the abandoned mule barn. The blacksmith's shop next door was also empty. The silent tipple loomed large, towering over a group of men milling around the gated gangway. Though the mine was idle, coal dust still layered the sidewalk, rooftops and trees. Martha brushed at the sleeve of her chambray dress, now speckled with black, her shoes a dusty orange.

"There's the garage." Klara pointed to a windowless, one-story building of corrugated steel, the padlocked door draped with a heavy chain and a "No Trespassing" sign. "Jakob!" she called and waved her arm.

Half a dozen men turned, paused their pacing. Martha recognized Jakob immediately. Same winsome grin, blue eyes with a mischievous glint, dark hair without a trace of gray. She suspected he was popular with widows of all ages.

Jakob lowered his hand-painted sign of "you can't dig coal with bayonets" to the ground and walked towards Martha, his smile widening. He slapped his chest and thighs, dust flying, and pulled her into a hug. "Mouthy Martha, you're as pretty as the day I left you at the trolley stand." He held her at arm's length, the grin unwavering.

Klara stepped closer, put a hand on Jakob's arm. "Martha's in trouble."

"Again? Little old, ain't you?" He looked at Martha's belly, let out a snigger.

Martha felt the heat rise to her cheeks, but she giggled, her youngest brother's laugh still infectious. She gave his arm a playful slap. "Not that kind of trouble, wise guy."

"It's her car," Klara said, unsmiling, and explained Martha's plight.

Jakob nodded. "I know Bob Grimes—good man. Worked with him on a company truck. I can get my hands on a couple gas rations, and," he turned slightly, shrugged a shoulder towards the picketing men. "Remy might be convinced to give up a bit of rubber." He put his hand on Martha's shoulder. "You stay with me for the night and I'll get you back on the road tomorrow."

Martha let out a long breath, the muscles in her neck loosening. She smiled, her first real smile since George died.

CHAPTER TWENTY-EIGHT

June 1943
New Kensington, Pennsylvania

It was late afternoon when Martha jerked to a stop on the Ferguson farm in the old Hudson. She waved out the open window at her daughter, standing in the middle of a garden in faded overalls. *No wonder she's in overalls, her belly is huge,* Martha thought, smiling. *Her grandchild.* When she learned the news, she had been glad, but her joy turned to disappointment. Disappointment that Frances wouldn't finish college, but most of her dismay was because she wouldn't be there for the birth. Martha didn't know when she would see the baby. But here she was. Truly free from George's rules. Free from Russell's ridicule, Joan's scorn. She fought tears as Frances ambled towards the car.

"Mom, I've been so worried," Frances said, panting slightly, a hand on the car. "Where have you been?"

"Sorry, Sunshine. Ran into a bit of trouble," Martha said. With no phone at Jakob's house, she couldn't tell Frances about her delay. She pushed the car door open and swung her feet to the ground. "You look wonderful."

"No, I don't." Frances laughed and wagged her hand towards the barn. "I'm as big as the cows."

Martha tried to pull her daughter into a hug but Frances was far too pregnant for anyone to wrap their arms around her. They both giggled as Frances turned from side to side, flaunting her full girth, finally laying her head on Martha's shoulder. When the screen door slammed, they separated, and watched Sarah Ferguson walk towards them, Rags limping behind.

"Joe's grandmother," Frances whispered.

"Mrs. Ferguson, very nice to meet you," Martha said. "I can't thank you enough for allowing me to stay here." She wrapped her arm around her Frances's shoulder. "And thank you, for taking such good care of my daughter."

"Our pleasure." Sarah nodded, cleared her throat. "My sympathies, Mrs. Pickett, on your loss. Burying two husbands is quite unfair."

"Yes," Martha said, cheeks heating. "Please, call me Martha."

Taking a step to the side, Sarah looked at the Hudson, eyeing the back seat heaped with clothes and baskets of belongings. "Bill and Joe will be here for lunch soon. They will get your things. And call me Sarah." She turned to Frances. "Show your mother where to wash up. I'm sure she would like to rest up before supper." Another nod, and she walked back to the house.

Martha watched her go. She liked Sarah Ferguson immediately. No pretense, her words forthright, a sincerity rarely found in the Pickett social circle. She looked down at the dog, leaning against Frances's leg. "Who's this?"

"Rags." Frances gave the grizzled muzzle a scratch. "I haven't told Joe about my real father," she said, her gaze on the dog, her voice soft. "Everyone just assumed you were married to him before he died. I didn't correct them."

Martha took in a long breath. *The past.* There was no escaping it. The sins of the father, she thought, remembering the reference in her white Bible of one generation passing their misdeeds to the next. *The sins of the mother.* She let out her breath, turned her attention to the green pastures, savoring the freshness.

So different from the coal patch. And the city. She pulled her attention from the field and followed her daughter.

At the pump, Frances worked the handle up and down, explaining the mechanism. Martha chuckled and put a hand on her daughter's. "I know how to use a pump, Sunshine."

"Right." Frances paused, then pointed to a small building squeezed between the house and the woodshed. "That's the bathroom." She lowered her voice. "An outhouse. Sorry."

"It's fine. I grew up with one," Martha said, hoping it was less fragrant than her brother's privy in Webster Hill. She rinsed her hands and followed Frances to the broad front porch, a collection of mismatched chairs scattered about. They stepped inside to a spacious living room, the long floorboards covered by oval rugs of braided rags, a large heating stove at the far end. The couch, a knitted afghan draped over the back, and several chairs were grouped around the floor-standing radio.

"The kitchen is through that door." Frances pointed to her left but stepped to her right. "Let's go this way, through the dining room."

Stretching nearly from one wall to the other, a long table with a low bench on each side filled the room. A steep staircase adjoined the dining room, the bare wood creaking beneath their feet as they climbed to the second floor, Frances leading her mother through the first door.

"This is my room," Frances said. She walked to a wood cradle in the corner, a rocking chair beside it. "Joe's grandfather made it. Sarah brought it down from the attic. She used it for Joe. And Joe's father. And Uncle Bill and Aunt Emily."

Martha ran her fingers along the cradle's smooth edge. "I have many names and faces to learn, don't I?" She smiled. Frances was finally surrounded by aunts and uncles, grandparents and cousins. Her grandchild would never be lonely, never wonder about his family. At least not about his father's side. Neither Klara nor Jakob mentioned another reunion and Martha didn't broach the idea. Klara didn't even come to see her off in the morning, saying a clipped goodbye when she left Martha yesterday afternoon with Jakob. Her evening with her brother was pleasant, he was a surprisingly good cook and did most of the talking, his passion for the miners' union obvious in his animated face and hands. Their conversation never turned to family. Jakob wasn't interested in Martha's life, he asked no questions about her child or husband, and when she inquired after Jakob Junior, he simply repeated what she had already learned—he was somewhere overseas. Martha doubted her nephews and niece knew she existed.

"Yes. It's a big family," Frances said. She pointed out the window. "That's Joe's father's house. And Uncle Bill and Aunt Louise's house, and behind it is Bill Junior's house. We're going to build a house on the other side. Near that big elm. Joe's going to hang a swing in it for the kids." She paused when her voice hitched.

"What's wrong, Sunshine?" Martha put her hand on her daughter's back, moving it in circles as she did when Frances was a small girl.

"Nothing." Frances shook her head. "Everything. The doctor said all is well, but I carry around this feeling of uneasiness and dread. A cranky chicken made me cry this morning. Then I found a hornworm on a tomato plant and cried again."

"I was the same way before you were born," Martha said. "Dottie had to calm me down more than once." In the months leading up to Frances's birth, Martha was able to keep her paralyzing thoughts at bay during the day, but at night she would lie awake, missing her mother, and wondering how she would raise a child on her own. She often poured out her fears and regrets to Dottie.

252

"Can't change what's been done, Martha," Dottie had said. "Tomorrow gonna come 'round no matter what you do, and I'm betting it'll be better than today."

Dottie once possessed unfettered optimism. Martha swallowed, pushing away the thoughts of her lost friend.

"Your bedroom is next door." Frances led her down the hall, stopping at the next doorway. "I know it's too warm for your quilt but I thought it would make you feel at home." She put her hand on Martha's arm. "Are you doing all right, Mom? Why did it take so long to get here?"

"I am fine, Sunshine," Martha said, moving to the bed and running her hand over the yellow bonnet on her childhood quilt. She sat, patting the bed beside her. "I had a flat tire, ended up in Webster Hill. Stayed at my brother's house. Saw my sister."

Frances's eyebrows shot up and her mouth fell open. "Bet they were surprised. Were they happy to see you?"

Martha nodded, chuckled. "Jakob, my brother, took it all in stride. Acted like it was last month he saw me, not twenty-five years ago. But, Klara, my sister, she was definitely surprised." Martha's smile slipped away. She wasn't going to tell her daughter that Klara was still narrow-minded, intolerant. That it was her sister who told her to give up her baby to save the family's reputation. In Klara's eyes, Frances was a mistake. "My sister never was one for surprises," Martha said. "Klara likes routine. Likes everything to be in its proper place. Just like my mother."

"What about your mother? Did you see her?" Frances asked.

Martha focused on the quilt, danced her fingertips across the blue bonnet. "She died four years ago."

"I'm sorry," Frances said. "And your father?"

"Has black lung and doesn't leave his bedroom." Martha kept her gaze on the quilt, moving her hand to the pink bonnet.

"I'm sorry," Frances repeated.

Martha raised her chin, looked her daughter in the eye. "Don't be. He refused to see me."

CHAPTER TWENTY-NINE

December 1943
New Kensington, Pennsylvania

It was noon on Christmas Day and the entire Ferguson family was packed into Sarah's house. The air was scented with cloves and rosemary, the dining room table creaking under a large ham, two roast chickens and platters of vegetables. The kitchen table was loaded with desserts. Martha hadn't stopped smiling since she got up at daybreak to help. It felt good to be surrounded by kind, generous people. People she had the luxury of calling family. She took a bite of melon and, surprised by the sweetness, let out a whoop.

Faces turned her way.

Martha laughed and blotted her chin with her napkin. "Delicious," she said. "I had no idea you could keep a melon this long."

"I planted it," Frances said, patting her chest with obvious pride.

"Frances planted the tomatoes, too," Sarah said. She sat at her customary place in the lone chair at the head of the table of adults, the youngsters creating their own fun at two makeshift tables in the living room. "Your daughter also did a good job weeding and keeping pests away, until she had to go and have this beautiful baby." Sarah winked at Frances and pinched the flushed cheek of six-month-old Joe Ferguson, the fourth, confined to a highchair wedged between his great grandmother and mother.

Baby Joe, as Sarah called him, was born on the last day of July at the hospital in town. Sarah thought the baby should come into the world at home with the help of a midwife, but Martha, recalling the unpleasantness of the Webster Hill midwife, lobbied for the hospital. She kept the Hudson fueled, never using it for herself, so it would be ready to take her daughter to town when the time came. Every day she kicked the tires, started the engine, and listened closely to the familiar rattle and hum. If anything were amiss, she would alert Joe Senior, who seemed able to fix anything. Frances's labor was short, but intense, Martha pacing outside the delivery room door. Baby Joe was born with a head full of caramel-colored curls and blue eyes, but his eyes had since settled into his dad's unique, ever-changing hazel hue. Martha smiled at her grandson. Today, his eyes were nearly as green as the Christmas sweater he wore, a sweater knitted by Sarah for her own grandson years ago.

"We bury the melons in the granary. Keeps them fresh," Joe Senior explained to Martha.

"We've always been lucky to have plenty of food at the farm," added Bill, sitting across from his brother. He leaned back in his chair and winked at his sister. "Including desserts."

Emily shook her head, but she was smiling. "I brought pumpkin pie. And cookies," she said. "But the cookies aren't up to my usual standards. I used molasses. No sugar. And I used oleo, instead of butter."

"Oleo? Psst," Sarah said, waving a dismissive hand in front of her face. "They say it's as good as butter but I don't believe it for a minute. It's not even yellow."

"Comes with yellow food coloring, Mom," Emily said. "I heard Carlson's Market is getting in a shipment of sugar tomorrow. I'll be first in line. Taking my tin of grease. You know you get two red stamps and four cents for each pound of grease now."

"Red—that includes fish, right?" Sarah asked. "Let me know if the market has haddock and I'll turn in my grease."

The government urged housewives to save excess cooking fat since it contained glycerin, and glycerin was needed to make explosives. Printed propaganda and advertisements on the radio touted, "a skillet of bacon grease is a little munitions factory." Sarah still did most of the cooking in her house but on those rare occasions when Martha fried ham or bacon, she made sure to save the leftover grease, straining it, since the propaganda warned, "no bacon bits in the bombs."

"What I really miss is coffee," said Emily with a loud sigh.

A collective moan filled the room, for once the entire table agreeing. Coffee drinkers could buy only a pound every five weeks.

"I brought a cake," Lucille, Bill's oldest daughter, said. A year younger than her brother, Bill Junior, Lucille was nearly as tall and had Junior's wavy, blond locks. She pushed one of her wayward curls from her eyes. "It's a recipe being shared at the plant. No eggs, no butter, no milk."

Bill shook his head, grimaced, and opened his mouth to protest but his wife, Louise, silenced him with a hand on his arm. "I'll try a piece, Lucille," she said. "Busy at the plant?"

Lucille, and her younger sister, Susan, lived in a small apartment in town, both working at the aluminum plant since their graduation from high school. She nodded. "They're moving workers around. Making us learn different jobs so when we're short in one area someone else can step in."

"I'm operating a crane this week," Susan said. She was the opposite of her sister, short and dark-haired.

"Martha is making filters and Marion is learning to weld."

Since Sarah needed little help around the house, Martha went to work at the aluminum plant in town a month after Little Joe was born. The plant, like most factories, was in desperate need of help since losing thousands of male employees to the war and Martha wanted, needed, to be useful. And just like she did when she went to work at the Pickett house as a young mother, she enjoyed having a purpose, and a small paycheck.

"Weld?" Bill Junior looked at his wife. "That sounds dangerous."

"We teach them how to be safe," Lucille said. She had worked her way up to supervisor, now overseeing the training department. "It's funny what some gals come to work in. High heels, rings and bracelets. We tell them to wear short sleeves, hair pulled up. And no jewelry to get caught in the machinery." She shook her head, curls bouncing, and smiled at Marion. "Marion's smart. Learns fast."

"That's why I married her. Smart and pretty." Bill Junior wrapped an arm around Marion. "But I still hate you working at the plant."

"But it's all right your sisters work there?" Susan said, eyebrows raised.

Lucille and her mother looked at Bill Junior, who turned towards his father.

"Don't look at me for help," Bill Senior said, throwing his hands up. "Not the first time that mouth of yours has gotten you in trouble."

Bill Junior looked up as Emily walked from the kitchen with a pie in each hand. "Perfect timing, Aunt Emily. Let's all have pie," he said, his sisters and mother groaning.

"What'd I miss?" Emily asked.

"Nothing worth repeating," Sarah said. "I will be happy when this war is over, and things can go back to normal."

"You mean us girls staying at home, Grandma?" Susan asked. "I was at the plant before the war and I want to stay on after."

"How about a husband and babies?" Sarah asked, frowning, eyes narrowed.

"Pretty slim pickings for husbands, Grandma."

Sarah flapped her hand. "All those boys will be coming back soon. Girl as pretty as you will find a fella. You too, Lucille," she said.

"Lucille has a fella."

"Be quiet, Susan," Lucille said, her voice a hiss.

"Mr. Bellson. At the plant." Susan aimed a wry smile at her sister.

"Benjamin Bellson? Why he's nearly as old as me," Bill Senior said. "Lost his wife a few years back. Horrible accident on Freeport Road."

"I just had dinner with him," Lucille said, glaring at her sister.

"I think he's too old for you," Louise said.

"I'm not getting any younger, Mom." Lucille pushed her curls back from her forehead, turned a triumphant smile towards Susan. "Unlike my sister, I do want kids."

"You don't want children, Susan?" Louise's mouth hung open.

"I don't know, Mother. Maybe. Someday." Susan's cheeks bloomed crimson, head drooping, attention on her slice of pie.

With far less conservation, dessert was over in minutes.

Sarah stood and carried her plate into the kitchen, the other women following. Sarah orchestrated the clean-up, quick and efficient with eight pair of hands, and filled two baskets with eggs, milk and butter. "For Stephanie and her mother," she said, passing a basket to Martha.

Frances insisted that Martha go with her today to Stephanie's, house. "I want you to meet her mother. I

259

know you two will hit it off," Frances had said that morning.

Martha agreed, although she would have preferred to spend a quiet afternoon reading. She liked Stephanie, although she was a tad serious, especially when compared to Christy. Stephanie visited nearly every weekend and she and Frances had long conversations composed of words Martha couldn't pronounce. When Stephanie's remarks turned to college, Martha could see the yearning in her daughter's eyes and she still held out hope that Frances would someday return to school.

Sarah handed the other basket to Marion as a present for her folks, and Marion, Martha, Frances, with Baby Joe in her arms, climbed into the delivery truck for the fifteen-minute ride into town.

"Pick you up in two hours," Bill Junior said to Martha as he pulled the truck to the curb in front of the Kwolek house.

Martha waved at the truck, turned toward the house when the door opened.

"Merry Christmas," Stephanie called from her porch. She ran down the sidewalk and encouraged Baby Joe into her arms. "I loooove your sweater," she cooed, prompting a giggle from the baby.

Inside the small house, Martha lowered the basket to the floor and walked to the squat pine adorned with strands of gold fabric and homemade decorations. It made her think of the sparse trees she had decorated at the Pike Street apartment with her own crude creations. Two of her ornaments, a horse made of clothespins and brown yarn, and a red sled created from popsicle sticks, survived her move to the Pickett house but the humble ornaments were never displayed next to Ruth Pickett's hand-blown glass bulbs. Once Joan took over the Christmas decorating, the trees grew more embellished with new bulbs commissioned every year to match Joan's color scheme. Martha's smile faded. In her haste to leave the Pickett house, she had left the homemade horse and sled behind. She didn't think often of that house, or its occupants, surprised at how easily the years with George and Russell became distant memories, no longer able to hurt or haunt her. She looked around the cramped room. The Pickett parlor would be poshly decorated and filled with fashionable people. Her smile returned. No question, she would rather be here, in a modest room filled with love.

Snatching a small bundle wrapped in red fabric from under the tree, Stephanie handed it to Frances. "For Baby Joe. My mother and I made it."

Frances, sitting on the couch, pulled on the raw edges of the fabric wrap and held up a miniature jacket of plaid wool with a matching cap.

"You like?" Nellie Kwolek, Stephanie's mother, stood at the doorway.

"Very much," Frances said, running her hand down the front of the jacket, fingering each small button covered with brown leather. A matching button topped the small cap. She looked up at Martha, her eyes misting. "This is my mother, Mrs. Kwolek. Martha."

Martha smiled a greeting and took the shrunken jacket from her daughter's hand. "Beautiful," she said. Frances had told her that Stephanie's mother was an exceptional seamstress, bringing the talent with her from her native Poland. She was right. The stitches on the jacket were perfect, better than any store-bought garment. Martha returned the jacket to Frances and retrieved the basket she left by the door. "For you," she said, and passed the basket to Nellie, noting the woman's knotted knuckles and calloused hands. Martha didn't know what Nellie did at the aluminum plant but whatever the tasks, she knew the conditions were harsh, the hours long. Her back pained and her hands were raw from just four months at the plant so her heart ached for Nellie who had been working there more than ten years, forced into a factory job when she became a widow.

Nellie peeked under the white cloth covering the basket and squealed. "Butter! Eggs and milk, too. I haven't had an egg in weeks. Thank you." She looked up, eyes welling. "We will have milk with the chalka I made this morning."

The minute the word came out of Nellie's mouth, Martha could smell the sweet bread, remembering ancient Mrs. Olinski sliding fresh loaves from the humped oven in their Webster Hill backyard. What became of the Olinski family, she wondered, berating herself that she never thought to ask Klara.

Martha returned to the tree, rubbing the needles between her fingers, releasing the pine scent. "Your tree is lovely," she said.

"Thank you. My husband, John, he made the decorations." Nellie sat on the couch beside Frances, wagged her fingers at Baby Joe. "John liked to collect leaves and flowers and seeds."

Stephanie moved beside Martha, pointing at an owl fashioned out of pinecones. "That's my favorite," she said. "I used to walk the woods with my father. He came home from the steel mill gloomy, said he needed a walk to cheer up. Said he was shedding his steelworker skin, like the snakes shed their skins every spring. I still have some of those skins in my bedroom."

"*Niesmak!*" Nellie said, her voice sharp but her mouth turned up, her eyes twinkling. "I did not like those skins. Your father scared me with them."

Martha looked at Frances. She was sorry her daughter didn't have any happy memories of her father to share. Peter would have been a good father. A good provider. And he would have adored Frances. Their home would have been filled with laughter. And singing. Peter loved to sing. *Patrick, too.* She couldn't think of Peter without Patrick clouding her memories.

"Come," Nellie stood. "Let's eat."

Though she wasn't hungry, Martha followed her to the kitchen and settled into a chair just as Stephanie's seventeen-year-old brother, Stanley, burst through the back door, a block of ice on his shoulder.

"Twenty pounds. This should last until Monday, Mother," he said, opening the top of the ice box and sliding the block inside. He turned, noticing Martha.

"This is Frances's mother, Mrs. Pickett," Nellie said.

Martha smiled, in spite of the "Mrs. Pickett" tag.

"Nice to meet you," Stanley said. He tossed the cardboard ice card on the table. "Won't need this anymore. We're finally getting a refrigerator. I think we're the last house in town to get one." He also tossed a lumpy burlap bag on the table. "Butternuts. Not the same as chestnuts but that's all I could find, Mom." He stuffed a chunk of bread in his mouth and walked from the room, calling out a greeting to Frances.

Nellie looked at the doorway, her eyes filling. "I worry so about my Stanley. I pray war is over before they can take him from me."

Not wanting to meet Nellie's eyes, Martha concentrated on her slice of chalka. *War.* Two young men she loved were lost to wars. Randolph was officially classified as "Missing in Action" but Martha didn't expect to see him again. Lily, on the other hand, would not give up and traveled to London, determined to report on the war, and look for Randolph. So far, she had been disappointed in both attempts, her letters becoming less hopeful, bitterness pushing through. Martha didn't understand Lily's desire to write about the war. She certainly didn't need another war story. The radio was full of them, *Life Magazine* thick with photographs of dead soldiers and vacant-eyed refugees. Every day, she read in the *Dispatch* the names of the town's soldiers who died, many of the last names now familiar. When working the line at the factory, or in the market, or at church, she would look at the faces, wondering who's lost a son, or a husband, or a father, and her heart skipping when she thought, who's next?

She turned, catching a glimpse of Frances on the couch. What would become of her daughter if Joe didn't return? Would she be left a shell, like Frederic's mother, a little more of her slipping away each day? She leaned back and looked at her grandson, sound asleep in his mother's arms. The tightness in her chest eased. Frances would survive for her son's sake; children made you stronger than you ever thought possible.

CHAPTER THIRTY

October 1945
New Kensington, Pennsylvania

Baby Joe was a typical toddler. He babbled non-stop when he was awake, and if he wasn't running on his stubby legs, he was fidgeting in his chair. Now thirty pounds, he was a load for Frances and the crowded Penn Station had captured the two-year-old's curiosity. He kicked and wiggled in Frances's arms, begging to be put down.

"Here. Let me hold him," Joe's father said, pulling the toddler from Frances.

Her fingers wrapped around her son's ankle, Frances squeezed, as much to halt Baby Joe's kicks, as to calm her quaking hand. Her entire body was shaking. Her husband was coming home. Joe made it through the war.

***

Gathered around the radio five months ago listening to President Truman announce victory in Europe, Joe Senior had let out a bellow that sent Baby Joe running from the room. Frances wept as her mother chased after the toddler and Sarah bowed her head in silent thanks. Bill, Louise and Bill Junior cheered. The room quieted as the president reminded, "our victory is only half over." But people couldn't contain their jubilation. Thousands gathered in New York's Times Square and celebrations took place across the country. In New Kensington, church bells rang, stores closed and people danced in the streets. Frances was finally able to sleep through an entire night and, during her waking hours, she couldn't stop smiling. A month later her high spirits were dashed when she learned Joe was headed to the Pacific. Frances turned her disappointment inward but Sarah had no intention of keeping her dismay to herself. She was angry.

"Three years is enough. My grandson needs to come home," Sarah said, as the family gathered for a Sunday supper. She glanced around the table, her eyes locking on Louise's. "Any word from Todd?"

Louise shook her head.

Sarah stood so quickly her chair toppled over. Nobody said a word as she stomped to the kitchen, leaving her upturned chair on the floor. Frances released her son from his highchair and looked at her mother. "Will you take the baby?"

"I got him. Come here, Baby Joe," Joe Senior said. He swept the toddler up and moved into the living room.

A moment later, static, then voices spilled from the radio.

"I'll get the dishes tonight," Martha said, nudging Louise towards the living room.

Her hands full of plates and bowls, Frances followed her mother into the kitchen. Despite the distressing news, Frances smiled at her mother. Having her here had kept Frances upright, kept her from wallowing in self-pity. The Ferguson's were kind, welcoming, doing their best to make her feel a part of the family, but Frances hadn't realized how much she missed her mother until the day Martha drove onto the farm. A great weight was lifted from her chest that day and

Frances found herself humming verses she last sang at the monastery.

Sarah shook her head at the plates, several with food still on them. "Rags would have made out very well tonight. Look at all these scraps."

Two weeks earlier, Sarah had buried her beloved dog. Frances tried to help but Sarah turned her away. When she expressed concern, Joe Senior brushed it off.

"That's the third dog she's buried," he said with a shrug. "Always insists on doing it herself. Guess it's her way of saying 'goodbye.'"

The three women worked in the kitchen in silence, the sounds of the radio competing with the crickets' chorus spilling through the screen door. Frances and Martha stood at the sink, their backs towards the table where Sarah poured applesauce into wide-mouthed jars. When glass shattered on the floor, Frances and Martha turned to find Sarah slumped at the table, her lifeless eyes gone dark.

Joe Senior and Emily decided they didn't want the news of Sarah's passing shared with their sons while they were still at war. Didn't want their boys learning the news in a letter. "Better to tell them in person," Joe Senior said. "It'll soften the blow." The rest of the Ferguson's agreed. Frances did not, but she kept her opinion to herself, going along with their wishes, as always. Stoic at the church and cemetery after Sarah's funeral, Frances sobbed that night after Baby Joe was asleep. She wept for her son, who would not remember his great-grandmother. Wept for herself. She would miss Sarah's unconditional affection and wise advice, her calming aura. But, mostly, she wept for her husband. Every letter she received from Joe mentioned Sarah, he never failed to ask about his grandmother. He would be heartbroken.

Two months after Sarah died, Japan surrendered. Another two months passed before Joe boarded a ship for America. He called Frances from New York to tell her when his train would be arriving in Pittsburgh, the sound of his voice sending her to her knees and she alternately laughed and cried during the brief conversation. Joe said there was a line a mile long waiting to use the phone and he ended the call with a hushed "I love you." Her hand shook far too much to hold a pen so, between hiccups and snuffles, she relayed the details to Joe's father to record, but he dismissed Joe's plan of taking the train from Pittsburgh to New Kensington and announced that he would take Frances and Baby Joe in the delivery truck to greet Joe at the Pittsburgh station.

***

"He's going to be surprised to see us," Joe Senior said, his eyes scanning the platform.

Frances nodded. She had played the reunion scene over and over in her mind, vowing to be strong, keep her emotions in check, but when the doors of the train opened and a crowd of soldiers surged on to the platform, Frances panicked. *Maybe I won't recognize my husband? Maybe he won't recognize me?* Her father-in-law tensed and she heard him call Joe's name, but she remained frozen, people swarming, jostling, Baby Joe whimpering. A solider stepped in front of her and she stepped back as the man's hand reached for her.

"Joe?" she mouthed. If hadn't been for his dimple and crooked smile, Frances wouldn't have recognized her husband. He was thin, his face sharp angles and hollows, the lines at the corners of his mouth etched deep, but it was his eyes that had changed the most. The sparkle was gone, replaced by a wariness that made the hair on the back of her neck prickle, made her want to turn around and search for the danger his eyes saw. Her hand was ripped from her son's ankle as Joe pulled her forward, crushing his lips to hers. She tasted salty tears, and the tang of blood. Parting, she touched her tongue to her split lip and introduced her husband to his son.

Joe leaned down, tapped his fingertip on Baby Joe's foot. "Hello."

The toddler turned his head, burying his face in his grandfather's chest, twisting a handful of plaid flannel in his small fist.

Joe Senior patted the toddler's head and smiled, his lopsided grin mimicking Joe's. "You're looking well, Son," he said.

"You too, Dad." Joe's voice was barely audible above the din on the platform.

Frances took Baby Joe into her arms and nudged her father-in-law towards Joe. She dug in her pocket for her handkerchief and blotted her bleeding lip as the two men embraced, Joe patting his father's back with one hand, his duffle bag in the other.

"I didn't expect this welcome," Joe said as he took a step back, giving his eyes a quick swipe with his sleeve.

Joe Senior shrugged, his eyes moist, his grin fixed. He put a hand on Frances's back. "Let's go home."

They fought their way through the boisterous mob, Frances moving her son to her other hip.

"You want me to carry him?" Joe asked.

She shook her head. "He can be shy with strangers." Frances regretted her words when Joe's face clouded. Every day, since her son was born, she had shown him a photograph of Joe. "This is Daddy," she said. "Just like in the picture, honey." She looked up at Joe. "Your high school graduation picture. Your grandmother gave it to me." Her heart skipped, inwardly admonishing herself for mentioning Sarah.

"He'll warm up to you, Son. Give it time," Joe Senior said. "Here, I'll take him." He extended his arms and Baby Joe crawled into them.

"He looks like you," Joe said to Frances, slipping his arm around her waist. He chuckled. "I'm glad."

Frances smiled. "He's got your eyes."

"Grandma's eyes," Joe said. "Can't wait to see her."

She glanced at her father-in-law, who gave his head a quick shake. Her smile faded and perspiration dotted her upper lip, stinging when it dripped into the small split. The deceit of Sarah's death made Frances uneasy as she knew when the truth came out it would be painful.

As they neared the truck, Joe Senior dug the keys from his pocket and dangled them in Joe's face. "You want to drive?" He handed Baby Joe back to Frances.

Joe shook his head. "Haven't driven since I left. Probably a little rusty." He heaved his duffle bag into the truck and helped Frances inside, Baby Joe clinging to her neck. He slid in next to her and pulled the door closed, cranking the window open and taking a deep breath. "I dreamed about these hills." The truck lurched forward and Joe turned from the window. "How's the farm doing, Dad?"

"Good," Joe Senior said. "Hate to say it, but we've prospered."

During the war, the government urged Americans to drink more milk since meat was scarce, and ice cream was promoted as an alternative to sugary desserts. Dairy farms across the country were thriving.

"Does that mean Grandma will finally put in a bathroom at her house?" Joe prodded Frances's arm with his elbow. "How are you getting along with the outhouse?"

Frances felt her cheeks burn. "Fine." In truth, she immensely disliked the outhouse, especially when the temperatures dipped below freezing. She was looking forward to their new house, with an indoor bathroom, but she had resigned herself to one more winter in the outhouse since their home wouldn't be built until spring. Her mother didn't seem to mind the outhouse nearly as much as she did. She glanced at Joe, wondering how he felt about her mother living with them. For their new house, he had proposed a large living room and dining room, wrote about the wide porch and big yard he had in mind, but he never mentioned the number of bedrooms, or the size of the kitchen.

"We put electric in the milk shed. Refrigerated tanks, now," Joe Senior said. "Bill Junior wants to make ice cream. It's very popular. Folks were aching for something sweet."

"Hmm," Joe said, his face toward the open window. He turned, took Frances hand in his and brought it to his lips. "Frances wrote me about cakes made without sugar. Has Grandma found a way to bake her pies without sugar?" He dropped Frances's hand and rubbed his palms together, Baby Joe raising his head at the raspy sound. "I'm home just in time for apple pie season."

Frances refused to look at her father-in-law, keeping her face on her son's curls. His grandmother's death was going to ruin his homecoming. She wished she had followed her heart for once and let him know. He wasn't a child. He could have handled the news, would have appreciated the time to absorb the shock before facing his waiting family.

"Son," Joe Senior said, his voice shaking, his weathered hands squeezing the steering wheel. He cleared his throat and tried again. "Son, I'm sorry to tell you...your grandmother is gone. She died in June."

"What?" Joe stiffened and turned in his seat, dark eyes glaring at Frances. "Why didn't you tell me?"

Startled, Baby Joe dropped his face to Frances's chest, his arms wrapped around her neck. She loosened her son's grip, patted his head, hesitating, seeking the right words. "We, ah, I, didn't want you..."

"I told her not to," Joe Senior said. "We didn't tell you or Todd." He sighed. "Your grandmother died quick. At home, just as she wanted."

Joe gave Frances another look, one she couldn't read, and pulled a pack of Lucky Strikes from his pocket. He faced forward and shook out a cigarette.

Her mouth fell open—she had never seen her husband smoke—but she closed it without saying a word.

The smell reminded her of Russell, her sloven stepbrother seldom without a cigarette, overflowing ashtrays his calling card.

"Any news on Todd?" Joe asked, face still forward, smoke circling.

"He'll be home by Christmas," Joe Senior said.

Joe finished his cigarette, lit another, turned towards the open window. Baby Joe napped, his body a dead weight, Frances's legs going numb. She wanted to fill the awkward silence, but she was tongue-tied and apprehensive, feeling as if she was sitting next to a stranger.

***

They arrived at the farm to dozens of family members, clapping and cheering. Joe barely got his feet on the ground before Lucille, seven months pregnant, pushed into his arms.

"Good golly, Lulu, I can barely get my arms around you!" Joe said.

"Looks like she gained all the weight you lost." Uncle Bill laughed and pulled Joe into an embrace.

Aunt Louise and Aunt Emily moved in, hugging Joe at the same time.

Emily stepped back, wiped her eyes and nudged her fourteen-year-old daughter forward. "Sheila, say hello to your cousin."

Still rail thin, with long arms and legs, Sheila nodded a shy hello.

"Even my husband took time off today," Emily said. She pointed at her husband in his fireman's uniform, his arm raised in a salute.

Several other relatives and friends on the porch, aged eight to eighty, waved as Bill Junior and his brother Marvin, his one-year-old in his arms, descended the steps.

Joe lay a hand on Marvin's shoulder. "Congratulations on your son," he said and grinned at Bill Junior. "Your turn, Junior." He slapped his red-faced cousin on the back.

Frances stood to the side, Baby Joe's hand in hers. Her son sucked on his thumb, his small brow puckered, watching his familiar relatives enthusiastically greet a man he'd never met before. She lifted the confused toddler into her arms, patting his back. Her eyes found her mother's, standing on the porch among the crowd, waiting patiently. This would be the first time her mother and Joe met. Would she like him? Would he like her? Martha charmed the other Fergusons, talking and laughing as if she had known them all her life so she pushed her concerns aside as her mother moved down the stairs, coming to a stop in front of Joe.

"Hello. I'm Martha," she said and spread her arms.

After just the slightest hesitation, Joe stepped into them.

Frances let out a breath and pointed. "See, your grandma just met your daddy. And she likes him." She kissed Baby Joe's forehead and walked towards the house.

"Let's eat," Martha said, looping her arm through Joe's.

Frances swallowed, a sudden sadness tightening her throat. Those would have been Sarah's first words. Joe's grandmother believed a full belly was fundamental. Always generous with the farm's bounty, a hungry soul was never turned away from Sarah Ferguson's table.

Joe stopped at the door to the dining room, shaking his head at the food-laden table, a tall pitcher of milk at each end. "This sure beats c-rations," he said.

The family filed in behind him, jockeying for seats, but leaving the chair at the head of the table empty.

CHAPTER THIRTY-ONE

October 1945
New Kensington, Pennsylvania

Frances sat on the couch in the living room of the farmhouse, Baby Joe asleep in her lap and Joe beside her. It was early evening, Joe Senior the only one remaining of the boisterous Ferguson welcoming crew and he seemed reluctant to leave. He sat in the chair closest to the couch, reaching out, touching Joe's arm whenever he spoke, as if making sure Joe was real.

Martha walked in from the kitchen. "Let me take Baby Joe upstairs," she said to Frances. The toddler let out a whimper as she pulled him into her arms but he settled his head on her shoulder without opening his eyes.

Joe Senior patted the arms of his chair. "Guess I better be going, too." He stood, laying his hand on Joe's shoulder. "Good to have you home, Son. See you in the morning." He walked to the dining room door, paused, turned and gave Joe one more look before rounding the corner.

"Just you and me," Joe said to Frances. He pushed to his feet, retrieved his duffel bag, and bounded up the stairs.

Frances followed, her body tense with nerves and anticipation. "That's usually where Baby Joe's crib is," she said, flapping her hand towards the corner of the bedroom. She and her mother had pulled the crib into Martha's bedroom that morning.

Joe sat on the bed and dug into the mouth of his bag, pulling out a stuffed bear. "I think our son is too old for this. He's not a baby. I'm going to call him 'Little Joe.'"

She started to say it was his grandmother who gave his son the nickname, but closed her mouth and nodded, remaining rooted at the doorway.

He patted the bed. "Come here. Close the door. This is for you," he said, handing her a small box with a red bow.

Hands shaking, she worked to untie the ribbon. "Perfume!" She held the delicate bottle as if it were a small bird and pulled the stopper. "It smells wonderful. Lilac. Like the bush out back."

"Is that the one by the outhouse?" He frowned. "Great. Now I'll think of the outhouse every time I smell it. Bad choice."

"No. It's lovely. Thank you." She leaned to kiss him but he bent forward, pulling more items from his bag.

"I have candy for your mother. And this was for Grandma." He put a small box on the bed between them. "It's yours now." He shrugged. "Or give it to your mother."

Inside was a tortoise hair comb. "It's beautiful," Frances said, her voice hitching. She pictured the comb in Sarah's silver hair.

Joe dragged his duffel to the bureau and opened a drawer. It was full. He opened the next drawer. He opened all the drawers to find each bursting with clothes.

"They're Baby Joe's," she explained, jumping to her feet and pulling small shirts from the drawer, tossing

276

them on a chair. She reached for Joe's duffel, crying out when he snared her wrist.

"I'll get it," he said, releasing her arm. "How can a two-year-old have so many clothes?"

"Hand-me-downs from Aunt Emily. And gifts. Stephanie and her mother made clothes for the baby, too." As she rubbed her wrist, glancing at her husband's profile from the corner of her eye, she had the same troubling feeling as in the ride home from the train station that he was a stranger.

"Stephanie Kwolek?" he asked. "She wrote to me. We got letters from lots of gals. She still in college?"

"Yes. Graduates next year." She watched in horror as Joe reached for the closet door. "Wait!" she called, knowing the cramped closet was more precariously jammed than the overflowing dresser drawers.

"What the hell!" Joe said, taking a quick step back.

Half a dozen cigar boxes tumbled out, letters spilling to the floor. She dropped to her knees at Joe's feet, gathering the envelopes and stuffing them back into the frayed boxes. Frances had first discovered the colorful containers in Mickey's apartment when she was a child. Emblazoned with the navy and orange stogie logo where Dottie worked, Mickey filled his box with marbles, pebbles and spin tops, his mother keeping one by the stove for matches, thread and scissors. Salvaged from the stogie factory's rejects pile, Dottie brought one home for Frances to fill with crayons, and, eventually, stacks of the boxes could be found in both apartments on Pike Street, filled with everything from clothespins and yarn, to scraps of paper with scribbled recipes. The humble boxes survived Martha's move to the Pickett house and Frances took them when she left the house for the final time.

Joe plucked an envelope from her hand and scowled. The letter was from him. He let it fall to the floor. "Get rid of them. I don't need reminders of where I've been." Turning away, he unbuttoned his shirt and sat on the bed, pulling his trousers off and draping them and his shirt over the headboard. In his boxer shorts, he sat on the bed and tugged his undershirt over his head and smiled, motioning Frances towards him.

She stepped between his knees, fumbling with the buttons on her blouse.

With a finger he raised her chin. "Hello, Mrs. Ferguson." He eased her skirt to her ankles and slid his hand under her slip, running his fingertips up her leg. His smile faded into a frown. "No stockings?"

She shook her head. "They're hard to get so we paint the line on. See?" She gave her finger a lick and rubbed at the black line painted down the back of her leg. She turned off the lamp.

"Turn that back on," he said, his voice sharp. "I want to see you."

"Shush. Baby Joe is next door." Frances held her breath, hoping her son didn't wake but she heard his first, faint cry and knew it would get louder. Her mother's muffled voice, trying to comfort the toddler, carried through the wall, but the wails continued. Baby Joe was used to sleeping in his mother's bed.

"I'll be back." Frances stepped into her skirt and buttoned her blouse. Ten minutes later she returned to find Joe stretched out under the covers. When he lifted the linens, her breath hitched at his nakedness. She undressed and slipped between the sheets.

"You are so beautiful," he said, his hands roaming. His thumb found her nipple, and she responded with a small cry. He silenced her with a rough hand over her mouth. "Don't wake the baby again," he said, his hand still over her mouth as he tried to enter her. After several failed attempts, he rolled to his back, arm across his eyes. "Guess I'm tired."

"It has been a long day," Frances whispered, running the tip of her tongue over her aching lip. Joe didn't respond. She lay in the darkness, wondering what she did wrong, her body craving the same pleasure and tenderness as her brief honeymoon. She wanted to touch him, talk to him, but he turned on his side, away from her. Tomorrow night will be better, she told herself. It wasn't. And the next night was even worse, Joe stalking from the room, Frances listening to his footsteps on the stairs. She slipped her nightgown over her head and padded to the window. It was dark, the sliver of moon shrouded in thick clouds, but she finally spotted the glowing tip of her husband's cigarette. She switched on the lamp and stared at the mirror hanging over the dresser. Face inches from the silvered glass, she patted her cheeks, pulled the skin taut. She combed her fingers through her thick hair, the red-gold tresses kinked from the day's plaiting. Maybe it was time to get it cut and curled into one of the more fashionable styles, she thought. She lifted her nightgown and stared at her body, a finger tracing the tracks stretched across her belly. With a sigh, she let the nightgown fall, and turned off the light. When Joe returned to bed twenty minutes later, she stayed curled on her side, pretending to be asleep.

***

In the morning, Frances awoke to an empty bed. She dressed and went downstairs, expecting to find Joe in the kitchen, but it was her mother she found, pushing split wood into the stove. Dressed in overalls, her thick plait wrapped around her head and covered by a red bandana knotted at her forehead, Martha was ready for her day at the factory.

"Good morning." Her mother smiled. "Joe awake?"

"Yes. He must be outside," Frances said, not meeting her mother's gaze. "Baby Joe, ah Little Joe, still sleeping?"

Martha nodded. The back door opened and Joe and his father walked in, followed by Bill Junior. Joe's mouth fell open when he saw Martha's attire.

279

She laughed and tugged at her bandana. "Working at the aluminum plant today."

"But not much longer, thank goodness," Joe Senior said. "Next week will be the last for Martha and Marion at the plant. Now that the boys are coming home they can take their jobs back."

"What about Susan?" Joe asked.

"She was there before the war, wants to stay on," Martha said, opening the oven door and pulling out two round pans of golden biscuits. "Frances, take that ham off the stove."

"I got it," Joe said. He lifted the iron skillet and dumped the ham onto the platter in Frances's hands. His fingertips brushed hers as he took the large dish from her and he gave her a quick smile.

Frances followed Joe into the dining room, pausing at the bottom of the stairs, her ear tuned to sounds of her son. Hearing none, she slipped into the chair beside her husband.

"We're cutting the hay in the south field today," Joe Senior said, spearing a slice of ham. "Joe wants to try out the new tractor."

Bill Junior nodded, his face downturned, eyes on his plate.

"Buck and Duke are through, huh?" Joe asked, drizzling honey over a biscuit.

"They were ready to retire. Last time we hooked them up was early spring, when gas got really tight," Joe Senior said.

Frances was glad to hear the two draft horses wouldn't be pulling the heavy plow anymore. She had grown fond of the gentle giants, sneaking carrots and apples to them as they pawed in their pen outside the barn.

"Thought I'd take a look at your Hudson this afternoon, Martha. See if I can get it running again," Joe Senior said.

280

"It doesn't run?" Joe raised his head, dabbing his napkin at the yellow yolk caught at the corner of his mouth.

"Don't know." Joe Senior shrugged. "Hasn't had gas in it for a year. And the tires were bad, so we put it up on blocks. Now that rationing is over, I'm hoping we can get her running again."

"Maybe it's time to retire it, too," Joe said. "What are you driving these days, Junior?"

Studying his plate, Bill Junior pushed half a biscuit in his mouth. "The delivery truck." He didn't look up.

"Heard Detroit's making cars again. Benton's has a new Chevy in their window," Joe Senior said. "You thinking about buying a car, Son?"

Joe pulled his frown from Bill Junior and grinned at Frances. "Unless my wife spent all the money I sent home."

She smiled and shook her head.

"She couldn't spend it if she tried. Nothing to buy except war bonds and oleo," Joe Senior said.

Bill Junior stood. "Let's go, Martha."

"What's with him?" Joe asked after Bill Junior and Martha left.

Joe Senior shrugged. He picked up his plate and disappeared into the kitchen.

Joe looked at Frances.

"Marion," she said. "She's been living in town with Susan. Moved there after Lucille got married. Because of her job at the plant she says it's easier to stay in town."

"So, she'll be back now that her job's done?"

Frances shrugged. "Marion doesn't talk much to me." The relationship between herself and Marion cooled after Martha moved in, Marion becoming downright chilly after Baby Joe was born. Frances wondered what she had done, or said, to raise Marion's ire but her mother chocked it up to jealousy, reminding Frances that Marion wanted a baby. Now Marion was focusing her rancor on Bill Junior.

"What about Susan?" Joe asked. "What does she think about all this?"

Frances lifted a shoulder again. "Susan has other things to worry about. Been seeing her boyfriend from high school. He's back from the war."

"Ricky? Ricky Thompson? Can't believe Susan would go out again with that sad sack. Where was he? Europe? Pacific?"

Frances shook her head. "Don't know. He's in a wheelchair, now."

"Oh." Joe fell quiet and concentrated on his ham slice, the only sound the scraping of his knife against the china. When his plate was empty, he stood and walked into the kitchen, putting a hand on his father's shoulder. "Let's go, old man."

The table cleared and dishes in the sink, Frances went upstairs. Tiptoeing across her mother's bedroom to the crib, she peered down at her sleeping son, resisting the urge to push the matted curls from his forehead. She moved to the window and closed her eyes, the breeze drying the tears tracing down her cheeks. A rooster called from the coop, his cry faint. When she opened her eyes, Joe stood at the small corral housing the horses. One of the horses—Frances thought it was Duke but she couldn't be sure from this distance—nosed Joe's shoulder and he rewarded the beefy animal with a scratch between the eyes. The tractor surged from the shed and both horses bolted inside, Little Joe waking with a wail at the engine's roar.

"Good morning!" Frances lifted the toddler from the crib, bouncing him on her hip as she walked back to the window. The tractor had already moved from her view as it chugged to the outlying fields, the sound of the engine fading, growing dimmer, just like her dream of the perfect reunion with her husband.

CHAPTER THIRTY-TWO

May 1946
New Kensington, Pennsylvania

Frances held Joe's new suit jacket at arm's length, scrutinizing the charcoal wool for specks of dirt and lint, running the stiff brush down a sleeve. He had looked so handsome today, she noticed other women admiring him. She felt the longing, the now familiar ache low in her belly. Joe had been home seven months and had still not made love to her. It had been weeks since he even tried. She turned to her husband, lying on the bed. "I like how you look in this suit."

Joe raised himself to an elbow and stubbed out his cigarette in the ashtray on the bedside table. "Waste of money," he said. "I'll never wear it again. Too hot."

It had been hot at Stephanie's graduation ceremony. The day was warm and the Syria Mosque auditorium was stifling, though the venue wasn't half full. The war took a toll on the size of the graduating classes from all colleges. As Stephanie crossed the stage to collect her diploma, Frances thought her friend must be roasting in her heavy gown and cap, but Stephanie didn't seem to mind. She wore a huge smile and a corsage of roses, waving her rolled diploma like it was a magic wand. The sharp bite of jealousy surprised Frances. She was happy for Stephanie—she really was—but her mind was full of what-ifs. What if she hadn't gotten pregnant? But she couldn't imagine life without Little Joe. What if you could go to college while you were expecting? She nearly laughed out loud, imagining her bumbling, pregnant-self knocking glass beakers and test tubes to the laboratory floor. There were several professors she recognized at the ceremony, including Dr. Robinson. He remembered Frances, approaching her after the ceremony as she and Joe stood on the steps of the Mosque with Stephanie's mother and brother.

"Miss Albrecht?" he called.

"It's Ferguson now, Dr. Robinson," she said, laying a hand on Joe's arm. "You remember my husband, Joe?"

He nodded and shook Joe's hand. "Returning to school this fall, Mr. Ferguson? We're looking forward to a record class this coming year. Many men coming to school under the G.I. Bill."

Joe shrugged. "Haven't decided."

Dr. Robinson returned his attention to Frances. "How about you, Mrs. Ferguson. You coming back? I remember you were a good student."

"Our son keeps her busy," Joe said.

Even if she wanted to return to school there would not be enough money as Joe spent their entire savings, and took out a loan, for a new car, two bathrooms and a coal furnace. Instead of building a new house next to his father's as planned, Joe, and his family, decided he and Frances would stay at the farmhouse. She and Joe moved into Sarah's old bedroom, and her mother moved into Frances's room. Little Joe was settled into Martha's old room, waking up most mornings in his grandmother's bed.

Frances gave Joe's jacket one more brush and hung it in the closet. "Did you turn on Little Joe's nightlight?" She slipped her nightgown over her head and sat at the vanity that was once Sarah's.

"Yes. But I still think that boy's old enough to sleep without a light. And he needs to stay the whole night in his own bed."

"He's not used to sleeping in a room by himself yet." Frances squinted at her distorted reflection in the aged mirror as she tried to run a comb through her crown of tight curls. She pulled one of the coils, released it, and watched it spring back to her head.

"How long will your hair stay curled? It's kind of like a sheep," Joe said, with a chuckle.

"I don't know." Frances sighed. She regretted her decision to cut her hair the minute the first foot-long strand fell to the beauty shop floor. "Marion said they'll relax soon."

"Marion. Hmm. Wouldn't listen to much she says."

Sporting the latest fashions, her dark hair crimped into waves, Marion moved back to Bill Junior's house a few days after Joe and Frances settled into Sarah's bedroom. Marion and Bill Junior quibbled and picked at each other throughout their meals at the farmhouse, and at last week's dinner, Marion stormed out, leaving behind an untouched plate of food. Frances had stood, intending to follow her, but Joe grabbed her wrist.

"Let her go. It's more pleasant without her," Joe had said.

His palm slamming on the table hard enough to make dishes jump, Bill Junior glared at Joe. "You want me to leave, too?"

"We're all tired of your bickering," Joe said, eyes narrowed.

Bill Junior had dropped his fork and left without another word, and he and Marion hadn't been back to the farmhouse since.

Frances looked at Joe in the mirror. "You and Bill Junior talking again?"

"No." He switched off the light by the bed and rolled on his side, facing away from Frances.

She turned off the small lamp on the vanity and crawled into bed. Joe didn't stir. "Joe, am I not pretty anymore?" she asked, her voice catching.

"Frances, you're beautiful." He let out a long breath and rolled on to his back, reaching for Frances's hand. "You'll always be beautiful."

She let out a sob as he kissed her fingertips. "I'm sorry I got my hair cut. I thought it would make me more attractive to you. Make you want me again."

Joe's other hand reached to the table by the bed, returning with a cigarette. He dropped Frances's hand and flicked his wrist, the silver lighter clicking open, a flame erupting. "It's not you, Frances." He puffed out a ring of smoke along with a heavy sigh.

She turned on her side and put a hand on his chest. "What is it, then?"

"I can't forget what I saw over there. What I felt. The fear. The cold. I thought I lost my fingers and toes to frostbite." He paused, the tip of his cigarette brightening, then fading as he exhaled. "I had to shoot boys. I swear the Nazis grabbed kids off the street and put guns in their hands. They were younger than my nephew Robert, for chrissake." He inhaled again, exhaled. "I won't shoot another living thing. Bill Junior laughed when I wouldn't take down a buck. He wasn't over there. He doesn't understand. Todd does."

Todd was living with his parents and working on the farm but the family didn't see much of him. He disappeared for days with no explanation. When Todd did come for dinner, he said very little, and afterwards, he and Joe isolated themselves on the porch, drinking beer and smoking, closing down their conversation when anyone came into earshot.

"What can I do?" Frances whispered.

Joe's cigarette glowed, dimmed. It glowed again, then he stubbed it out. "Junior bought six new calves. Holsteins. We've always had Jerseys."

Frances rolled on to her back, staring at the ceiling. The last thing she wanted to talk about was cows but it was better than no conversation. "What's the difference?"

"Holsteins produce more milk but our Jerseys' milk is better. More butterfat. Junior's still harping on making ice cream. Wants a new building. Tear down the milk house, he said." Joe paused to light another cigarette. "You know, when I was a boy, most of our milk was thrown to the pigs. We separated it and only kept the cream. Churned some butter and sold the rest to a creamery. It was Uncle Bill's idea to store whole milk. Started delivering it to people in town. Fresh water had to be running all the time to keep the milk from spoiling. Now the electric keeps the tanks cold." Joe exhaled, continued in a sharper tone. "Bill Junior's got wires running everywhere in that milk house. It's jammed with equipment. Pasteurizer. Homogenizer. He's even got an ice cream freezer in there. Dad doesn't say a word. Allows Uncle Bill and Junior to spend all the money." He sucked in a large breath, exhaled slowly, his voice less strident. "They even got Todd on board now. He's going to that new vocational school down in Blawnox. Going to learn how to fix refrigerators and freezers."

"Maybe that'll be good for Todd," Frances said. "Susan thinks he's running with the wrong crowd."

"Susan said? How would she know? Probably came from that cock-eyed husband of hers. Where'd you see her?"

"In town. At the store." Frances regretted mentioning Susan, now a family outcast since she married Ricky Thompson. Susan brought Ricky to the farm once, his wheelchair stuffed in the backseat of her old car. It took three men to get Ricky and his wheelchair up the porch steps and into the farmhouse. His purple heart pinned on his chest, Ricky ranted about God's injustice, questioned Joe's and Todd's service since they had no visible scars, and announced he was an atheist.

287

After several beers, Ricky passed out in his chair and Bill and Bill Junior deposited him in Susan's car, with firm instructions to not bring the man back.

Joe stubbed his cigarette out and rolled on to his side, away from Frances. "Good night," he said.

When she heard her husband's soft snore, Frances eased from the bed and crept downstairs. She wrapped an afghan around her shoulders and curled up on the couch in the living room, her mind on a loop, asking over and over, will my husband ever be the same? She missed the man she fell in love with and was heartsick that her son and mother may never meet that man.

***

The next morning Frances was off the couch and dressed before her mother came downstairs. Joe strode into the kitchen, giving her a quick kiss on the cheek before sitting down at the small table. She poured him a cup of coffee, wondering if he noticed she hadn't slept in their bed. Her mother came into the kitchen a few minutes later, Little Joe's hand in hers.

"When is Stephanie moving to Buffalo?" Martha asked as she busied herself at the stove.

Joe looked up. "Buffalo? Stephanie is moving?"

Frances nodded and lifted Little Joe into his highchair. "She took a job with a chemical company. Will be working in their research laboratory." She watched Joe's jaw tense, the muscles twitching, his cheeks reddening. She hoped his envy might spur him back to school. At least one of them should finish college. "She moves next week," she said. "Can we visit her this summer? Wouldn't you like to see Niagara Falls?"

He shrugged. "We'll see." He stood, half the food on his plate untouched, and walked out the door, giving Little Joe's hair a ruffling as he passed his squirming son.

"Winston!" Little Joe yelled as a yellow and white puppy pushed his nose against the screen door. "Go play, mamma?" He turned his eyes, the color of grass today, towards Frances.

"Finish your eggs."

"Go play," Little Joe repeated, his arms pumping, stumpy legs kicking.

Not up for an argument, Frances lifted her son from his chair and he ran out the door, Winston nipping at his heels. Joe came home with the puppy last month, telling her a boy in town had a boxful of pups and was giving them away. She put up a half-hearted fight, but the truth was she'd grown fond of Rags and missed having a dog around. Joe named it "Winston" and the puppy and Little Joe quickly became inseparable.

"Maybe it's best we don't take another trip, anyway," Frances said as she cleared the dishes from the table.

Martha laughed. "At least there wouldn't be snow in the summer."

Frances nodded, a sly smile tugging at the corner of her mouth. A week before Christmas, Joe had loaded everyone into his sleek, new Fleetline and headed for Donora to visit Christy. Two inches of fresh snow covered the roads and Frances wanted to turn around after witnessing a nasty collision of crunching metal and burning rubber. Joe kept going, slowing a bit but still driving fast enough that she gripped the dashboard with both hands. He scoffed at her suggestion to stop for directions and they drove aimlessly for miles, arriving at Christy's house two hours later than expected.

Her smile faded as she walked to the back door and watched her son kick a ball across the yard, Winston in hot pursuit. "Do you regret not having more children?" she asked.

"George didn't want any more, thank goodness," Martha said. "I did the best I could with Russell and Randolph, but I feel I failed with Russell." She smiled. "I do like being a grandmother. Can't wait for the next one."

Frances turned back to the door, peered at the outlying hills. She couldn't bring herself to tell her mother there was little chance of another grandchild.

CHAPTER THIRTY-THREE

August 1946
Buffalo, New York

Frances waved, a lump in her throat, tears threatening. Happy tears. Her son was head-to-toe yellow, rubber pants, boots and jacket, the hood pulled tight around his face. Flanked by Joe and Martha, both dressed in the same yellow attire, Little Joe was beaming. The trio stood on a wood landing halfway down the many stairs to the base of Niagara Falls. Her mother dropped Little Joe's hand long enough for him to wave back.

"He's grown since I last saw him," Stephanie said.

Frances nodded and watched her family move down another set of stairs. For Little Joe's third birthday, Joe finally agreed to visit Stephanie and they were spending the day at Niagara Falls. She was hoping the change of scenery might have a restoring effect on Joe. He sometimes blamed the summer heat for his lack of effort in the bedroom but he had given up long before the warm weather arrived. She didn't know what to do. Didn't know if this was normal, but who to ask? She would be mortified talking to her doctor about such a private act. He might think her a hussy, wanting sex, and what if word got out? New Kensington was a small town that liked to gossip. The question had been on the tip of her tongue several times when alone with her mother but she just couldn't bring herself to ask, fearing her mother might think ill of Joe. They got on so well and Frances wouldn't say anything that might change that relationship.

"You sure you don't want to go with them, Stephanie?" Frances asked, leaning close to be heard over the roar of the falls. She had no desire to traipse down the 500 steps to the river's edge, and Stephanie, who made the hike once before, stayed atop with her. "I'll be fine by myself."

Stephanie shook her head and led the way to a nearby bench. "No. Once was enough."

"When were you here?" Frances asked, settling in on the damp wood.

"Two months ago. Just after I moved to Buffalo," she said. "I came with the other gals from the lab."

"I didn't notice any women when we were there yesterday," Frances said. She stopped by the laboratory where Stephanie worked while her mother lounged at the hotel and her husband and son explored downtown Buffalo. Frances had felt right at home in the lab, the acrid smells pleasing. Her hands in her pockets to keep her fingers from the glass tubes and flasks, she read each label on the chemical jars, their symbols as clear in her mind as her final day of college.

"I'm the only woman left," Stephanie said. "Ester got married and Barbara took a teaching job."

"You like Buffalo?" Frances asked.

"It's fine." Stephanie shrugged. "I don't go out much. Saving money."

Stephanie lived in one room at a women's boarding house, telling Frances the house was clean, the owner pleasant, and the other boarders quiet, so she never found a reason to search for another place. She had also said the price was right.

"I apologize again that you had to stay at a hotel," Stephanie said.

Frances laughed. "Don't be sorry. Little Joe and Mom are loving the hotel." Her family spent the night in one of the 450 rooms at the grand Hotel Statler in downtown Buffalo, Martha and Frances in one bed, Joe and Little Joe in the other. It was an event for all of them, the first time since Joe left for the war that she had been in a hotel, and the first time ever her son stayed overnight anywhere besides the farm. Little Joe's first ride in the elevator was daunting—he complained of grasshoppers in his belly—but his apprehension evaporated the minute the door opened and he sprinted down the hall, little fingers trailing the textured walls. His eyes bugged at the shower in their bathroom and he spent five minutes flipping the switch for the light in the closet. Her son would be talking about this trip for months.

"To be honest with you, I didn't think I would last this long," Stephanie said, shaking her head. "Dr. Klein— the man who interviewed me back in May—didn't want to hire me in the first place. Said I lacked experience. I think he didn't want to hire me because I'm a woman. At least the man interviewing me for the job in Pittsburgh was honest. Said he didn't believe a woman would be the right fit." She smiled, nudged Frances with her elbow. "Dr. Klein said he would get back to me but I told him I needed an answer. Told him I had another offer. It wasn't true, but there weren't many men graduating with chemistry degrees so I figured he had to be getting desperate." She shrugged. "So was I. I knew I could do the work. Just needed the chance." She looked at her hands in her lap and sighed. "There are some days I do regret being so bold."

"You can't do the job?" Frances asked, surprised. Stephanie was smart and hard-working, she couldn't imagine her not succeeding.

"It's not that. I can do the work just fine." Stephanie hesitated, raising her chin, her attention drawn to the Horseshoe Falls across the border. "Unrealistic goals. Tight deadlines. My boss questions every experiment I do. Belittles my findings in front of my colleagues. My

293

male colleagues. Did the same thing to Barbara and Ester." She pushed a limp curl from her forehead, the mist rising from the falls dampening every surface. "Not long after Barbara left, leaving me as the only woman in the lab, I found a newspaper in my locker. It was folded to the help wanted section, a job for science teacher at Buffalo Public School Number Forty Three circled in red." She snorted. "I never did find out who put it in there."

Frances turned, studying Stephanie. "Why do you stay?"

"I like what I do." Stephanie shook her head and smiled. "No, I love what I do. The experiments are fascinating."

"What are you working on?"

"Polymers. Synthetic fibers," Stephanie said. "The goal is a thread strong enough to put in tires so the rubber will last longer. Can you imagine?" She raised her hands, palms up, her voice resounding with enthusiasm. "Think how many tires are sold every year. The company wants to repeat the success of nylon."

"Nylon?" Frances asked.

Stephanie nodded. "It was the company's first synthetic fiber. Polymer 66. The older chemists in the lab told me it was first called 'nuron.' That's 'no run' spelled backwards." She chuckled. "The name evolved into 'nylon.' They introduced nylon stockings at the World's Fair, and, well, they were an instant success. You remember how easily silk stockings tore? But, during the war, all the nylon the company could made went to the army for parachutes, ropes, tents and uniforms. Now they're making stockings again. Women can't get enough."

Frances had read in the *Dispatch* that 40,000 people lined up at Kaufmann's Department Store in downtown Pittsburgh just before Christmas to buy nylon stockings, the line stretching a mile down Fifth Avenue. It never occurred to her that Stephanie's company made the stockings. "How can you make thread from a liquid?" she asked, intrigued.

"We use a machine. A spinner." Stephanie extended her index finger, rotating it into a pirouette. "Chemical fibers are pushed through small holes and the threads come out the other side." She smacked her palms together.

"Hmm," Frances said. She turned her face back towards the falls and closed her eyes against the mist, breathing in the sodden air that smelled of lichen and dank stone. Her neck was tight, a headache starting. *Jealousy. And a bit of anger.* She recognized the feelings. It was why she didn't answer Lily's letters for months. Lily wrote of busy days full of interesting people, fascinating sights, and new discoveries, an eagerness for her future emerging. On the other hand, Frances answered Christy's mundane letters of banal tasks and family member tales within days. She knew she shouldn't be jealous. Living on the farm was comforting—safe—and she loved being a mother. She should be happy, like the women in the *McCall's* magazine advertisements. Smiling housewives in flowered aprons, their red fingernails pointing at the latest refrigerator or washing machine. But a small part of her wanted more. She shook her head and opened her eyes, forcing herself to be cordial.

"Will you stay here for medical school?" Frances asked, pushing aside her jealousy, reminding herself it was not Stephanie's fault Frances hadn't finished college, reminding herself Stephanie had no husband, no children. But that was Stephanie's choice, wasn't it? She had always been more interested in chemistry than people.

Pensive, Stephanie was quiet for a few moments, looking again at the Canadian shore. "I don't think I am going to medical school."

"What?" Frances frowned, genuinely concerned. "Why not?"

"Things are going to get better here. I'll have a new supervisor by the end of the year. I've met him. Paul Morgan. A nice man. And he's interested in his own ambitions. Wants to make a name for himself so I think he will leave me alone. Let me do my own research in my own time." She paused, leaned closer, her voice hushed. "There are rumors of a new research laboratory. The company has land in Delaware. Lots of land. Mr. Morgan says there's a good chance we could be in a brand new lab in a few years." She straightened, her voice brightening. "I can make it another two or three years here. Someday, I'll have my own team."

"But, you wanted to be a doctor," Frances said.

"I also wanted to be a fashion designer." Stephanie laughed. "I belong in a lab, not a hospital."

Frances turned away and watched the Maid of the Mist chug towards the falls. Where do I belong? she wondered. What happened to that ambitious girl wanting to invent the next, great piece of glass? She looked down at her palm, almost expecting to see the tiny glass marble she created in Sister Mayme's chemistry class years ago. But her hand was empty, the palm calloused by kitchen utensils and garden tools, the faded dream slipping through her fingers.

PART FIVE:
HEALING ALCHEMY
1950 – 1965

CHAPTER THIRTY-FOUR

November 1950
Wilmington, Delaware

Two days before Thanksgiving, Joe stomped into the kitchen, slamming the door behind him. "That's it. Pack up your clothes. Little Joe's clothes. We're moving to Wilmington."

Frances, sitting at the table, flour sifter in hand, looked at her mother. Since his father's death the month before, Joe had been unpredictable. On day much too warm for October, Joe Senior noticed smoke seeping out beneath the milk house door. With a bucket of water in his hands, he ran into the building and tossed the water on the flames licking the sides of the ice cream freezer. The electric line to the freezer was never properly grounded and Joe Senior was electrocuted, dying instantly.

With another glance at her mother, Frances lowered the sifter and stood, running her hands down her apron. She reached behind to untie the strings, pulled the apron over her head and followed her husband up the stairs.

In their bedroom, Joe was stuffing clothes into his duffel bag. "Stephanie invited us to stay with her anytime. Maybe she can get us jobs where she works. We'll start over. I can't be at this farm any longer. Grandma's gone. Dad's gone. Junior just blamed Dad for his own death. Said he had no business being in the milk house. No business? It's his farm for chrissake!" He dropped the duffel and sank to the bed. "Was his farm."

Frances sat beside him. "I miss your father, too, but this is your farm, Joe. You love it here."

He shook his head. "Ever since we agreed to majority rules, Dad and I haven't had a chance. Uncle Bill will always side with Junior. Marvin goes along with whatever his dad says. And now Todd's doing the same. Next thing they'll be giving Bill the third a vote."

Six weeks after Bill and Marion parted ways permanently in June of forty-six, Bill Junior brought his new eighteen-year-old girlfriend to the farm. They married the following month, and a year later William Ferguson III was born.

"What about Little Joe?" Frances asked. "He loves it here."

"He'll learn to like wherever he is." Joe stood as he picked up his duffel, and moved to the dresser, jerking a drawer open. He grabbed a handful of underwear and pushed the garments into his bag. "Pack up your trunk. Whatever fits in the car is what we'll take." He looked at Frances, his eyes dark. "Call Stephanie. We leave in the morning."

Frances went back downstairs. "He'll change his mind," she told her mother, her arms stretched behind to re-tie her apron.

Joe did not change his mind. When Little Joe came home from school he told his son they were going on a trip.

"Who?" Little Joe asked, sitting at the kitchen table, snacking on milk and cookies.

"You, me, your mom and grandma," Joe said.

Frances was relieved to hear her mother was included in his half-baked plan.

"Can Winston come?" Little Joe asked.

"Of course."

"Can I take my bike?"

"If it fits," Joe said. He turned to Frances. "Where's the bank book? I'm going to town. We'll be in Wilmington by nightfall tomorrow."

***

Frances turned in her seat to smile when Little Joe cheered, and Winston barked, as they drove out of the Blue Mountain Tunnel. It was the seventh, and final, tunnel on the drive across Pennsylvania on the new turnpike. The seven-year-old, and his dog, were wedged between Martha and the steamer trunk on the back seat of the big Chevy, her mother doing her best to keep Little Joe entertained on the long journey. They played "I Spy" and counted cows, Little Joe expertly pointing out the difference between the black and white Holsteins and the brown and white Herefords and Guernseys. When he spotted a field of light brown cows he yelled "Jersey's, just like ours, right Dad?"

"Yes," Joe said, his hands tight on the steering wheel. His voice was husky from his non-stop smoking since leaving the farm at sunrise nearly seven hours ago.

Frances looked sideways at her husband. His jaw was clenched, his knuckles white. She turned to the clock next to the overflowing ashtray on the dash. "Can we stop, please?"

He nodded, lighting another cigarette, but as he sped up to overtake a stretch of slow-moving cars he passed by the next service station.

Not saying a word, Frances turned towards her window, studying each car they passed. Most were filled with families, and she imagined them reuniting with relatives for a happy Thanksgiving celebration. She closed her eyes and pictured the pumpkin and apple pies on the table in the kitchen at the farmhouse. She and her mother started baking days ago, pretending it would be an ordinary Thanksgiving with the Ferguson's gathered for dinner at Sarah's long table, putting aside their differences for a few hours. She brought two of the loaves of freshly-baked bread, plus a box of jarred vegetables and fruit preserves, but there wasn't room in the car for more food. From the minute they drove off the farm, she had been agonizing over the many things left behind. The many things she would never see again.

Joe turned off the turnpike and headed south, the light fading as he turned into the housing development where Stephanie lived in a three-bedroom, split-level home. He slowed and squinted at each house. "Can you see the numbers?"

Frances shook her head. "She said it's yellow. Number fifty-eight."

"I can't see the colors of the houses," he snapped. "They all look the same."

The neighborhood was one of the new, planned communities springing up in the suburbs across the east coast, a part of the postwar building boom. After winding through the development twice, Frances finally spotted Stephanie's house number in a flash of the headlights. Joe pulled to the curb.

The light by the door flicked on and Stephanie stepped out on to her stoop.

Frances jumped from the car and ran up the sidewalk. She stood at the bottom of the three concrete steps, her hand on the iron railing. "I'm so sorry to intrude on you like this," she said, her voice cracking. She knew this was pushing the boundaries of their friendship.

"It's fine." Stephanie put a hand to her mouth, stifling a yawn. "I said you were welcome any time. I just hope you like my cooking. I've never roasted a whole turkey by myself."

Frances's sighed, her heart heavy. She feared she was disrupting Stephanie plans for her holiday. "I'm sorry. We're spoiling your plans. Maybe we could find a hotel?" Her voice hitched again and she turned away, watching Joe wrangle Little Joe's sleeping body from the back seat, Winston bounding out behind.

Stephanie came down the steps and put a hand on Frances's arm, encouraging her to look her way. "The more the merrier. I have two friends, a couple, coming for dinner and they won't mind at all that you are here. There's plenty of food." Stephanie paused, her eyes widening when she saw Winston.

Martha had looped a rope around the dog's neck and stood beside him as he watered a nearby tree.

"Sorry. Little Joe loves his dog. We couldn't leave him behind," Frances said. She swallowed hard. "I'm sorry," she repeated, glancing at the light coming on at the house across the street.

"It's fine." Stephanie stepped aside as Joe came up the walk, Little Joe draped over his shoulder.

"Thank you for having us," Joe said, his eyes not quite meeting Stephanie's.

Stephanie ran up the steps, pushed the door open. "Come in." She led the way across a small foyer, up a short flight of stairs, and down the hall to the first bedroom.

"Mommy?" Little Joe rubbed his eyes as Joe lowered him to a narrow bed against the wall.

"I'm here, Little Joe." Frances kissed her son's smooth forehead and slipped his shoes off. "Go back to sleep."

"I need to say my prayers."

"You can skip tonight. Say double tomorrow," Frances said. The thought of tomorrow made her stomach turn. She kissed Little Joe once more and he closed his eyes, rolling to his side and curling into a tight ball.

"There's another spare bedroom across the hall. With a larger bed," Stephanie said.

"You and your mother can take the bedroom," Joe said to Frances. "I'll sleep on the couch." He shouldered past Stephanie and disappeared down the hall.

Mouthing "sorry," Frances followed Joe. How many times had she apologized? She went outside and knelt beside a whining Winston, running her hand over the blocky head. The dog had grown into fifty pounds of short gold fur with a white face and liquid brown eyes.

Stephanie came to Frances's side. "Never had a dog," she said, eyeing Winston. She raised her head and looked at Martha. "Go on inside. Take the dog with you. The living room is at the top of the stairs. I'll help Joe and Frances."

After ten minutes the car was unloaded and Stephanie's living room was cluttered with boxes and a mishmash of luggage.

"That's everything," Joe said, arching his back as he surveyed the room.

"Are you hungry?" Stephanie asked.

"No." Joe shook his head, his attention focused on the sheets and pillow stacked at one end of a green tweed couch stretched in front of the living room's large window. "I'm tired." He grasped a sheet and snapped it open.

Embarrassed by her husband's curtness, Frances cringed, her cheeks warming. All day she had put up with Joe's incivility, her admonishments unspoken. She took a step towards Joe, eyes narrowed. "Joe..."

Her mother pushed up from the easy chair, clearing her throat. "It has been a long day," Martha said. She lay her hand on Frances's shoulder and turned to Stephanie. "Good night, dear. And thank you once again. We'll see you in the morning."

Frances followed her mother to the bedroom. "It's bad enough Joe uses a sharp tone with me but he shouldn't speak to Stephanie like that," she said and dropped to the bed.

"You're right," Martha said. "But it's not the time to get into a loud argument. It would only embarrass Stephanie. And unsettle Little Joe." She let out a long breath and sat on the bed. "Things will look better in the morning."

Frances broke, face crumbling, tears falling. She jammed her fist in her mouth to keep the sounds from escaping.

***

Early the next morning, just before the sun rose, Frances woke, head aching, eyes puffy. She dressed and crept down the hall, stopping at the end of couch to stare down at her husband. Her hands curled into fists, last night's shame and sorrow morphing to anger. Joe, sleeping soundly with his face buried into the back of couch, didn't stir but Winston, stretched in front of the couch, jumped up and followed her into the kitchen. His toenails clicked on the linoleum as he tracked her around the small room. The percolator pot filled, Frances turned the knob on the gas range and titled her head, adjusting the flame. She opened the refrigerator, searching the crowded shelves for milk. The bottle, looking very much like a Ferguson Dairy quart, brought tears to her eyes. She thought of the barn, the smell of manure and sweet alfalfa. She thought of the cows, their jaws working, bloated udders swaying, their wide hooves pawing at the hay. Little Joe loved the barn. Loved the animals that called it home. Startled by Winston's quick bark, Frances nearly dropped the bottle. She turned to find

Stephanie frozen at the door, a pink cardigan pulled tight over her brown jumper, her wide eyes on Winston.

Frances giggled. "Sorry." She shouldn't laugh but someone being afraid of Winston was funny. The poor dog ran from scolding squirrels. "It's all right, Winston." She put the cream on the table and laid her hand on the furry head. She scratched behind Winston's ears. "He won't hurt you."

The dog wagged and moved to the back door, his nose prodding the knob.

"I need to take him outside," Frances said, hurrying out the door. She looked to the sky as Winston wandered across the rectangle of matted grass. The rising sun, a hint of red on the horizon, was much more anxious to start the day than she was. She coaxed the dog back to Stephanie's small back porch and sat on a step. *How could Joe do this to them?* Their plans for the future gone. Tossed away on his bitter whim. Winston nudged her knee. She looked at the drooping tail and trusting eyes. "It's going to be fine," she whispered, repeating her mother's words from the night before. She scratched the dog's head, repeated the words once more to herself, then stood and walked inside.

Her mother was circling the table, lowering plates and silverware, Stephanie manned the range. Joe sat at the table, reading a newspaper and sipping coffee. He didn't look up. Little Joe stood on his toes, his fingers hooked on the edge of the counter, staring at his reflection in the silver toaster.

"Hiya, Winston," Little Joe said. "Mommy, watch this. Bread is going to come out of there." He pointed a squat finger. With a lusty pop, the toaster belched out a browned slice and Little Joe clapped, Winston adding a bark.

Frances couldn't help but smile. "We don't have a toaster," she explained to Stephanie. "I'll get a jar of jam."

Joe lowered his newspaper to the table. "I'll get it. Do you know which box?"

"No. I'll get it," Frances said. She pushed past her husband, not allowing him the chance to search her trunk. Hidden beneath her blouses and skirts were three cigar boxes filled with letters: box number one stuffed with letters from Joe, number two full of letters from her mother, and the third box filled with Randolph's and Christy letters. When Joe came into the bedroom last night while she was packing, he was furious when he saw she was putting her boxes of letters into the trunk.

"We don't have room for letters. Leave them," he had said.

"I can't leave them here for your family to read. They're personal."

"I'll burn them." Joe grabbed a box.

"No." Frances snatched it back. "I'll do it." She sat beside the stove in the farmhouse's living room until midnight, going through every box, reading each letter. She wanted—needed—to remember the Joe of his letters and kept them all. It was difficult to decide which letters to keep from Randolph and Christy. Reading the letters from Randolph hurt but the years had dulled the ache of losing him. Christy's letters left Frances raw. Two years ago, she got a late-night phone call from one of Christy's sisters. Her dear friend was dead, along with twenty of her neighbors, from a toxic fog that engulfed their town for four days. Joe and Frances went to the funeral and finally got to meet Christy's husband as he stood at the casket crying, his tears landing on his six-month-old son cradled in his arms.

Finally locating a jar of peach jam and a can of dog food, Frances returned to Stephanie's kitchen, forcing a smile on her face.

"Can opener?" She held up the dog food.

Stephanie nodded at the cabinet beside the sink. "Top drawer."

"How is Stanley?" Frances asked, cranking the opener's handle, keeping her fingers from the can's ragged edge.

"Fine. Still with...LaVonne." Stephanie said the name with a French accent, making Frances chuckle.

"How far is it to your job?" Joe asked, stubbing out his cigarette and squinting through the smoke at Stephanie.

"Eight miles."

"Can you get me a job there?" he asked, no hesitation.

Stephanie glanced at Frances. "Maybe." She looked at Joe. "You would have to finish college."

"I need a job now." He tapped the newspaper. "They need help building houses. I can do that." He stood. "I'm going to explore the neighborhood."

"Can I come, Daddy?" Little Joe stuffed the last of his toast into his mouth and looked at his father, eyes wide and shining.

Frances held her breath, stared at her husband. She hoped his discontentment and harsh words were not going to be extended to Little Joe.

Joe returned Frances's gaze. Finally, he nodded and smiled. "Sure. We'll take Winston with us."

Frances waved to Little Joe and slipped into the chair Joe left behind. "I am sorry, Stephanie. Joe's been so angry since his father died. He took it very hard and..." She paused, her voice hitching.

"Such a waste. Joe Senior was a good man." Martha pushed to her feet and carried her plate to the sink, standing with her back towards Frances and Stephanie.

"I'm sorry," Frances repeated, not sure if her apology was for her husband's behavior, her father-in-law's death, or the tears she couldn't contain. "I promise we won't stay long. Maybe I could get a job at your company. I'll do anything," she said. The sound of her own voice made her cringe, despair and desperation taking it to a high pitch.

"They're always looking for help in the secretary pool," Stephanie said as she pulled the turkey from the refrigerator and dropped it into an oval baking pan, one wing catching on the side. She poked at the wing, turned and looked at Frances. "Can you type?"

Frances shook her head and wiped her cheeks with the handkerchief her mother slipped into her hand. "I haven't typed since college, and I was never good at it."

"You were good at chemistry," Stephanie said. "I need someone like you on my team at the lab. We're not

308

getting the results we want." She rearranged the turkey, a leg now sticking over the edge.

Martha stepped to Stephanie's side. "Here, let me do. Sit down. Chop some onions and celery for the stuffing."

Stephanie pulled an onion from the wood bin on the counter and sat beside Frances. "It's frustrating," she said, peeling the yellow skin. "Half those young men they hire for the laboratory—with degrees from the best schools—don't know a polyamide from a lanthanide." She leaned towards Frances. "Go back to college. Come work for me."

Frances threw a quick glance at her mother. Martha had encouraged her to go back to college more than once, volunteering to care for Little Joe while she attended class. Frances used up all her excuses and finally had to tell her mother that even if she wanted to return to college, she couldn't because Joe had spent all their money. She gave Stephanie a tight smile. "Maybe someday."

CHAPTER THIRTY-FIVE

May 1951
Wilmington, Delaware

Frances sat on the bed in their rented duplex and watched Joe button his brown work shirt. "What about Mass?" she asked. They had lived here for three months and Joe had gone to church twice.

"Not this week. Time-and-a-half on Sunday," he said, kneeling to lace his boots.

"You said that last week." Frances sighed, rolling her aching shoulders. While staying at Stephanie's, Joe found a job in construction and Frances went to work at the chemical company as a secretary. Joe was content in his new profession, Frances was not. When they moved across town to this duplex, Frances took a job at a nearby grocery store, waiting on customers like she once did at Wanamaker's department store in Philadelphia. She worked long hours and fretted that she wasn't there to greet Little Joe when he came home from school. Joe worked even longer hours, leaving the house at sunrise and returning after dark, and he worked most weekends.

"Little Joe thinks he shouldn't have to go to Mass every week, too," Frances said. "He doesn't want to be an altar boy, now." She pushed her swollen feet into her black pumps and stood.

Joe shrugged. "Maybe he's right."

"You were an altar boy."

"And look where it got me. Working day and night, after spending three and a half years shooting people I didn't know. Where was God during the war?"

Frances had no answer. She went down the stairs, avoiding the third step from the top and the fifth step from the bottom so their creaking wouldn't wake her mother and son. She filled a pot with water and turned the knob on the stove. Nothing. She tried the other three knobs. Nothing. "The stove isn't working again," she said as Joe came into the kitchen.

He got on a knee and pushed the range from the wall. A mouse scurried along the baseboard and disappeared into a crack in the corner. "Damn it!" He wedged his head and arms behind the appliance. "Try it again," he said, his voice muffled.

She turned the knob. "Nothing."

"Try again."

"No. Nothing."

Joe sat back on his heels. "Call Jergerson. Tell him to fix the damn stove or get us a new one. I'll set another mouse trap tonight." He heaved himself to his feet and walked out the back door.

Through the small window above the sink, she saw Joe stop in the ankle-high grass, lift a foot, and shake his head. His mouth worked but she was glad she couldn't hear. Little Joe did a poor job of cleaning up after Winston. She twisted the hot water faucet, watching the sink fill. Since it was early, and the neighbors weren't awake yet to use up all the hot water, it didn't take long. She pulled bowls, plates and glasses from the shelf above and dunked them in the lukewarm water. Unlatching the bread bin, she took out a loaf wrapped in waxed brown paper and a box of corn flakes, scrutinizing both for holes. Satisfied no rodent had found a way into the tin box, she unwrapped the bread and sliced it. She gathered

312

a bottle of milk, three oranges and a slab of butter from the refrigerator and put them on the table.

"Good morning, Sunshine." Her mother came into the kitchen, Winston behind her, tail wagging.

Frances gave her mother a small smile and scratched the dog's head. "The stove's not working. Bread and cereal for breakfast. I'll take Winston out."

After a short walk around the small yard, she came back inside to find that her mother had squeezed the oranges into juice and filled the bowls with cereal.

"They're at it early," Martha said, jutting her chin towards the shared wall.

Angry voices, a woman's and a man's, filled the room. The couple living in the other half of the duplex made no attempt to keep their fights, and their makeup sessions, quiet. When they moved to the duplex, her mother warned that living in the same house as strangers could be challenging. "The walls are thin, and people, especially children will intentionally eavesdrop," Martha had said with a sheepish smile. "I did."

The neighbors had two kids, a boy and a girl, with various other people—Frances assumed they were relatives—staying in the house for days at a time. The girl, Fay, was thirteen going on thirty, as tall as Frances and with shoulders nearly as broad as Joe's. Fay ignored everyone including her ten-year-old brother, Simon. Simon was repeating second grade, after two years in first grade. He was two years older, and at least a head taller, than all the other second graders in Little Joe's class.

"Good morning!" Frances said, putting on a cheery voice for her son.

Little Joe, dressed in navy pants and a white shirt, grunted and slumped into a chair. He tossed his clip-on tie on the table. "I don't want to go to Mass."

Frances pushed a bowl of cereal in front of her son and poured milk on top. "You want strawberry or grape jam?"

"Grape."

Martha sat beside Little Joe, Frances nibbling on a slice of bread as she stood at the sink. Nobody spoke, even the usually chipper Martha was silent, the only sounds coming from the neighbors.

"I'm going outside," Little Joe said, his bowl still half-full. "Come on, Winston."

"Don't get those clothes dirty," Frances said. She watched her son go out the door, his shoulders rounded, his head hanging. "He doesn't like it here." She picked up her son's tie and ran it through her fingers. "He was such a happy kid at the farm."

"Any news from the farm?" Martha asked.

"Got a letter yesterday. Todd's wife had a boy. Todd Junior."

Without Joe's knowledge, Frances kept in touch with their niece, Nancy. About the same time Nancy's younger sister became a mother, Todd moved with his wife into the farmhouse. It made Frances angry to think of another woman in her kitchen, cooking with her pots, tending to her garden, using the bathrooms Joe was so proud of. She wondered what Todd's wife did with the clothes she and her mother left behind. Did they fit her? Does Todd Junior wear Little Joe's baby clothes, left neatly folded in the old dresser with the broken handle on the top left drawer?

Winston's barking brought Frances to her feet. A few seconds later, Little Joe's anguished cries sent her and her mother running out the door. Little Joe was sitting on the ground and Simon was atop Little Joe's bike, one leg on the pedals. Winston had a mouthful of Simon's other pant leg, pulling hard, and Simon balled his hand and punched Winston's ear. The dog yelped and let go. At Winston's cry, Little Joe sprang up and launched himself at Simon, sending both boys and the bike to the muddy ground.

"Stop!" Frances yelled, pulling Little Joe up and pushing his body behind her legs.

314

Simon jumped up and moved towards Little Joe, but Frances stopped him with a hand to his chest.

"He pushed me off my bike," Little Joe said.

"I just wanted to try it out," Simon said. "Take a little ride. That's all."

Frances looked towards the door of her neighbor's, hoping for some help from Simon's parents, but if they heard the commotion, they were ignoring it.

"Go inside, Little Joe. Time for church," Frances said.

"Yeah, *Little* Joe. Time for *church*," Simon mocked.

Jaw clenched, Frances ignored Simon's taunts. She led her son upstairs to the tiny bathroom that smelled of mold, no matter how often she scrubbed. "Hold still, Little Joe," she said, rubbing a washcloth on his face.

"Stop calling me 'Little.'" He jerked from her grasp. "The kids in school make fun of me. They tell me I should go back to the farm." He stalked out, slamming the door of the bedroom he shared with his grandmother.

Frances sat on the scarred lip of the old bathtub and let her tears fall to the cracked linoleum. She hated that her son was being tormented by classmates. She looked at her mother, standing in the doorway. "He's an outcast, just like I was."

Martha moved into the tight space and sat beside Frances. "Kids are resilient. He'll be fine."

Frances wanted to disagree, wanted to remind her mother of the misery she quietly endured, the loneliness she was forced to live with, but throwing salt in old wounds wouldn't bring any good. Instead, she dropped her head to her mother's shoulder. "I don't want to be here, either. This place is terrible. It's dirty. Nothing works right. And even with my job we're barely able to pay the bills."

"I'll find a job," Martha said.

"No!" Frances jerked upright. "Someone has to be here for Little Joe." She stood, wadding up toilet paper and blowing her nose. "Nancy said the farm is doing well. Very well. Joe should be compensated. The farm was his inheritance, too."

"Would Joe take the money?" Her mother asked.

"He has to. We can't go on like this."

***

Three weeks later Bill Ferguson stood on Frances's doorstep, his plaid shirt out of place in the city. He pulled her into a hug, and despite her best efforts, she cried. He smelled of the farm and she shed even more tears, dampening the worn flannel.

"Where's Little Joe?" he asked.

Frances took a step back, embarrassed. "At Stephanie's. With Mom. He doesn't know you're here."

Bill nodded. He sat on the couch, absently scratching Winston's head. "Joe doesn't know I'm coming, does he?"

Frances shook her head. She had written to Bill, explaining their situation, and asked him to draw up papers for Joe's part of the farm.

"I won't tell him you wrote me, Frances."

She pushed back to her feet. "I'm sorry. You must be hungry. Come on, I'll fix you something to eat. Make some coffee."

They were sitting in the kitchen when Joe came home. He was speechless.

"I'll leave you two alone," Frances said and retreated to the living room. She picked up the newspaper but after reading the same paragraph twice, she put it aside. Five minutes later Bill came into the room and handed her a check.

"He signed the papers, but he won't take the money. Told me to leave." Bill paused when his voice quavered. "Take care of yourself, Frances. And Little Joe." He gave her shoulder a quick squeeze and walked out the door.

It took Frances a week to convince Joe to put the check in the bank. A week after that, her husband came home with an old pickup truck and Ferguson & McLaughlin Construction Company was born.

CHAPTER THIRTY-SIX

August 1952
Wilmington, Delaware

Frances squinted out the streaked window of Joe's truck. It was the day after Little Joe's ninth birthday and she was fuming. "An hour?" She turned and glared at her husband. "That's all you could spare for your son's birthday?" After Little Joe's dismal birthday last year, Frances swore her son would never suffer through another cheerless celebration but yesterday was worse than the year before. She had sat in the duplex's living room and watched Little Joe open presents, eat cake and drink sugary punch, but her son barely managed a smile. He wasn't happy. She could see it in his dulled eyes, their hue nearly always a muddy brown. His shuffled his feet, head down and he often came home from school with unexplained scrapes and bruises. His only friend was Winston.

"I've been working on a surprise," Joe said. He pulled to the curb in front of a red brick Victorian with a yellow and black "for sale" sign tacked to the wrought-iron fence.

Frances frowned at the sign, whipped her head towards Joe. "No," she said.

"Yes! Come on, let me show you our new house." He pulled his key ring from the ignition and dangled a tarnished barrel key. He ran around the truck and yanked the "for sale" sign off the fence and pushed open the rusty gate hanging by one hinge. After a run up the herringboned brick walk, he took the porch steps two at a time and tossed the sign to the worn boards. He turned and waved.

Frances opened the door, stared at the house. The age and color reminded her of the Pickett house but this one was smaller. It had an interesting roof line with a sharply-peaked gothic gable in front and a half-moon skylight set high in the attic near the roof. She frowned at the stained glass window on the first floor, remembering the dark windows at the Pickett house. She eyed the porch. Not nearly as large as the wrap-around on the farmhouse, but it was a good-sized porch, badly in need of paint. With a closer look, she spotted sagging where the porch curved around the right side of the house and several balusters were missing from the railing. She remained beside the truck, arms crossed, mouth in a tight line, fuming. Her husband made another life-changing decision without her input. She shook her head, angry at herself for believing he had learned his lesson. A few days after they moved east, Joe admitted that leaving the farm had been rash, coming very close to an apology. She had asked why he didn't talk to her beforehand.

"You were the one always telling me to 'speak up' in college," Frances said during a late-night argument in Stephanie's living room a few nights after they arrived. "What about Little Joe? Doesn't he have a say?"

"A child does what his parents say," Joe had said.

"Parents, Joe. You said parents, with an 's,'" Frances snapped.

"Keep your voice down," Joe said, lowering his own to a whisper. "Let's make the best of it. I'll make sure we don't regret the decision to move to Delaware."

"Your decision," Frances said. "Not 'the' decision, it was 'your' decision."

Joe had stared at her, his eyes dark. For the next few months, he was extra agreeable. Consulted her about the duplex, she agreeing it was time to move out of Stephanie's, but within the year he was back to his old ways, starting a construction company on his own, buying a truck. Is this what marriage was supposed to be, she wondered. The husband making the decisions, the wife going along with it? That was how it was with her mother, no question George called all the shots, but what she saw of Randolph's and Lily's brief marriage was different. Her stepbrother had asked for Lily's opinion, valued it. Did Frances's thoughts mean nothing to Joe?

Standing next to the open door of the Victorian, Joe clapped. "Come on!" He opened his arms, beckoned her towards him.

With a resigned sigh, she moved up the uneven walk, the smooth soles of her loafers slipping on the moss-covered bricks. The banister wobbled under her hand as she made her way up the steps to Joe's side.

He lifted her into his arms. "Never did get to carry you over the threshold when we got married." Kissing her twice, he stepped into the house and lowered her feet to the floor of checkered tiles of black and white octagons. He ran a hand over the intricate pattern of vines and leaves carved into the thick wood of the door. "Look at this. Solid oak." He grasped Frances's hand and led her out of the small entrance to a long hallway and stomped his foot. "All new carpet. That's the living room." His wagged his hand to the left at a large room with faded wallpaper rising to the six-inch crown molding and plasterwork ceiling. "It just needs a coat of paint." He took several steps and stopped, chin titled up, right hand resting on the dark oak mantle above a green-tiled fireplace. "Look at this staircase. Three stories."

Frances studied the handrail as it curved up the stairs, sunlight slanting through the broad windows on the generous landing.

"Here's the dining room," Joe called from the next room.

Frances forced her feet forward. Shoulder-high oak paneling connected a built-in sideboard on one wall to a fireplace surrounded by burgundy tile on the opposite wall. Dust dulled the chandelier, three tiers of beveled crystals on tarnished brass arms. Another set of stairs, narrow and unadorned, separated the dining room from the kitchen.

"This is a bathroom. But it needs work," Joe said, opening and closing a door beneath the back stairs. "What do you think of the kitchen? A good size, isn't it? And that door goes to another porch and there's a backyard. Not real big, but Winston and Little Joe will love it."

At the gas range, Frances bent and opened the oven door, wrinkling her nose at layers of burnt grease, her eyes watering at the caustic smell. She twisted both the hot and cold water handles but only a drip fell to the porcelain stippled with rust. She squinted at the crack running across the ceiling, a triangle of brown filling one corner.

"I can fix that," Joe said, following her gaze. "We'll get a new stove and refrigerator. And sink. But the tile's in great shape."

She looked at the white rectangular tile covering the bottom half of the wall, searching for blemishes or cracks, but, trying hard, she found none.

"Let's go upstairs." Joe bounded up the back staircase. "I think your mom will like this bedroom," he said, his voice raised to be heard over the groaning boards.

Frances didn't move. If he had asked her—his wife—what she wanted in a house, she would have said a place where the floors didn't creak and the ceiling wasn't cracked. A new house. That's what they had planned at the farm. But she didn't say a word when Joe told her they would stay in the farmhouse. Didn't say a word when he insisted on two new bathrooms, leaving no funds to bring the kitchen up to date. Not one complaint. "Follow the rules, listen, don't talk," the nuns had said. "It's best to stay quiet, don't upset George or Russell," her mother had said. Trained to keep her thoughts to herself, she had a lifetime of unsaid words.

She sucked in her breath and walked up the bare stairs into a long room, the floor covered with the same olive green carpet as the downstairs hall. The room's lone window was covered by a shade and she tugged the pull ring. The oiled cloth didn't budge. She lifted an edge from the window and looked out at the narrow yard bordered by a rusting fence. A pebbled alley marked the back boundary.

"I'll build a garage," Joe said, his head ducked behind the opposite side of the shade. He smiled at Frances across the glass, dimple winking.

The cloth fell from her fingers and she stepped back. That dimple was not going to charm her, she thought, even though she rarely saw it these days. She stomped to the adjoining room, a bathroom with a large tub surrounded by a wall of the same white tile as in the kitchen.

"Look a shower," Joe said. He stood at the doorway, his smile intact. "Just like in the hotel in Buffalo. Little Joe will love it. And that's his bedroom." He pointed and disappeared through the door at the opposite side of the bathroom.

She stepped into the next room, slightly smaller than the first bedroom, the hardwood floor bare. It would be a good room for her son, she admitted to herself. Getting Little Joe out of their current neighborhood was very appealing.

"When he gets older Little Joe can move to the third floor," Joe said. "I'll fix it up. Add a bathroom." He walked out the second door of the bedroom and down the hall towards the front of the house. "Come see the other bathroom."

Larger than the first bathroom, this one was also tiled in white but what caught her eye was the window above the deep, claw-foot tub. It was the first stained-glass window she saw that she liked. No dark reds or burgundies, this window was pale blue with flowers of lavender petals on slim green stems. Orchids, like the ones in the conservatory where she and Joe shared their first kiss.

"Imagine taking a bath in that tub," he nudged her with his elbow. "Room for both of us."

Frances stared at the tub, face warming as she allowed herself to imagine the romantic scene. If only, she thought, and moved back into the hall.

Joe brushed past her through the next door. "This is our bedroom." He stood in the middle of a spacious room, grinning.

It was the grin she fell in love with, the grin she hadn't seen in many months. It could still make her legs weak, her heart thump. She turned away, didn't want him to see her flushed cheeks, and walked to one of the two windows. It wouldn't open.

"Here, let me help." Joe said, his hand on hers.

She pulled her hand away and moved to the other window, the gauzy leaves of a large maple inches from the glass. Her shoulder against the pane, she pushed and the heavy casement eventually slid up with a moan, the outside air rushing in, carrying the smell of mowed grass and something blooming, roses perhaps. She heard the sound of traffic, but it was faint, barely audible over the trilling birds, their notes sharp and sweet. This could be a fresh start, in and out of the bedroom. The heat from her cheeks spread downward and she couldn't help but smile.

Joe punched his palm with his fist. "I knew you'd like it! I know it needs work but it's sturdy," he said, stomping his foot on the thick carpeting. "All brick. A solid foundation. I'll do the work myself."

"But, Joe, how can we afford this?"

"I used the rest of the money from Uncle Bill for a down payment. The company is doing great. We just hired another fella. And with the money from your job we'll be fine." He laid a hand on Frances's shoulder and smiled at her, his eyes as green as the leaves outside the window." I used the G.I. bill for the mortgage. Why pay rent to someone else? Let's get on with our life." He pulled her into his arms and kissed her.

The heat was undeniable, as if a flame had been lit in Joe. He teased her lips apart, tongue probing, his hand sliding her dress up her thigh, rose-scented breeze grazing her bare buttocks. She unbuttoned his shirt, fingers flying, her lips on his bare chest. He spread his shirt on the carpet and they dropped to the floor, Frances finally getting her long-awaited, second honeymoon.

CHAPTER THIRTY-SEVEN

October 1954
Wilmington, Delaware

"Ouch!" Little Joe yelped.

"Sorry. Stand still," Martha mumbled through the pins clamped between her lips. She and Stephanie were crouched Frances's living room, sewing the final touches to the eleven-year-old's Halloween costume.

"It's not funny, Tuck," Little Joe said, pointing at his friend, Tommy Tucker.

Tommy laughed harder and spun around, the fringe on his vest and pants flapping. He and Little Joe were dressing up as cowboys for Halloween and Stephanie made their costumes, with Martha's help.

Martha smiled at her grandson's friend, glad that Little Joe finally found an ally. It had been heartbreaking to watch the boy struggle through those first years in Wilmington. His life had been upended, thrown into turmoil, through no fault of his own. It brought back painful memories of Frances in the monastery. She knew all too well that a child can't understand why they were removed from the only home they ever had and tossed into a new world full of strangers. She had thought a brother or sister would have been good for Little Joe but she never asked Frances about it. As close as they were, there were some things they didn't talk about.

"Looks good, Little Joe," Frances said, walking into the living room with a plate of cookies, the scent of vanilla and cinnamon trailing.

Martha studied Frances as Little Joe and Tommy followed the plate to the coffee table. She wondered what scars Frances carried from her childhood trauma. Her daughter could fall into days of melancholy and Martha was unsure if it was just France's introspective nature or unhealed wounds from those precarious months in the monastery.

Tommy murmured something that Martha didn't catch but it made her grandson double over with laughter. Music to her ears, Little Joe's laugh made her heart soar.

"You and Tommy take a cookie upstairs and get back into your play clothes," Frances said. She turned to Stephanie. "How can I thank you for doing this? I know how busy you are."

"I was glad for the excuse to leave the lab at a decent hour. I am stymied." Stephanie worked to her feet and sat beside Frances on the couch, tugging her skirt over her knees.

"Things not going well?" Frances asked.

Stephanie shook her head. "Three years I've been testing polymers. Thousands of chains. None of them with the results the company wants."

"Organic or synthetic monomers?"

"We've tried both, but we get a better inter-molecular bond with synthetic."

"What about the bond between carbonyl groups and centers?"

Martha shook her head, letting out an exaggerated sigh.

"What?" Frances turned, eyebrows raised.

"You are wasting your talents at the grocery store, Sunshine."

"Not much longer," Frances said. "Joe said the company is doing fine and I don't need to work. I'm just staying on until they can find someone to replace me."

Thank goodness, Martha thought. The grocery store was no place for her daughter. Frances could have found a job closer to the Victorian but she was loyal, grateful to the store's owner who gave her a job when they moved to the duplex and were desperate for income. Martha's thoughts clouded. She had been angry at Joe for months after dragging them to Wilmington. Could barely look him in the eye. But she was also beholden to him. From the day he came home from the war, Joe had been gracious to her. Treated her as family, never complained about her presence. Many men would not be so charitable to their mother-in-law.

"Will you go back to college?" Stephanie asked.

"Not now. I want to be here for Little Joe. Maybe when he goes to high school."

Martha knew her daughter wanted to make up for the past four years when she wasn't here to greet Little Joe when he came home from school. It was Martha who dried the boy's tears. Helped him with homework. Tossed the ball to him in the back yard.

A knock at the door interrupted her thoughts. She stood. "I'll get it."

Joe's business partner, Frank McLaughlin, stood on the front porch, a pumpkin in one hand, a brown paper bag in the other. "Hello, Martha. You're looking especially beautiful today."

"Hallo, Frank." Martha's cheeks warmed. She stepped back and followed him to the living room.

"Hello, ladies," Frank said, bending at the waist into a slight bow.

"Frank!" Little Joe yelled as he bounded down the stairs, Tommy on his heels. "What you got there?"

Frank held up the pumpkin. "Hi boys. Anyone want to make a jack o-lantern?"

Little Joe and Tommy chattered and skittered around Frank, Winston joining in the melee with a howl. Martha herded the group to the kitchen, the room spacious and comfortable, with all new appliances, just as Joe had promised when they moved in two years ago.

"I brought everything we need." Frank lowered the pumpkin to the table and pulled a large knife and a candle from the bag. "Don't touch that," he said, pointing to the long blade. Frank had been Joe's foreman on the first construction job he worked after their move to Wilmington and despite their age difference—Frank was twenty years older than Joe—the two men hit it off. Frank was impressed with Joe's skills and drive, and when Joe confided his desire to start his own company, Frank proposed a partnership. He was good with numbers, Joe was a meticulous craftsman, and the business thrived.

Kneeling on the chairs, Little Joe and Tommy watched as Martha spread newspaper across the table. They knocked on the pumpkin, laughing at the hollow sound.

"That's a really big one, Frank," Little Joe said.

"Aw, that's nothing." Tommy waved his hand. "Back home we used to grow pumpkins bigger than Winston." Tommy was a transplant, too, uprooted from Ohio.

"I'll cut off the top, and you boys scoop out the seeds," Frank said, pushing the knife into the pumpkin's flesh, an earthy, ripe scent filling the room.

Martha leaned on the counter to oversee the carving, a content smile on her face.

A widower for four years before joining forces with Joe, Frank let everyone know he was smitten with Martha from the day he met her. When the company was in its infancy, Joe and Frank spent evenings in the kitchen at the rented duplex, scheming and dreaming. At first, Martha resisted Frank's advances. He didn't give up. He wrangled invitations from Joe for family dinners at the Ferguson house, always bringing a gift for Martha.

Always ready with a joke, and a compliment. But it was the way he treated Little Joe that finally won Martha's heart. When Frank took his own grandchildren to the zoo or the park, or ice skating in the winter, he also included Little Joe. No matter how busy the company got, he always made time for the children in his life.

Winston circled the table, pouncing on a scrap. He chewed and spat it out, deciding it wasn't the usual gourmet fare gracing the kitchen floor. The boys giggled as they pulled handfuls of orange muck from the big gourd, seeds caught in the stringy pulp like minnows in a fisherman's net.

Frank looked up, his eyes finding Martha's. He smiled. "I have something for you." He walked to her side and dug in his chest pocket, pulling out a small box tied with a pink ribbon.

"Oh, Frank, another gift?" Martha said, face flushing. "You just gave me one for my birthday." Two weeks ago, when Frances insisted on a party for Martha's fifty-fifth birthday, complete with a three-layer cake, balloons and paper streamers hanging from the chandelier in the dining room, Frank had given her a transistor radio. The portable novelty quickly became a favorite of Little Joe's, her grandson and Tuck singing and barking to "Doggie in the Window" as they carried the little, red radio around the house.

"What is it, Grandma?" Little Joe asked, watching her slip the ribbon from the box, anticipating another present he could enjoy.

She smiled. "A pumpkin."

"What?"

Martha held up a gold brooch, in the shape of a pumpkin, with two small emeralds as a stem. "It's lovely, Frank. Thank you."

He leaned in and gave her a quick kiss on the cheek. She felt her blush deepen, just as it always did when Frank showed affection in front of her family, but she had grown to like frank's special ministrations.

"Guess we're eating in the dining room." Frances stood at the door of the kitchen, surveying the mess. "Tommy, you want to stay for supper? I'll call your mother. Frank, how about you?"

"Sure." Frank pushed on a triangle he cut into the pumpkin. "There's the other eye, boys." He turned the pumpkin towards Little Joe and Tommy. "Now the mouth. Jack needs some teeth."

"Do you know what time Joe will be home?" Frances asked.

"He wants to finish the Rawlings' basement tonight." Frank paused, his knife poised over the pumpkin. "He told me to tell you not to hold dinner."

"He hasn't been home for dinner in a week," Frances said. She pulled a tall pot from a cabinet. "Wonder if he'll make it home for Halloween tomorrow night."

"He promised to take us trick-or-treating," Little Joe said.

Frank returned his attention to the pumpkin, cut a final square. "I can take the boys through the neighborhood tomorrow night if Joe can't make it home."

"Thank you," Frances said, shaking dry noodles into the pot.

"I told your husband to slow down, have some fun," Frank said. "Joe said there'll be plenty of time for fun later. I thought the same thing." He straightened, looked at Martha. "So now I have to make up for all those lost adventures, and I found the perfect gal."

Martha snorted. She was far from perfect but Frank made her believe she could be happy.

CHAPTER THIRTY-EIGHT

November 1954
Wilmington, Delaware

Martha stood at the window in the kitchen, sipping coffee, watching two cardinals pick through the fallen leaves, their scarlet feathers bright against the faded grass. This was still her favorite season. And early morning, just after dawn, was her favorite time of the day. She had volunteered to rise extra early today to get the turkey stuffed and in the oven so it would be ready for the noon feast. The birds suddenly took flight and the yellow Hy-Point Dairy truck appeared in the alley. She opened the door. "Happy Thanksgiving, Mr. Meany."

He extended his own greeting as she took the crate from his hands, the bottles rattling against the aluminum bars.

She put one bottle on the table and loaded the remaining quarts into the refrigerator, straightening at the sound of footsteps on the bare boards of the back stairs.

"Good morning!" Frances said, her slippers slapping against the kitchen tiles as she stalked the coffee pot simmering on the stovetop.

"Happy Thanksgiving, Sunshine." Martha held out her cup out for a refill. "Cinnamon rolls will be ready soon."

Frances frowned "What about the turkey?"

Martha laughed. "It's in the oven, too. I thought if I made cinnamon rolls and put them in the living room it would keep Little Joe out of the way."

"And, Big Joe, too," Frances said.

"What about Big Joe?" Joe asked. He stood at the bottom of the stairs in his bathrobe, running a hand over his stubbled chin.

Frances poured a cup of coffee, added a splash of milk, and handed it to him. "You and Little Joe can eat breakfast in the living room." She kissed his cheek and turned him towards the doorway, giving his bottom a quick pat.

Martha smiled at the exchange, laughing when Frances caught her watching and blushed to a shade nearly as bright as birds in the yard. Martha walked to her daughter and kissed her cheek. "It's lovely to see you happy." Frances's blush deepened.

They both turned at the noise on the stairs, Little Joe and Winston spilling into the kitchen.

"What are you wearing?" Frances shook her head at Little Joe's cowboy costume. "Halloween was last month."

Little Joe smiled, his emerging dimple on display. "Cowboys have Thanksgiving, too, Mom." With a finger, he pushed his hat up his forehead, his eyes twinkling.

Martha laughed.

Frances shrugged. "Guess he should wear it while he can. The way he's growing, it will be too small in a month or two." She poured a glass of milk and handed it to Little Joe "Take this with you. Grandma made cinnamon rolls. You and your father can eat them in the living room."

"Oh boy! Cinnamon rolls," Little Joe yelled, yanking the toy gun from the holster on his hip and aiming it at Winston. He clicked the trigger, Winston barking.

Frances pushed the gun's barrel up, directing it towards the ceiling. "What did I tell you about pointing that gun at anyone, including Winston? Go on. "She turned him around and nudged him towards the living room. "I'll take Winston outside."

Martha removed the pan of rolls from the oven, the warm scent of cinnamon filling the room. She swirled white icing across the top and carried the pan to the living room, lowering it to the table in front of the sofa. The room was warm, Joe had built a fire in the fireplace, and the television buzzed, fuzzy, gray images moving across the screen.

Joe lowered his newspaper and grinned, a mischievous glint in his eyes. "Beautiful day, isn't it Martha?"

Martha nodded, watched Little Joe devour a cinnamon roll in three bites, licking his fingers before grabbing another. "Yes. Yes, it is." She returned Joe's smile, raised her eyebrow, waiting for whatever it was Joe was hinting at.

"Frank finagled another invitation out of me. He's bringing wine and some kind of Jell-o thing his daughter makes," Joe said, leaning forward to nab a roll.

Martha frowned. "I thought he was eating at his daughter's."

"Oh, he is. His daughter's having dinner at five. Frank found a way to have two Thanksgiving meals." Joe kept grinning, roll in hand.

Martha shrugged, but inside she was smiling. "Well, we certainly have plenty. Did you buy the biggest turkey A & P had?"

Joe laughed, bit his roll in half, and swallowed. "You can never have too much leftover turkey. Especially the drumsticks." He looked at Little Joe. "Right?"

Little Joe nodded, eyes wide, mouth full.

"Hmm," Joe said, a crease etching between his eyes but his mouth turned up at one end. "Hope I won't have to fight Frank for a drumstick."

Martha shook her head with a laugh and walked away. She paused in the dining room, watching Frances smooth the orange tablecloth across the table. She smiled. Ruth Pickett would have been horrified at the colored cloth. "You'll need to set one more, Sunshine. Joe just told me Frank is coming."

"Oh, is he?" Frances said, her attention focused on the table.

Martha gave her daughter a sideways glance and moved on to the kitchen. She turned the dial on the transistor radio in the windowsill and settled at the table with her coffee cup and potato peeler. "Do you think I should make biscuits?" she asked when Frances walked into the kitchen.

"Stephanie is bringing bread," Frances said, sitting across from her mother, paring knife in hand. "That should be plenty, even with Frank coming."

"Well-ll," Martha said, drawing out the word. She loved Stephanie, had come to think of her as family, appreciated her kindness and generosity, but the truth was, Stephanie couldn't cook to save her life. From that Thanksgiving Day four years ago when they moved in, invaded Stephanie's house, Martha had taken charge of the small kitchen. She snorted, remembering Stephanie, one of the smartest people she had ever met, trying, unsuccessfully, to fit the turkey in the roasting pan.

"What?" Frances asked. She giggled. "Stop worrying, Mom. Stephanie visited New Kensington last week and brought back loaves of that bread her mother bakes."

Martha smiled, picked up another potato, searched for bad spots. "Chalka. That's what the bread is called."

"Uh-huh," Frances mumbled and snapped a green bean in half. She started humming to the radio.

Martha frowned. Her daughter seemed preoccupied. She was about to ask when Joe wandered into the kitchen and picked up the empty coffee pot. "I'll make another pot," Martha said.

"No hurry," Joe said. "I'm going to shower and shave. Need to look spiffy for the big day." He bent, kissed Frances on the cheek. "Little Joe is in front of the television but I don't expect him to sit still much longer." Straightening, back arched, arms overhead, he looked at the window. "I'll take him and Winston outside."

Joe disappeared up the stairs and Little Joe bounded into the kitchen, Winston and Stephanie on his heels.

"Aunt Stephanie is here," Little Joe yelled.

"Shush." Frances shook her head. "I see that. Happy Thanksgiving, Stephanie."

Martha moved from the range, took the two loaves from Stephanie's hands, and pulled her into a hug. Whatever she lacked in cooking skills, she made up for it with her fashion sense, always sporting the latest styles and trendy colors. Today, she wore a navy swing dress, a Swiss-dot scarf knotted at her neck. "How is your mother, Stephanie?" Martha asked.

"She's fine." Stephanie sighed. "Still working, though both Stanley and I think she should retire."

Martha took a deep breath, the bread wrapped in waxed paper inches from her nose. "I'll never tire of this smell."

Little Joe slipped into the chair beside his mother. "Can I have another roll and more milk?"

"Yes but go get the glass you left in the living room," Frances said. She turned her attention to Stephanie, nodded at a chair. "How was New Kensington?"

"Fine," Stephanie said and reached for one of the rolls. "I ran into Nancy Ferguson at Jackson's. They're tearing down the farmhouse."

"What?" Frances looked stricken.

Stephanie shrugged. "Whoever is living there now is building a new house."

"Todd," Frances said with a sigh. "Todd and his wife live there."

The percolator bubbled and Martha pulled the pot from the stove. She poured a cup for Stephanie, refilled Frances's and her own.

"Thank you," Stephanie said. She turned to Frances. "Nancy gave me a box of clothes. Little Joe's clothes. She thought you might want them."

"Clothes for me?" Little Joe stood at the door, empty glass in his hand.

Frances jumped up, took the glass and filled it with milk. "Old clothes. They don't fit you anymore." She pulled out a chair. "Sit." She glanced at the stairs again, put a roll in front of Little Joe. "We'll talk about it later," she said to Stephanie, her voice low.

"Hello!" Joe stepped into the kitchen, after-shave generously applied, the scent of citrus and cloves replacing the cinnamon smell. "Happy Thanksgiving, Stephanie," he said. He jutted his clean-shaven chin towards Little Joe. "Drink your milk, cowboy, and meet me in the backyard. We have leaves to rake."

***

"More turkey, Frank?" Joe asked, long knife in hand. "I'll fight you for the drumstick."

They had finished the meal, most having seconds of everything except Frank's orange Jell-o salad.

Frank shook his head. "I can't eat another thing." He nodded at the salad, more than half of the orange ring remaining. "I am leaving that here. It would hurt my daughter's feelings if I took it back with me. She said the salad was all the rage."

Martha stood. "It wasn't bad. We just have too much food. Including pie." She picked up Frank's empty plate and her own and carried them into the kitchen.

Frances followed with her plate, Joe's and Little Joe's in her hands, Winston on her heels. She tossed turkey scraps into the dog's bowl in the corner of the room. "I'll get the other bottle of wine, you bring the pie."

"More wine? I've never seen you drink more than one glass, Sunshine."

"Oh, well, I don't want to offend Frank, since he brought two bottles."

"What can I do?" Stephanie walked to the sink and stacked her plate with the others.

"Nothing, right now. It's time for dessert," Frances said, nudging Stephanie back towards the dining room. "Come on, Mom."

Frank stood when the women returned to the room, pulling the chair out for Martha. He opened the wine, refilled all the glasses.

"Who wants pie?" Martha asked, picking up a knife. "Oh," she said, jumping to her feet. "Forgot the whipped cream."

"Wait!" Frank put a hand on Martha's shoulder. "I have something to say before we cut the pie anyway." He cleared his throat, raised both hands to Martha's shoulders. "Martha, I love you."

"Yuck," Little Joe said. "He's getting mushy."

"Shush." Frances put a hand on Little Joe's arm.

Frank smiled at Little Joe. "Fine, I'll get right to it then. Martha, will you marry me?" He pulled a black box from his pocket and flipped it open, the diamond sparkling.

Throat tight, Martha lowered her head, concentrating on the uncut pie. She didn't think it was possible, never believed she deserved such a chance, but for the second time in her life, she was in love with a good man, who loved her back. "Yes," she said, raising her head, her gaze locking on Frank's. "Yes."

The room erupted in claps and laughter, Martha turning her attention to Frances. "You knew?"

Frances nodded. "Joe told me."

Martha looked at Frank, eyebrow raised. "So, I was the last to know?"

Frank shrugged. "Well, now, I couldn't ask your father for permission so I went with the next best thing."

Martha told Frank both her parents were dead and she had lost contact with her siblings. Both were true.

Klara sent a brief note two months after her stay in Webster Hill to let her know their father had passed. Martha felt little, the same lack of emotion as when George died. She told Frank she lost Frances's father in the first world war, letting him believe they were married. Frances refused to tell Joe she was born out of wedlock, saying it was too late now to change the story, and Martha couldn't take the chance that Frank might let it slip to Joe if she told the truth. Her smile wavered as she looked at Frank, wondering what he would think of her if he knew. And Joe? Would he think less of her? She could bear the disapproval from both men but the thought of letting down Little Joe was unacceptable. In her grandson's eyes, she could do no wrong.

"It's a dandy of a ring, don't you think, Martha?" Joe said. "Now I'm going to have to get my wife a diamond. Can't be outdone by an old fogey."

"How old are you, Frank?" Little Joe asked.

"Fifty-five," Frank said with a wink.

Little Joe let out a long whistle. "Wow, that is old."

Martha laughed. She looked at Joe and he winked. She smiled at Stephanie and Little Joe, then turned her gaze back to Frances. Joyful tears slide down her daughter's cheeks, and Martha was no longer able to contain her own.

CHAPTER THIRTY-NINE

September 1959
Wilmington, Delaware

Frances felt deserted. Her mother was out of town with Frank, Joe was on a job, and Little Joe was cruising in his new Corvair. She wasn't happy that Joe bought their son a car for his sixteenth birthday six weeks ago, but her husband was determined to give Little Joe everything he himself had been denied as a young man. When Stephanie invited her to take a drive, Frances gladly accepted.

"Where are we going?" She asked as she settled into Stephanie's long estate car. Her friend had an affinity for station wagons, telling Frances that you never knew when you might need the room. Frances had never once seen her friend fill her car.

"To the university. I want to show you how close it is to your house." Stephanie flipped her signal with a loud click and turned on to the sprawling campus. "You told me you couldn't go back to college until Little Joe was in high school. Well, Little Joe's in high school."

"I don't know. I've forgotten much of what I learned at Tech," Frances said as they wound through the campus. She had thought of returning to college more than once but always found an excuse to delay that final semester. They passed a sleek, two-story building, the glass shimmering in the autumn sun. Next to it was a stocky brick structure, students skipping down the stone steps.

"You've forgotten more than most of my new assistants ever knew about chemistry," Stephanie said and worked her long vehicle into a parking space in front of a three-story, gothic-looking structure. She shut down the car and faced Frances. "I sent for your transcripts. We have a meeting with the head of the chemistry department at four o'clock."

"What? No. I'm not dressed for a meeting." Frances leaned left, catching a glimpse of herself in the rearview mirror.

"You look fine," Stephanie said.

Easy for her to say, Frances thought and gave her friend a sideways glance. Stephanie never left her house looking passé, fashion magazines her guilty pleasure. She frowned at the mirror. "My hair is a mess."

"Stop making excuses. Come on," Stephanie said. "It can't hurt to talk with him."

Dr. Geoffrey Linden, head of the Chemistry Department, stood when she and Stephanie were led into his office. He raised his arm, frowning at his watch. "I have a meeting across campus at four-thirty, Miss Kwolek."

"We won't take up much of your time, Doctor," Stephanie said. "Have you reviewed Mrs. Ferguson's transcripts?"

Dr. Linden sighed and sat back down, waving a hand towards the chairs in front of his desk. "Mrs. Ferguson would need to take basic chemistry, and calculus, before she can even be considered for the organic and physical chemistry courses." He pulled his glasses off and rubbed his eyes.

"She had basic chemistry at Carnegie Tech. And organic chemistry," Stephanie said, crossing her arms across her chest. "Mrs. Ferguson was an exceptional student."

342

The professor let out another sigh, this one louder and longer than the last, and leaned forward, elbows on his desk. "The chemistry requirements have changed since you attended college, Mrs. Ferguson." His chin dropped and he peered over the top of the lenses at Frances. "Perhaps you would be more comfortable in another course of study? One that would offer more employment opportunities for a woman of your station in life. Our teaching curriculum is excellent."

"She already has employment opportunities. At our Research Laboratory." Stephanie lowered her hands to the arms of the chair and leaned forward. "Perhaps you've heard of it? We are quite generous to the University."

Frances put a hand on Stephanie arm to quiet her. "I was hoping to complete my studies in one semester."

Dr. Linden shook his head. "That won't be possible. If you can't devote the time necessary..."

"She can." Stephanie pushed to her feet. "Thank you. We'll take a look around."

They wandered the building, walking into an empty lecture hall large enough to hold a hundred students. Frances examined a painted wood model of molecules and squinted at the five-foot wide periodic table suspended from the ceiling. She breathed in, the scent of chalk dust and nervous sweat transporting her back to her days at Carnegie Tech. She had been so anxious in those first weeks at college, Christy cracking jokes to calm her.

"It says the Science Building has been renovated and modernized to meet the requirements for today's exacting scientific work." Stephanie stood by the chalkboard and read from the college catalog. "There are two lecture halls, eight classrooms and three laboratories incorporating the most efficient exhaust hood system available today." She looked up and winked. "So any fires you start will be whisked away by the exhaust hood."

"Don't say that!" Frances said.

343

"I'm joking. Let's look at a laboratory."

Frances sighed. Now it was Stephanie cracking jokes to calm her. Wrangling in the kernel of doubt grazing in the pit of her stomach, she followed her friend through the long hallway and down the stairs.

"Looks like the lab at Tech," Stephanie said.

It did remind Frances of her college lab, and she was relieved. Stephanie's research laboratory was overwhelming to her. It was large—covering several acres—and full of unfamiliar equipment, but this lab was comfortable, the wood counters topped by two-inch black slate in the familiar u-shape, a Bunsen burner every six feet. Another, slightly smaller version of the periodic table hung next to the chalkboard. She walked to the wall of wood shelves, staring up at the empty glass beakers, flasks and tubes, her fingers twisting the diamond ring on her left hand. Joe had been true to his word at her mother's engagement and bought Frances a gold ring with one large diamond set between two smaller ones.

"Frances," Stephanie called, waving a map. "Let's get to the admission office before it closes."

As they crossed the grassy quadrangle, Stephanie came to an abrupt stop, lowering her head and throwing up an arm as a plastic disc flew overhead.

"Sorry, ma'am." A young man in sneakers and t-shirt, his blue jeans rolled to mid-calf, jogged by. He pushed his hair from his eyes and bent to retrieve the toy, flinging it toward a group of young men several yards away. All were casually dressed, many barefoot. Not far from the men, two young women in shorts and bathing suit tops stretched out on towels spread over the grass, a transistor radio blaring tunes she didn't recognize.

"Things sure have changed since we were students," Stephanie said.

Frances nodded, remembering Christy's daily, hour-long preening before she left their dorm room. "You never know who you might run into," she had always said, admonishing Frances over her scuffed oxfords and unflattering skirts. Most of the women in their dormitory were just as fastidious as Christy and would have been appalled by the scantily-clad students. Frances picked up her pace, shaking her head at that familiar feeling of being out of place.

***

It took Frances a week to get up the nerve to talk to Joe about returning to college.

"How much?" he asked.

She slid a list of the college costs across the kitchen table as Joe pushed his coffee cup aside, flipping his silver zippo open to light a cigarette. He drummed his fingers on the table, scanning the page. "And then you'll go work for Stephanie?" He asked through a cloud of smoke.

She nodded.

"Every day?"

"Little Joe doesn't need me anymore."

"I need you," Joe said. He smiled. "You're lucky. You don't need to work."

She returned the smile, but it slid away when Joe shook open the newspaper and disappeared behind it. She wandered into the dining room, blowing dust from the mantle, and continued into the hallway. In the living room, she curled up in her favorite chair by the window. Since her mother married and moved out, and Winston died, the house seemed so empty. Joe still worked long hours and Little Joe was busy in his teenage world. She sighed, her husband was right. She didn't need to work. College was a silly idea.

After a week of dodging Stephanie's calls, she finally admitted to her friend that she hadn't moved forward with her plans.

345

"Frances, please. I need you on my team," Stephanie said. "And I know you want back in the laboratory. I could see it in your eyes when we were at the college lab."

Frances dismissed Stephanie's comments but after another long day wandering the quiet house, she sat down to complete the admission forms. She got as far as her address when the phone rang. It was Frank, breathless and rambling. Joe collapsed and was rushed to the hospital. He had lung cancer.

CHAPTER FORTY

November 1959
Wilmington, Delaware

"Why? Why did he get sick?" Frances asked the doctor. She and her mother stood outside Joe's hospital room where he had laid, comatose, under an oxygen tent for the past five days.

The doctor lifted a shoulder. "There is no exact cause."

"When will he wake up?" Frances probed.

"I don't know when, or if, he will regain consciousness," he said. "It's the morphine. But without it, the pain would be unbearable."

Since the diagnosis six weeks ago, Joe had seen four different doctors, and all gave him the same answer, "there is nothing we can do." He kept working, until a bout of coughing left him doubled over in pain, blood dripping down his chin. Frank drove him home and Joe dropped to the couch in the living room, too weak to climb the stairs to the bedroom. Frances spent her nights on the floor beside him, her days cooking his favorite foods. He barely ate, even broth was difficult to swallow, but Frances wouldn't give up. She was determined to feed the cancer from him, believing, just as Joe's grandmother taught her, that food was a salve for any ailment. Sniffles? Chicken and dumplings. Backache? Roast beef and mashed potatoes. Feeling blue? Ham and eggs, sunny-side up.

On his last morning home Joe refused all food, grasping Frances's hand as she tried to spoon broth in his mouth. "I'm sorry, Frances," he said, his voice a croak. "I know I don't say it much but I do love you. I don't want to leave you."

She dropped the spoon in the bowl and pushed it aside. Finally meeting his eyes, emerald green that day, she merely nodded. Moments later, he went into a violent coughing fit. She called Frank. Frank called an ambulance.

It was the last time Joe was conscious. She should have told him there was no reason to be sorry. Or simply, "I love you, too." She would regret her silence for the rest of her life. Beside her, she felt the doctor shift his weight, starting his retreat. Her mother stopped him with a hand to his wrist.

"How long?" Martha asked.

The doctor hesitated. "A day. Maybe." He focused on a point above Martha's head, refusing to meet her eyes, or Frances's. "More likely, a few hours." He turned away, his white coat flapping around his legs as he escaped down the hall.

"I'll call Frank," Martha said.

"No!" Frances grabbed Martha's arm. "Don't leave me."

Martha turned, glared at a trio of gawking nurses. She nudged Frances towards Joe's room and they stood at the doorway, watching a nurse remove the plastic that had been tented over her husband's face and torso.

"What are you doing?" Frances demanded, her nails digging into Martha's skin.

"Dr. Irving said there's no further need for the oxygen tent," the nurse said, carefully folding the plastic. She pulled a chair close to the bed and gave Frances a tired smile. "Sit down, Mrs. Ferguson. Talk to him, if you like."

Martha extracted her arm from Frances's grip and walked to the chair, helping Frances into it. She lay her hand on Joe's for a moment, then knelt beside Frances. "I'll be right back, Sunshine." She stood and walked to the nurse. "I need to call my husband," she whispered.

The nurse nodded and Martha slipped out the door.

"Can he hear me?" Frances asked.

"I think so." The nurse's shoes squeaked as she moved across the polished floor, stopping to tap the bottle hanging near Joe's head.

Frances slid her hand under Joe's, her thumb mapping the familiar terrain of his calloused palm. She willed his eyes to open, wondering what color they would be today. His eyes were often a reflection of his surroundings but this room was colorless, a sterile mixture of whites and grays. She tried to think of something profound to say. Or perhaps a fond memory to make them both smile. Nothing. Her mind was blank, refusing to cooperate. She shook her head. "No. I won't let you go. I can't live without you. Wake up. Wake up, now. Wake up."

She got louder with each command, the nurse scurrying from the room and returning with Martha.

"Frances, let's step outside." Her mother leaned close, whispering in her ear. "The priest is here."

Horrified to see Father John standing at the door with his bible, chalice, pyx and paten in his arms, Frances pushed to her feet. "No," she said, jerking her head from side to side, her vision blurring. She took a wobbly step, dropped back to the chair. Her eyes filled and her vision blurred again. She blindly reached for Joe's hand, holding tight as his skin cooled beneath her fingertips.

***

349

The grief was all-consuming. Smothering. Five days passed and Frances was still unable to eat, sleep or utter a coherent sentence. Her mother moved back into her old bedroom, cooking, cleaning, and reminding Frances to breathe. Frances stared out the window of the bedroom she had shared with Joe, twisting her ring, a thousand "what-if's" filling her head. *What if they stayed at the farm? Maybe the city air dirtied his lungs. Could it have been the cigarettes? No, the army wouldn't have given the soldiers something bad. Maybe the war caused it? He never should have enlisted. They would have drafted him anyway.* Her thoughts looped, overlapped, tangled and knotted. She couldn't control them.

Little Joe had no idea what to do with his grief. He was sent home twice from school for fighting and when he was home, he locked himself in his bedroom. Martha climbed the stairs to the third floor with trays of food, coaxing him to eat.

Despite Frances's objections, her mother planned a Thanksgiving Day feast, recruiting Stephanie's help to get the meal on the dining room table at noon. Frances stayed in bed until eleven, wanted to stay in bed the remainder of the day, but her mother was persistent.

"Joe loved Thanksgiving. He wouldn't want you to miss it," Martha said, pulling a blouse from the closet.

She rolled away from her mother and stared at the window, remembering her first time in this room. The house turned out to be a fresh start for both of them. They found happiness again. She squeezed her eyes closed, pushing away the memory.

"Sunshine." Her mother sat beside her, her hand on Frances's shoulder. "I wish I had words to ease your pain." Martha paused, continued in a soft voice. "When Frederic died, I didn't think I would ever feel right again."

Frances turned and looked at her mother, incredulous. "Now, you talk about Frederic? When I asked about him years ago you had nothing to say."

"It hurt to talk about Frederic," Martha said. "It still hurts." She lay her hand on her chest. "You learn to live with it."

Frances rolled her head back towards the window. *Live with the pain.* That's the best her mother could come up with? She closed her eyes again, her hands rolled into fists. "Go away." The bed moved.

"No," her mother said from across the room, obviously back in the closet. "Your son needs you." She tossed a skirt and blouse on the bed. "You are the reason I survived Frederic's death. I am forever grateful to Peter, your father, for giving me the best possible reason to go on." She patted Frances's ankle beneath the blanket, prompting Frances to open her eyes. "Just get up for an hour. Put on some clothes, brush your hair. You don't have to eat. But you do need to show Little Joe that you are trying." She walked to the door, paused, turning back to give Frances a small smile, and left the room, closing the door behind her.

When Frances made it to the dining room, Frank was leaning over the steaming turkey, a long knife in his right hand and a large, two-pronged fork in his left. He lowered the knife and fork, looked at Frances expectantly.

Frances shook her head. She wasn't going to say grace. Wasn't going to thank God. She slipped into her chair. "Let's eat," she said, her voice hollow, an inky murkiness threatening to overwhelm. She stared at the fork beside her plate, doubting she had the strength to lift it.

"My dad always carves the turkey." Little Joe jumped from his chair. "Let me do it." He reached for the knife just as Frank withdrew the blade and Little Joe ended up with a three-inch slice across his palm.

Her son's cries cut through her fog and Frances sprang from the chair. She cradled Little Joe's hand in hers, pressing napkins to the gash. "We are going to the

351

hospital," she announced. When everyone at the table stood she gave her head a strong shake. "Just me and my son."

She sat beside Little Joe in the emergency room while the young doctor stitched his palm, and, though he was sixteen years old and physically a man at six feet tall, Frances still saw her little boy, wincing each time the needle pierced his skin.

He leaned his head on her shoulder and let her comfort him as if he was five.

"I'm sorry your father died," Frances said.

"Me, too."

She stared at the row of black stitches zipping across his palm and wished it was her hand that was slashed. Wished her pain was on the outside. A laceration heals, the pain lessening with each day, but her pain, the pain on the inside, wasn't easing. It wasn't going away. And now, her mother's words echoing, she knew it never would. *Learn to live with it.*

That Sunday after Thanksgiving, Frances forced herself back to church, staring at the crucifix over Father John's head throughout the service. Little Joe did not go with her.

CHAPTER FORTY-ONE

December 1960
Wilmington, Delaware

Frances took a step back and scanned the eight-foot pine, searching for the perfect spot for her prized Santa ornament. She climbed two stairs on the step ladder and stretched her arm to hang the bulb on a branch near the top. A gift from Joe on their first Christmas in the Victorian, she refused to hang the bulb on the tree last year. It was the first year without Joe and she couldn't bear the sight of it. If she had her way last year, there wouldn't have been any Christmas decorations in the house but her mother put up the tree, arranged pine boughs on all the mantles and cooked a Christmas meal. Her mother stayed at the house until the middle of January, finally moving back to the homey ranch house Frank had built when they married.

The bulb against her palm, she admired the details of the painted face, the cherry-red lips, the bright blue eyes that reminded her of Joe's. Her breath hitched, the knotted ache in her chest tightening, threatening to unravel and strangle her. Just when she thought she was during fine, proud of her progress, a reminder would send her spiraling. She backed down the ladder and fell into the chair by the front window, searching for something, anything, to distract her darkening thoughts. She stared at the carpet, counting the loops as the early afternoon sun slanted across the gray wool. The house was warm today, unlike that first winter in the aging house when Frances was never without her sweater and she wore two pairs of socks to bed. Cold air had crept in through every ill-fitting window, some gaps as wide as her finger, and frost glazed the panes, inside and out. Joe replaced the windows, one by one, starting with the bedrooms. He had finally gotten to the windows in the living room the summer before he died.

She turned and watched Little Joe pull his car to the curb and hop out, carefully closing and latching the fence gate behind him. Frances smiled. She spent years scolding her son for leaving the gate open and allowing Winston to escape. Out of habit, she glanced at the floor by the window on the south wall, one of Winston's favorite napping spots.

Bursting through the door, stomping his feet, Little Joe paused at the doorway to the living room. "Hiya, Mom." He nodded at the tree. "Looks good."

"Thanks, Little Joe." She never did learn to call her son something besides 'Little,' even though he corrected her daily in his pre-teen years. "You hungry?"

"Of course," he said, following Frances to the kitchen. He sniffed the vanilla-scented air. "You've been busy, Mom."

Baking had become a welcome distraction for Frances, the counters and table crowded with dozens of cookies stacked on silver trays and covered with cellophane. Little Joe stuffed an iced cookie in his mouth, swallowing it whole. He grabbed another and sat at the table. "We going to Grandma's for Christmas dinner again this year?"

She shook her head. "Your grandmother and Frank are coming here. His daughter, Rebecca, and her husband and daughter, will be coming, too."

"Melinda's coming, huh?" Little Joe grinned.

"Yes, Frank's granddaughter will be here." Frances gave her head another shake. "You should be thinking more about your grades, less about girls. Did you complete the forms for Widener?"

Quiet for a moment, Little Joe studied the trays, finally settling on a cookie shaped like a bell and sprinkled with red sugar. "I was thinking of taking a year off before going to college."

Not wanting an argument, or to alienate, Frances considered her words. At times, Little Joe took the opposite stance from hers for no obvious reason except to prove his bullheadedness. "What would you do?" she finally asked.

"Elliot's going to work at a hotel in the Poconos for the summer. When it closes for the season, he's going to Florida."

"You want to spend your life working at a hotel?"

"Not the rest of my life, Mom. I just want to see some new places. Meet some new people."

"You'll meet new people at college," Frances said. "Your father saved for your schooling. It was important to him."

"Dad never graduated from college," he said, lifting one shoulder. "You didn't graduate from college. Both of you did just fine."

"I regret I never got my degree."

"Yeah, yeah. I know. You had me instead. I've heard the story." He grinned, the dimple in his chin deep. "Say, how 'bout you use the money. Go to college instead of me."

This wasn't the first argument they had had about college. Little Joe's grades weren't great, slightly better than average, but he would be accepted at many colleges. Frances hoped her son would take an interest in Ferguson and McLaughlin Construction but he had shown little aptitude for neither hands-on work, nor management of the business. Frances brightened. "All

355

right. We're both going to college," she announced. "If I go, you go."

His mouth fell open. "I'm not going to college with my mother. I mean, I love you, Mom, but..."

She shook her head. "I don't mean the same school. But if I go back, you have to promise me you'll go." She extended her right arm, her eyebrows raised and a smile pulling at the corners of her mouth.

He stood, let out a long, low whistle and grasped her hand. "I just got bamboozled." He shook his head, grinning. "Well-played, Mom." He kissed the top of her head. "I'm going to Tuck's. See you at dinner."

Frances went to the desk in the small office under the main staircase and opened a drawer, withdrawing the partially-completed university admission form. She stared at the paper, her eyes blurring at the date on the top of the page. The date she learned Joe had cancer. She dropped the form to the desk and sat back. Time was now measured by Joe's death. Before Joe died, after Joe died. One day after Joe died. Two days. One week. Weeks became months. Then it was twelve months. She twisted the diamond on her finger, shaking her head. A year since Joe died. A year since she learned to change a light bulb, adjust the television antenna, balance a checkbook. Joe had taken care of everything. Before he died, her biggest decision was chicken or beef for dinner. She didn't vote in last month's election because she couldn't decide who to vote for. Joe always told her who was the best candidate.

Frances returned to the kitchen, pulling pots and pans from the cabinets, milk and cheese from the refrigerator. She imagined each new dish to be an experiment in a laboratory—mix together basic ingredients, add heat, and something different emerged. She filled a large pot with water, added a dash of salt, and put it on the stove. Seven minutes to boil. Twenty-four seconds longer than it took for the water to boil at the farm. She could still see Sister Mayme's hand

356

scratching across the blackboard in her high school's chemistry laboratory. *As altitude increases...* The sister drew an arrow pointing to the top of the board. *The boiling point of water decreases.* Sister Mayme drew another arrow pointing down. Her chemistry teacher had been so proud when Frances had been accepted at Carnegie Tech, what would Sister Mayme think of her now?

As the cheese melted in the warmed milk, Frances stood over the pan, watching the orange cubes disappear, just like the life as a chemist she had once dreamed of. She turned off both burners and walked back to the office. Settling into the desk chair, she completed the admission form, crossing out the old date and replacing it with today's.

CHAPTER FORTY-TWO

September 1961
Wilmington, Delaware

Frances dabbed a tissue at her leaking eyes. "What will I do without Little Joe?"

Her mother, sitting across from her at the kitchen table, raised an eyebrow but didn't say a word.

Frances was glad her mother kept her thoughts to herself, for once. She pushed up from her chair and walked to the window, watching a leaf drift to the grass. The knee-high maple sapling Joe planted the year they bought the house was now a twelve-foot tree, the leaves just beginning to take on their scarlet hue. Her son was leaving for college the next morning and she was regretting her doggedness in getting him there. "Chester is too far away," she said, shaking her head. "I don't care what he says, he can go to the same school as me. Live at home and drive to his classes every day."

"No," Martha said.

Frances wheeled around, glaring at her mother. "What? You want him to go away?"

"No, of course I don't want him to go away," Martha said. "But it's time. When you went to college, I survived. As will you. You will be busy with your own schooling."

Frances turned back to the window. "I made a

mistake. I can't go to college. I don't know what I was thinking." She watched another leaf fall as her thoughts turned to Joe. She remembered well the day she approached him about a return to college, and he had discouraged her. She had been hurt, and a little angry. But maybe he had just been trying to protect her from failure.

"Little Joe is going away," Martha said. "Sitting at home missing him will not do either of you any good."

Frances kept her back to her mother. "What if I fail? What kind of an example will that be?"

"A good one. Little Joe will know you tried. Stop fretting, Sunshine. The sky is not falling. The sun will come up tomorrow."

She turned, locked eyes with her mother.

"You-will-be-fine," Martha said, drawing out each word.

Frances wanted to believe it, but some days, she felt fragile, as if she might shatter like a piece of glass.

Her mother reached across the table and lay her hand on Frances's. "There are still going to be bad days. Moving through grief is not an uphill journey. There are valleys, some of them quite wide, but as long as there are more good days than bad days, you're all right."

Frances didn't fret about the valleys, she could work her way through them, find a path up the shadowed slopes like she did when Randolph and Christy died. It was the deep pit of depression she found herself in after Joe's death that terrified her. It was a dark place with steep, jagged walls. She could not go there again, the strength to climb out wasn't in her.

***

The next morning, Frances lay in bed staring at the window, thinking of Joe, just as she did every morning. The old steamer trunk was pushed against the wall below the window and she padded to it, running her hand

360

along the slats, worn smooth from decades of use. She offered it to Little Joe to take to college but he had declined with a laugh. Her palm against the glass pane, she pushed the window up, the leaves of the stout maple rustling, a warm breeze caressing her face. Despite the heat, she shivered, fearing the day ahead.

Dressed, and a smile pasted on, Frances got busy in the kitchen. As the batter sputtered on the hot griddle, she wondered when she would again make pancakes for her son. He breath caught as she realized she would never again pack her son's lunch or pace her bedroom late at night waiting for him to return from a high school dance.

"Hiya, Mom." Little Joe came up behind, dropping his suitcase to the kitchen floor with a thud.

She wiped her eyes and turned, doing her best to hold her quivering smile. "Good morning...Joe."

He laughed. "Now that I'm leaving you drop the Little?"

She burst into tears.

Little Joe shook his head. "Aww, Mom, no crying. You promised."

She nodded, ran her hand across her eyes again, and turned back to the stove, flipping the pancakes on to a plate. "You want juice or milk?"

"Neither. I'll have coffee," he said, drowning the pancakes in maple syrup.

France sat across from her son, watching him eat, still marveling at how fast, and how much he could push into his mouth. She jumped when a horn sounded in the alley at the back of the house.

"Frank's here," Little Joe said, pushing to his feet. He put his plate in the sink and grabbed his suitcase. "Let's go, Mom."

Frances rode with Little Joe in his car, Frank and Martha following in his big Buick. When they arrived at the dormitory, Little Joe's unknown roommate was nowhere in sight, but he had claimed the bed by the window, his belongings strewn around and on the bed. It reminded her of the first time she met Christy and tears prickled, but somehow, she kept her promise and did not cry, leaving her son in his dorm room after just one hug.

On the drive home, she sat in the back seat of Frank's car, her eyes closed against the wind from the open windows, making no attempt to join in her mother's and Frank's conversation. Her thoughts turned to Joe. This should be a day of celebration. Joe had missed so many milestones in Little Joe's life. Always working. Always vowing he'd be there next time. She swallowed hard, pushed the anger aside. She hated her anger. It did no good, only made her feel guilty, but there were times when anger was the only thing she could feel.

Her mother hauled her from her thoughts when they pulled to the front of Frances's house. "Would you like us to come in for a bit?"

She looked at the Victorian, remembering the first time she saw it. It looked far better, but the problem with these old houses—Joe had said more than once—was that they needed constant upkeep. The paint on the porch railings and gables was peeling, the roof stippled with moss and mildew. The downspout leaked. Inside, the refrigerator hummed and clicked, the hot-water faucet in the master bedroom dripped. Nothing that needed immediate attention. "Thanks. But, I'll be fine," Frances said, hoping it was true.

***

Her mother was right, the sun did come up the next day, but it didn't seem as bright. Little Joe's college was less than thirty miles away, but it could have been on the other side of the country as far as she was concerned. She brewed a cup of coffee and stood at the window in the kitchen, sipping slowly. When the phone rang for the second time in ten minutes, she lunged, hoping it was her son.

"Big day today!" Stephanie said.

"Yes," Frances said through gritted teeth. Stephanie's voice was far too cheery, just as her mother's had been ten minutes ago.

"General Chemistry at eleven. Library Science at one thirty." Stephanie had memorized Frances's schedule of courses. "What are you wearing?"

"I don't know." Frances shook her head and rolled her eyes, never understanding Stephanie affection for fashion and fabrics. "I'll call you when I get home this afternoon."

In her bedroom, she pulled a blue cotton blouse out of her closet and stepped in front of the full-length mirror, holding the shirt under her chin. She did the same with a red blouse, and a silky one of green and black checks. An hour later she left the house in a white blouse and brown skirt, sensible loafers on her feet, and arrived fifteen minutes early for her first lecture in the science building.

A young man, not much older than Little Joe, sorted papers on the instructor's desk. He looked up and frowned. "Are you lost, ma'am?"

She glanced at the chalkboard where "General Chemistry" was scribbled, dismayed to see "Dr. Linden" written below. After considering a run for the door, she nodded at the board and said, "I'm registered for this class. Frances Ferguson. Are there assigned seats?"

The young man ran his finger down a page. "Yes. There's your name. Hmm, I was expecting..." He paused and shrugged. "I'm Charles Goff, Dr. Linden's graduate assistant. You can sit anywhere, ma'am."

She knew the young man was being respectful but every time he said "ma'am," her skin prickled. "My forms have Professor Wendt listed as the instructor," she said.

"Professor Wendt took a position at another college so Dr. Linden is filling in. You're lucky. He's an excellent teacher."

Yes, lucky, Frances thought sourly. She climbed

three rows and wedged into the first seat, her books and notebooks balanced on her knees. After a humiliating struggle with the raised arm of the writing desk, she was finally able to lower it. She kept her head down as students filed into the room but she could feel the curious eyes on her. Her worry about her fashion choice being scrutinized by other female students was pointless since she was the only woman in the class.

Dr. Linden strode in and perused the room, his gaze lingering on Frances. He lectured for twenty minutes, Charles keeping pace with the transparencies on the overhead projector, then announced a quiz. Dr. Linden left the room as Frances and the other seventy students bent over the sweet-smelling mimeographed page, scribbling words and formulas until Charles called, "time's up."

***

In Stephanie's kitchen that evening, Frances lamented to her friend. "I knew most of the answers but I wasn't quick enough on the formulas." She didn't mention that it took her five minutes to figure out how the desk worked.

"You'll get faster," Stephanie said and pushed chopsticks into her plate of chicken chow mein from the small restaurant around the corner. She never did improve her cooking skills, extolling the culinary virtues of take-out food and frozen TV dinners. "How was the Library Science class?" she asked, drizzling sweet sauce on an egg roll.

Frances shrugged. "At least I wasn't the only woman. Every freshman has to take Library Science. It's one class I'll pass." She chased noodles around her plate with a chopstick, finally giving up and digging in with a fork.

Stephanie stood. "I'll be right back. I might have something to make you smile."

364

Frances frowned as her friend returned, a small stack of clothes in her hands.

"I know you said you didn't want any of Little Joe's old clothes that Nancy Ferguson sent back with me but I thought you might get a kick out of seeing this again." Stephanie held up the plaid jacket she and her mother had made for Little Joe when he was an infant.

"Oh my goodness!" Frances pushed her plate aside and pulled the jacket into her hands. She looked at Stephanie. "You kept it all these years?"

Stephanie nodded. "I went through the box a couple years ago. Pulled out this and a few other things that I thought you might want to see." She shrugged. "But, then Joe died and I thought the memories might upset you."

Frances murmured her thanks. She ran a hand over the tiny buttons, looked up. "Do you still have the box?"

Stephanie nodded. "Yes, it's in my basement."

"I'll take the whole box," Frances said. "My mother's church has been collecting donations for the Florence Crittenton Home in Wilmington." She kept her eyes on Stephanie's, waiting for a reaction. "It's a home for unwed mothers. I was born at one."

Stephanie stared, wide-eyed, and Frances tried to read her friend's expression. Was it surprise or distain? Frances looked to the side, taking her bottom lip between her teeth. She had trusted Stephanie, would she regret it? "I don't know why I'm telling you." She paused, shook her head. "I just don't want to be dishonest with you anymore. You've been such a good friend." She let out a long breath, looked at the jacket in her lap. "No one knows. I never even told Joe. I didn't want him to think less of my mother. Or me." She raised her chin, leaned forward. "Little Joe doesn't know so please don't tell him."

"I wouldn't," Stephanie said and put her hand on Frances's, a rare show of affection. "It's nobody's business." She smiled. "But I do appreciate that you told me. Makes me feel special."

Frances chuckled. "You are easy to please."

"That's not what they say at the laboratory."

Frances laughed harder. "Guess I'll find out soon enough." She let her smile fade. "Well, in for a penny, in for a pound. You want to hear my whole story?"

Stephanie nodded. "Yes. I do."

Frances told her of the confusing year at the monastery and her tormented days at the academy. Told her of her mother's loveless marriage to a stepfather who never once spoke her name, a stepbrother who bedeviled her and her mother for fifteen years. She relayed the humiliating moment Joan divulged Frances's secret, and the heartbreak of losing her two childhood friends, Mickey and Pamela.

Stephanie shook her head. "Back in college, when I met you, I was jealous. I thought you had the perfect childhood. A big house, private school. All those pretty dresses."

"That I never wore," Frances said with a laugh. She rolled her neck, took a deep breath. Just like when Randolph learned the truth, she felt lighter, stronger. "You don't hate me, or my mother, do you?"

"No. Of course not." Stephanie shook her head. "Doesn't make a bit of difference to me."

Frances returned her attention to the pile of old clothes. She held up a pair of red corduroy pants. "I'm keeping the jacket but these can go to the Crittenton Home." As she folded the small legs, she wondered about the baby that would be wearing them. What did the future hold for him? Would he be adopted and never know of his roots? Or raised by a courageous single mother, both mother and child routinely rejected by family and friends and facing a lifetime of scrutiny? She sighed, caressed the soft fabric with her fingertips. "Maybe someday the shame and stigma of illegitimacy will disappear."

366

CHAPTER FORTY-THREE

April 1962
Ocean City, New Jersey

A seagull caught Martha's attention as it flapped furiously to join a flock, then, wings extended, floated into the colony. She rolled the passenger seat window down, just a crack, so she could hear the gulls' cries and smell the briny air. She turned, her face towards the windshield, stealing glances at Frank's profile, his eyes hidden behind dark glasses. Her was attention drawn to his hands gripping the steering wheel, left one at ten o'clock, right at two o'clock, and she smiled. Always in the same position when he drove. His fingers were long, tapered, the nails freshly cut and buffed. No sharp edges on those nails, she had filed them herself this morning. One of the many things she enjoyed doing for her husband.

Frank stopped the car in front of a three-story, cedar-shingled house. "Let's have a look," he said.

Martha twisted, squinted at her daughter and grandson in the back seat. Neither had spoken more than a dozen words during the two-hour drive to Ocean City.

"I'll wait here," Little Joe said, closing his eyes and leaning his head back.

Frances pushed her door open and stomped up the

sidewalk.

Martha studied Little Joe. Her grandson was not happy, and hadn't been for the past five months since, at the Thanksgiving table, he announced he was quitting school after just one semester.

"College isn't for me," he had said to a stunned Frances. "You'll see when my grades come. No sense wasting any more money."

"What will you do?" Frances asked.

Little Joe grinned at Frank. "Thought I'd take another shot at running the company. Dad's old office still empty?"

With a sideways glance at Frances, Frank chewed slowly, swallowed, and lowered his fork to the table. He looked at Little Joe. "We have a good offer from the Smith brothers. They've been trying to buy us for years. Your mother and I decided to accept the offer."

Little Joe looked from Frank to his mother and back to Frank. "You're selling Dad's company?"

"I'm getting old, Little Joe," Frank had said and pulled Martha's hand into his. "I have a heart problem, nothing real serious yet, but I want to spend time with your grandmother. Travel a bit."

Little Joe had turned to his mother. "Dad loved his company. How can you sell it?"

"Little Joe..."

"Don't call me 'Little.'"

Martha had helplessly watched her grandson storm from the room, wondering if her family would ever make it through another Thanksgiving meal without drama.

***

With his share of the money from the sale of Ferguson and McLaughlin, Frank decided to buy a home at the shore. His search narrowed to three houses, he planned a trip with Martha to make the final decision, and Martha, after weeks of pleading, had convinced Frances and Little Joe to join them. She now wished she hadn't been so persistent.

After one more look at her sullen grandson, Martha swung her legs from the car. She grasped Frank's outstretched hand and walked towards the house's small porch where Frances waited, arm crossed, foot tapping. She ignored her daughter's obvious impatience and slowed her steps, smiling at her husband. They were the same height—just as she and George had been—but unlike George Pickett, Frank showed no self-consciousness. Their height was the only thing George and Frank had in common. Frank laughed easily and often and sought Martha's opinion in every conversation. Seven years of marriage had only deepened her love for Frank and she relished her role as stepmother and step-grandmother to his two adult daughters and four grandchildren. Most mornings she awoke early to watch her husband sleep, feeling a contentment she hadn't known possible.

"After you, ladies," Frank said, unlocking the front door and pushing it open.

All three strolled through the house, stopping in the kitchen.

"Nice size," Frances said.

"Martha?" Frank asked.

"It's fine." She nodded and moved to the window. "Big yard, too."

They wandered upstairs, finding many good qualities, but after considering the price Frank decided it was too much to pay for something so far from the beach. He drove to Asbury Avenue and the three of them toured another, smaller house. The price was better but it was still four blocks from the coast. The next house was close to the beach and the price was right, but it needed major repairs.

"First thing would be a new roof," Frank said. "And one bathroom would never be enough." He stood on the sidewalk looking at the narrow house, Frances and

Martha at his side. It was four stories, the main entrance on the second level, white-pillared porches stretching across the second and third levels. The top floor was an open space with a dormer window in front of a sharply pitched roof.

Little Joe eventually came to stand beside Frank.

"The top porch lists to the right," Little Joe said, tilting his head.

"Luckily, I know of some good construction fellas. Bobby Johnson's looking for work. You remember him?" Frank asked.

Little Joe nodded. "Thought he stayed on at the company when you sold it?"

"Yes—when your mother and I sold the company—Bobby stayed on, but he didn't like the new management. Bobby's good, but he doesn't take direction well." Frank laughed. "Your dad and Bobby had several rows. Bobby would stomp out of the office, then come back an hour later like nothing happened. Your dad would make a joke and they'd move on." Frank paused, squinting at the house. "Never met a man who didn't like your dad," he said, his voice hushed. "He was a good man, Little Joe. I miss him. Once he died, the company was never the same."

Quiet for a moment, contemplating the house, Little Joe finally nodded. "Let's go look around inside."

"Great!" Frank tossed the key and snatched it out of the air with a grin at Martha.

"We'll wait in the car," she said, nudging Frances into the back seat.

"He worries me, Mom," Frances said after Frank and Little Joe walked away.

"I'm guessing you mean Little Joe, not Frank."

"Yes. But I worry about Frank, too," Frances said, turning towards Martha. "He makes you happy."

"Yes, he does." She patted Frances's hand. "Little Joe will be fine."

"Losing his father was hard on him."

"And you."

Frances took in a deep breath, let it out slowly. "After Joe Senior died and Joe dragged us here, I never thought we would be happy again." She paused when her voice hitched. "But we were." She paused again and looked out the window, a hint of a smile on her face. "Lots of good memories in this town."

Martha nodded. When Frank said he wanted to buy a house at the shore, and she realized there was no talking him out of it, she suggested Ocean City. Her first trip to the beach town was the summer after Joe bought the Victorian, and he loaded everyone, including Winston, into the car for a drive to the New Jersey coast. It was the first time she, Frances and Little Joe saw the ocean. Unfortunately, Winston was not welcome at the crowded Atlantic City beach, so they drove south to Ocean City, and after a two-hour search, finally found a one-bedroom apartment that allowed dogs. After she and Frances gave the place a proper cleaning, they thoroughly enjoyed their trip, pledging to return next summer. They did return, every year for the next six summers, making two trips to the shore on what turned out to be Joe's final summer. On that second trip, Martha noticed her son-in-law spent much of his time in a canvas chair under the boardwalk, but when she questioned him he said he had a sore toe, claiming he dropped a ball-peen hammer on it.

"Some days, I still can't believe Joe's gone," Frances said.

Martha ran words through her head, trying to find ones to comfort her daughter, but she knew only time, and love, would bring the healing Frances sought. She had run to the arms of another man after Frederic died, but it didn't mend her broken heart. Frances had made her whole. Once her daughter was born, there wasn't room in her heart for grief.

Frank got behind the wheel and Little Joe slipped into the passenger seat. "That's the one!" He turned and winked at Martha, gave his watch a glance. "Four o'clock. Watson's is open." He drove three blocks to the popular restaurant and they settled into their seats at a square table in the Marine Room, schools of pink fish swimming by on the blue wallpaper. "Order the prime rib, Little Joe," Frank said. "Frances, Martha, go for the lobster. We're celebrating." He smiled at the couple seated nearby, the only other occupied table.

It was still off-season so the restaurant wasn't the bustling place Martha was accustomed to. She wanted to remind Frank of his doctor's suggestion to eat less meat but she bit her tongue, not wanting to say anything that might take the shine off her husband's glow. And after the day's rocky start with her grandson she was delighted to see Little Joe smiling. "How are things going at the newspaper, Little Joe?" she asked. Since quitting college, her grandson had worked at a hotel, two restaurants, and was now employed at the newspaper.

He shrugged. "Working the presses isn't for me. I've been watching the reporters. And the photographers. Think I might try my hand at journalism. Applied at Rutgers. Tuck and I will room together."

"What?" Frances dropped her fork. "Why didn't you tell me?"

"Didn't want to get your hopes up." He shrugged again. "I'm not as good a student as you."

"Your mother was always a good student." Martha laid her hand on Frances's. "I've waited a long time to see you graduate from college, Sunshine. Can't wait to watch you get that diploma."

Frances shook her head. "Mom, I'm not going to the graduation ceremony. I'm too old to wear a cap and gown."

"Nonsense," Martha said. "You will go and we will all be there to watch, cheering loudly, and doing our best to embarrass you."

372

CHAPTER FORTY-FOUR

July 1963
Wilmington, Delaware

Frances sat behind her desk, Stephanie standing at her shoulder, and recorded another long chain of chemicals. She remained quiet, respecting her boss's thought process.

"We'll add more terephthaloyl chloride next time," Stephanie finally said, and dropped into the chair next to the desk. She squinted at the clock on the wall. "Tomorrow."

The week after she received her college degree last year, Frances went to work at the research laboratory. Her team—led by Stephanie—had made and tested ten thousand polymer chains, none of them producing threads strong enough to replace steel.

"I can stay," Frances volunteered. She didn't mind working long hours, avoiding her lonely house whenever possible. And she liked the laboratory, surrounded by bright and creative people, each day interesting. When she first started at the lab she had been intimidated but slowly she found her place among the virtuosos of chemistry. What would that doubting man she encountered on her school field trip to the glass factory have to say about her skills now? She wondered if Mickey still worked at that factory. Wondered where he lived, if he married, had children. After his betrayal, she never saw him again but he still intruded in her thoughts from time to time.

"Let's call it a day," Stephanie said, pulling her glasses off and rubbing her eyes. "Little Joe still coming home this week for Frank's Fourth of July party?"

"I'll believe it when I see him." Frances stood and shrugged out of her white lab coat, hanging it on a hook on the wall behind the desk. "You sure you don't want to come to Ocean City? Mom would love to see you."

"Thanks, but I'm going to the fireworks in Philadelphia." Stephanie pushed her glasses back on her nose and stood. "Little Joe still in New York?"

Frances nodded. Now at City College in New York City, his third college in two years, her son hadn't been home for six months.

***

After Little Joe and Tommy Tucker started the semester at Rutgers last September, Frances didn't see her son again until December. She had been thrilled to see Little Joe so happy when he walked into the kitchen a few days before Christmas.

"He's in love," Tommy explained, standing in the Ferguson kitchen picking through the trays of cookies. He sidestepped an elbow aimed at his ribs from Little Joe.

"For your mother." Frances handed a tin of cookies to Tommy.

"Thanks, Mrs. Ferguson. Merry Christmas." Tommy leaned to plant a kiss on Frances's cheek.

"Hold it!" Little Joe grabbed his camera from the bag on his shoulder, twisting the focus ring and pressing the shutter.

"One more," he said to his mother as Tommy ducked out the back door. The black Nikon raised, he inched left, then right, bent his knees for another angle.

"There. You're beautiful!"

Frances waved a hand across her face and moved to the refrigerator. She poured a glass of milk and slid it across the table. "Sit. Have a cookie."

He devoured an orange cookie and drained his glass with one gulp.

"More?" Frances pushed her chair back.

He put a hand on her arm. "Think I'll have coffee instead. I'll get it. You want some?"

She nodded and picked up the camera. "This is heavier than it looks."

Little Joe poured two cups of coffee and sat, nudging his chair next to Frances. "This is the view finder." He pointed. "Look through there. Then turn this wheel until it's focused."

The camera to her eye, she looked through the small pane of glass at her son. Gone were his chubby cheeks, replaced by a lean face with a shadow of beard rising in the late day light, his coffee-colored hair curling against the collar of his leather jacket. His eyes were as brown as his hair, with a twinkle that made her heart ache with memories of his father's smiling eyes. She lowered the camera.

"Tell me about her," she said.

"Her name is Ginny. Virginia. But everybody calls her Ginny," Little Joe said, his hands animated, eyes shining. "We met in New York City. Tuck and I went to a party and there she was. She's a journalist. Well, she will be, once she finishes school."

Frances thought of Lily and her life in journalism. Still in London, Lily was always chasing a story, jumping on a plane or a train to faraway places where violence was the headline. Randolph's remains were identified shortly after the war ended and buried in Cambridge so Lily stayed in England, wanting to be near Randolph. She liked her life of adventure. Rarely visiting the United States, Lily kept in touch with Frances through letters and the occasional phone call.

375

"I'm transferring to New York University," Little Joe said. "Taking photography. Photojournalism. Ginny and I want to travel."

"What?" Frances pulled her drifting mind back to her son.

"I'm moving to New York."

"Where will you live?"

"An apartment." He suddenly became very interested in his coffee.

Frances frowned. "By yourself?"

Little Joe paused, dipped a spoon in his cup. "No. I'm moving in with Ginny. She lives with two other couples in Greenwich Village."

"You are not married," Frances said, her voice stern. "You cannot live with a woman who is not your wife."

"Ginny doesn't want to get married." He looked up, lifted a shoulder. "She doesn't believe in marriage. Her parents divorced when she was a kid and she was shuttled between them."

"What would Father John say?"

He shrugged again. "I haven't been to mass since Dad died. I'm not going back."

Their eyes locked, neither looking away. Little Joe's eyes had turned a shade darker, his mouth a thin line. He was ready for an argument. One Frances couldn't win. Her son had his own money—thanks to the trust fund Frank created when the company was sold—but Little Joe's access to the money was restricted until he turned thirty. She was glad for the restriction. Young men make rash decisions. She blinked. Not just young men. Little Joe's father made many hasty choices, expecting her to deal with the consequences in silence. She forced a smile. "When do I get to meet Ginny?"

"Soon." Little Joe had stood and pulled the camera into his hands, whistling as he walked from the room.

***

376

Frances was finally getting the chance to meet Ginny. Early on the Fourth of July, she drove to Frank and Martha's house at the shore. Still the prudent businessman, Frank rented the property to vacationers in June and August but stayed at the house in July, hosting a large Independence Day party every year. Her mother was in the kitchen of the beach house when she arrived, spooning creamed yolk into halved hardboiled eggs. Frances stuffed one of the deviled eggs into her mouth.

"How is it?" Martha asked. "More mustard?"

Frances shook her head. "It's fine. You hear from Little Joe?"

"Called last night," Martha said, filling another egg. "He promised to be here by suppertime."

Frances sat and forked pickles from a jar onto a relish tray. She wondered about the mysterious Ginny. Why didn't she want to marry Little Joe?

"Hello!" A tall woman, ponytail swinging, breezed into the kitchen, two young children in tow. "I brought coleslaw." She walked to the refrigerator, obviously familiar with the room.

"This is my daughter, Frances," Martha said. "This is our neighbor, Audrey. And her children, Dennis and Charlotte."

"Lottie." The girl said and ran out the back door, her mother and brother following.

Half an hour later, the house and backyard were crowded with more neighbors and Frank's relatives.

"You have a houseful," Frances said to her mother, tossing buns into a basket. "Maybe I should drive home tonight?"

"There's plenty of room. Frank carpeted the bottom floor so the youngsters can stay there," Martha said. She pulled on red-checked oven mitts and retrieved a long cake from the oven.

"Hiya!" Little Joe stood at the door, his camera on a multicolored strap around his neck.

Martha nearly dropped the cake in her rush to wrap her arms around Little Joe. She took a step back and held him at arm's length. "Don't you eat? You're too skinny."

"You can fatten me up, Grandma." He held his camera to his eye and pressed the shutter.

Frances studied her son. He was thin, and he needed a haircut. She turned her attention to the young woman poised in the doorway. She was a few inches shorter than Frances with kohl-rimmed eyes blinking beneath long bangs. Her sleek hair, the color of molasses, hung to her waist.

Little Joe turned, pulling the young woman forward. "This is Ginny."

Her heart in her throat, Frances choked out a gasp. Ginny was at least seven months pregnant.

Martha stepped between Frances and Ginny, put her arm around the young woman's shoulders. "Lovely to meet you, Ginny." She looked at Little Joe. "Frank is in the back yard. Come on." She ushered the couple out the door.

Frances stood at the window, arms crossed, watching her son and his girlfriend make their way across the yard to the picnic table. Frank welcomed them with open arms and Little Joe backed up, camera aimed, Ginny smiling seductively for each shot. Frances dropped to a chair, fuming. She was still seething ten minutes later, when Little Joe walked back in.

"Sorry," he said, shrugging. "I wanted to tell you but Ginny said it would be better in person."

"When are you getting married?"

"Mom, I told you. Ginny doesn't want to get married."

"Even with a baby?"

He shrugged again.

Frances stood. "Little Joe..." she paused when the door opened. Seeing it was her mother she continued, voice shrill. "You have to get married. Now. Before that child is born." She turned to her mother. "Tell him, Mom."

Martha lowered an empty basket to the table, turned to Frances. "It's his and Ginny's decision. Not yours."

"What?" Frances exploded. "How can you say that?" From the corner of her eye she caught Little Joe inching towards the door and stopped him with a hand to his wrist. "You are ruining your life!"

Little Joe pulled his arm from her grasp, narrowed his dark eyes at Frances, and escaped out the door.

"Calm down, Frances," Martha said. "Having a child won't ruin his life. It will, however, make life more difficult. He'll need our help. Our support."

Frances stared at the door where her son had just disappeared, shook her head. "This is wrong. He wasn't raised that way."

"You sound like my mother," Martha hissed. "Just before she sent me away."

Frances turned and opened her mouth but her mother didn't give her the chance to speak.

"Do you want to lose your son as my mother lost me? Your grandmother never got to spend one minute with you. I pitied her. I was the lucky one." Martha poked a finger into her own chest, a flush burning high on her cheekbones. "Not one day did I ever regret having you. Never did I feel my life was ruined." She snatched the basket from the table, grabbed the bag of hot dog buns, and stormed out the door.

Frances dropped back to the chair, elbows on the table, face in her hands. It wasn't easy for her mother to raise a child on her own, she knew that. Choices were limited, her mother forced to live with secrets and lies. But Frances had to live with the secrets, too. She always felt flawed, through no fault of her own, and didn't want her grandchild to go through life with that same feeling.

CHAPTER FORTY-FIVE

June 1965
Wilmington, Delaware

"Hello?" Frances called as she walked through her back door. She found her mother in the living room, Frank on the couch beside her. He threw a hand up in greeting, his focus on the television screen.

"Sorry, I'm so late," Frances said. Thought we had a breakthrough at the lab today." She shrugged. "Turned out to be another false alarm."

"Shush." Martha put a finger to her lips. "I put Hope down a half hour ago."

Frances slumped into one of the easy chairs, disappointed her granddaughter was already in bed. When she left the house this morning, twenty-two-month old Hope was wide awake and had a firm grasp of Martha's plait. Frances's attempt to pry the braid out of Hope's hands was met with ear-piercing squeals, and a cookie bribe fared no better. Frances had wished her mother luck and left the house just as the sun stoked the morning sky a deep red.

Gunfire erupted from the television, men on horses galloping across the screen, gleaming pistols in hand. Frances stood and made her way back to the kitchen, avoiding one of Frank's lengthy explanations of the show and who was a good guy and who was a bad guy. Her mother followed.

"He loves those westerns," Martha said, her voice muffled as she dug in the refrigerator. "I'll heat up some spaghetti for you. I think Hope had more on her than she ate." She paused. "Little Joe called. He's back in London. Staying at Lily's."

"Ginny with him?" Frances asked.

Martha shook her head. "Still in Vietnam. Hope said 'DaDa' on the phone but she was looking at Frank when she said it."

"No wonder," Frances said. "Hope has spent far more time with Frank than with her father."

Frances had been frustrated by her son's choices since the day he brought Ginny to the Fourth of July party two years ago. She convinced them to stay with her in Wilmington until the baby was born but within days she regretted the invitation. Remembering Sarah Ferguson's kindness when she moved to the farm, pregnant and scared, Frances did her best to provide Ginny the same safe haven. While at the Ferguson farm, Frances never questioned Sarah's ways and slipped into the household quietly, but Ginny wasn't one to keep her opinions to herself, and Little Joe never disagreed. Frances spent the rest of that summer working long hours, escaping to her mother's house whenever Ginny got under her skin.

"I made your Wiener Schnitzel recipe and Ginny was horrified when I told her it was veal. She won't eat meat," Frances had said as she sat in Martha's living room a week before Hope was born. "I made her liver, told her it was good for the baby, but she refused to eat it. She nibbles on carrots and celery, talks of tofu and bean sprouts. Plays odd music on Joe's phonograph."

Martha had shrugged, unfazed. "Guess she feels secure enough to express her ideas. Since I was always living in someone else's home, I spent most of my life keeping my thoughts to myself."

382

Frank, sitting on the couch beside Martha, had laughed. "Not anymore."

***

Hope was born on a scorching day in August, greeted by Little Joe, Frances, Martha and Frank, Ginny's family noticeably absent.

"I wish your father was here," Frances whispered to Little Joe as she held Hope in her arms for the first time.

"Me, too."

The first month of Hope's life passed happily. Then Ginny announced she was returning to New York, with Hope.

"I think Hope's too young to be exposed to all those strangers," Frances said. "Leave her here. Your grandmother would be happy to watch the baby while I'm at the lab."

Little Joe hesitated, raising an eyebrow at Ginny. She finally nodded.

"All right," Little Joe agreed. "We'll only be gone for one night."

One night stretched to five nights. Ginny got a job at *Newsday* and went on her first assignment as Little Joe drove back to Wilmington to pack up their things.

"You can't live with a baby in an apartment full of people coming and going at all hours," Frances said as she watched Joe stuff clothes into his father's old duffel bag.

"It's just until I can find an apartment for the three of us."

Frances cried as Little Joe drove away with Hope. He was back in a week, grudgingly admitting Frances was right—the apartment was no place for a baby.

"Ginny's so busy and I can't leave Hope alone. Nobody in the apartment volunteered to watch the baby," Little Joe said. "And really, I wouldn't leave Hope with any of them anyway. Can you watch her while I

383

search for a new place to live? A week, I'm guessing. Two weeks, tops."

Three weeks after that conversation, Little Joe and Ginny left Frances heartbroken again when they took Hope to their studio apartment in the Bronx. Frances didn't see her granddaughter for another eight weeks, until Christmas, when Joe and Ginny announced their plan to move to London.

"With the baby?" Frances asked.

"Of course," said Little Joe. "We'll be staying with Lily, but only for a month or so. *Newsday* wants Ginny to write stories about Americans in Europe, and I'm going to take their photographs. It's a great opportunity."

"And while you're both working who will be watching Hope? You can't expect that of Lily." Frances pointed out.

Little Joe and Ginny exchanged glances.

"You'll leave Hope here," Frances had said, and left the room before either could answer.

Little Joe and Ginny returned from Europe in early summer, but not to stay. Ginny was going to Vietnam to cover the war and Joe was heading to Africa to take photographs, happily announcing he had landed a dream assignment from *National Geographic*. After a month in Wilmington, they left again without their daughter.

Frances welcomed 1965 with Hope on her lap, turning the pages of the glossy magazine, her index finger tapping a vivid photograph of sunset on the plains of Kenya, a herd of elephants silhouetted against the fiery sky. "Your daddy took that," she said, planting a kiss on Hope's forehead. It was difficult to understand her son's decisions but she was proud of his work. Ginny was also making her mark, one of her stories about a village in South Vietnam was reprinted in *Time*. The article was far too depressing for Frances's taste but Frank was impressed, and told Ginny so, when she and Little Joe came home this past March. They stayed for six weeks, then headed overseas, leaving Hope behind, once again.

***

Martha put the reheated spaghetti on kitchen table and Frances nodded her thanks. She breathed in the comforting scent of basil and garlic, twirled long noodles around the tines of her fork. "Remember when Lily taught me how to do this?" she asked, raising her fork, inspecting the ball of pasta.

Martha chuckled. "I tried it with Hope but ended up using a knife and fork."

"Joe never did get the hang of it. He always cut it into pieces." Frances chewed slowly, thinking of her husband, wondering what he would say about their son's nomadic life.

"You want me to make coffee?" her mother asked. "I miss having a cup after dinner but the doctor told Frank to cut back so I only make one pot in the morning now."

Frances shook her head. "No, thank you. How is Frank? Looks like he's gained some weight."

After a heart attack the previous year, Frank spent a week in the hospital. It was a mild attack, but there was some damage to his heart, and the doctor told him to take it easy. Frank did the opposite, taking Martha to California for a month.

Martha shrugged, but she was smiling. "He seems fine. Says he's going to enjoy whatever time he has left."

"It's good to see you so happy," Frances said and pushed another spaghetti orb into her mouth.

"Love will do that. Maybe you ought to give it another try, Sunshine."

Frances nearly choked. "Me? Heavens no." She shook her head and looked at her plate, tears blurring her vision. Joe had been gone nearly six years but still, when Frances awoke at night, she reached out for him, longing for his touch. They had talked of another baby but it never happened and Frances was secretly glad her

385

son was an only child. She loved Little Joe. Loved him fiercely. If anything happened to him, she would simply not go on. She was terrified of losing those she loved. That's why she would never fall in love again. She wouldn't even get another dog. It was silly, she knew, to fret over things beyond her control but try as she might, her thoughts often ran wild. Except at work. When she was in the laboratory—mixing, calculating, discovering— her mind was totally focused, occupied only by the task at hand.

Martha laid her fingertips on Frances's arm.

Frances looked up, covered her mother's hand with her own. She managed a smile, her tears averted. At her age, and without words, her mother was a comfort, still able to chase the sadness and doubts away. Who would do that for Hope?

CHAPTER FORTY-SIX

July 1965
Wilmington, Delaware

This is different, Frances thought. She straightened, blinked, returned her focus to the microscope. Definitely different. Dipping a glass rod into the beaker, she stirred the cloudy solution and held it up towards the laboratory's bright ceiling lights. She called Stephanie over and the two of them gaped at the shimmering liquid.

"Look at it under the microscope," Frances said.

Stephanie bent and peered into the eyepiece. "I've never seen anything like it. Parts of the chemical chains are perpendicular bars. And they're aligned." She lifted her head. "Let's do it again."

Meticulously following the formula pinned to the cork board, they measured, mixed and heated. The result was the same.

"I'm taking it to the spinner." Stephanie picked up the beaker.

Frances watched her hurry from the lab. She wanted to believe this was the one but after three years and thousands of failed formulas, it was difficult to be optimistic. Most of the liquids they produced were clear and flowed languidly, like syrup, a few spun into threads, but none produced the desired results. It was disheartening, day after day of disappointments. She shook her head, marveling at Stephanie's confident tenacity.

Back within five minutes, Stephanie was flustered, her cheeks splotched. "Mr. Quinn won't spin it. He assumed the cloudiness was because of particles and said it would plug up the holes of his spinneret. He said it doesn't have the viscosity of regular polymer solutions." She paused, sucking in a breath. "Can you talk to him, please?"

"Me? Why would he listen to me?" Frances asked.

"Oh, Frances, you know Tim Quinn is sweet on you. He's been flirting with you since the day you walked in this building."

Frances let out a snort, frowning and waving a hand in front of her face. Timothy Quinn was the manager of the spinner unit. He was well-liked, known for his easy-going manner and silly jokes. In her first weeks at the lab, when Frances ate lunch at the company's cafeteria, Tim would run to her side, offering to buy her meal, following her to a table. Frances was embarrassed by the attention and didn't find his jokes amusing, turning down his every invitation to get together outside of work. After a month of Tim's overtures, Frances brought her lunch in from home and ate at her desk in the lab, but since Hope came along and Frances's mornings were hectic, she often didn't have the time to prepare lunch and ventured back to the cafeteria. Maybe his jokes had gotten funnier, or maybe she wasn't as uptight, but Frances found her aversion towards Mr. Timothy Quinn had eased.

"Please?" Stephanie asked again, her voice pleading.

Face burning, Frances took the beaker from Stephanie's hand and marched down the hall. She paused outside the door to the spinner room, took a breath and opened the door. "Hello, Mr. Quinn," she said, planting her feet in front of his desk.

He jerked his head up, his hand instinctively covering the half-dollar spot of bare skin on his crown. "Missus Ferguson! Lovely to see you." He smiled.

"I want to send this through the spinner," Frances said, forcing a smile. She thrust the beaker towards him.

He stood. "I already told Miss Kwolek 'no.' Those particles will gum up the spinneret. I'm very sorry, but unplugging that valuable machine is time-consuming. Costly."

Frances gave the beaker a gentle shake, watching the contents, thin as water, roil against the glass. She held the beaker out. "There are no particles."

He laughed. "Of course there are. Look. It's cloudy."

"There are no particles," she repeated, scanning the room. "Where's a microscope. I'll show you."

He hesitated, then stepped from behind his desk and walked across the room, Frances following. Dipping a pipette in the beaker he withdrew .05 milliliter, dropping it on a microscope slide. Once the second glass slide was added, he examined the sandwiched fluid under the lens, rotating the magnifying turret twice. He looked at Frances, eyebrows raised. "Interesting."

Frances nodded.

"All right. I'll spin it, if you will have dinner with me."

"What?" Frances's hand went to her chest. "That's not fair," she stammered.

Tim smiled. "I'm joking. I will spin it." He walked off with the beaker in his hand, paused to look back. "But I really would like to take you to dinner."

Embarrassed, Frances looked around the room but thankfully no one was in ear shot. She noticed Stephanie standing by the door and motioned her over.

"Make him take you to Buckley's," Stephanie whispered. "Best restaurant in town."

Frances stalked off after Tim, face burning, heart thumping, Stephanie following. When the spinning

389

began, she held her breath, but there were no problems. Grasping one of the freshly-spun fibers, she pulled and twisted, Stephanie doing the same, but unlike all the previous fibers they created, this one would not break.

"Aha!" Stephanie yelled, grabbing Frances by the shoulders. "This could be it!" She tossed her head back and laughed, pulling Frances into a hug. She even embraced a startled Timothy Quinn before skipping out of the spinning room, her new-fangled thread dangling from her hand.

CHAPTER FORTY-SEVEN

August 1965
Wilmington, Delaware

"Go see Grandma?" Hope asked, her small hand in Martha's, face upturned.

Martha nodded. She was following a guard through the chemical company's building to Stephanie's office, guaranteeing Frances a few minutes with Hope on her second birthday. For the past month, since announcing a promising discovery at the laboratory, Frances had been working from sunrise to sunset. Martha volunteered to take charge of Hope, once again spending her days and nights at Frances's home. When she managed to catch sight of her daughter, Martha had noticed a lightness in Frances's step, a sparkle in her eyes. Whatever this new finding was, it had brought about a change, an uplifting, to her daughter's entire demeanor.

Happy Birthday!" Frances jumped from a chair and landed a noisy kiss on Hope's lemon curls.

Stephanie smiled and let her pencil fall to her desk. "Happy Birthday, Hope."

Hope giggled, blue eyes shining.

"We're having a party this Sunday. You're coming, right Stephanie?" Martha asked.

"Wouldn't miss it."

Dropping back to her chair, Frances spread her

arms and Hope crawled into her grandmother's lap, petticoat rustling.

"You look very pretty, Hope. I love your dress," Stephanie said.

"I'm sure her mother wouldn't approve." Frances adjusted the white bow cinching Hope's waist. "Ginny prefers a more modern look. She sent white go-go boots for Hope's birthday."

Martha chuckled. "It was a battle this morning to not have her wear the boots today." She bent, wiping a scuff from the toe of Hope's black patent Mary Jane with her thumb.

"Wish I had time to make you a dress." Stephanie rubbed the dress's pink satin between her fingers. I loved making clothes for your daddy when he was a baby."

Frances looked at Martha. "Did her daddy call?"

"This morning. He and Ginny both got on the phone. They are in London. Coming home at Thanksgiving." Martha paused. "Maybe to stay."

Frances sucked in her breath and Martha put a hand on her shoulder. "A child needs her mother," she whispered.

"Even if she's a bad mother?" Frances snapped.

Martha narrowed her eyes, brow knitted. "We don't know yet what kind of mother Ginny will be," she said, her voice low. "When she has been around, she has been good with Hope."

"That's my point, when she's around. What kind of mother traipses off to another continent, abandoning her daughter?"

"Frances, she didn't abandon Hope. She left her daughter with family," Martha said, taking a step back. "Ginny knows Hope is better off here. I imagine she misses her daughter terribly, but she shouldn't have to give up her dreams because she has a child."

"I did," Frances said. She looked down at Hope's puzzled face. "Let's go see the colors."

Martha watched her daughter lead Hope to the

other side of the office and point to a shelf of glass jars, their contents rich hues of violets, yellows and blues. Frances perched the toddler on a chair and slipped a slide in the microscope and guided Hope's eyes to the lens, laughing at the delighted squeals. Something caught Frances's eyes and she straightened, raising a finger to her lips. Martha followed her daughter's gaze to a tall man in a white coat striding across the laboratory floor.

The man stopped at the door of the office, taking in the unusual occupants. "Paul Morgan," he said to Martha with a nod.

"My mother," Frances said and put a hand on Hope's head. "And granddaughter."

Martha had never met the director of the laboratory but she had heard from both Frances and Stephanie about his grueling work ethic and brilliant mind and was expecting a somber man. But Paul Morgan was smiling.

He extended documents to Stephanie. "Here are the final test results. And the patent. Congratulations." He looked at Frances, Hope now in her arms. "Nice work, Missus Ferguson." He gave Hope a quick wave and walked away.

"I knew that fiber was different," Stephanie said as she squinted at one of the documents. She put a hand on Frances's arm. "It's nine times stiffer than any thread previously tested. Five times stronger than steel."

Martha pulled Hope into her arms and watched Frances and Stephanie celebrate, watched them put the frustrating years of near-misses, setbacks and failures behind them. Their work in this laboratory was a mirror of life, Martha thought. Challenging and uncertain, often messy, decidedly not linear. Full of ups and downs with joyful triumphs, large and small, and losses that knock you to your knees. Choices made, regrets borne. She put her lips to her great-granddaughter's ear. "Never give up, my beautiful girl. Be brave and hold tight to your dreams."

The End

APPENDIX

Dr. Kate Waller Barrett (1857-1925) was a prominent physician, social reformer, humanitarian, and leader of the National Florence Crittenton Mission, a progressive organization established in 1883 to assist unwed mothers. More than 70 Crittenton homes operated in the United States and abroad at the time of her death. Today, the Crittenton family of agencies works collaboratively with each other and The National Crittenton Foundation on national research, communication, and advocacy efforts designed to improve the well-being of girls and young women. More than 10 million people have been served since 1883.

Stephanie Louise Kwolek (1925-2004) was a pioneering chemist, whose discovery led to the creation of Kevlar. She was inducted into the National Inventors Hall of Fame in 1994 and the National Women's Hall of Fame in 2003. In 1996, she was awarded the National Medal of Technology and in 1997 the Perkin Medal from the Society of Chemical Industry. Stephanie didn't fulfill her dream of becoming a doctor but she did save countless lives with her invention of Kevlar®, now used worldwide as body armor for police and the military.

The Donora inversion of 1948, one of the worst air pollution disasters in U.S. history, left 20 people dead and 7,000 sickened. Within a month, another 50 residents died of respiratory illnesses. The inversion eventually led to the Clean Air Act and state and federal agencies that regulate pollution.

War Cake Recipe
2 cups brown sugar
2 tablespoons shortening or lard
1 teaspoon salt
1/2 package raisins
2 cups hot water
1 teaspoon ground cinnamon
1 teaspoon ground cloves
Boil above ingredients for five minutes after they begin
    to bubble.

When cold, add:
1 teaspoon baking soda
1 teaspoon hot water
3 cups flour

Beat together good. Bake in slow oven for 45 minutes.
Note: slow oven temperatures range from 300-325
    degrees Fahrenheit

ACKNOWLEDGEMENTS

When I decided to write Stoking Hope, I started with research on Dr. Kate Waller Barrett and found two vintage books helpful. *Some Practical Suggestions on the Conduct of a Rescue Home*, was published as a pamphlet by the National Florence Crittenton Mission in 1903. It was combined with *The Life of Dr. Kate Waller Barrett*, written in 1933 by Otto Wilson, and reprinted as part of the *Women in America, From Colonial Times to the 20th Century* series in 1974. *Fifty Years Work with Girls* was also written in 1933 by Otto Wilson, in collaboration with Dr. Barrett's oldest son, Robert S. Barrett.

Stephanie Kwolek was a dedicated and pioneering chemist who forged a remarkable career in an industry that offered few opportunities for a woman of her time. A slim book, *Stopping Bullets with a Thread* by Edwin Brit Wyckoff, along with published interviews and media articles, helped bring Stephanie to life.

My research included several visits to The Coal and Coke Heritage Center at Penn State Fayette, The Eberly Campus, where I met with Dr. Evelyn A. Hovanec. Dr. Hovanec compiled, wrote and edited *Common Lives of Uncommon Strength: The Women of the Coal and Coke Era of Southwestern Pennsylvania 1880-1970*. Thank you to Dr. Hovanec, and also to Amanda Peters, Coal and Coke Heritage Center Archivist.

Two other books on coal mining I found helpful were *Cloud by Day, The Story of Coal and Coke and People* by Muriel Earley Sheppard, and *Coal, A Human History* by Barbara Freese.

For hands-on coal mining experience, I visited the Exhibition Coal Mine in Beckley, West Virginia, and I hitched a ride with a group from our local chamber of commerce for a tour of a working coal mine in West Virginia's northern panhandle.

The Sisters of our Lady of Charity operated a monastery and school for girls in Wheeling, West Virginia, from 1900 until 1970. The historic building has found new life as a nursing home. Sister James came to the monastery in 1950 and she graciously shared her memories while leading me through the labyrinth of hallways and re-configured rooms, transporting me back to the time when the building was full of young girls and dedicated nuns. Articles from the *Wheeling Intelligencer* in 1900 and the *Wheeling News-Register* in 1938 and 1960 also provided insight on the sisters and their school.

Ms. Martha Atwell graduated from the Margaret Morrison Carnegie College at the Carnegie Institute of Technology (now Carnegie Mellon University) in 1941 and she shared with me her college publications, photographs and recollections of her years at Carnegie Tech. Thank you to Lindie Droulia, Associate Director for University Events and Engagement/University Advancement at Carnegie Mellon University for putting me in touch with Ms. Atwell.

Special appreciation goes to the members of my writers' groups: Sylvia Adams, Linda Lee Blakemore, Jennifer Collins, Barb d'Souza, Howie Ehrilichman, Peter W.J. Hayes, Lilly Kauffman, Janet McClintock, Steve

Sharpnack and Judy Smitley. All talented writers, their insights, suggestions and encouragement kept me going.

And, last but not least, thank you to Daniel Willis, publisher, D. X. Varos, Ltd., for taking a chance on *Stoking Hope* and for his patient guidance throughout the publishing process.

ABOUT THE AUTHOR

A Pennsylvania native, C. K. McDonough has a journalism degree and twenty years' experience in the communications industry. A self-proclaimed history nerd, Caren has turned her love of research and the written word into her first novel, *Stoking Hope*.

Other Exquisite Fiction from
D. X. Varos, Ltd.

Chad Bordes
The Ruination of Dylan Forbes

S. W. Capps
Runaway Train

Courtney Davis
A Werewolf in Women's Clothes

Therese Doucet
The Prisoner of the Castle of
Enlightenment

Samuel Ebeid
The Heiress of Egypt
The Queen of Egypt

G. P. Gottlieb
Battered
Smothered

Wayne E. Haley
Sean P. Haley
An Apology to Lucifer *(Feb. 2022)*

Jeanne Matthews
Devil by the Tail

Phillip Otts
A Storm Before the War
The Soul of a Stranger
The Price of Betrayal